D1044104

The Library Paradox

THE LIBRARY
PARADOX

Catherine Shaw

All the characters and events portrayed in this work are fictitious.

THE LIBRARY PARADOX

A Felony & Mayhem mystery

PRINTING HISTORY
First UK edition (Allison & Busby): 2006
Felony & Mayhem edition: 2008

Copyright © 2006 by Catherine Shaw
All rights reserved

Published by arrangement with Allison & Busby

ISBN: 978-1-934609-11-8

Manufactured in the United States of America

For my sister, who provided the greater part
of my education on the subject.

The icon above says you're holding a copy of a book in the Felony &
Mayhem "Historical" category, which ranges from the ancient world
up through the 1940s. If you enjoy this book, you may well like other
"Historical" titles from Felony & Mayhem Press, including:

The Smoke, by Tony Broadbent
Spectres in the Smoke, by Tony Broadbent
City of the Horizon, by Anton Gill
City of Dreams, by Anton Gill
City of the Dead, by Anton Gill
Man's Illegal Life, by Keith Heller
Bertie and the Seven Bodies, by Peter Lovesey
Bertie and the Crime of Passion, by Peter Lovesey
The Blackheath Poisonings, by Julian Symons
Ovid, by David Wishart
Germanicus, by David Wishart

For more about these books, and other Felony & Mayhem titles, or to
place an order, please visit our website at

www.FelonyAndMayhem.com

or contact us at

Felony and Mayhem Press
156 Waverly Place
New York, NY 10014

The Library Paradox

Pages from
Vanessa Weatherburn's Diary
of March 1896

Cambridge, Wednesday, March 11th, 1896

We were sitting in the front room, Arthur and I. I had not told him about the telegram. I rather thought that nothing might come of it, and in that case there wouldn't have been any point. But when I perceived, through the window, a little group of gentlemen coming up the path, I felt it might have been better to have mentioned it before.

Arthur was reading the newspaper, and I was peacefully engaged in mending a tiny torn sleeve, while Cedric tried to climb upon my knees and Cecily dug through my workbasket and flung out all the spools. We had come in but shortly before from our outing; the late afternoon sun was still gleaming through the crisp cold air, and the children's cheeks were still flushed from their exertions of toddling, usually in opposite directions, and what with tumbling down rather frequently and trying to climb up on anything pointy or lumpy, we came home with a fair crop of scrapes, tears and dirty spots.

The cheerfully crackling fire was most welcome, and I had just put on the kettle and taken up my mending, when a shadow darkened the window and the three gentlemen came up and stood hesitating outside. Arthur glanced up at my gesture of surprise, and saw them also. I hastily rescued the telegram from my workbasket, where Cecily had only just discovered it, and handed it to him wordlessly.

Dear Vanessa some friends of mine will possibly visit you shortly asking for help please do help them if at all possible very urgent please thank you thank you stop Emily.

'I see,' said Arthur with a very faint smile, looking from the telegram to the window to me.

I rose from my place, put down my sewing (or rather, put it up, in a place high enough for little hands not to pull it down and prick themselves on the needle), and arrived at the front door just as the bell rang, Cecily and Cedric frothing about my skirts in an effervescent mixture of shyness and curiosity. Three grave, somewhat embarrassed scholarly faces looked into mine and there was a short silence.

'How do you do?' I said politely.

'Very well,' said one of the gentlemen, a little shortly, I thought. 'We would like to speak with Mrs Weatherburn, if you please.'

'Oh! She is me, I mean I am she,' I said, realising he must have taken me for a housekeeper. 'Please do come in, of course.' And I stood away from the door, shooing the twins a little distance off so that they should not be trodden upon. Cecily took one look at the gentleman who entered first and burst into tears, while her brother, apparently deciding that the visit had already lasted sufficiently long, directed the word 'Bye-bye' to the newcomer in a firm, ringing tone, while waving his little hand in an unmistakable gesture of dismissal. The gentleman glanced at my upset workbox, the scattered mess upon the floor and the weeping tot with frank dismay. I was just about to take some drastic measures, when the door from the kitchen opened, and Sarah entered, back early from her half-day out.

All three gentlemen brightened up considerably. How something so diminutive, so fresh, and so pretty can also be so efficient and so energetic, always delightful, always cheerful in spite of the endless round of cooking, cleaning and taking care of the children, is quite beyond me. And what is more, she does it all on vegetables alone! Sarah neither eats nor prepares meat, but at least she allows the mistress of the house to fiddle about the kitchen (so many cooks do not) so that I can easily put on a roast or some chops to accompany her lovely spinach soufflés or rice-stuffed tomatoes. That such a thing should have found its way into my household is a blessing; surely it must have been a stroke of Divine Aid.

In less than no time, Cecily was gathered up and consoled, her tears dried, and the spools and cottons swept out of sight, while Cedric was momentarily controlled with a small cake. I pulled forward chairs for the visitors and tried to pretend that noise, chaos and disorder were phenomena perfectly unknown to me.

'I'll take them up to the nursery,' said Sarah, sweeping Cecily under one arm and trundling her away in great contentment, followed by Cedric snugly wedged in his father's left arm. I sighed with relief and turned my full attention to my visitors. Three pairs of eyes were fixed upon me with doubtful expressions. I breathed again.

'There,' I said firmly, in the hopes of dispelling possible poor impressions. 'Now I do hope you will tell me how I can be of help to you.'

There was some shuffling and looking at each other, and the most senior of the three gentlemen began to speak.

'Let us introduce ourselves,' he said gravely. 'I am Professor Hudson and this is Professor Taylor, of King's College in London. This young man is Mr Sachs, a student of mathematics. We have had a—a difficulty, a problem, at our university; you may have heard something of it. It is the kind of problem which…' and his face took on a more doubtful expression than ever, 'which apparently you have had some success in solving before, or so we have heard.'

'From Emily Burke-Jones,' timidly interjected the youthful Mr Sachs. 'She's a good friend of mine.'

It began to dawn on me that the problem about to be set before me might be more important than I had bargained for. Certainly, Emily is aware of the half-dozen or so little investigations I have undertaken since my marriage left me without any professional occupation, in most of which I succeeded in unearthing the truth by what always appeared to me to be a fortunate mixture of good luck and coincidence. Considering the lengthy miens in front of me, I felt sure that she must have exaggerated my accomplishments to the point at which they had expected to encounter someone quite different from myself. But I felt curious. No, it was more than curiosity. Clearly something very serious had happened, and I felt an urgent desire to know more about it.

'Please tell me about the problem,' I said quietly.

There was some hemming and hawing and looking at each other. Then Professor Hudson cleared his throat.

'The problem concerns the death of a colleague of ours, a

professor at King's,' he said. 'Ahem, it appears to be undoubtedly a case of murder.'

'Murder!' said Arthur, returning to the room exactly in time to catch this particular word. In spite of his best efforts to hide it, I cannot help being aware that Arthur suffers from a feeling of visceral horror and repulsion in respect of my work as a detective. Yet he has long since given up trying to dissuade me from it, and indeed I can count on his doing his utmost to help me if he can.

I did not speak, but the word *murder* awakened an echo of violence and terror inside me, which certainly mirrored his. This immediate reaction was, however, instantly overcome by an impulse to interfere quite as powerful as any I might have felt had I observed someone being murdered in front of my very eyes.

'Ah, Weatherburn,' said Professor Hudson with an air of relief at this sight of a familiar face, shaking Arthur's hand cordially. 'How do you do? Good work that last article of yours. Yes, yes indeed. You've heard about our problem down at King's, I suppose? No? Well, it isn't in the Mathematics Department. It's a strange thing.' The pleasant light went out of his eyes and a wrinkle appeared on his forehead as he recalled himself to his task of information.

'The circumstances of the murder are most mysterious; one might even call them paradoxical. And the police appear to be making no headway. The whole situation has created innumerable difficulties at the College; the atmosphere is heavy, students are withdrawing, trustees are making remarks. The case is in imminent danger of being drawn to the notice of the Queen, in which case I fear that the College may come in for serious sanctions.' He coughed again, uncomfortably, and threw a glance into a corner where, my eyes following his, I perceived Cecily's favourite rag doll lying with her legs tossed unconcernedly over her head.

'Professor Taylor, here,' he continued, 'is the Head of the History Department and as such was one of the closest colleagues of Professor Gerard Ralston, the murdered man. The History Department is of course the one most affected. My student Mr Sachs, however, was one of the three who discovered the body. Because he has been questioned by police and is directly concerned in the case, we decided to approach Professor Taylor about the possibility of consulting a private detective, someone who would be entirely discreet and devote his energy uniquely to the case in hand in the hopes of arriving at a satisfactory and rapid solution.' He coughed once again. 'As it happens, we were not acquainted with any such person, but Mr Sachs, as he said, had heard about your achievements in this line, Mrs Weatherburn, from a friend of his.'

'People often have recourse to the famous detective of Baker Street in cases as important as this one, do they not?' I murmured, perceiving his discomfort with, as I supposed, my dissimilarity to his preconceived idea of a successful detective.

'Holmes?' Professor Taylor spoke up, an expression of disgust on his face. 'The publicity, the publicity! I have no doubts of his capacities, and surely he is discretion itself during a case, but when all is over—why, his associate publishes detailed descriptions of all the most interesting cases in the *Strand Magazine*! Which, by the by, explains his immense renown at least as much as his successes do. No, no, we cannot consider such a thing. Much better to remain closer to home. My being acquainted with your husband keeps it all in the family, as it were.'

'I see,' I said thoughtfully. Certainly, I am neither experienced nor famous nor brilliant, and yet, there was a period, after I married and stopped teaching, where if some interesting problems had not come my way, I should have fallen into gloom out of sheer boredom—indeed, there is quite simply a part of my brain which is not fulfilled by the plain enjoyment of domestic pleasures and yearns to touch the rougher spots of life's texture. And I have, after all, been able to untangle several rather complex situations. Still, most of those were not murders, but rather, less drastic if equally mysterious disappearances and robberies. I cannot feel certain of success when undertaking a case; yet there is no room for error in a situation like this, where lives may hang in the balance.

'Before deciding anything at all,' I said, firmly putting these considerations away for later, 'I would be grateful to have as many details of the case as you can give me.'

'Certainly,' answered Professor Hudson. 'I will give you the circumstances as precisely as I know them, and you will see at once that it all appears to be quite inexplicable. To begin with, you must know that Professor Ralston, a Professor of History, worked so extensively with texts that he had collected a considerable library of his own, consisting of thousands of historical volumes. Upon an agreement with the College dating back several years, he donated the whole of his library to the College on certain conditions; the new library was to be situated on the ground floor of a building belonging to the College, which had been used hitherto for the lodging of lecturers. This building lies a few hundred yards down the Victoria Embankment from the main building of King's College, in a strip of grounds giving onto Adelphi Street, with a back gate to these grounds on John Street. Professor Ralston was lodged on the upper floor of the house, with a study on the ground floor giving directly onto the library. In this way, he was able to continue to treat the library as his own, while the whole of the body of students and professors was also able to take advantage of it during the day; Professor Ralston continued to add to the library as fast as he acquired new tomes, and the College added to it from its own funds as well.

'The interior of the house was altered according to these arrangements. The front door now leads directly into the library, which occupies the whole ground floor of the building as a single vast space, except for the one room, which was preserved as Professor Ralston's study. Shelves of books line the walls of the room from floor to ceiling all the way around, and there are a few desks and lamps in the centre for readers. The stairs to the upper part of the house where Professor Ralston resided lead up from inside his study. The house itself is situated in the middle of a grassy quadrangle, which is some thirty yards wide, with buildings on either side of it. The length of the quadrangle stretching between the two parallel streets is longer, probably about eighty yards. It is entirely surrounded by a tall wrought-iron grille and one can enter only by the two gates. A path leads from the front gate directly up to the house, a distance of about thirty yards. This path then skirts the house to either side, and continues straight on to the back gate. The back gate is locked at five o'clock each evening, by a caretaker of the College on his rounds, whereas the front gate remains open in general unless Professor Ralston is away.'

Taking up a paper, the Professor made a quick sketch of the grounds, the buildings and the adjacent streets, which I reproduce here.

'Now,' he continued, 'although the official library hours were from nine to five o'clock, Professor Ralston was not strict about this rule, and had no particular objection to people remain-

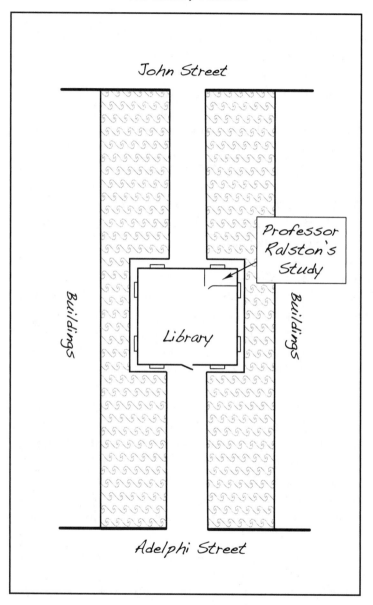

ing in the library for a little while after five o'clock; generally, he did not bother to lock the front door of the house until he went upstairs to get ready for the evening meal at seven. Knowing this, two students from his Department, Matthew Mason and Edward Chapman, needing to consult some texts, headed to the library after their last class of the day: we are talking about the 6th of March, the Friday of the murder. It was already nearing five o'clock; indeed, the students arrived at the back gate at five o'clock precisely, exactly at the same time as the caretaker, who walked with them for the last part of the distance and allowed them to enter before locking the gate behind them.

'The two young men walked down the back path and had just turned left along the house to go around to the front, so that they were passing under the window of Professor Ralston's study, when they heard a tremendous noise of shouting and crashing of furniture coming from within. They stopped for what they describe as a few moments, listening and hesitating, and then they heard the sound of a shot followed by total silence. Immediately and together, the two students dashed around to the front of the house and rushed into the front door, which was closed but unlocked.

'As they came around the corner of the front of the house, they caught sight of this young man here, Mr Sachs, who was walking up the front path towards the door and had heard nothing of the commotion within. Mr Sachs, perhaps it would be better if you would recount to Mrs Weatherburn what happened next.'

Professor Hudson folded his wrinkled hands and sat back with a small sigh of relief. Mr Sachs looked shy, but quickly began to speak.

'I was coming up the path to the house to use the library,' he said. 'I wouldn't be able to tell the time exactly, but they tell me it was just on five o'clock and that seems about right. I was too far to hear any sounds of a struggle, and as for the shot, I don't think I heard it, but there was plenty of noise behind me, what with people and carriages passing in the street. At any rate, I walked up the path towards the house, and when I was about halfway there, about fifteen yards off I should say, I saw Mason and Chapman come tearing around the side of the house. They saw me as well, and shouted something like "There's a fight going on in there!" and then they ran inside together. I rushed up after them and followed them in. One of them was already inside the professor's study, and the other was in the doorway of it. The one inside, I think it was Mason, was bent over the professor's body, feeling his pulse. He said, "I think he's dead." The other fellow reacted very quickly. He glanced around the library, then ran back to the main door and looked outside. No one was in sight. He ran around the house to the left and, understanding that he was looking for the murderer, I ran out with him and went round it to the right, but we saw each other coming around the back; there was nobody in the quadrangle at all. I swear it was absolutely empty; it's only grass, there isn't a corner where anyone could hide. Then they asked me if I had seen anybody going out as I came in. Now, this is the funny thing.' He hesitated, glanced up at me quickly, and continued. 'I had seen someone going out as I came in, and it was a very odd sort of person to see in a place like that. I don't know if you know the kind of person I mean, but it was an elderly gentleman of the Orthodox Jewish persuasion, dressed in traditional garb, with a long black overcoat that hung open, a black jacket beneath it from under which hung the fringes of his prayer shawl, and a large wheel-shaped fur hat on his head.'

'Ah,' I said.

'Well, at first the police were all for tracking this person down,' continued Mr Sachs. 'In fact, they soon found that he was seen by other people as he approached the library grounds along Adelphi Street at about four thirty, and then as he left it just on five o'clock. He was seen taking an omnibus in the direction of the East End. The police have been searching for him, but it's like looking for a needle in a haystack; if you're not from there, no one will talk to you, and most of them hardly speak English anyway. At any rate, after trying to reconstruct the crime, it turned out that it didn't seem possible for him to have been the murderer.'

'Why not?' I said, surprised.

'Because I crossed him just as I was entering the gate from the street. The timing is wrong. As soon as they heard the shot, Mason and Chapman ran around to the front of the house. The house is a square about twenty yards long on each side, and they had only to run halfway around, so they can't have taken more than nine or ten seconds to reach the front door. When I saw them coming around, I must have been about halfway to the house, which means a distance of fifteen yards or so from the street. I had walked those fifteen yards at a normal pace, say in eight or ten seconds, and I'd seen the man leaving as I came in. What that means is that I saw him going out the gate to the street at virtually the same moment that the others heard the shot. He'd have had to get there in no time at all, after the shot—not even a champion sprinter could do it! Besides, when I saw him, he was just walking normally out of the gate, not running. I didn't notice him being out of breath or anything like that, either. The police have gone over it again and again with me, but it just never seems to add up.'

'Couldn't the other two gentlemen have run around the house more slowly than they thought?' I asked.

'The police had them do it again as they thought they had done it, and timed them. Nine or ten seconds.'

'Well, then there must have been someone else in the library,' I said.

'We did think that someone might still have been in the library when we all dashed in, but he could not have done otherwise than be plainly visible. There is no place to hide in that large room. Still, even supposing that he managed it, and then slipped out during the moment we were all looking into Professor Ralston's study, it would take him ten seconds or more to run out of the room and down the path to the main gate. But I'm sure much less than ten seconds went by before Chapman ran out the front door to look around. You see, Mason and Chapman were a few seconds ahead of me going into the front door, so they got into the study before I did, and Mason was saying that Professor Ralston was dead just as I put my head in at the door. And I certainly saw no one. But Chapman ran outside as soon as he heard Mason's words, and I followed him immediately. There was no one there, absolutely not a soul. On top of this, the police have managed to locate a handful of people who were outside in Adelphi Street around that time, and although more than one observed the old Jew and saw me entering as well, nobody observed anyone else coming out of the gate.' He stopped, bewildered, and looked at me expectantly.

'Perhaps the murderer rushed up the stairs leading to Professor Ralston's private quarters,' I suggested.

'The police thought of that,' intervened Professor Taylor, opening his mouth only for the second time. He was a tall, rather dry man of reserved appearance, who seemed reluctant to take part in the conversation even as he spoke. However, as he knew the deceased Professor much better than the other two, he was clearly aware of many relevant facts. 'The door to the stairs was locked and the key was in the Professor's pocket.'

'Why would he lock the door to his rooms while he was sitting in his study?' I said. 'Doesn't that seem a little strange? Surely he went in and out?'

'He did, but he had the habit of locking that door always. For he also left his study frequently to go to look up books in the library, or even to have an informal chat outside with a colleague, and he disliked the idea that someone could slip in and go upstairs during those times. So he had it fitted with a lock that locked itself automatically whenever he came out and shut the door, and if he wanted to go back upstairs, he would just unlock it.'

'Is it possible that there was another key to the door? People usually have a spare.'

'He had exactly one spare; his housekeeper knew that. She told us he kept it in his bedside-table drawer, and it was there.'

'Was the housekeeper in the rooms upstairs?'

'No, she leaves every day at three. There was no one at all in the flat.'

I remained silent for a moment, reflecting on the peculiar arrangement of the facts.

'Was any weapon found?' I asked.

'Yes, indeed, the gun was on the floor. Professor Ralston was lying on the floor behind his desk, which had been pushed over. The chair opposite had also fallen, and the desk was partly propped up on the chair. Books and papers had slipped off the falling desk, and one or two things, a chair for instance, had been thrown violently across the room.'

'And where was the gun?'

'It was lying on the floor near the door of the study. We presume the murderer dropped it as he fled.'

'The police believe that he was shot from the doorway?'

'Ah no, he was shot at point-blank range. The police believe the murderer fled instantly, dropping or tossing the gun.'

'And have they tried to trace the gun?'

'The gun belonged to Professor Ralston, and was habitually kept in his desk drawer.'

'Oh! It was his gun? Why did he have a gun in his study?'

There was an embarrassed silence, during which everybody looked at somebody else. Both mathematicians ended up looking at Professor Taylor with silent firmness, so he resigned himself to speaking once again.

'Professor Ralston was a very special kind of person,' he said, choosing his words carefully. 'He had...let us say that through his researches, he had made a certain number of enemies, and was aware of it. I always found him a very suspicious and perhaps even rather paranoiac individual, although given what happened his fears appear to have been justified. In any case, he cared very much about his library being freely accessible to researchers, but at the same time, this put him in a rather risky position with respect to anyone who might wish to harm him. That is why he purchased a pistol and in fact learnt to use it and kept it by him at all times.'

'So he may have had the pistol out, and it must have been snatched from him during the struggle,' I visualised.

'That is what we assume must have happened. But it seems impossible to understand what occurred next.'

'Were there fingerprints on the gun?'

'There were smudged traces of Ralston's own fingerprints, which is normal enough, but according to police, they were much smeared over as though the gun had been somehow loosely wiped.'

'Did anything interesting come up at the inquest?'

'Nothing we have not already told you, I believe. Naturally, they brought in a verdict of murder by person or persons unknown.'

We sat silently for some moments, each engaged in trying to form some picture of the violent events he was describing. It was strange indeed, that the obvious and straightforward explanation seemed excluded merely by a bother over a few seconds. No other solution appeared possible, so there simply must be some way to arrange the timing in order to understand how the old man could have shot the Professor and so quickly arrived at the gate. Unless it were not he, but a different person, who had managed to hide himself somewhere in the room (under the overturned desk, perhaps?) and darted out later. Perhaps the most urgent aspect was to try to discover the motive for the crime, and form some idea of who could have borne a personal grudge against the man.

'The case sounds most interesting,' I began. 'I really think one must concentrate on the question of motive. Is it possible for you to give me a thumbnail sketch of Professor Ralston's circle of family and friends?'

'It is only too easy,' said Professor Taylor with dry displeasure. 'He was a single and very lonely man, with an acrid and vinegary nature. He lived entirely alone, with a housekeeper who came in by the day, but who had already left the building and is known to have been at home at the time of the murder. His father is a well-known historian, but in an area quite remote from that of his son; he studies the royal history of France and Poland at the time of Catherine de Medici. Their joint history, you know; her son Henri was chosen King of Poland before becoming Henri III of France. The Professor travels to the Continent quite often; indeed, he was away on a journey at the time of his son's murder, and it is taking the police some little time to locate him. The telegram has been following him about Europe, but it is expected to reach him and bring him back to England within a few days. Ralston's mother died, from what I have heard, when he was a small boy. She was a foreigner; his father had met and married her on his travels. He had no other family. His social life was essentially restricted to his professional contacts at the College; he rarely ate at home, preferring the company and opportunity for open discussion at High Table twice a day. I have lunched and dined with him frequently, by which I mean that I have actually sat next to him and spent the hour listening to what he had to say; he was not one to listen much to other points of view. He also had students whose research he guided. But I cannot say that I knew him to have any particular friends. It is true that he travelled on occasion, visiting other universities, and he also had a lot of contact with journalists, not all of it friendly, for apart from scholarly articles, he was a great contributor to political newspapers and magazines. He had an enormous correspondence and published reams of Letters to the Editor in both British and French newspapers.'

'From what you say, it sounds like there are people who may have had a professional motive of resentment against Professor Ralston. Perhaps it would help to know more details about his writings. Of course, I suppose the police are already working on all these angles.'

Professor Taylor sighed rather loudly.

'These are not easy questions,' he observed. 'You see, some of Professor Ralston's research...was of a very special nature. Not everything he did, naturally,' he added hastily. 'He was a specialist of Christian history, particularly medieval history: medieval saints, you know, and the Spanish Inquisition. His collection of books was to a large extent concentrated around that period of time. But he...'

His voice trailed off, and he once again looked embarrassed.

'He had bitter relations with the Semitic community,' put

in Professor Hudson firmly. 'You see, he published a continuous stream of articles on the role of Jews in medieval and modern society. His views on the subject were quite radical. They were more than views, as it happens; he had built up an entire theory attributing, shall we say, many of the ills of modern British society to the agency of its Jews and their occult but fundamental, as he believed, role in its development. In defending such views he was certainly not alone, although it isolated him within the University.'

'He published virulent articles refuting Herzl, and several on the Dreyfus affair as well,' put in Professor Taylor. I felt a little dismayed, hoping the Professor did not assume that I recognised these names as a matter of course. If this constituted a motive, then I feared I would have difficulty penetrating its depths. However, the Professor was still speaking.

'You know of Theodore Herzl, of course,' he said, in a tone, which clearly implied that he was well aware that I did not. 'An Austrian journalist, but based in Paris. Ralston knew him personally and was fundamentally opposed to his vision. This Herzl came out very recently with a most inflammatory pamphlet on the subject of the Jewish State, whose thesis asserts, essentially, that the sufferings and persecutions of the Jewish people, together with the perceived ills they cause to the fabric of society in the many European countries which harbour them, could all be resolved in a single blow if the people were to be given an independent State of their own, located in their historic land of Palestine. The subject is not my speciality, of course—my research concerns Guilds and Apprenticeships—but the thing was in the newspapers. Anyway, I had only too many opportunities of becoming familiar with Ralston's attitude to these things.' He made a face rather as if he had tasted a lemon, but continued valiantly. 'You see,

The Library Paradox

Ralston was convinced, as a great many people seem to be, that the Jewish community in England, as in each European country, wields power and influence far out of proportion to its relative size. It is no secret that the proportion of Jews among intellectuals and financiers is greater than that of the general population; I have frequently heard this fact attributed to the ancient tradition of study of that people, and possibly also to the fact that in certain countries, they have been forbidden access to the land and to many of the manual employments. I have no claim to being a specialist, and personally do not have any realistic idea as to whether the disproportionate presence of members of that race in the professions relating to money is a consequence of some natural propensity or simply of the many social restrictions imposed upon them. In any case, it is not to be denied that they have made a success of it, in what concerns their profit at least, if not in what concerns their popularity as a group. At any rate, Ralston was filled with resentment against what he perceived as their undue influence, and very fired up with concrete plans to diminish it. It is a natural thought that might occur to anyone, that if the Jewish people were given a State of their own, a large number of them would certainly depart thither, and that in fact by various pressures and persecutions, that number might be augmented, so that many of those—and there are many—who share Ralston's point of view welcomed the ideas in Herzl's paper with alacrity. But Ralston did not; he was very acrid about what he considered such foolishness. Since the recent appearance of Herzl's pamphlet, Ralston discoursed upon the subject at practically every opportunity. His view was that the role of the Jewish community within a given country, England for instance, would be comparable on a world scale with the role of a Jewish State among the states of the world, and that therefore, if a State of its own were to be attributed to the Jewish people, it would soon come to wield among the nations of the world the same undue and disproportionate influence and power as he perceived is wielded by the local community. This appeared to him as a far graver ill, for it would threaten global peace and not merely the well-being and cohesion of each population separately. His view was positively doomsday and even apocalyptic; he was convinced that, not content with seeking peace, well-being and profit for themselves, the Jews have a natural desire to foment discord and failure in others. Ceaselessly he cited example after example from history, from ancient to modern times. And such examples are easy enough to come by, especially if one is willing to be tendentious in one's interpretations. Consider merely the books of the Old Testament. Time and again, after their escape from bondage in Egypt, the arrival of the Jewish people sowed trouble and discord in other lands.'

'Really,' put in Arthur, whose mind had wandered away during this discourse, but who was brought back to earth suddenly by the words 'Old Testament', a topic which fascinates him. 'I should have said that the Bible portrays the Hebrews as a much persecuted people. I mean, enslaved by the Egyptians, exiled to Babylon, invaded by the Greeks, conquered by the Romans; it never seemed to stop.'

'But think of the older stories; Dinah and the Hivites, for example, or the Amalekites, or the Canaanites,' sighed the Professor, 'and all the other nations the Hebrews were commanded to destroy...in Deuteronomy 7, is it not? Certainly, these conquests are depicted as a necessary struggle for the survival of the chosen people, but it is all easily open to many interpretations. Ralston interpreted—but he was never crude. He would never, for instance, have made scholarly use of the popular notion amongst ignorant Christians that "the Jews killed Jesus". Instead, he taught a course on early Christianity in which he gave an analysis of the role of Saint Paul as a dissident Jew within his own community; something which would quietly sustain his thesis by focusing on what he considered the quintessentially Jewish procedure for gaining influence, while fully respecting the nuances of history and the beauties and glories of Christianity. His teachings were always outwardly irreproachable, and in fact the students unanimously claim that they learnt an enormous amount from him. However, he allowed himself to be much more inflammatory and demagogic in his newspaper and magazine articles, something which would not have been acceptable within the College walls.'

'And were not the newspaper articles harmful for his scholarly reputation?' I asked.

'For his reputation as an individual, perhaps, but not as a scholar,' he replied. 'His articles were invariably serious and carefully thought-out works. His political views may have been dangerous, radical and to some extent even rabble-rousing, but he expressed them very solidly. His strong suit, he always claimed, was logic. He was particularly apt to phrase his theses in terms of deductions and syllogisms, so as to make them appear infallible. As a matter of fact, he was sincerely fascinated by logic as a science, and followed lectures on the subject.'

'That is how I became acquainted with him,' explained Professor Hudson. 'He followed the introductory courses on logic several years ago, and continued to come back occasionally for the more advanced levels. He was quite good actually; he took the trouble to work out the problems to the last detail and he penetrated the language and style of reasoning as well as the best of the students. I've talked over one of his pet topics many a time over dinner: the role of morality in the sciences, and in logic in particular. He very much enjoyed constructing complicated paradoxes, which somehow proved his moral or historical point. I could not accept his views, but I was invariably forced to respect his insight and the solidity with which he constructed his arguments. He was a highly intelligent man, and his articles were incomparably better than the average journalistic fare. It is really a great pity that…'

He stopped, frowning. Mr Sachs rolled his eyes. Professor Taylor sighed.

'Do you think we could actually dig a specific motive out of all this?' I asked.

'We all agree that Professor Ralston's activities in this domain were aggressive and reprehensible, and they certainly earned him many enemies,' observed Professor Taylor. 'But it is hard to imagine that someone can have been provoked by them to the point of murder. And why now?'

'There was something,' said Professor Hudson. 'I don't know what its bearing on the case may be, but it is certain that Professor Ralston was very concerned about it in the last days preceding his unfortunate demise. I cannot tell you exactly what it is, because he did not really tell me, and I am not even certain of how much he himself knew. But on the very day before his death, he was fulminating at the table about some new development in the Dreyfus affair. Professor Taylor has also published articles on the affair, following the news of his scandalous secret trial, something over a year ago, was it not? But his views on the subject are diametrically opposite to those Ralston entertained.'

'That is very interesting,' I said, looking at Professor Taylor. But he did not appear to have much to contribute.

'He said nothing to me of this "latest development",' he grumbled, looking at me as though to gauge the extent of my ignorance of the topic to which he referred, which, alas, was

The Library Paradox

complete. Newspapers find their way only sporadically into my hands, though Arthur reads them rather regularly, and my knowledge of current world news is no better than that of most young mothers with babies in the nursery.

'Alfred Dreyfus,' explained Professor Hudson, having obviously understood the state of affairs, 'was a captain in the French Army, who was accused in November 1894 of spying for the Germans, after the discovery of a letter containing classified information found in a wastebasket in the German embassy. The letter in question was not signed, and the judgement was based on an absurd and controversial comparison of handwritings. He was court-martialled, and condemned to be publicly dishonoured and deported to perpetual solitary confinement in the Devil's Island prison off the coast of French Guyana, where he remains to this day. He has never ceased for a moment to declare his innocence, and his family—together with a handful of lawyers, journalists and other associates—is working as energetically as possible to discover the true culprit and obtain a reopening of the case. They have made but little progress, unfortunately, until now. However, from what Ralston said to me the day before his death, something new appears to have turned up. Ralston had involved himself deeply in the public commentaries on the case from the start, and as far as it was in his power as a kind of intellectual journalist, he did what he could to sway public opinion against Captain Dreyfus. As a matter of fact, it would appear that Dreyfus was selected to be the culprit, on totally unsatisfactory evidence, simply because he was Jewish. His enemies and detractors in the French press have been generic anti-Semites for the most part, led by that rabid creature Drumont and his inflamed Parisian newspaper, *La Libre Parole*. Well, Ralston thought that attempting to sweep anti-Dreyfusism under the general blanket of anti-Semitism was a bad thing, sufficient to convince idiots but not anyone with an independent, thinking mind. The trouble was that the very nature of the Drumont articles clearly indicated that anti-Semitism alone was the fundamental basis of conviction. So Ralston devoted himself to publishing a series of articles specifically demonstrating Dreyfus' guilt according to a "logical" examination of the evidence. He spent time in Paris and met and disputed publicly or in print with a number of the people connected with the events. He came to know most of these people personally, and I assume it was for this reason that he always seemed to be in possession of the very latest rumours on the case. What he learnt shortly before his death must have been something of this sort. From what he told me, I gathered that some secret document or other has turned up which some interpret as showing that the spying business is still going on even though Dreyfus has been mouldering on Devil's Island for the last year. I dined sitting next to him on the 3rd, and he was simply steaming, rolling up his sleeves to begin the battle. Well, all I can say is that even if all this actually turns out to have some bearing on the case, in terms of motive, it still fails to shed any light whatsoever on the means.'

'Could you make any guess as to the person who gave Professor Ralston the information?' I asked.

'I don't know who gave it to him,' he answered. 'I wish I did, but he did not mention the name. However, I did get the impression quite strongly that he had not received it from a friend, but rather from someone who had communicated with him for the express purpose of proving him wrong, someone who was probably a strong believer in Dreyfus' innocence. It could be that journalist, what was his name? A French Jew who stood up for Dreyfus throughout, and who exchanged a number of letters and polemical articles with Ralston after the condemnation. Ralston seemed to be permanently angry with him. I can't remember his name. But he is very passionate about the case, and works continuously with the family on suing for a retrial. If anything new has turned up in Dreyfus' favour, it seems likely that he would know about it, and not inconceivable that he might tell Ralston, just to thumb his nose.'

'Ralston's influence against the Jewish community was growing,' said Professor Hudson. 'That explains why it seems as though he might have had any number of enemies. It must, I suppose, be considered possible that some fanatic may have wished to put an end to him and his work, without being personally acquainted with him. The police obviously considered at first that the Orthodox Jew seen by Mr Sachs was a prime suspect of this nature. It would really be an almost unthinkable coincidence that someone else could be murdering Ralston exactly at the same moment as the curious but not entirely unbelievable visit by this unexpected personage. But to put it bluntly, the police are flummoxed by the time element. No one can understand how the man could have done it and got himself to the gate in so little time, or how someone else could have managed it without being seen.'

There was a brief silence, during which I felt, perhaps exaggeratedly, that all three gentlemen were waiting for me to explain how the thing might have happened. But nothing came to my mind, except that further investigation would be needed. I hesitated. Arthur was on the point of leaving on a trip to France—I was supposed to be spending two weeks alone with the babies...

'This needs further investigation!' I said.

'We are at our wits' end, Mrs Weatherburn,' said Professor Hudson, leaning forward anxiously. 'The College is suffering.'

I longed to accept the case immediately, dash to London,

and set about learning about Professor Ralston, his private life, his nasty articles, his enemies, and their apparently rather good reasons for hating him.

'Unfortunately, I am leaving tomorrow morning to spend two weeks in Paris,' said Arthur, not looking particularly displeased. 'I don't see how you can get away, Vanessa.'

I felt a minuscule pang of rebellion. Over the past few years, Arthur has ended up becoming used to my investigations, and has even, on occasion, actively lent me a helping hand. But he rightly considers murder something different and far more dangerous than the run-of-the-mill case, for one who has killed may well kill again, by choice the person who is on his track...

How could I manage it? I listened to the sounds of happy thumping and laughing echoing dimly from upstairs. I am needed here, I know it. And even if I were to go, would I really be able to help? Might not a case of murder, based, perhaps, not on personal feelings but on causes of an international and political nature, be beyond my modest capacities?

I am so taken with the babies that I sometimes fear that my horizons, never immense, have now shrunk definitively to within the four walls of their nursery, and I find myself envying Arthur, who although of course the most devoted of fathers, still allows himself the occasional jaunt to London or even to the Continent, upon important mathematical occasions, not to mention the many hours spent at his work in Trinity College.

I write honestly the thoughts and doubts that went through my mind, but I do not pretend to deny that underneath them, I enjoyed a perfectly solid conviction that I should be setting out to London shortly, by hook or by crook. As I said before, I could no more refrain from investigating this murder than if it were being done in front of me. I looked at Arthur and he looked gravely back at me.

'It will be difficult,' I said politely to the visitors. 'I must think about it. I will send you a telegram tomorrow morning.'

They took their leave, courteously abstaining from insisting. Professor Taylor actually seemed a little relieved. I then proceeded to devote myself to domestic affairs with no further mention of the case. Arthur glanced at me suspiciously but did not say anything. Together with Sarah, we bathed and fed the twins and entertained them until it was time for them to settle like little droplets into their cribs to sleep. Then we sat down to our own evening meal. It was only then that I caught a significant glance from Arthur.

'Vanessa, dear, I really don't see how...' he began.

'Oh, don't worry about it,' I said, hastily changing the subject.

I wonder if Dora and John would not enjoy spending a few days playing at being loving and doting aunt and uncle for a little while. After all, it might give them some practice for the future—might it not? I could send the twins down to them on the train tomorrow morning, with Sarah. With Sarah there, it should be manageable, and then, Sarah could teach Dora how to vary her husband's diet with some of her unusual ways of preparing food, such as putting cheese and mushroom sauce over cauliflower, instead of a juicy roast of mutton. And perhaps, seeing that Dora's face is so exactly like mine, the twins would not suffer too much from an absence of several days at least; certainly longer than any they have ever known. Could I do it?

I shall do it! Tomorrow morning I shall send Dora a telegram, and another to Emily, to see if I may stay with her in London. And as soon as I have received answers, I shall send another to Professor Taylor. He is not expecting me to come, I think, but he shall be surprised!

I will write down everything in this diary exactly as

it occurs, and it shall be for you, Arthur, to read upon your return and discover the full record of my failures or successes. For even when you are away, there is nothing I do not wish to share with you, and nothing that we can share can ever be deeper than that which we share already. If I do not want you to know that my decision is already firmly taken at this very moment, it is because you look so tranquil and happy sitting across from me, scribbling formulae in the golden glow of the lamp. I do not want you to leave England fearing for me; I do not want your stay in France to be undermined by worry. Go peacefully, and we shall see what we shall see.

London, Thursday, March 12th, 1896

I was awakened this morning by Arthur's gentle kiss on my forehead; he had risen in the early darkness, and dressed in total silence. We did not exchange a single word; his clasp and his lips told me everything; I knew his thoughts and he knew mine. There is so much that it is really better not to put into words.

Yet even with his tacit seal of acceptance of whatever I should decide, I spent a long moment of doubt and anxiety, as I sat in the train to London, all telegrams having been expedited and answered during the morning. I have often noted that forced inactivity engenders this state within me, and have never yet truly managed to discover an effective antidote. I found I could not fix my mind on the poor Professor's murder, for I really do not have anything to go on. Instead, my mind was filled with the image of my last sight of Cecily and Cedric, as they stood framed in the doorway of the train, clinging to Sarah's skirts with their little fists, and watching me, their eyes wide with doubt and suspicion and the corners of their little mouths beginning to descend sorrowfully.

When they awoke this morning, and I went to fetch them out of their little beds and gathered their tender bodies in my arms, still all warm and soft from a night of sleep, with flushed cheeks and heavy eyes, I could not help asking myself if I was not making a mistake; if the right place for me at that moment was not, quite simply, exactly where I was. And I had a sudden and most displeasing vision of myself, thrusting the children into the care of others and gallivanting off to London. I love them so much, yet there is something in me which longs to emerge, if only occasionally, from the tender cocoon of motherhood, and confront the brutal realities of life. I suppose it must be quite normal, yet I find myself racked with doubts.

The arrival of Sarah bearing warm milk and buns relieved me of some of the weight of these thoughts. The babies opened their mouths like little birds in a nest, and while I sat upon the carpet holding them, Sarah, who had already been out to send off my telegrams, had begun preparing for the trip, under the assumption of replies in the positive, and filling a capacious bag with tiny morsels of clothing, and sundry indispensable cloths and scraps. Having finished her breakfast, Cecily, whose eighteen-month-old little mind is already very sharp, stood up, collected a favourite sheep in one hand and her pillow in the other, and prepared to follow Sarah on the trip she was obviously about to take, lining up behind her and imitating her movements with accuracy. Cedric, equally fascinated by the packing procedure, attempted to contribute by taking things out of the bag as fast as Sarah put them in, and throwing them upon the floor, until she lifted the bag onto the table, and forestalled the noise about to emerge from his widely protesting mouth by popping a biscuit into it. And when finally the bag was filled and closed and the children washed and dressed, Dora's eager response to my telegram had arrived, and it was already time to leave for the station. With no time to feel regrets...

How excited the babies were by this unusual excursion, by the noise and bustle of the station, the train's long whistle as it approached, and the footboard connecting the platform to the carriage, into which they were energetically hoisted by a passing porter in a uniform with bright buttons. The effect of it all was that they were in a state of effervescent delight until the very moment when calm returned, the whistle blew once again and the porter arrived to close the door, which separated them from their mother. Only then did the beginnings of dismay appear upon their little features, but there was no time to react, for the door clunked shut upon them, and I was left alone, feeling guilty and sorrowful, and infinitely grateful for knowing that after myself, nobody in the world could care for them better than Sarah.

I could not accustom myself to the separation, the first of more than a few hours since their birth. I boarded my own train, to London, and sat in it nostalgically recalling all the months during which I carried them within me, full of hope and astonishment and dawning suspicion, reliving the hours of pain and ecstasy which brought them forth, and remembering Arthur's face when the nurse finally opened the door to allow him entry to the bedroom, and confronted him proudly, carrying two little snugly wrapped bundles, one in each arm.

These things are the pearls hidden at the heart of the outwardly dull-seeming oyster.

And yet, there have been moments—many of them—when I have felt imprisoned by the walls of domesticity, and yearned for something more. Since I gave up teaching to be a respectable matron, it has happened to me, on occasion, to be submerged with ennui. More than once, since then, I have been saved from this state by people who, referred to me by other people in a quietly expanding chain, have brought me strange little problems to solve: a man who read his wife's diary and found himself cold with fear at what he saw there; a lady who slipped out of her own life, leaving no trace behind; a woman who lost her emerald, and never recovered it—for when I realised who had taken it and followed her onto the boat on which she meant to depart forever, she saw me approaching, understood instantly and, slipping it out of her pocket, flung it impetuously into the flashing waves.

But murder is something that I have not encountered since the strange case of Mr Granger's death before my marriage. My mind roved into the past, remembering the facts of that case, and then, four years earlier, those other murders through which I first met Arthur. Eight years! It is hard to believe. My mind wandered on to Emily and the telegram I had just received from her. She was just a child of thirteen back then. I remember her so well, already grave and intelligent far beyond her years, a penetrating intellect and an innate, unswerving sense of justice. I have not seen her much since my marriage, and not at all since last summer, when she shocked her mother by announcing her intention to continue her studies at the University of London.

Cambridge, of course, does not allow women to obtain doctorates, even if they *do* achieve Wrangler status at the Tripos. One of the best young women students of mathematics in Cambridge ever, Grace Chisholm, who had completed her undergraduate course of study at Girton three years earlier than

Emily, was obliged to leave for Germany in order to obtain a doctorate. I had thought that Emily would follow in her footsteps, but she has other ideas. Having discovered that women may earn a doctorate at the University of London by enrolling at Queen's College, she has decided to follow this path. Indeed, she has realised that although this College itself is actually destined for the training of highly educated governesses, enterprising young women may manage to follow courses or receive tutoring from Professors at King's or at Cambridge, and thus proceed to the highest levels of study. Certainly few girls have accomplished this feat as yet, but Charlotte Scott of Girton did it more than ten years ago, and is now teaching in America!

Emily's mother was more shocked by the idea of her daughter's renting a flat in London than of her travelling all the distance to Germany and living unsupervised in a foreign land. Like any other matron, Mrs Burke-Jones feels that London is a Gehenna, and that her daughter may be led to perdition there. However, Emily held firm, and her mother ended by consenting to give her a modest allowance, on the condition that she share her flat with an older lady by way of a chaperone. The allowance perhaps strains her means a little, but clearly she finds it preferable to tolerating the humiliation of having Emily go out to work. Emily's results at Girton were quite brilliant, and even her mother feels that it would be a great waste to force her to stop her studies now and vegetate here in Cambridge, a place which, while being a shining light of erudition, is such a lamentable backwater as to progress and social issues, and particularly the rights and abilities of our sex. So Emily has set up house in London, and to all appearances she is very happy there. I am most eager to see her again; her welcoming reply to my telegram was sparing in words (youth is always short of money) but not in feelings.

Tavistock Street—the words gave me a pleasant little shiver of anticipation. London again! Its streets, its bustle, its vigorous life, its frenetic activity, its easy freedom; a taste of it is like a taste of vibrant red wine.

These were my thoughts as the train pulled into Liverpool Street. An electric tension swept through me as I stood up; my bag was reached down by a helpful gentleman traveller who ushered me politely onto the platform ahead of himself. The moment I emerged, the very air of London struck me as different, and my excitement increased as I scanned the small group of people waiting to welcome the passengers, to see if I could spot Professor Taylor, who had confirmed that he would fetch me. Before I saw him, he was coming towards me and taking my valise out of my hand.

'I cannot thank you enough for accepting my invitation,' he said gravely, as though he had prepared the words. I could not help feeling a twinge of worry as to whether he truly believed in the success of my enterprise. I myself was, as always, tremendously uncertain about the outcome, meaning only to try my best.

'Have you already arranged for a place to stay, or will you need a hotel?' he continued solicitously.

'I will be staying with a friend,' I responded quietly. 'But it is enough for me to go to her flat this evening. My case is not heavy; I can carry it with me, and I am ready to start working immediately.'

'How exactly do you intend to begin?' he said, looking slightly taken aback. 'I am ready to help you in any way I can, but I must admit that I have not the faintest idea how a detective goes about his—er—or her work. I had thought of organising a small dinner party at my home, with several of my colleagues from the department, as soon as I can manage to send out the invitations. You may possibly learn something useful from them, although it may essentially come down to the fact that Gerard Ralston had but few friends and, as far as we know, no private life at all. What else were you thinking of doing?'

'Well,' I said, 'ideally, if it were possible, the very first thing I would do would be to look through all of Professor Ralston's papers. I meant to ask you where they are now, and if such a thing is feasible. I hope the police have not seized them?'

'As far as I know, the police have not actually taken any papers. Ralston kept all his papers in his study, and the police have looked through everything and sealed the place off. They asked me a number of questions and I did not get the impression that they had found anything conclusive. Indeed, I am afraid you are likely to find more drafts of articles and notes on research than revealing private letters. I cannot believe he had much in the way of non-professional correspondence. On the other hand, I cannot quite persuade myself that he was murdered, either; yet it is a fact that he was, so chances are that something may turn up.'

'Would he not have kept personal papers in his flat rather than in his study?' I asked.

'Apparently not. The lady who came daily to clean and cook for him claims there wasn't so much as a scrap in the house. But that's normal enough, after all; his study was not really separate from his flat, it was just below it. He had a couple of large cabinets in his study, in which he piled and filed everything except whatever he was working on at the moment, which he kept in his desk.'

'I see,' I said. 'All this makes me feel that I would dearly like to have a look around in his study. But I suppose it is hopeless, since you said that the police have sealed off the room.'

'Well—at any rate they have locked it and carried off the key,' he said.

'And the spare one as well, I suppose,' I replied. 'Was there really no other?'

'The police believe so,' he replied with an indefinable expression, which might have been very slightly smug. 'That is what the lady who did for him told them. But as a matter of fact, there is another. Ralston actually had his key copied, and he gave the copy to me on the eve of a trip to the Continent that he took one or two years ago. Of course he packed every document he thought he would need, but he still worried that once over there, he might realise that something he had left behind was absolutely indispensable after all. He wanted me to be able to fetch it out and send it to him in case that happened.'

'And did he end up asking you to do so?'

'No, he did not. In fact, I rather believe that he forgot about it altogether. He was a very possessive man, and I am quite certain that if he had remembered about the key, he would have asked me for it immediately upon his return. I forgot all about it myself, as a matter of fact. I simply added it to the ring of keys I usually keep at home. But I remembered it suddenly yesterday, when I got your telegram, and have brought the ring with me.' And he proceeded to extract it from a leather case he carried. 'I would be hard put to tell you which one it is on sight,' he added, looking at the tightly crowded congregation of keys of all shapes and sizes, 'but it must be here, and we shall find it. I only hope that our action cannot be considered illegal.'

He flagged a cab and we climbed in and directed the driver to Adelphi Street. He occupied the drive in giving me sundry details and thumbnail sketches of the members of the Department. I paid special attention to any mention of past conflicts, and retained a few names for further investigation. At length, the cab drew up in front of the library and we stepped out.

It was peculiar to confront the tall iron grille, the impressive gate opening onto the street, and the wide path leading up between two narrow green swards to the heavy, square stone house, with the images that I had formed in my mind while listening to the descriptions of the place given to me in my own home. It was not really dissimilar to what I had imagined, yet it possessed the inexplicable additional sharpness of reality, which also distinguishes familiar figures seen in dreams from their actual embodiments.

We walked up the path slowly. I tried to estimate how much time it took us, and to imagine suddenly seeing the two students come tearing around the corner of the house, and myself running to follow them inside. I wondered if the sequence of events could really be so impossible to adjust as the professors and police seemed to imagine, and if it would be possible, at some point, to make some experiments myself.

We entered. The vast, square room with its enormous windows looking out in all directions was peopled only by two lonely figures. One, a young man with spectacles, sat at a desk just within the main door, a pile of books before him.

'This is Edmund Bryant,' said the Professor, pausing briefly before the desk to introduce me to him. 'Our Department has hired him to watch the library by day, so that it may continue to be used by students and faculty.' I greeted him quietly, observing with interest his pale face equipped with a rather long, very narrow nose, a high forehead and oddly light eyes which seemed to emerge with difficulty from a state of deep concentration.

'You are studying?' I asked him.

'I am working on my dissertation,' he replied, and something like a flash of resentment appeared briefly in his eyes and disappeared immediately as he turned to his books again.

The other occupant of the library, a student with disarranged clothes and tousled hair, stood on a ladder fetching down a book from a high shelf. Upon hearing us enter, he descended. At the sight of Professor Taylor, he turned somewhat pale.

'Ah, Randall,' said the Professor with a vinegary smile. 'I am indeed pleased to have encountered you. How fortuitous. I believe you have something for me, do you not? It is already somewhat late.'

'Oh, um, ahem, yes, of course,' mumbled the student in deep embarrassment. 'It is…that is…it is at home, I…I have not had time yet to…'

'Please do give it to me at the first opportunity,' said Professor Taylor. 'I am beginning to correct them today.' And he continued to stand fixing the student with his sharp eyes. Completely flustered, the poor young man murmured a hasty assent, and putting the book he had selected down on the nearest table, left the library as quickly as he could.

'One of the students in my advanced Medieval Commerce class,' said the Professor with some annoyance. 'Brilliant, but disorganised and permanently late. He has still not given me his draft on Early Apprenticeships in the Art of Metalworking, and has been avoiding me lately because of it. I expect he has not completed it yet. Well, he is gone now; to finish it, I hope. Now for the other one.' He turned to the studious gentleman at the front desk.

'I will be remaining here for some time, Bryant,' he said. 'You may leave for the afternoon. Leave me the keys to the front door and the main gate; I will lock up, and you can get them back tomorrow morning if you come to me before classes.'

'Yes, sir,' said Edmund respectfully but reluctantly, beginning to gather up his things. He looked put out, as though he had been perfectly happy where he was, and did not particularly want to be sent away, and piled his books with distinct lack of energy. He seemed about to say something, but the Professor forestalled him.

'Oh, and will you be going to the main building? You couldn't stop off and put this note into Professor Hudson's letterbox, could you? It would be most helpful.' Taking up a notepad, he wrote something upon the first page, folded it carefully and handed it over. Edmund could not but take it, and I admired the Professor's dexterity.

'I wrote out the dinner invitation for Sunday to Hudson,' he confided to me when Edmund had disappeared down the path and out of the main gate. 'Why not? This way it's done, and Bryant is got rid of. Now let us deal with anyone else who might choose to appear.'

He wrote *THE LIBRARY IS CLOSED TODAY* in large letters on the notepad, tore off the page, and pinned it to the heavy wooden front door, then closed it and locked it from the inside with the key he had authoritatively removed from Edmund's possession.

'Here we are, then,' he said.

It took him several minutes of patience, trying the keys on his ring in the keyhole of the locked door to Professor Ralston's study in turn, but he eventually located the right one and the door swung open.

'Ah, there we go,' he said with satisfaction.

The study presented a peculiar sight. The police had apparently left the furniture exactly as it had been when the murder took place. There was not much of it, in fact; apart from two large, solid oaken cabinets on either side of the large window looking out over the grass at the back of the house, the study had been furnished only with an impressive, massive desk and two black wooden chairs, one with arms and one without. Probably the Professor had one chair behind his desk and the other was for visitors, but it was not possible to tell immediately which chair had occupied which position, for they had apparently been flung about the room. The smaller of the two appeared to have crashed against the wall, smashing the glass of a picture, which still lay among the shards. The desk had been pushed over, but had not fallen entirely to the floor, having partially and crookedly come to rest upon the other chair, which lay flat on its back on the floor, rather miserably upholding the full weight of the desk on the edge of its upthrust seat. The desk was a handsome one; its burnished wooden surface was free since everything on it had slid to the ground. I spotted a little dent in its centre, as though it had received rather a sharp blow from a heavy object. I peered closely at this dent. It seemed to have been newly made; infinitesimal splinters of wood showed, clean and fresh, at its edges. The papers and pens which had been lying on the desk lay scattered on the floor, as did a nearly empty inkpot and an elegant brass lamp, its shade awry. A thick carpet covered the central section of the floor. Before the tragedy, the study must have been quite a pleasant place to be.

'You see how the floor is raised above garden level,' observed Professor Taylor. 'One goes up several steps from the path to the front door; the higher level keeps out the damp. It means that the windows are quite high; they are at waist level in here, as you see, and thus above head level outside. That is why the students who heard the sounds of the struggle which produced all this'—he indicated the mess with a wave of his hand—'could not simply peer within to ascertain what was going on.'

'It is a pity,' I said thoughtfully, 'that they did not think of climbing on each other's shoulders.'

'Peering in windows goes against the grain, instinctively, doesn't it?' he replied. 'It probably did not even occur to them. I think that in their place I should have done exactly the same as they did.'

I walked rather tentatively around the fallen desk and looked at the spot where Professor Ralston had presumably been wont to sit.

'This is where his body was found,' said the Professor. 'He was apparently shot at very close range while standing behind his desk. There was not much blood. The police took away samples, I expect, to do whatever they do with them in their chemical laboratories, but I don't believe it yielded anything unexpected. The gun was over there,' he added, indicating a position one or two yards in front of the fallen desk, rather near the door. He then turned to the cabinets, and tried a drawer. 'Perhaps we should begin by having a look at these?'

It had not occurred to me that he might actually intend to offer me his collaboration. I would much have preferred to work alone. It was my habit; after all, one could never tell who might be involved in the events one was trying to uncover, or at least have a secret interest in them. But he was already opening some drawers and peering inside them, and for the life of me I could not see how to send him away.

'This one holds drafts of his own papers and articles, and copies of newspapers and magazines containing things that interested him,' he remarked, lifting out some of the contents.

'I think I will begin by inspecting the desk,' I said, and leaning down, I began to look at the papers that lay upon the floor. 'I don't suppose we had better disarrange things too much, had we? I mean, the police will be expecting to find this room as they left it.'

'True, true,' he said, quickly putting the papers he had spread out on the floor in front of the window back into a neat pile. Then he changed his mind. 'Well, it's not likely they'll have memorised the exact order of every paper, is it? I don't suppose it matters much. I'll look at them drawer by drawer. Dear me, look at this—most interesting! Quite a collection of copies of original documents from the Spanish Inquisition! Notes from a trial, here… Not surprising, I suppose,' he added, leafing through an article he had discovered, and looking as pleased as a cat with a saucer of cream. 'Yes, I suppose that makes sense, with his interests, doesn't it? Most interesting, this,' and he continued reading busily. Within a few minutes he was utterly absorbed. It did not seem that he was going to be much of a disturbance to me after all.

Quietly, I picked up the few sheets from the floor and began to peruse them. One contained a careful outline of a lecture, and a couple of others contained a list of what looked like possible topics for dissertations. Besides this, there was a letter in French addressed to Professor Ralston, and a final sheet, which appeared to be the beginning of an answer to this letter. I picked it up quickly, my heart beating. It seemed likely that this was the very last thing he ever wrote.

Dear Lazare,

I have received your news. Surely you realise that vague nonsense concerning rumours of a lost or found "petit bleu" is unlikely to have the slightest effect on the Affair. If the thing really exists, which appears highly doubtful to me, it is almost certain to be a forgery…

The Library Paradox

I could not help imagining the Professor seated at his desk, writing these lines with a pinched expression on his face, pausing for a moment to consider his next words…and hearing a knock at the door.

Picking up the letter in French, I read it carefully. It was extremely short, and from what I could judge, the tone seemed to be aggressive, almost accusatory. However, it was too telegraphic in style for me to be able to understand what it referred to.

Vous allez pouvoir arrêter vos agissements. Un nouveau document est apparu, cette fois définitif; il s'agit d'un petit bleu trouvé au même endroit que le bordereau, mais cette fois avec mention explicite d'un nom: celui du vrai coupable. La justice suivra son cours.

Bien à vous. B.L.

'Do you know what this is all about?' I asked Professor Taylor, carrying the letters over to where he knelt upon the parquet.

'Eh? What's that?' he said, emerging with difficulty from the profound concentration inspired in him by the yellowed articles into which he was plunged.

'Look at this,' I said, pushing the documents under his nose. 'Do you have any idea what it is all about?'

'I've often wondered how a detective works,' mused the Professor unexpectedly, paying no attention to the papers I was holding out to him. 'I mean, there must be such a wealth of information; far too much, one would think. Just look at all the papers in this room. Looking for a clue is like looking for a needle in a haystack, isn't it? And the talking with people— why, what can one hope to discover by talking with my colleagues, for instance? I mean, I know them all very well, and can already imagine everything they will probably say. And I must say I can't see what use any of it could possibly be in elucidating Professor Ralston's death.'

His words distracted me momentarily from Lazare's letter.

'It is hard to explain exactly how I proceed,' I admitted, quelling the slight feeling of worry that his words aroused in me. 'I really don't know just what I am trying to do. Maybe the best description would be that I form a picture in my mind of what constituted the normality of the situation I am investigating, and once I have developed a clear enough picture, I notice anything that stands out, and restrict myself to investigating that. Now, of course, it is still too early for me to have formed a picture. Examining the papers in this room will help me to start. These particular letters strike me as very interesting. Please do have a look.' And I thrust them towards him once again. The Professor pushed his glasses up on his nose.

'Most embarrassing, this looking at other people's letters,' he murmured uncomfortably, taking them and squinting at the Frenchman's rather difficult handwriting. 'This letter must be about the Dreyfus affair,' he added after a moment, brightening visibly. 'It simply has to be the very one he mentioned to me.' This thought, or the exciting nature of the documents, appeared to relieve him of some of his scruples. 'By that journalist I told you about, whose name I couldn't remember. Lazare—yes, that's it, Bernard Lazare, a French journalist much in the public eye. It is certainly he, and he does seem to assert that a new document has appeared, which apparently indicates another person as the guilty party. Dear me, this *is* exciting—I simply must find out more about it! Do you know, I must show you my dossier on the Dreyfus case when you come to the house for dinner. It's a shocking business, you cannot imagine. I've been in contact with the family; they're grateful to anyone who will show a bit of support. They'd give their right arms to make some progress in finding the true culprit. Perhaps this will finally turn out to be a break in the case, though it's all rather cryptic. What exactly is a *"petit bleu"*?'

'It's a handwritten telegram on a standard blue postal form,' I told him. 'But he doesn't say from whom to whom. It sounds exciting to me, too, but apparently this letter didn't have that effect on Professor Ralston. He appears to have decided to dismiss the whole thing out of hand.'

'Well, that would be typical, I should say. Once he had got his opinion on something fixed, it was virtually impossible to make him change it. A pity. Such rigidity is not a professional advantage. Here, for instance,' he added, taking up one of the papers he had been inspecting, 'in this text, he absolutely insists on defending what is really now considered an outdated interpretation of some remarks by Torquemada…'

I left him to his studies, and after taking a few moments to copy down the contents of the two letters in my notebook, I replaced them more or less where I had found them and turned my attention to the drawers of the overturned desk. They yielded nothing of interest, however. There were only four of them, and two of those contained writing implements and blank sheets. The other two contained only work related to his teaching: carefully organised folders contained outlines of lectures and courses, and also lists of undergraduates and doctoral students, accompanied by personal commentaries, generally of a sour nature, such as: 'no insight, destined to fail' or 'unpleasantly obsequious although hard-working'. My eye caught a familiar name: 'Edmund Bryant: persists in stubbornly developing wrong ideas.' I felt a brief flash of sympathy for the pale-eyed youth.

After this, I spent more than two hours looking through

the drawers of the heavy oak cabinet containing so-called personal papers, although I must observe that anything less personal I have rarely witnessed. I peered through many years of pass books from the bank, vigilant for the appearance (or disappearance) of the unexpected lump sum, which could denote blackmail, or other activities of a doubtful nature. I have kept regularly to this habit ever since the day when such a discovery led me to the true reasons for the inexplicable behaviour of a certain man whose wife had come to me in distress, having incomprehensibly been offered a diamond bracelet in spite of living on straitened means. But there was nothing of the kind in Professor Ralston's financial life. His monthly stipend appeared with clockwork regularity, and his expenses were relatively few. A larger sum spent in December 1894 was attributed by Professor Taylor to the aforementioned trip to France. Nor could I find anything in the least bit untoward in the neatly organised piles of bills.

I read rapidly and indiscreetly through a fairly copious correspondence, but there were no personal letters in it at all; they were all more or less official. I discovered that the firm of lawyers representing Professor Ralston was one Gumbadge, Gumbadge & Upp, a fact that I stored away in my mind for future reference. I also found two previous letters from Bernard Lazare, dating from last year; one of them contained an impassioned argument for the innocence of Dreyfus, and the other a carefully developed essay criticising the social ills produced by anti-Semitism. Although Professor Ralston's replies were not to hand, I was beginning to be able to form an idea of what they were probably like.

In a separate drawer, I did come upon a small packet of handwritten letters, which I snatched up eagerly, but they were merely from Professor Ralston's father, and contained little of interest. They were few and far between, sent from various places during his periods of travel; mostly from Poland, but occasionally from Romania, Bulgaria or Paris. Their tone was formally affectionate but not warm, and they contented themselves with some remarks concerning the author's travels, some concerning his health, and kind queries as to his son's welfare. Every now and then I came upon a slight variation, such as an answer to something the Professor had asked, or an amusing anecdote or complaint. But there was absolutely nothing which seemed to have a bearing on the murder. I scanned the most recent letter, written one month ago in Warsaw, with particular attention, but it remained opaque, so I put all the letters together and, slipping them back into their drawer, I turned to the other cabinet.

Professor Taylor had gone through much of it already, but although he was very eager to help me, it turned out to be perfectly impossible to make him understand the kind of thing I was seeking; the more so as I found it difficult to explain even to myself. Not only did he fail to understand, but he had an irresistible tendency to latch onto various things, which *he* found peculiar, such as the complete lack of critical analysis which apparently struck Professor Ralston, like a blindness, when confronting certain specific questions such as the effect on commerce of the exclusion of the Jews from the silk-making Guild, a trade in which they had developed great expertise. He went into the peculiarity of these views at great length, criticising Ralston and distracting me from advancing in my task. However, he took no offence at the fact that I continued to rustle papers while he talked, and I kept one ear on what he was saying, and one eye on the contents of each drawer.

'Look at this,' I said suddenly, interrupting his stream of remarks, and lifting out a leather document holder from the bottom of one of the lowest drawers, I showed it to him. It was inscribed 'B.L.', and although by the worn shape of it, it had once contained a thick pile of documents, it appeared to contain nothing now.

'He emptied this one out,' observed the Professor.

I opened it. It was indeed empty, except for a single small sheet, which had got stuck under the metal clasp of the folder.

'That's odd,' I remarked. 'I found letters from Bernard Lazare in the other cabinet. What can this have been?' I shook the folder to dislodge the little sheet, but it did not fall out. I did not want to detach it by force, for I was afraid that the police might have already noticed its existence, but the blank, back side of the paper was all that was visible. However, by peeling it back delicately and turning the folder around, I was able to read over the contents. Although unfamiliar to me and not very precise, they generated a spontaneous feeling of disgust and faint horror within me.

'What an awful man Professor Ralston must have been,' I said.

The paper contained a handwritten list, which ran as follows.

> 1144: William of Norwich (England). Jewish
>   leaders executed.
> 1171: Blois, France. Thirty-one Jews killed.
> 1180–1200: Bury St Edmunds, Bristol, Winchester
> 1199: 1235: Erfurt, Bischofsheim, Lauda,
>   Fulda (Germany)
> 1244: London: Jewish citizens heavily fined (?)
> 1255: Little St Hugh (Chaucer). 100 hanged
> 1462: Anderl von Rinn
> 1475: Saint Simon of Trent

The Library Paradox

1490: Torquemada, LaGuardia trial: 8 Jews burnt
1840: Murder of Padre Tommaso of Damascus
1853: The incident in Saratova, Russia
1880–1890: large influx of Eastern European
    Jews to London
1886: James Wilson
For recently published Catholic analyses, see:
    Bishop Martin of Paderborn, 1872
    Roman Catholic journal Civiltà Cattolica, 1881

The last dated entry in the list, mentioning James Wilson, had been pencilled in underneath the rest, and underlined heavily. The Professor took the folder from me, and read the list with his glasses pushed to the tip of his nose.

'This is Ralston's handwriting,' he said. 'I am not sure exactly what information he has been collecting here. It looks rather sensationalistic and certainly anti-Jewish. I cannot say that I am entirely surprised. At any rate, this may well be quite old since he seems to have lost interest and emptied out the rest of the contents, presumably into the bin. This list obviously just got stuck here by mistake.' And he shook the folder out, as I had done, without dislodging it.

'I don't know if there's much to be made of it,' he said.

'Perhaps Bernard Lazare will know,' I answered, copying it into my notebook. 'After all, this seems to have been his folder. I really must manage to make his acquaintance somehow.'

'Ah, that is an idea,' he answered with alacrity. 'You are right. It might be most enlightening. Do you know, I don't see why I shouldn't invite him to give us a lecture here at King's. He's becoming rather a well-known fellow; there's a lot he could tell us that would be interesting. I shan't ask him to talk directly about the Dreyfus affair, of course. We'll pump him on all of that over dinner, if he'll come.'

I was pleased.

'Can you write to him as soon as possible, or even telegraph?' I said hopefully. 'I am in a great hurry, you know. I don't have much time.'

'What is the rush?' he said, surprised.

A vision of babies toddling in the sunshine swam in front of me.

'Oh, ah, well, the trail is growing cold, you know,' I said hastily. 'It is always best to act quickly.'

'Yes, of course,' he agreed, turning back to his explorations. And we completed the work of examining the contents of the drawers in silence.

The shadows were lengthening rapidly, and dusk was upon us by the time we had finished. I had found absolutely nothing else that I could consider remarkable or significant, and dared not take the little that I had found away with me. The Professor muffled himself up in his coat and hat, wound his scarf many times about his neck, locked up the door to the study and then the main door of the library. We walked together to the main gate leading onto the street.

'It is late enough to lock this one up as well,' he observed, glancing at his watch. 'As head of the department, I have my own keys to the gate and library,' he added, smiling. 'I only borrowed Edmund's to make sure he wouldn't return unexpectedly. I shall return them to him tomorrow morning, but I expect you might temporarily want to have mine, and the key to Ralston's study as well. Do take good care of them, and make sure to return them to me as soon as you do not need them any more.' He handed them to me with a cheerful and carefree gesture that contrasted greatly with the doubtful mien he had worn when welcoming me at the station. I wondered what had transpired to ease his mind. I was just basking in the flattering assumption that observation of my methods might have increased his confidence in my success and removed his doubts when it suddenly flashed across my mind that he might—just possibly—have managed to locate and subtract some incriminating document from Ralston's study without my noticing it. My eyes went automatically to his briefcase, and my mind leapt ahead, moving faster than the reasoning brain, asking and answering its own questions in the flash of an eye. Why would the Professor have waited for me to be there in the study with him if he wanted to search for some paper? Well, Edmund might have found it suspicious if he went in all alone, whereas with me, who could always be explained as an officially retained detective, he had a valid reason. But why could he not have gone quietly alone at night? Too dangerous; he would need to count on several hours of searching and the policeman on the beat would surely notice the light. This sudden, friendly offer of the keys—did it mean that there was nothing more to search for in the tumbled study?

Unaware of my thoughts, the Professor was still smiling and holding the keys out towards me. I accepted them as gratefully as I could, reassuring myself that it was most unlikely that the tall and distinguished figure in front of me could be the murderer, and that after all, he was probably merely being helpful. 'I am sure they will be useful,' I told him. 'I will come to see you if I need anything else. Please let me know if you succeed in getting Lazare to come down. In the meantime, you may be certain that I will be devoting myself entirely to the case.' And I left him and continued in the direction of Tavistock Street, concentrating on keeping a firmly open mind.

It was fully evening by the time I arrived at Emily's little flat. I rang, the door was flung open, and she welcomed me eagerly with a shining face.

'Vanessa!' she squealed joyfully. 'We've been waiting ever so long. Do, do come in at once.'

After my marriage, Emily found herself quite unable to call me Mrs Weatherburn; she was too much used to the 'Miss Duncan' of her schooldays. But by the time of my wedding she was already a young lady, and a dear friend of mine to boot; her days as my pupil were long past, so I persuaded her to call me by my Christian name.

I entered within, and admired her quarters, which though small, were bright and comfortable, with a warm fire dancing in the grate and enough comfortable armchairs and pillows to make a number of people welcome. Indeed, Emily was not alone, for young Mr Sachs rose from a chair to greet me, accompanied by a slender, dark young lady.

'This is Jonathan Sachs whom you've already met, and this is his sister Amy, who shares the flat with me,' she explained. 'You remember how pleased Mother was when I told her that I had found a lady to room with me.'

I observed Amy Sachs intently. While certainly older than Emily, I found it hard to believe that she was thirty, as Emily had told Mrs Burke-Jones in order to reassure her as to the serious and elderly nature of her chaperone. She looked like a girl who, while not quite young any more, has preserved her youth by continuing to live it, and avoiding the barrier which, once passed, leads inevitably to matronhood.

Emily, who knows me very well, divined my thoughts immediately. 'Amy exaggerated her age a little bit when we talked to Mother,' she said quickly. 'But not all that much, really! Just a couple of years. I'm so glad I met Amy, for at first I didn't know a soul here with whom Mother would have considered letting me share rooms. Luckily Jonathan, whom I knew from classes, told me that his sister was also seeking to move away from home and try the experiment of living independently in London. Amy is a writer,' she added proudly, drawing her friend forward by the hand.

'A hopeful writer,' corrected the young lady modestly.

'Oh, she has already published things! Haven't you, Amy? She's published some stories in magazines, and some poems. No novels yet, but they're sure to come, aren't they? Well, do come into the bedroom and put down your things.'

'I hope you will do me the honours of your flat,' I said, following her and most interested to see all the details of the unusual and independent living arrangements.

'Oh, certainly. But there isn't much to see. This is my bedroom and the other one is Amy's. This little room over here will be yours. It's too small to be useful for anything much; it's not much more than a big closet, really. At least, that's what we use it for. But we've moved in the sofa, as you see, and made it up as a bed for you. I do hope you will be all right.'

'This is perfect,' I said, contemplating with delight the narrow quarters where I was to spend my London nights, and putting my case down on the bed proprietarily.

'Then let's go back and have tea,' she said, and we returned to the sitting room where she immediately put on the kettle.

'I do hope you won't find us too forward, Mrs Weatherburn,' said Amy Sachs, suddenly and unexpectedly adopting a leadership role in the conversation. 'You see, we are very excited about meeting a real detective. Emily has told us so much about you.'

I writhed a little at these words. I have never, but never thought of myself as a 'real detective'. An amateur, a pure amateur, with a little talent, perhaps, for feeling out the unusual, and for guessing people's feelings and intentions.

Unaware of my embarrassment, Amy continued to strike ahead.

'While we were waiting here for you, the three of us came to a decision together; we want to help you solve the murder, if we can. We would like to be your council of war. I don't know exactly what we could do, but we have had one or two ideas. Do you think we might be able to help you? Can you tell us anything about what you are trying to discover?'

Although there was perhaps something shocking about it, I did not dislike her forthrightness; she spoke only what was uppermost in my own mind. I had been wondering if we should have to avoid the subject of the murder and make small talk throughout the evening, and finally, I found this preferable to that. After only the briefest of hesitations, I decided to ignore my embarrassment and a certain natural reluctance to share the progress (as yet near zero) of my investigation, and accept the proffered help for what it might be worth.

'All right, let it be so,' I said. 'If you are willing to help me, then let me begin by asking you some questions. I need some information, and one never knows who may turn out helpful. However, if this is a war council, we must start off on an equal footing. I hope you will call me Vanessa.'

'And Amy and Jonathan, then,' she replied, continuing very naturally in her position as leader of her little committee. Emily poured out tea, and we all settled together in front of the fire. I felt a sense of warmth, comfort and friendship quite incongruous with the task I had come to London to perform. It was all I could do not to feel guilty.

'I have two questions to start with,' I began. 'The first one is this: do any of you know anything about a certain French gentleman called Bernard Lazare, who, as far as I know, is a journalist?'

Emily looked blank, but Amy and Jonathan appeared to be familiar with the name.

'Why yes, I know who he is,' said Jonathan. 'He was the big name in the Dreyfus affair a year or so ago; a Jewish journalist who stuck up for Dreyfus after he was condemned for high treason. Our parents follow his writings and mention him now and again, don't they, Amy?'

'Yes, they do,' she confirmed. 'I've read him too. He's a journalist and a writer as well. Before Dreyfus, he actually wrote some rather irritating things about Jews and assimilation into contemporary society. But what on earth is his connection with Professor Ralston's murder?'

'Perhaps none,' I admitted. 'But Professor Ralston corresponded with him, and may have been actually in the process of writing to him when he was killed. At any rate, an unfinished letter to him remained on his desk. That does not prove a connection, obviously, any more than if he had been correcting papers when he met his death. Still, there is something special: Lazare had sent him a piece of news about the Dreyfus case, which seemed to have annoyed him seriously just a day or two before his death.'

'Really? What kind of news?'

'The letter from Mr Lazare is not very detailed, but apparently a telegram appeared somewhere which would seem to indicate that somebody else was the traitor.'

'Ah, if only Dreyfus were to be proved innocent—it would save us!' exclaimed Amy dramatically. Her words surprised me.

'Save you? What do you mean?' I asked.

'His condemnation has been a disaster, an immeasurable international disaster for us, for our community,' she replied impatiently. 'Surely you realise that we are Jews, Jonathan and I?'

'Well, no, in fact. How could I have?' I answered, taken aback by the edge in her tone.

'How could she have, indeed? Don't be so sharp, Amy,' said Jonathan soothingly. 'Do you know, Vanessa—we encounter so much anti-Semitism in our lives, in school, at university, and in a polite, underhanded way, even in society, that we are sometimes unconsciously led to believe that an Englishman cannot see a Jew without thinking: "Ah, a Jew". Our name, Sachs, is such a typical one that we never manage to pass unperceived. To meet someone like you is actually very refreshing. We were going to talk about it anyway, as it has something to do with the help we want to offer you. But ask us your other questions first, as I don't think there is much more we can tell you about Bernard Lazare.'

'I hope to learn more by meeting him,' I told him. 'Professor Taylor has kindly suggested inviting him down for a lecture.'

Amy's eyes shone with pleasure at this news, but she said nothing. I saw that the peculiar interest she took in the death of a man she had very probably never met, which I had at first put down to curiosity for the sensational, was in fact nothing of the kind. Observing her more closely, it seemed clear that it stemmed rather from a desire to defend the community she felt she belonged to from the accusation of murder. My sympathy for her increased greatly forthwith.

'My other question concerns someone called James Wilson, and an event that took place in the year 1886,' I said. 'Have any of you heard anything about this? Of course you were all rather young at the time.'

I felt something like an electric shock pass through the air, or a sudden peak of tension. But three blank faces stared back at me, and three heads slowly and rather sadly shook from side to side.

'Oh, well, then,' I said. 'I shall try to get information from the old newspapers at the British Library. It is a technique I have found remarkably successful in the past. I have to admit that these are my only leads for the present. Since I cannot follow them up this very instant, let me hear your ideas now.'

'One thing we thought we could do is a reconstruction of the crime,' said Jonathan with alacrity.

'A reconstruction?'

'Yes—you know,' intervened Emily, 'try to figure out how the old man could have come out so fast.'

'Or how somebody else could have been there as well,' corrected Jonathan. 'Look, there are enough of us to play all the roles: Ralston is not needed; the murderer and the three witnesses make four. Shall we try it, Vanessa? Could we actually use the library to do it?'

'Yes,' I said. 'We can and should do it, but with discretion and in silence. Preferably in the evening.'

'But the library is locked in the evening,' said Amy.

'I have the keys,' I said. 'Shall we do it tomorrow night?'

'Yes—tomorrow night,' said Amy. 'Let us all meet here and go together.' She looked around to check that everyone was in agreement, then took a deep breath. 'Now, about the other thing. Jonathan—you tell her.'

He shifted about on his seat, unwound his long legs and knotted them differently, looking uncomfortable. After a moment's silence, he looked at his sister. She looked back at him.

'It is awkward,' he said. 'I hate doing it. I suppose I had better explain to you straight out, Vanessa, how bad I feel at the idea of pursuing the old man that I saw coming out of the library that day. I...I have to say that I don't believe he is the murderer, yet I don't understand how it could be anybody else. But not him—it just doesn't seem possible. That kind of person does not, cannot…' He stopped and again looked at his sister for help.

'We feel that trying to hunt him down as the murderer would be wrong,' said she. 'We think we *must* hunt for him, but without prejudice. As a witness, as someone who certainly will be able to explain something about the mystery. About what he may have seen while he was there, I mean.'

'I understand what you are saying,' I said. 'For reasons I am ignorant of, above and beyond the peculiar timing element, you are deeply convinced of his innocence. Perhaps you should begin by telling me why.'

'He was a Hassid, Vanessa. Hassidim do not commit murder.'

'Perhaps you had better explain to me more precisely exactly what a Hassid is,' I said.

Jonathan and Amy looked at each other.

'Hassidim are a group of Jews who practise their religion according to particular rites and rituals not shared by all Jews,' began Jonathan sagely. 'It isn't easy to explain superficially. If I tell you that they are of Ashkenazi origin, meaning from the Eastern and not the Southern countries; that they respect articles of a dress code not of Biblical or Talmudic origin, but established down to the slightest details by last-century rabbis; that they form little groups, each around what they call a "rebbe"—this is not exactly the same as what you would probably know as a rabbi, but a tsaddik, a truly wise and righteous man, whom they treat as their link to God, and from whose lips pure wisdom falls; that while praying they lose themselves in rocking back and forth and wild singing and dancing, all this does not really begin to describe the soul of the movement. The word Hesed means "grace"; these Jews feel that they have been touched by the grace of God. They are not approved by certain other groups of Jews, who consider their practices backwards, obscurantist, medieval. I am not speaking only of Enlightenment Jews who have assimilated into European societies for generations, but even of other Jews living in the very same remote Polish and Russian villages as these Hassidim, but who, however, are wary of the shade of fanaticism that accompanies their devotion.'

'How could you be sure that you recognise a Hassid when you see one simply walking down the street?' I asked.

'They have that very particular code of dress,' said Amy. 'The black coat, the sidelocks, and either the black hat or the big *shtreimel*, the fur-bordered hat that this man was wearing.'

'But perhaps the man you saw was wearing those clothes as a disguise,' I proposed.

'No!' said Jonathan. 'I wish I could believe that. Then we could assume that he *was* the murderer, and we would have only to hunt for him and solve the time puzzle. But it is impossible. The man was a real Hassid. There is no doubt about it.'

'But how can you tell?'

'I've grown up among them. It would be easy enough to put on the clothing, but I don't think even the most extraordinary actor could learn to walk with that special gait, carry his books and papers just that way, sweep aside his prayer curls with that gesture, mumble in Yiddish as he passed through the gate. Not in just that very way. I've gone over it in my mind again and again. He was a real Hassid.'

'You are absolutely certain?'

'I only wish I weren't!' he replied. 'But it's just impossible. Believe me, their manner of holding themselves, speaking, moving, the look in their eyes is unmistakable, and I don't see how one could act it. Maybe it wouldn't be so difficult to imitate one of the younger ones, who are sometimes a little forced in their efforts, but the man I saw was a true rebbe. He was old, and he had the authority. There is no question about it.'

'He was himself a rabbi?' I said, feeling a little awkward about using the unfamiliar term, although I had heeded his explanations.

'In the Hassidic sense—I should say definitely,' he replied.

'Then that should make it easier to trace him,' I observed. 'How many of them can there be in London, I wonder?'

'That is the point,' he said. 'That is exactly what we were going to talk to you about. You see, it would not be easy to count the rebbes who live in London's East End, because it is not an official status, such as being a priest would be. One is not ordained officially as a rebbe, so there is no list. On the other hand, while there are a great many of them, probably several dozen if not hundreds, still, if one has a contact within the tightly knit community who lives in that area, it seems to us', he glanced at his sister, 'that perhaps one could learn something. And that is what we believe we have.'

'It is not that we believe it; we actually have it,' intervened Amy. 'We have a cousin who married a man from that area. It is a strange story. Rivka was brought up in London, exactly as we were. She knew no Yiddish and as a child, she went to synagogue only occasionally, on the holiest days. But later she and her mother became more religious. She met this young man, David Mendel, after the services for the High Holy Days in September, three years ago. It was impossible to tell anything about his origins; his English was perfect. He is very handsome, and he and Rivka fell in love. Then came the surprise. David turned out to be from a Hassidic family living in the East End. They had emigrated from a *shtetl*—that is what they call their villages in the Yiddish dialect—in Poland some ten years earlier, when he was only a boy. An enormous number of immigrants started coming then—they're still coming, in fact—because of the pogroms, vicious attacks on Jewish villages by the local population.'

I remembered seeing a mention of the wave of immigration on Professor Ralston's list.

'Some of the *shtetl* families who arrived in London tried to continue living according to their customs, bringing up their children as they did at home, sending them only to *heder* and *yeshiva*, the schools for Jewish studies, and not to state schools. However, most of the people, the non-Hassidic Jews and a few among the Hassidim also, were more broadminded, and sent their children to the Jewish Free School in Bell Lane. That was the school that David attended, and he did so well there that he was awarded a scholarship to a grammar school to finish his studies. By the time he was sixteen or seventeen, you couldn't tell his English from that of a native. I don't think he ever told his schoolmates anything about his origins, or let them know that he spent his evenings in, as it were, a different world. When he finished school, he began an apprenticeship in a bank in the City, and eventually rose to a position of responsibility there. Yet he still lived at home with his parents, and remained at heart a practising Hassid; why, he even wears his prayer shawl underneath his city suit, although he hides the fringes during the day.'

'Such a double life must be wearying,' I said.

'It was before, for he could really say nothing about his life in the City at home, nor even use the language he spoke there, and even less the other way. The meeting with our cousin was a blessing. David was afraid that she would not agree to move to the East End and adopt the way of life of a Hassidic woman, but she said that she was ready to do it. And she did it. She has borne two children since their marriage three years ago. She almost never leaves the rickety little flat in Settles Street, and spends all of her energies in making a home for her family. On top of this, she has had to struggle to learn Yiddish, and the many religious rituals she is expected to know. She says she still feels like an outsider, but things have become progressively better for her thanks to motherhood, and to all of her efforts and good will. As for David, she is a godsend, since of course he is able to talk to her about the different aspects of his life, and she can help and advise him in what you may call the strictly British aspect as no *shtetl* woman ever could.'

'But do you suppose that your cousin and her husband would be willing or able to help us look for the mysterious rabbi?' I asked doubtfully.

'It depends,' intervened Jonathan. 'We have not seen them much recently, but we were debating in what way we could ask them for help. It would have to be a question of finding the rebbe in order to warn or exonerate him, and not in order to turn him over to the police—their help would certainly only be on that condition, Vanessa! Anyway, that is what I want, myself. I cannot believe for one moment, not for one single second that the rebbe I saw murdered that awful Professor.'

'And yet…' I said.

'I know, I know,' he answered quickly. 'Yet the strange time element remains in his defence.'

'The reconstruction of the crime will help us determine what might really have happened,' said Emily eagerly. 'Perhaps we shall come up with a new possibility!'

We separated upon this, and I retired to my room to write my impressions of the day. We have decided to attempt the reconstruction tomorrow night, just as soon as it is late enough for the streets to be empty and the light gone. Furthermore, Jonathan and Amy have agreed to pay a visit to their cousins tomorrow, in order to explain the situation, and to suitably prepare the ground so that they may receive me the day after tomorrow, should they be willing to help us.

My goal for tomorrow, before the evening, is to devote myself to searching out anything I can about James Wilson from the newspapers of 1886, as well as trying to find and read whatever I can locate of Professor Ralston's own writings. The task will be time-consuming and arduous, I know it from having performed similar ones in the past, but experience has shown me that it can be astonishingly rewarding. The amount of 'secret' knowledge which is actually in the public domain is, seemingly, immeasurable.

London, Friday, March 13th, 1896

I arose eagerly this morning, ready to begin with my projects. Emily and her friend were already up when I entered the tiny kitchen, preparing a modest breakfast of toast and tea, improved by a pot of homemade jam from Amy's parents. We did not dally long, nor even exchange many words; even while devoting a corner of my mind to the pleasure of finding myself in London, I was girding myself up mentally for the day that lay ahead of me. Emily was on her way to a class, and Amy to see an editor, so we all three left the house together, and separated in the street below. I made my way immediately to the British Library.

After three hours of research amongst fusty yellow pages from a decade ago, I began to feel the need for a light meal, and I considered taking a break even though I had as yet found absolutely nothing on the subject of James Wilson. I had, however, come across an article or two by Professor

Ralston, which I had read with great attention. Alas, while confirming all the unpleasant impressions I had already received from various sources, they seemed far too general in content to yield any insight on what might have led to his murder.

I wandered out into the pale March sunshine and searched for a place where a lady alone could pass relatively unnoticed while restoring herself. I saw a number of restaurants of all descriptions, all of which were entirely unsuitable, and into which I could not think of penetrating. I was beginning to seriously miss Cambridge, and compare the metropolis most unfavourably with it, when I spotted a lady as isolated as I myself, entering a place called Zoedone's. I followed her at once, and discovered an odd style of restaurant, very crowded, very full of noise and people, very adept at abruptly slapping down in front of one the food which had to be ordered over a counter at great speed, almost shouting to be heard over the din. All this was rather stressful for one of quiet habits, but had the advantage that no one in the place appeared to have any time to notice anyone else. Having gone through the ordeal of ordering, I therefore sat down to eat my meal feeling quite triumphant and most pleasingly modern, in spite of its mediocre quality. I would have dearly liked to continue strolling about the streets afterwards, but duty called me, and I bent my steps firmly back to the library.

After exploring a number of newspapers, I concentrated my main efforts on the *Illustrated London News*, whose unusual use of coloured engravings lends somewhat more of a popular and sensational light to the articles than when they are merely printed in narrow columns upon the page. And it was there that I finally struck gold. The article was in a copy dating from the month of June in the year 1886. As I read it, I was gripped by an increasingly powerful feeling of horror.

JAMES WILSON'S MURDERERS CONDEMNED

The trial of brothers Menachem and Baruch Gad for the murder of little James Wilson, an eleven-year old boy found stabbed to death behind a London warehouse in early April, came to an end today. The two brothers' defence was based on the lack of motive, as they were not previously acquainted with the child, who had no family or regular sleeping place, and who, according to testimony, apparently eked out a living, if it may be called that, by minor acts of stealing, either for his own benefit or that of unidentified employers of his talents. Opportunity, however, had been convincingly demonstrated from the very first days of the trial, as the brothers lodged in a building whose windows gave directly over the warehouse where the child was often to be seen, and where his little body was found. Defending counsel having raised the thorny question of lack of motive, their opponents responded with the time-honoured accusation of ritual murder of Christian children at the season of the Jewish Passover festival. The claim is that the blood of a Christian is an essential ingredient in the making of the traditional Passover flatbread. The Judge, and seemingly the public also, initially treated this motive with some disdain, but the prosecution then produced a witness whose erudition in such matters was clearly immense, and who gave an apparently convincing exposition of the history, the reality and the relevance of the purported motive. The witness, claiming fear of revenge, asked to remain anonymous to all but the Judge, who cleared the Court to hear his testimony and gave the Jury his own personal assurance of the witness' high qualifications. The witness was then escorted out unobtrusively, and the public was allowed to re-enter for the concluding statements, which gave a brief but clear summary of the witness' declarations. His statements obviously had the effect of causing the Jury to accept the motive as a valid explanation of the murderous act. The Jury deliberated only an hour and a half. Menachem Gad was condemned to the gallows, and his brother Baruch, presumed to have been his accomplice, to ten years' imprisonment.

Ritual murder? Christian blood in bread? Horrible! I thought. Could such a thing be true? such a horror really exist? It was difficult to believe—very difficult, indeed *too* difficult. And yet, the article unambiguously showed that twelve honest citizens *could* believe it. That such a thing as this can take place in London, England, at the end of the enlightened nineteenth century! Yet such a thing as what exactly? Ritual murder itself, or merely the belief in it? I remained stunned for some time, trying to collect my thoughts, unable to reconcile myself with the reality. What, I wondered, had Professor Ralston's interest been in this affair? I felt that I hardly wanted to know the answer; I balked at the idea of penetrating further into this story of suffering. Yet I knew that it could not be avoided. Why was James Wilson's name found in a strange list containing other names and dates from medieval times? Why was the folder marked 'B.L.'? What possible connection could there be with a French journalist called Bernard Lazare?

The very fact that the list, written by the Professor himself, explicitly contained a reference to a murder struck me as significant. Certainly, Professor Ralston was an historian, and obviously one who gloried in tales, such as this one, which seemed to support his pet hatred. Yet this might also indicate something deeper. For one thing, Professor Ralston took the trouble to dispose of the papers in that file. What could they have been? He did not seem to be a person who habitually destroyed his old papers, which appeared for the most part to be classified in apple-pie order. Why were these removed?

I forced myself to spend another hour searching for confirmatory articles in other newspapers, but discovered essentially nothing more than what I had learnt from the *Illustrated London News*. I then sat back, and began to reflect again on the Professor's list. I decided that the best thing for me to do next was to try to learn as much as I could about the other cases mentioned in it, and thought it should be possible to look them up in books, insofar as they represented historical rather than recent events. I glanced around, wondering where, in all of the enormous library, I should begin, when a voice spoke up within me, as clearly as the ringing of a little bell: *Professor Ralston's library*. Why, of course—I should be much better off there! It was smaller, and largely devoted to medieval history; it seemed more than likely that I should find everything I wanted, and much faster.

I left the British Library and made my way immediately to Adelphi Street. It was late in the afternoon, but not yet closing time. The door was unlocked, and Edmund Bryant was at his post, seated at his desk with his spectacles upon his nose, lost in piles of books and papers as was apparently his habit. I could not resist wondering, momentarily, if he were engaged in the stubborn development of wrong ideas, but dismissed the notion at once, as it appeared to me that if anyone's ideas could be qualified as wrong, they were those of the author of that statement. I stood for a moment contemplating Edmund, while removing my gloves one finger at a time. Eventually, feeling my gaze, he raised his head.

'Do you need something particular?' he enquired politely.

'Yes,' I said slowly. I thought that Edmund ought, with his knowledge of the library, to be able to direct me very quickly to the books that would best inform me of what I needed to know; I wanted to talk to Edmund in any case, and it seemed a perfect opportunity. Yet I hesitated, and for the following reason: I was embarrassed to take out the list that I had copied from the Professor's paper and show it to him. The terms of the list itself, together with what I had read about James Wilson, made me feel as though my notebook contained something violent, vile and shameful, and I loathed the idea that Edmund might think I was interested in such things of my own accord.

'I—I need to learn about Saint Simon of Trent,' I stammered, remembering a name from the list which I hoped would not immediately arouse any associations.

'Saint Simon of Trent,' he repeated slowly. 'Do you know what period he is from? Early Christian? Medieval?'

'Medieval,' I said quickly, remembering the date of 1475.

'Books about saints in the Middle Ages would be here,' said Edmund, rising and directing me to a certain set of shelves in one corner of the large room.

I set down my things on one of the tables scattered about,

and began to browse among the books on the shelves in the area he had indicated to me. I soon found a passage, in a book called *Lives of the Saints*, concerning Saint Simon; I found it all the more easily as the book I was holding fell open naturally at that place. I marked the page with a bit of paper, set the book on my chosen desk, and laying my notebook next to it open at the page containing the copied list, I began to search for references concerning the other names it contained. Whenever I found something, I marked the place and added the book to the growing pile on the desk, to be examined once a sufficient number had been collected. It was only after I had managed to find references to the stories of Padre Tommaso and Anderl von Rinn that I took notice of what I had only half-consciously perceived before: many of the passages which interested me had been studied before; they were frequently underlined in pencil or marked out in the margin and, without even realising it, I had been searching rather for these pencil marks than for the relevant names as I flipped through the pages. When I had constituted a pile of some eight books, I stopped my search and began to study the case of Saint Simon.

It did not take me long to discover that this saint was no more than a tiny boy of two and a half, whose murdered little body was discovered floating in the river near the city of Trent, in Italy. I skipped hastily through loathsomely detailed descriptions of the tortures he was alleged to have undergone, and read on through accounts of the accusations levelled at the Jews of the community, their trial, the many appeals, protests and retrials; and at last, the final trial before Pope Sixtus IV himself, ending in the burning at the stake of the entire community. I read citations of contemporary accounts of the event, some of which were viciously hostile, others objective and even quite sceptical, still others levelling all manner of ferocious accusations, and plunging without regret into demonisation and fanaticism, all the while tearfully bemoaning and mourning over the tender age of the murdered innocent, the blacker to paint his presumed murderers.

I read all manner of variations of the so-called 'ritual murder' accusation I had seen in the *Illustrated London News*, alleging that the Israelites *use the blood of a Christian child in the baking of their Passover unleavened bread.* I tried to imagine how Arthur would react if he heard of such a thing, and immediately visualised his faint smile of disgust at the very vulgarity, the loudness, the sensationalism of it. Indeed, I could not imagine a single sane person giving credence to the idea even for an instant. And yet, of course they do not—not most of them, anyway—not as individuals. The phenomenon is essentially a collective one. Only a crowd, I think, has the power to unleash such vicious madness in otherwise quite ordinary people. And who motivates these crowds? Just a very few people, with very special interests in mind—the ruin and annihilation of Jewish communities.

The alleged victims of ritual murder (said one book) were invariably stabbed, in order to collect the blood which thus ran. The murders were made to coincide with the date, in early April, upon which the Israelites yearly celebrate their own archaic form of Easter, the Passover, which commemorates their escape from slavery in Egypt recounted in the Old Testament. The book went on to mention the ten plagues of Egypt of the Old Testament, which God caused to fall upon the Egyptians when Pharaoh refused to let the Hebrews depart, and recalled in particular the death of the first-born male in each Egyptian household, which finally broke his resistance. The author explained that on the Passover festival, the Jews eat unleavened bread to commemorate the suddenness of their flight from Egypt under the leadership of Moses, for which the bread they had prepared had no time to rise. He argued that the tradition of using blood originated in the fact that some of the blood of the first-born children, during the tenth plague, ran into their unleavened bread before it was carried off, which surprised me as the Bible explicitly states that the children were smitten by the hand of God, without any mention of flowing blood. That those smitten first-borns, had they lived, would have been brought up in the worship of Anubis and Horus and Thoth, thus making it difficult to understand why Christian blood should be felt to be necessary today, was a further inconsistency which the author failed to address.

I began to wonder who had marked the passages I was reading, and if it had been the Professor himself. His name was inscribed on the flyleaf, and it seemed natural to suppose that none but the proprietor would mark a book. It made sense, since I assumed that he must have done research on the entries in his list, research that had perhaps been stored in the thick, now empty 'B.L.' folder. Putting down the *Lives of the Saints* and taking up a second book in which I had seen a mention of Saint Simon, I began searching directly for the marked passages. Alas, they were numerous and contained descriptions of the tortures inflicted on the child and the pain he had suffered before which the accounts in the preceding book paled.

I felt myself growing flushed and faint with anguish, and the sweat dripped off my brow until I could bear it no longer, and dropping the book upon the desk, I leaned back in my chair. I wished to reflect upon the meaning of what I had just learnt, but I could think of nothing but little Cedric's tender body, his sweet limbs, his fat dimpled hands, and the blood circulating within him like the juice of a sweet fresh cherry. I wanted to hold him in my arms more desperately than I ever did when he was actually playing around my legs. I wanted him to be the happiest little boy that ever lived, so that he could perhaps make a little gift of some of the precious drops of his delight to the little dead boy in Heaven. The trial of the Jews in Trent obviously appeared to be no more significant or credible than any of those innumerable sickening farces played out during the Spanish Inquisition, which was initiated by the same Pope merely three years later. Yet it was an undoubted fact that the little boy himself had died, and a vision of his cherub's face, superimposed upon little Cedric's, would not leave my mind. How such a tiny creature, who had done nothing in this world apart from dying miserably, could be canonised was mysterious to me, until I read that visitors to his tomb claimed to have experienced hundreds of miracles.

My mind wandered irresistibly to the house of my childhood, with its nooks and crannies and its wild garden. Dora and her husband are very happy there, and it is certainly a heavenly place for the twins...and yet...anything can happen.

The air of the library suddenly seemed to have become unbearably thick and stuffy. I felt that if I could not get some air instantly, I would certainly faint. Leaping up, I rushed outside, ran to the gate, and running into the street, I began to walk rapidly, farther and farther from the hateful library, until I spotted a post office. Entering it quickly, I spent some money on a few words of tenderness and anxiety which I expedited to Dora with a demand for instant response; the act relieved me of some of my tension, and I turned to walk to Emily's house in the quickly falling, still wintry dusk.

She was home when I arrived, and the kettle was boiling over a merry fire. My spirits lifted slightly at the sight of her rosy face.

'Oh, here you are! Have you discovered anything? Are our plans still good for tonight? Vanessa, what is the matter? How pale you look!' she added, glancing up at me from the tea tray she was busily arranging.

'I have been reading some frightful things,' I said. 'I don't want to talk about them; they are too awful. And they are not exactly pertinent to the investigation; they are from the Middle Ages. But there is a link to the little boy called James Wilson. I cannot talk about it now; it is really too horrible and I do not know enough yet. I don't even know why Professor Ralston was interested in all this, and if it has any connection with his murder. But he was certainly a strange man with a rather horrid mind. Ugh.' I sat down gloomily, still feeling the frustrating emptiness in my arms where a plump toddler ought to be firmly wedged.

I saw that Emily longed to ask questions, but my frowning brow discouraged the idea. We remained for some time in silence.

'I told Amy to come home around now, if she could, and bring Jonathan with her,' she said after a while, with an effort at brightness. 'I expect them any minute. They are very keen on making a serious effort to understand and exactly explain the seeming contradiction in the timing. Jonathan says that an impossibility is itself an impossibility, and therefore a solution must exist. What do you think?'

I smiled faintly, and shaking myself slightly, I gathered my spirits together.

'I quite agree with Jonathan's principle,' I said. 'Whether our modest capacities can actually discover the solution is another question. We shall certainly try our best. I wonder what will come of it? Perhaps we really shall see something; it is, after all, impossible to fully grasp a situation on the basis of a mere explanation, no matter how detailed. By the way, do you have a good watch or clock to do the timing with? We will need a second hand.'

'My watch has a second hand,' she said, showing me a dainty charm, which hung from her wrist on a thick chain of silver links. 'I believe that Amy has one as well. I wonder where she is? She and Jonathan should be here already.'

A ring at the door answered her words.

'There you go,' I said.

'But why on earth doesn't Amy use her key?' wondered Emily, going to open the door.

It was not Jonathan and Amy who stood waiting upon the mat, but a youth in blue with brass buttons.

'I have a telegram here for Mrs Weatherburn,' he said, holding out a paper. I rushed to the door, and snatching it from him, tore it open. Emily watched me breathlessly, and I saw the pleasure and relief in my own face matched in hers, as I read these comforting words: *Delightful babies full bloom enjoying tremendously Dora.*

'Ah, I am coming back to life,' I said with a sigh that arose from the depths of my lungs, as I fetched a coin for the boy.

'Is that why you looked so preoccupied?' said Emily. 'I hadn't realised it; were you worried about your babies?'

'It is the first time I have ever left them,' I admitted. 'But it was all exacerbated by these things I read today. Oh, this does make me happy!' and I folded up the precious paper and tucked it into my dress.

The Library Paradox

Jonathan and Amy appeared shortly afterwards, and we fell to preparing a modest supper together.

'Open this bottle of wine while we slice the vegetables,' said Emily, handing it to Jonathan; 'we purchased it especially for this evening. We thought that a little extra courage might not come amiss.'

'Anything you wish,' said Jonathan, gazing at her with a look which I suddenly realised could only be described as devotion. 'Give me a corkscrew.'

'A corkscrew? Oh!' said Emily with a slight blush. 'We didn't think of that. Do we have one, Amy?'

'Ah, I don't believe so,' said that young lady. 'We never drink wine. Jonathan, do invent something, I'm sure you can. As long as you don't let pieces of the cork fall into the wine! One always reads that that is disgusting.'

'Well, give me your workbasket,' he said cheerfully. 'I'll try it with this thing here, what do you call it,' he added, turning over the things, and discovering a crochet hook. 'I'll pierce it with this big needle first.'

He bent over the cork, and Amy, her hands covered with flour as she kneaded and rolled out a pie crust, turned to smile at Emily. But Emily, concentrating hard on her preparations, did not look up.

Wherever I go, I seem to perceive currents of emotion under the surface. Something is certainly going on here, and perhaps even several unspoken things, but as of yet, I do not really understand them. Unless, of course, it is all in my imagination...

While the girls prepared chicken pie and Jonathan made every effort to cause the broken bits of cork to move up and out rather than down into the bottle, I boiled up some milk and set it to simmer very slowly with rice for a pudding. Our cooking took some time, and by the time we sat down to dinner, a velvet darkness had fallen outside and we were very hungry. The meal together was light-hearted and lovely. I almost felt myself envying the enjoyable lives that students lead, with modest demands and few amenities except for the immeasurable one of independence and freedom.

'Let us tell her all about it, Jonathan,' said Amy, as we sat down around the table. 'We have done what we promised; we shall be able to introduce you to our cousin Rivka and her family. Tomorrow would be possible. What are your plans for tomorrow?'

'I need to go back to that library and finish my work there,' I said, repressing a shudder. 'And then, I must do something else very important; banal, perhaps, but the first thing that must be done in any investigation of this kind. I must find out what I can about Professor Ralston's last will and testament.'

'Do you have the right to see it?' said Amy in surprise. 'Wills are private, aren't they?'

'Actually, they are not. All wills eventually end up at Somerset House and may be consulted by the general public.'

'Somerset House? That's convenient—why, it's right next to the College! But I thought they had only marriages there.'

'Marriages, births, deaths, wills,' I answered. 'I have been there before, and it is most useful. But I will not be going tomorrow. Professor Ralston's will cannot be there yet; it is much too early. I have heard that his father is still travelling on the Continent and may not return to this country for another few days. The will must be opened and read in the presence of everyone concerned, so it may not even have been read as yet.'

'Then what can you expect to find out, and where will you go?'

'I shall go to see his lawyers. Probably I will not learn as much as I would like to. Lawyers are not forthcoming. But I hope that at the very least, I can find out if there is a will. And perhaps I can find out when the Professor's father is expected home.'

'That and the researches will not take up your evening, will it?' asked Amy eagerly. 'We asked Rivka if we could come tomorrow evening, and she invited us all for dinner. Will that be all right?'

'Oh, yes,' I exclaimed. 'I shall be happy to go there with you. In fact, I am most interested to meet them. Yet I still wonder—do you truly believe that they could somehow help us identify a completely unknown rabbi whose description could probably fit half the people in the East End?'

'Not half,' she smiled. 'Seriously, we think it is possible. Rivka may not be able to help much, as she does not know the extended community very well, and even their language still holds some difficulties for her. But her husband has lived there for many years, and has a thousand and one friends and acquaintances. It is a strange community: news spreads like wildfire within it, but information from the outside world doesn't always penetrate, and when it does, it is often given a very peculiar slant. People would be much more likely to know about the latest childbirth in the neighbouring street than about the fall of the Prime Minister, and if they did learn about it, they might attribute it to some curious cause that we would never imagine—the evil eye, for instance. Well, let me not exaggerate—they are more or less ordinary people, of course, and they read the newspapers just as we do. What I mean to say is that the community is as ingrown as a village and nobody's doings within it are likely to remain secret.'

'But what doings are we talking about? The man Jonathan saw may have done nothing more than simply taking an omnibus into town.'

'A trip into London might have been noticed by someone. We'll just have to feel our way—you are the detective, after all!'

'Well, I guess it will not be any foggier than the beginnings of a certain number of my previous investigations,' I remarked. 'We shall see when we get there. Now, if we have had enough of still-rather-liquid rice pudding and only-slightly-cork-flavoured wine, we had better think of going straight to Professor Ralston's library and attempting our experiment.'

The three young people leapt up with alacrity, and swept away the dishes in record time. Wrapping ourselves warmly against the pinch of March, we stepped outside and made our way on foot to Adelphi Street. It was by now nearly ten o'clock in the evening and dark as pitch; we had decided that this would be a good time, as it would be too late for many people to be about on the street, yet not so late that passersby or neighbours might get suspicious at the sight of lights and activity within, and call the police.

'The street gate is locked,' said Jonathan, rattling it as we drew up. 'Oh, Vanessa, this is annoying! I hadn't thought of it; they never used to lock it when the Professor lived here. How shall we get in?'

'I have the key,' I said, taking it out.

'Good work!' he said admiringly. 'Ho,' he added, glancing around, 'when I think that this is where it all happened! I was right here when the man came out, and just about in the middle there when I saw the other two.'

Having unlocked and opened the gate, I moved to the place he indicated, at a distance about halfway between the street and the building.

'How can you be sure of the exact spot?' I asked.

'I wasn't right near the street nor yet near the house,' he said, hesitating slightly. 'The path isn't long, so I must have been about here.'

'Well, that will give us a little leeway,' I observed. We walked up the path and entered the building. The great room was not in pitch darkness, for the sky vaguely shone its dim reflection of the city lights through the numerous large windows, which glowed pale in the darkness. Quickly, we lit a few candles we had had the foresight to bring with us. There was a lamp on Edmund's desk, and we lit that as well. It shed a warm glow, which lifted the shadows.

Half-consciously, I glanced at the desk in the corner where I had been working earlier in the afternoon.

'Oh, look,' I remarked, going over to it. 'I just remembered that I jumped up and rushed out, leaving a mess behind. I had forgotten all about it. Edmund must have piled everything neatly. Oh—I hadn't realised that I had left my notebook here as well!'

It lay upon the desk, still open to the page where I had left it, with Professor Ralston's repulsive list visible to any passers-by. My friends looked into it with interest. At the same time, I noticed to my surprise that the books arranged in a neat pile next to it each contained many more slips of paper as bookmarks than I had put into them myself, and that a few new books had actually been added to the pile.

'What has been happening here?' I wondered, taking up the top one, and opening it to the first marked passage.

An elderly Italian monk-priest, Padre Tommaso, disappeared in Damascus, Syria, after having visited the Jewish quarter in the city. Twelve Jewish leaders were arrested and tortured. Four died from the mistreatment; most of the rest confessed to involvement in a ritual murder.

'Someone has been doing my research for me,' I said. 'I suspect it must have been the young man who keeps the library. He seems very knowledgeable. Yet it was a strange thing to do.'

I turned to the flyleaf of the book, and saw a pasted-in *ex libris* label inscribed with the name Gerard Ralston and the year 1886. Putting it down, I picked up the one underneath it: *The Jew*, by Sir Richard Burton. Inside, at the place marked by another neat paper slip, I found a virulent and more detailed summary of the story of poor Padre Tommaso. With rising revulsion, I forced myself to glance quickly at the marked pages of the other books, and my companions gathered around the table and followed my example. All the items on the professor's list were references to accusations of ritual murder, and more than half the books bore the acquisition date of 1886, although others had been acquired earlier. Like those I had noticed earlier, many of the passages we read had been marked in pencil in the margin.

'This is disgusting!' said Emily, letting fall an account of the torture and disappearance of little Anderl von Rinn. 'What is all this about draining the blood of a Christian child for baking in their unleavened bread? It says here that

Jews do that—oh!' she added, embarrassed, glancing at her friends.

I thought that they could not but be pained by the horrific nature of the accusations against their people. But if they were, they restrained themselves from showing it.

'You shouldn't bother with all this rubbish,' said Amy simply, although a little loudly, slapping her book shut and dropping it on the table. 'It's ancient history, how can it help us? Even if Professor Ralston *were* interested in such things, which doesn't surprise me given all that we know about him, it's just some kind of research about the distant past, isn't it?'

'I don't know,' I hesitated. 'I would say you are right if it weren't for the story of James Wilson. That is too recent to be of interest to a medieval historian.'

'Yes, but the list makes it look as though he wanted to study all such cases. It would be normal for him to count that one in among the others,' she observed, pointing to my notebook.

'Perhaps,' I said. I did not wish to argue about it. Yet I remembered the list the way Professor Ralston had written it, and the heavily underscored words *James Wilson* added in at the very bottom. Was ritual murder the subject of his research, and was James Wilson just another case among many? Or was James Wilson, rather, the stimulating influence behind Professor Ralston's researches into ritual murder? Why had many of these books been purchased precisely in 1886? An idea began to form itself in my mind.

'I've just learnt far more than I ever wanted to know about the different ways of obtaining and using fresh human blood,' said Emily. 'Do let's start reconstructing the crime instead. At least the Professor was shot; that seems like an improvement over what I've just read.'

'Yes, let us do that,' I said. 'Only we had better leave all these books exactly the way we found them. We don't want anybody knowing that we came here in the night-time.' I piled them up neatly, and turning away from the loathsome heap with relief, I unlocked the door to the Professor's study.

'Oh—the furniture is still as it was,' said Jonathan in surprise.

'Yes. Is this exactly how it was when you saw it?'

He looked around carefully.

'Well, I didn't actually enter the study, you know. I came up to the doorway here, and just glanced in. I saw that fellow Mason bending over the body, which was mostly hidden behind the desk. But as far as I can remember, it was just like this.'

'Did you actually see the gun? Could you show me its exact position?'

'I did see it. I remember it shining. Let me see. It must have been right about here; just a yard or so inside the door, I should guess.'

'Well, we had better not move anything in here ourselves,' I said, carefully taking note of the position he indicated. 'Nobody touch anything. Now, let us see. When you first entered the library and saw this door, was it open?'

'Of course. Mason and Chapman had already gone in. I don't know whether they found it open or closed.'

'We'll try both ways. Let's leave it open now, to reduce the time necessary for the murderer to flee. Amy and Emily, you will be Mason and Chapman. I'll be Jonathan, and Jonathan will be the mur—let us say, the elderly Jew. We shall try to see whether there is any possibility that he might have been the murderer, and if not, how someone else could have been.'

The Library Paradox

I felt a little as though I had temporarily become the director of a theatre play. 'Emily and Amy, go and station yourselves under the window of this study here, at the back of the house. Jonathan, stay here, and when they are ready, make a noise for the shot; call out or something. The moment you hear it, girls, dash around the house and in at the front door. I will stay at the front gate, and start walking up the path towards the house as soon as Jonathan passes me there.'

We took up our stations; I went out to Adelphi Street and waited. The quiet moments that preceded our action were dense with their secret content; the dark blanket of the night and the pale, louring cloudbank overhead seemed so heavy as to stifle sound. The street was empty, but glancing up the path, I could make out the shapes of the large windows set into the black mass of the house, by the dim glow of the few candles we had lit within. The iron grille surrounding the grounds was thickly covered with ivy, so that if I stepped back onto the pavement, I could no longer see anything at all of what transpired inside. In order to lose no time, I moved back in and stood on the path itself. I heard nothing at all, until the front door of the library opened, and a black silhouette appeared outlined there for the briefest moment. The door closed behind him and I could no longer make out a thing, but I could easily hear Jonathan's footsteps as he came pelting towards me, his feet making a muffled scraping noise on the gravel. He winged past me onto the pavement, and I instantly began walking towards the house, but I had no sooner taken my first step than I heard Amy and Emily's running steps, and was able to make them out as they pulled open the door from which he had just emerged and piled inside, treading on each other's feet and laughing.

Jonathan and I returned to the library together.

'Where *exactly* did you and the man pass each other?' I said.

'Exactly at the gate, I told you. I turned in as he stepped out. I hadn't seen him before and didn't realise he was there till we nearly bumped into each other.'

'Did you pass left or right of him?'

'On the left. He passed right of me and turned right behind me down the street.'

'We'll do it more carefully next time,' I said.

'But it isn't just a matter of that,' he insisted, as we stepped into the library and joined the others. 'The man I saw simply wasn't running. I don't think he had been running before— he wasn't even breathing fast. At any rate, he certainly wasn't when he reached the gate. What I mean to say is: he was *old*, Vanessa. He was hale enough, but he just can't have been running like that at his age. Not like I just did.'

'How old would you guess that he was?' I asked.

'Well, it's hard to tell, but I would have said nearer eighty than seventy,' he replied.

'Nearer eighty than seventy!' I said in surprise. 'You didn't tell me he was as old as that. Are you sure?'

'He was old, I tell you.'

'Nearly eighty! Then I really don't see... Listen, let us give it one more try. Where in the study were you standing before you started running?'

'Right here near the door.'

'All right, stand just outside the doorway this time, with the door open, that's right. Then run anyway. But girls, you run more slowly this time. Imagine that it's slippery or some-thing, or that your shoes are tight. What I want is to see you come around the corner when I am already on the path.'

The Library Paradox

Once again, in the darkness, we went through the little scene. Jonathan came pounding down the gravel path, then skidded to a stop near me, so that we passed each other most civilly. Yet even so, I had barely taken three or four steps up the path when I heard Amy and Emily come trotting rather tentatively round the corner of the house.

'Bother!' I exclaimed. Instead of entering the library, they came towards us and we joined each other.

'Well, look,' I said to Jonathan hopefully. 'This is a little better already. They are coming around the house, and I am on the path.'

But he looked disgruntled.

'Well, you can believe me or not, but I was much farther up when I saw the other fellows, and they were dashing full speed, not tripping along like the girls are doing now.'

I sighed.

'I admit it doesn't work very well. It was easy for me to see that you had just been running when you reached me, even though you stopped before I could see you. And I could hear you awfully well, even though I realise that there is more noise around here during the day.'

'And when you've just shot someone, I don't suppose you have the time to think of things like stopping running just before the gate,' said Emily.

'I still don't think he was running at all.'

'And anyway, the major objection is Jonathan's claim that he was simply farther up the path when he saw the other two come around the house. Girls, let's time it separately. First we'll time how long it takes the murderer to rush to the gate and Jonathan to walk up to where he thinks he was. Then, we'll see how slowly you have to go to get to the front corner in that amount of time.'

For the third time, Jonathan dashed down the path and skidded to a walk, and I crossed his path at a quick clip and headed up to the point he had indicated to me as being the farthest one from the house he would accept.

'Twelve seconds,' I announced.

The girls then proceeded to the back of the house again and tried to come around to the front corner in twelve seconds. It was simply absurd. They trotted along as though going to the fair. It is amazing that over a short distance, three seconds signifies all the difference between racing and strolling.

'This is really not going to work,' I said finally. During the ensuing silence, we all looked at each other.

'You see?' said Jonathan. 'I know Mason and Chapman are no gymnasts, but they were running faster than that when I saw them. And I tell you, I think I was even farther up the path than where you stopped this time, and on top of that, I simply cannot believe that that old man had just been running at the speed I was going. It's not possible this way, Vanessa. It has to be something else.'

'All right,' I said. 'Let's proceed on the hypothesis of another murderer. Amy, that will be you. Jonathan will continue to be the elderly man. This time, let us suppose that Mason and Chapman circled the house in eight to nine seconds, running fast, and that the old man walked from the house to the gate at a normal speed, before the murder took place. Jonathan, walk from the gate to the house, and stop when you pass the point where you think you were when you saw them.'

He walked up the path; halfway up, he glanced over his shoulder and said, 'Here.'

'Eight seconds,' I said. 'That means that Jonathan would

have started walking exactly when Mason and Chapman started running, which was exactly when they heard the shot. What that means—pay attention to this—is that *the shot must have been fired at almost exactly the moment when Jonathan met the old man at the gate.* The old man would have left the library about seventeen seconds earlier. But remember that Mason and Chapman stood for a moment under the window before the shot, and they heard shouting and throwing of furniture. If that struggle lasted more than seventeen seconds, that means that the old man would still have been inside, and he would certainly have heard something of it. Perhaps that is even why he suddenly left. At any rate, he can hardly avoid knowing *something* about what was going on in Professor Ralston's room. Perhaps he could even see the murderer through the open door to the study. Or even if the door was closed, he might have seen someone go in, or heard something.'

'That's just why we think we must find him!' said Amy eagerly. But Jonathan's face was still cloudy.

'That's all very well,' he said. 'I wish that could be how it happened. But then, where did that other murderer go?'

Moving into the Professor's study, we all began looking around, trying to visualise the murderer's actions. The study itself was inexorably square and bare, devoid of dark corners, curtains, or complicated, angled furniture.

'In stories, the murderer hides behind the door!' said Amy with a sudden flash of eagerness, starting up.

'But this door opens outwards,' said Jonathan. 'I noticed that right away.'

'That's odd,' I said. 'Doors into rooms usually open inwards, don't they?'

'Well, this door opens *into* the library, so that doesn't

mean much. After all, it is also the exit door to Professor Ralston's private domain, so in that sense it's normal for it to open outwards. Maybe that's what they thought of when they were making the alterations to turn this place into a library.'

'So it's impossible to use it to hide,' sighed Amy. 'The murderer would have to run out of the study and flatten himself against the wall here to hope to be hidden by the opening door. But that's rubbish. Anyone coming into the library would see him at once. Is there really nowhere to hide in the whole of the library?'

The difficulty was the same; the space was vast and open, containing neither nooks nor crannies. There was no furniture at all beyond some plain chairs scattered around, and the five or six desks, which were actually rather high tables with four spindly legs. Amy crouched hopefully under one of them.

'It was still light at five o'clock,' said Jonathan, taking a candle and shedding some light in her direction. 'It's unthinkable that he could have slipped out and hidden under one of those, although one could almost get away with it at this hour. Not in the daytime, though—not when three different people actually came into the room. I myself am perfectly certain there was no one here, and the others say the same. You can take in this whole space at a glance, you know. And I didn't even go into the study itself. I turned around at once, as Chapman came out, and followed him back to the main door. We would have seen the fellow either staying or leaving.'

'It is disappointing,' I said. 'We have tried and tried, and I simply cannot see how it was done.'

'Do you think our reconstruction was in the least bit useful, then?' asked Emily, looking a little crushed at my words, as we extinguished the lamps, took up our candles and wraps, and locked up all the doors, preparatory to making our way back home.

'Oh, yes, indeed. It does clarify things. It shows at least what things are perfectly impossible.'

'And it proves definitively that the rebbe couldn't have *been* the murderer, yet must have been in the library during part of the time that the murderer was also there,' added Jonathan. 'Still, it's annoying. I wouldn't have believed that we could try all this without hitting on the actual solution. What on earth can have happened? It is really too provoking.'

'We simply must find that rabbi—perhaps he will give us the key to the missing clue,' said Emily with renewed optimism.

'Yes indeed. We have more than one string to our bow,' I said cheerfully. But my words did not really reflect my inmost feelings. To tell the truth, I felt a knot of tension and discouragement within me. It is not that I am generally overconfident of success in my endeavours, but I dislike nonetheless to be squarely confronted with failure, and failure is really the only honest description of this evening's experiment. Oh well! I refuse to yield to gloom; I shall *not* give up.

London, Saturday, March 14th, 1896

My first act this morning was to make my way to the offices of Gumbadge, Gumbadge & Upp. To be honest, I thought it most unlikely that I should obtain any useful information; in fact, I would almost have been content with arranging for an appointment at a later date. However, the lad at the front desk asked me not only my name and whom I wished to see, but also the purpose of my visit, and raising his eyebrows when I mentioned the name of Professor Ralston, he disappeared into the mysterious depths of the back offices, and returned after some little time, saying, 'Mr Upp will see you now. Come this way, please.'

I was led through corridors and down halls, and eventually ushered into a large room luxuriously furnished with a deep pile carpet in dark red, and a great deal of burnished mahogany. The discreet lad left us, closing the door, and Mr Upp, a small, spare and elderly gentleman, examined me with great interest.

'Do sit down,' he said at length. 'In what way can I be of service to you?'

'I suppose I may as well tell you directly that I am a private detective, investigating the murder of Professor Gerard Ralston of King's College,' I said. I tend to really prefer to keep this fact to myself during investigations, but it seemed that in this case, there was much to be gained by presenting myself in some kind of an official capacity.

'Ah,' he said. 'And who has retained you, if I may enquire?'

'A group of the Professor's colleagues, worried about the reputation of the university and of the department,' I replied. There was a short silence.

'Well, that is rather regrettable,' he said finally. 'I had hoped you were a clue. A young lady having some connection to Gerard Ralston—that would have been news indeed! But it is not to be. Have you made any progress in your investigations?'

'It is difficult,' I told him. 'I have some ideas, but it is not going to be easy for me to confirm them. I thought you might be of help to me on some of these matters.'

'Which ones, for instance?' he said, a little gleam in his eyes showing, to my relief, that curiosity about the case was going to get the better of the lawyer's habitual discretion.

'The question of a will, to begin with. The question of inheritance must necessarily be gone into in any case of murder.' I allowed my tone to reflect a wealth of experience and knowledge, which I do not really possess. But it was my intention to establish between us some feeling of professional comradeship.

'Professor Ralston left a will, which has not been officially opened yet,' he said. 'We must await the return of Professor Ralston senior from his travels, which should occur any day now. I know the contents, of course, as I wrote it myself, but I really cannot reveal them to you. It contains,' he coughed slightly, 'nothing surprising, I may say.' He coughed again.

'Just supposing that the will *did* contain something surprising, something that might constitute a clue,' I asked him, 'what would your duty be then? Would you or would you not be obliged to notify the police even though the will has not been officially opened yet, or would the choice be left up to you?'

He glanced up at me quickly, and hesitated a moment before speaking. When he did, his tone was level and poised. 'That is quite a subtle problem, dealing as it does with the question of what constitutes a clue,' he said. 'It would be largely a question of my personal discretion. But there is nothing of the kind *in this will*. Gerard Ralston'—he seemed to dislike referring to him as "the professor", a title he appeared to consider reserved for the father—'had no fortune to leave and no one very remarkable to leave it to. As you probably know, he had already presented his collection of books as a formal gift to the College. I really do not know that I can say any more. Perhaps you have some other ideas to follow up?'

'Well, I do,' I said. The peculiar emphasis on the words *in this will* intrigued me greatly; I felt that there was something he wished me to understand, but that he did not feel the moment ripe to speak of it openly. Not knowing how to open the oyster, I plunged ahead directly with my next question, hoping secretly that there might be some connection.

'There is something I would very much like to ask you. But I am not sure whether or not you actually know anything about it.'

'Fire ahead,' he said unexpectedly.

'It concerns the murder of a boy called James Wilson, for which a man was hanged, and another was condemned to ten years in prison for the murder,' I said.

'Aha, so you have come upon that!' he said, interest in the matter obviously getting the better of discretion. 'Good work, if I may say so.'

'So you do know something about it?'

'Something. And what about you?'

'Almost nothing. Except that a newspaper article says the two men were condemned on the testimony of an expert witness on the subject of ritual murder. An anonymous witness, whose identity was known only to the judge. And I have discovered that Professor Ralston did research on the subject of ritual murder, and he seems to have become interested in the subject in the year 1886; the very year of the murder.'

'How did you find that out? He never published anything on the subject.'

'He did not. I checked. That is what raised my suspicions. You see, I found a list of historical cases that he had written down, and when I studied the entries on the list to see what they were all about, I realised that they were all cases where people of the Jewish religion were accused of ritually murdering Christians. I looked up the cases in books, which were part of his own library, and I found that many of them had been heavily annotated by him, and that several of them had been purchased in the year of the trial. I did think at first that hearing about the murder trial might have stimulated his interest in the subject, but after looking up his published articles, it struck me as odd that he never actually wrote anything about it. So I began to wonder why he had gone to all that trouble.'

'And?'

'And I thought he himself might have been the anonymous witness,' I said bluntly.

'Mrs…Weatherburn,' he said, glancing down at the paper with my name on it which the boy had brought him, 'I will say this: I know the answer to your question. Yet, I am not sure that it would be right to discuss it here.' He hesitated, leaning his elbows on the table and tapping his lower lip with the tip of a lean index finger.

'It is not secret information, is it?' I said hopefully. 'I mean, it is not a legal secret, like the will. In the interest of discovering your client's murderer, would it not be best to communicate all the circumstances to me?'

'Certainly, if they had a bearing on his murder,' he replied. 'In that case, I would have also communicated them directly to the police. But as a matter of fact, I have come to the conclusion that they do not.'

'How can you tell that?'

'If I were to confirm your suspicion, what would your conclusion as to its relevance be?'

I had not wanted to put my ideas into words, much less aloud and in front of a third party, but it seemed as though this would be a necessary concession to obtain what I wanted. I consoled myself with the thought that Mr Upp had every appearance of being discretion itself.

'Well,' I admitted, 'the man who was condemned to prison in 1886, Baruch Gad, might have managed to discover the identity of the witness, perhaps through friends working for him on the outside. Now, he was condemned to ten years, so if he was freed recently, he might himself be the murderer. It would be understandable,' I added quickly, feeling a stab of guilt at thus tossing out accusations.

'That would indeed be the ideal solution, although I must take exception to your statement: murder is never understandable. However, I do not see how Baruch Gad could possibly have discovered the identity of the anonymous witness, and even if he had been able to learn it by some means that I cannot imagine, I must disappoint you by telling you that he has not yet been released. The murder took place in April, and as the term of his imprisonment is counted from when he was first arrested, he is due to be released in a little over one month from now.'

'Oh dear,' I sighed. 'Are you sure? I know that prisoners may sometimes obtain early release.'

'It was the very first thing I took care to ascertain when I heard of Gerard Ralston's death,' he responded immediately.

'Did you? Then it must have occurred to you as it did to me that he might have learnt about the identity of the witness somehow.'

'Unlikely though it appeared to me, the idea did cross my mind, and I felt it important to verify.'

'It's almost lucky for him that he was not released early,' I mused. 'He would certainly have been suspected and perhaps even rearrested, and he wouldn't have been the right person. The poor man may not even be the least bit interested in revenge.'

'Well, I will tell you what worried me,' he said, as though finally coming to a decision. 'Baruch Gad *was* interested in revenge. He did not know who the witness was, at least at the time of the trial, but he meant to find out if he could. And you are right. Gerard Ralston was indeed the witness, as you have correctly deduced. The fact is that in spite of his confidence that his anonymity had been preserved, Ralston was still somewhat nervous about Gad's imminent release.'

'How do you know that Baruch Gad was—or is—thinking of revenge?'

'Because of a letter he wrote. When his brother was hanged, he wrote to the judge who had presided over the trial, a letter in which he swore to him that he would spend the rest of his life, if necessary, tracking down the anonymous witness. The judge knew Ralston, of course, and had personally vouched for his credentials. His name was Sir William Colton; he died some years ago. He gave Gad's letter to Ralston, and told him he might need to use it some day. Ralston gave it to me, and told me that if he was murdered, I should use it to have Gad convicted. Obviously the first thing I did when he *was* murdered was to check on the fellow's whereabouts, but as it turns out, he is sitting in the same jail cell he has occupied for the last ten years. It wasn't he.'

'Do you think I could see his letter?' I asked timidly.

He hesitated.

'When the judge had this letter transmitted to Ralston,' he said, 'it worried him a great deal. He kept it for a while, and then brought it to me in order to consult me about what it would be best to do. I advised him to do nothing as long as Gad remained in prison, and to use the letter to obtain police protection, if necessary, when he should be released. He then gave it into my care, and we agreed that it should be unsealed and used only in the event that he should meet a violent death, in order to identify and convict the murderer. Naturally, Ralston did not suppose for a moment that he might meet a violent death at the hands of somebody else, and neither did I. And we made no provision for that contingency. The letter was to be *used to identify and convict the murderer*—and this, on the assumption that Baruch Gad *was* the murderer—it was *not* intended for any other use. As I told you, my first thought when I heard about the murder was that we had missed the train, somehow—that Baruch Gad must have been released a little early. I hastened to unseal the letter, reread its terms carefully to see if they were as I remembered them from ten years ago, and then, as I told you, I was easily able to verify that Gad was still in prison. So Ralston has met a violent death, and the letter has been unsealed, but it does not seem to be relevant. Legally speaking, it is not clear what course is to be taken in this regard.'

'But you told me that if his will contained some clue, you would have been almost duty bound to give the information to the police, even before his father arrived for the official unsealing. Should not the same be true of this letter?'

'Are we justified in considering that the letter contains a clue?' he asked. 'It is a threat of murder by a person who cannot have committed the murder.'

'Well…' I hesitated. Thoughts swirled in my mind, though I did not express them. I pictured someone from the family of the imprisoned man, perhaps a wife remaining faithful and loving year after year, realising that at the very moment of his release, he intended to forfeit the remainder of his ruined life by committing another murder, and taking the sin upon herself in order to offer him the gift of freedom. I hesitated, then said, 'Even if Gad is not the murderer, I still think the letter should be shown to the police.'

He smiled thinly.

'What the police know sometimes leaks into the newspapers,' he observed. 'If this Gad is not the murderer, then what is the point of letting the public know about Ralston's role in his trial? Let us be blunt; it was not a pretty thing. It would be a stain on his memory and on the College where he studied and taught. I very much doubt that those of his colleagues who retained your services would appreciate the result.' He paused a moment, thoughtfully. 'In general, we lawyers do not consider the police as allies. They have their own means of enquiry, and they are efficient and thorough at it. If you could discover Ralston's connection with the James Wilson case, then so can they. In this case, as I have explained to you, I do not consider the letter to contain a clue so flagrant as to warrant my transmitting it to them immediately. In fact, for the reasons I have just explained to you, I do not want to take the responsibility of giving them the letter at all. What I mean to do is to give the letter to its present rightful owner, Professor Ralston senior, upon his return, and wash my hands of the whole affair. I cannot predict what he will choose to do with it, but I will be very glad when the decision is off my shoulders and in his hands.'

'I seem to detect that you were not fond of Professor Gerard Ralston,' I observed.

'The man was a monster,' he answered simply. 'But we do not allow such personal opinions to interfere with the exercise of our profession in any way. Do you know,' he added suddenly, 'I am going to let you see the letter. After all, you already know the damning fact it contains. And if it were to turn out that it could shed any light whatsoever on the murder in spite of appearances, why, it would be a good thing if you were made aware of it, while remaining discreet. Discretion, after all, is the main reason for which people address themselves to private detectives, is it not?'

'It is often the reason, although there are others,' I concurred. 'Sometimes people are convinced that the obvious suspect, whom they consider innocent, will be arrested by the police. The detective at least has no power to do this. And the detective is expected to obtain full proof of his accusations, or at least enough to convince the person who hired him, whereas the police may content themselves with handing over their main suspect to judge and jury.'

'But in our case, the would-be main suspect cannot be guilty, and yet you seem to sincerely believe that his letter may nevertheless have some bearing on Ralston's murder,' he observed slowly.

'Yes. Instinctively, and by my imagination, I cannot help feeling that it may.'

'Imagination,' he repeated, in the tone of one who considers that faculty nothing but an annoyance and a troublemaker, and who is well content to need no part of it in his own work. 'Well,' he added dryly, 'I will not ask you to spin your tales. I will show you the letter.' And he rang a small bell to summon a freckled lad, somewhat younger than the one who guarded the entrance.

'Bring me Gerard Ralston's file,' he said, handing him a ring of keys. The boy dashed off and returned quickly, bearing the keys and a heavy folder. I secretly wished I could have a good look into its depths, but I said nothing. Mr Upp opened it only a crack, fingered the papers within, and eventually extracted a letter, written with a bad pen on a piece of poor quality paper, yet the handwriting of which showed traces of a decent education and a strong character.

To Sir William Colton,

I pray to G-d, Sir, that in your lifetime you have never committed and will never again commit an injustice as grievous as that which you have committed today. Because of today, your soul is black with murder, the murder of my brother condemned to death and also the murder of my soul condemned to despair.

In your summing up to the Jury and in your final judgment you were misled by the Devil. G-d forgive you. You emptied the Court to hear the Devil speak, but you could not empty the Court of the Jury nor of the Accused. Thus, although he turned his back to me, I saw the Devil with my own eyes.

I am writing to you so that you know and he knows that throughout the ten years of my incarceration, I will have no other thought than to find him one day and send him back to where he came from.

Baruch Gad

The letter was signed with an angry flourish, underlined with a wide streak that nearly rent the paper. The whole letter breathed out the state of a soul in agony. I stared at it silently for a long time, feeling rather bad.

'How old was Mr Gad at the trial?' I asked.

'I don't know exactly, thirty or so, and his brother several years older.'

'I—I suppose they really *were* guilty?' I asked Mr Upp hesitantly.

'How should I know?' he said dryly. 'I am in the habit of upholding the decisions of the Courts of Law insofar as possible. What I can assert with certainty, however, is that without Gerard Ralston's testimony, the accusation would have foundered for lack of motive. Opportunity had been proven, but the evidence was purely circumstantial, and the malice of the accusers was rather patent. The accused, naturally, never ceased protesting their total innocence.'

And what if they were innocent? I thought suddenly, reading the lines of the letter again and again, feeling the bitter despair behind the words echoing within me.

I took my leave of Mr Upp rather quietly. Once outside in the street again, I made my way to Hyde Park and, seating myself upon a bench, I took out my faithful notebook and wrote down the text of Baruch Gad's letter as exactly as I could remember it. I then put my notebook away and sat in the pale March sunshine, watching the birds pecking at crumbs on the green, the ladies and gentlemen walking, the nurses pushing perambulators along the paths. I felt seized by a sudden mixture of guilt and nostalgia and wanted Cecily and Cedric dreadfully. There is a magic circle around them, as around all tiny children, into which evil cannot penetrate; one feels so safe, so whole, so warm in their presence. Or at least, such is the illusion they give us, and the illusion perhaps creates some pale image of itself in reality. Yet it is pale indeed, for evil can touch children. I shivered, thinking of little James Wilson, who had been cruelly murdered, and whose killers may have been discovered and punished—or may have gone scot-free.

'This won't do,' I said to myself, jumping up from the bench and dusting off my skirts. 'Action, girl. No moping.' I felt very hungry and wandered the streets for a while, looking for a tea shop, but alas, as I had already discovered, tea shops in London where a woman can enjoy a peaceful cup or a quiet meal alone are distressingly rare. Again I thought lovingly of tranquil Cambridge, with its medley of little shops and tearooms. London is exciting, but what haste and bustle in its crowded, dirty streets! I am glad I do not live here. In the end I contented myself with purchasing a loaf of bread, and after having broken off and nibbled enough of it, in secret, to still the worst of the pangs, I put it away and hailed a passing growler.

Somerset House was my next destination.

The Library Paradox

I felt doubly on familiar ground as I approached the large stone building surrounding its two noble paved courtyards. The whole area around King's College was already beginning to feel like home; as for the place itself, I had already had occasion to visit it and knew the functioning of the inner sanctum. I entered the first courtyard, paused for a moment to admire its spacious breadth, and then made my way to the bureau of marriages, births and deaths. The young man behind the counter at the entrance waved me languidly within. A number of people were already busily consulting the large, alphabetically arranged ledgers, leaning them upon the slanted stands arranged between the bookshelves for that purpose. I moved first to the marriage section, in which the heavy tomes were bound in green. I wished to discover if either of the Gad brothers had been married.

'What were their Christian names again?' I asked myself, turning over the leaves of my notebook to recall the unfamiliar syllables. 'Ah yes, Baruch, of course, and Menachem was the one who was hanged.' I was uncertain of the exact pronunciation of these archaic appellations, and could not help smiling at the idea of their being described as 'Christian'.

A little calculation told me that if Baruch Gad was thirty years old in 1886, then he could hardly have been married before 1875 at the earliest. Mr Upp had said that his brother was 'several years older'. I decided to give him ten years, and begin searching from 1865 and continue until I found what I wanted, or reached the fatal year of 1886. I thought I had better note down every marriage in which one of the partners bore the name of Gad, for the family might have ramifications that I should know about.

The work took a long time, for each ledger covered but three months, so that I had to make an alphabetical search for the name "Gad" in some eighty different tomes. Each name appeared only with a reference number next to it, the year being inscribed on the binding of the volume and the month at the top of the page. To learn more about a given marriage, it was necessary to write down the reference number and carry it over to the part of the room where the marriage certificates were kept.

I was helped in my lengthy task by the rarity of the name of Gad, which actually failed to appear in the large majority of tomes, several dozen of which were thus back on the shelf within less than a minute of my having taken them down. In this way, I worked my way through more than thirty tomes, marking down nothing but the marriages of Nathan Gad in September 1865, Judith Gad in April 1867 and Eder Gad in June 1871—when I struck gold! In January 1874, I found the record of the marriage of Menachem Gad, and added it to my list in a trembling hand. So there was a Mrs Gad somewhere out there, after all—a woman whose husband had been hanged, whose life had been destroyed, a woman who had every reason to wish Gerard Ralston to burn in the fires of hell.

I restrained myself from rushing off immediately in my impatience to find out the name of this lady, and forced myself to doggedly continue my work through to the end of the year 1886. In this way I noted down the marriages of Charles Gad in March 1877 and Emory Gad in 1884; Baruch's name never appeared. I heaved the last tome back onto the shelf with relief, and carried my list of seven to the registers containing the marriage certificates, where my researches produced the following result:

Nathan Gad to Nehama Dan, September 1865
Judith Gad to Simon Sachs, April 1867
Eder Gad to Mary Ann Brittle, October 1871
Menachem Gad to Britta Rubinstein, January 1874
Charles Gad to Myra Stern, 1877
Emory Gad to Sarah Lewin, May 1884

I carried this list to the young man at the front desk.

'What can I do for you?' he asked kindly. Somerset House is a place where people largely take care of themselves, and perhaps he was thirsting for a little activity.

'I have this list of marriages,' I said, showing it to him. 'I am wondering if I could find out whether some or all of these people named Gad belonged to the same family. How do you think I could go about it?'

He took the list, scanned it and smiled. 'They don't go in much for intermarriage, do they?' he observed.

'What do you mean?' I said, surprised at this remark.

'Jews, aren't they?' he said impatiently.

'How do you know that?' I said, and immediately felt that it must be a stupid question. He laughed openly.

'I spend all my time working with names, don't I? I know names! I've seen a thousand names from every country in the world. This is London, the melting pot, isn't it? Why, half of these names here are nothing but the names of the twelve tribes, the sons of Jacob, you know: Dan, Gad, Benjamin, and Lewin, which is the same as Levy.'

'Very true,' I observed, struck by this simple remark, and feeling that I should have realised it by myself. 'But Eder's certificate says he was married in a church, whilst most of the others were married in a synagogue.'

'What was the father's profession?' he asked curiously.

'I noticed it particularly; his father was a horse-nail maker called Mark Gad,' I told him.

'Oh,' he said. 'Mark is very New Testament, isn't it? That means they could be converted several generations back, or maybe this particular Gad is a deformation of some other name. At any rate, the marriage certificate gives you the age of the bride and groom, and the names of their fathers. So what you can do is calculate their birth year up to a year or so from the age, and try to look up their birth records in the red books over there. Then, on their birth certificates you will find the names and ages of both parents, and you can try to work backwards. However, the information in our office may not go back far enough for your needs. Records before 1837 were not central, they used to be kept in the parishes, and somebody married in the Seventies might easily have been born before 1837. Also, if these people were not born on British soil, you won't find any birth records for them here. You'll just have to do the best you can with that.'

'I see,' I said. 'Yes, I suppose that I can at least try working backwards from their birth years. What a pity it is that they give the ages and addresses of the newlyweds on the certificate, but not their exact date of birth or the place where they were born! It would be so very helpful. Oh well, I will see what I can do. Thank you very much for your help.'

I moved now to the area containing birth records. The system was the same as for marriages: the names were listed in enormous ledgers—bound in dark red, these—and the certificates themselves were referred to by number. I looked up each one of my six Gads and their spouses as best I could, but found little. Nathan Gad, born in 1833, was too old to be in the register, whether or not he was born in England, as were Simon Sachs and Eder Gad. I calculated the birth years of the others, to within a year, and found 1845 for Nehama Dan, 1846 for Judith Gad, 1841 for Anna Gershon, who was a widow, and 1853 for the one who interested me more than any other, Britta Rubinstein. However, not one of these ladies appeared in the register. All must have been foreign-born. The same was true for Menachem Gad himself, whose year of birth I calculated to have been around 1851. I did discover that Charles and Emory were born in Bournemouth in 1851 and 1858, and were brothers, and that their wives were born, respectively, in London and in Devon. But Charles being born in the same year as Menachem seemed like a bad sign in terms of their being related, although I determined to contact the British Gad brothers if I could locate them and make some enquiries.

Having made notes of all my discoveries, I lifted the last volume back onto its shelf and was about to depart, when a thought suddenly struck me. Pulling down the ledger for the year 1874, the year of Menachem Gad's marriage, I began to search for entries under the name of Gad. It had occurred to me that he may have had a child. And amazingly, I found mention of a certain *Rebecca Gad* just two tomes later, born in April 1875. My heart pounding, I continued searching for births of little Gads through to the end of 1886, noted down a total of four, and rushed to the birth certificates to confirm my idea.

It was as I hoped. *Rebecca Gad was the daughter of Britta and Menachem.* The other three children had been born to Eder and Charles. Full of this knowledge, I emerged into the late afternoon, thinking intensely about a little girl called Rebecca who lost her father in a horrible way when she was only eleven.

My first act once I recovered my spirits was to stop at a library to enquire whether they carried a published Directory of London householders. I wished to attempt to find out if a Britta Gad, a Rebecca Gad or even a Britta or Rebecca Rubinstein were listed, though I was well aware of the unlikelihood of it all; would they have remained in London? Would they have kept the same name? Would they have the slightest chance of being registered householders, rather than mere lodgers? The answer to all of these questions was 'very probably not', and I was not surprised at the failure of my quest. What, I wondered, could I possibly do now to try to locate them?

Suddenly I thought of my old friend Inspector Reynolds of Scotland Yard. I have crossed his path more than once in the last few years, and he has always been most kind. I believe he took a particular liking to me once, when I realised that a colleague and rival of his was entirely on the wrong track, and our relations have been of the most cordial since then. Would he be able to help me?

Who else might know? Baruch Gad, of course, and I know well enough where to find *him*. I wonder if it would be possible to visit him in prison. What pretext could I imagine to obtain the right to a visit? Decidedly, I must visit Inspector Reynolds. I wrote this down in my notebook and, consulting the time, hastened my steps towards home.

Jonathan had already arrived when I reached the flat, and he and Amy were fermenting with excitement about our coming visit to their cousin. They exchanged frequent glances and their nervousness struck me oddly. We must, I thought, be going to a strange place indeed.

Emily was her usual self, tranquil as milk, perfectly well-bred, equally at home in any situation. We started out about an hour before sundown. The city was already grey with shadow.

'Are we getting out here?' I asked in surprise, as Amy stopped our cab in a part of London which, although not particularly familiar to me, did not seem to be the heart of the East End.

'Uh, we thought we would walk the rest of the way,' mumbled Jonathan.

'You see,' Amy said, speaking clearly, 'religious Jews are not allowed to take cabs on the Sabbath, that is from Friday sundown until Saturday sundown. We do it, of course, but we feel that it wouldn't be right to appear on a Saturday at Rivka and David's in a cab, or even to go driving into the East End where they all live. I hope you are not too tired to walk a short distance?'

'Oh no, it's quite all right,' I said hastily, although I had already walked a great deal that day. Still, comfortable shoes go a long way towards making such walks pleasant.

'I did not know that the Israelites rested on Saturday rather than Sunday,' I added, observing the quietness in the streets around me, which contrasted sharply with the busy Saturday bustle in the part of London I had just come from.

'They rest on the seventh day, observing the fourth commandment, just as Christians do,' she said dryly. 'Both traditions come straight from the book of Genesis and the Creation in six days, you know. We Jews just count the days differently. Sunday is the first day of the week for us. If it doesn't fall on the same seventh day as it does for Christians, why, I don't know where that comes from; the desire to differentiate themselves, no doubt. Don't you know anything about it? Does it say anything in your Bible about changing the Sabbath to Sunday?'

I felt a pang of guilt as I became uncomfortably aware that before her last words, I had stupidly and automatically applied the words 'the desire to differentiate themselves' to the Jews, imagining momentarily that they had chosen to rest on a different day than the Christians. I tried to imagine a time and place in which Judaism was the norm and to be a Christian was a recent fashion, adopted only by a few. The absolutism of Christian thought and Christian values is more deeply embedded into our unconscious minds than we realise. And oddly enough, we Christians often spontaneously think of Christianity as having been born in Rome rather than in Jerusalem, although Rome is really only the place of its flowering. But it is so convenient; there are no pagans left to reveal the original nature of Christianity as a choice among others. And the observance of Sunday worship seems to us as old as the religion itself...yet...

'No,' I admitted, thinking over any possible reference I could remember from the Gospels or the Epistles to Sunday. 'It was the day of Christ's resurrection from the dead, and it is indeed referred to as the "first" day of the week. But I have no idea when Christians actually chose to set that day aside for rest and worship.' I made a mental note to ask Arthur to find out for me. He has many very erudite friends.

My friends led me past Petticoat Lane, which was, they assured me, the very heart of the East End, and down the Whitechapel Road. We left it for Fieldgate Street, passing an old synagogue whose open doors revealed dim lights and a group of men within, crossed over to the other side, and ignoring a dingy little way on the right bearing the euphemistic denomination of Greenfield Road, we turned into narrow little Settles Street. There were not many people about, but those that were there, hurrying along, looked to me like folks from an ancient tale. There were stout, weary women wearing wigs and many ample layers of skirts, bearded men wearing heavy black coats and hats, with long locks of hair dangling quaintly on either side of their faces. The streets were muddy and lined with shabby tenements. The whole place oddly had the air of a rather tumbledown village, except that (in spite of the street names) I have rarely seen anything less reminiscent of fields and greens and gates.

Jonathan and Amy stopped in front of one of the tenement houses, entered the main door, which stood ajar, and knocked loudly at the door of a flat on the ground floor. We heard shuffling and children's voices, the door opened suddenly, and a young woman greeted Jonathan and Amy warmly, joyfully, beckoning us all inside. I was surprised and greatly struck by her appearance and manner.

Rivka Mendel is the most astonishing example I have ever seen of a woman living at the crossroads between two separate worlds. In the dim light of the hall, she seemed extremely young to me—no older than Emily, I should have said. But as we stepped into the firelit front room, I saw lines of weariness on her face that suddenly seemed to age her. Whether the round shape under her voluminous dress indicated that she was expecting a baby or had had one quite recently, or both, I could not be sure, but the room was soon invaded by a tiny boy hardly bigger than Cedric—I reached for him spontaneously—and a baby of some seven or eight months who crawled in upon hands and knees. Ignoring the guests, these arrivals climbed simultaneously upon their mother and proceeded to vociferate demands. Rivka sat down, somewhat heavily and, gathering them to her, indicated to us that we should take off our wraps and sit down. She did not excuse herself for the children, nor remove them to some distant region of the flat, nor even seem to see anything amiss in their noisy presence, as I realised that I often did with Cedric and Cecily when guests appeared and I thought they might be put out by the noisily joyful disorder and racket.

'Dovidl will be home any moment,' said Rivka with a voice whose slight echo of weariness did not cover a lilting note of happiness. 'It will be time for Havdalah, and then we'll have dinner. I am so happy to meet you,' she added, turning to Emily and to me. 'Look Samuel, look Eliel,' she added to the swarming boys, 'the lady is making shadow animals on the wall! Look—a wolf! A rabbit? Oh, that is pretty! You must show me how you do it!'

'Woof, woof,' said the intelligent tot, climbing off his mother and toddling over to the wall to touch the shadows I was making with my folded hands. It is an art that I have developed to some perfection in the nursery, and it never fails to fascinate children of all ages.

'Woof-woof DOG,' I informed him educationally.

'He doesn't speak much yet, though he is nearly two,' Rivka told me. 'It's probably because he is growing up in a mix of languages. I speak English with him, of course, but I am the only person who does so. His father and the rest of his family speak to him in Yiddish.'

'She doesn't know what Yiddish is,' said Amy. 'It's the language spoken by Jews from the East, from Poland and Germany and thereabouts. It's a kind of ancient hybrid German dialect full of Hebrew words, which is actually written out in the Hebrew letters, for those who can read them. But a person who knows German can understand at least something of spoken Yiddish.'

'And have you learnt to speak it?' I asked Rivka.

'I have learnt a lot,' she smiled, 'since I have been living here. I understand it reasonably well and can make myself understood. I'm not sure that the reading will ever come really easily to me, though.'

At this moment the front door banged to and a cheerful and eminently British voice shouted, 'Here I am, Rivkele! Time for the blessings!'

And a perfectly wonderful young man pushed aside the curtain, which hung in front of the door, and made his appearance with a smile of sheer delight on his face.

David Mendel's entrance into the low, crowded room was like a breath of fresh air. It provided an immediate and incontrovertible solution to the puzzle of the choice of this lovely girl, who had renounced a life of relatively carefree liberty (certainly, girls suffer a thousand restrictions in our decorous society, yet modern girls with character, such as Amy and Emily, are not absolutely prevented from carving out their lives much as they will) for a life of crowded poverty, straitened means and innumerable children, in a world foreign to her yet out of which she might virtually never step again. I suddenly remembered Shakespeare's odd words *and eke most lovely Jew*—I had always wondered what he meant. Anyone, I thought, might easily fall in love with this young man, in whom remarkable beauty, especially about the ardent black eyes, was conjugated with a radiant aura of tenderness, spirituality and inspiration. It is something which can be found only in deeply religious people. Seeing him made it clear to me at once that the traditional Christian discourse on the subject of Israelites and their religion much maligns them. I reminded myself anxiously that this handsome young man with the shining eyes, who swung his little boy up into his arms and laid his hand lovingly on his wife's shoulder, did not believe that Jesus Christ is our Saviour and Messiah, and the Son of God. But the thought had lost its usual power of provoking a feeling of shocked awe within me. Instead, I had a sudden, fleeting vision of the Heavenly Host laughing at our foolish enmities and rigid convictions. I smiled.

Wine and spices had been laid out on a white cloth, together with a lit, braided candle, on the small dining table in a corner of the room. We stood in a group around this table, Emily and I stealing awkward and respectful glances at the others to see how they behaved, while David pronounced a series of Hebrew blessings over these objects, touching the glass of wine, smelling the spices and holding his hand to the candlelight and then to the firelight as he chanted. The procedure was utterly foreign to me, and yet it did not seem strange, for he performed it with the same air of infinite familiarity that I feel when chanting 'Sing a song of sixpence' or 'Mary, Mary, quite contrary' for the twins.

Coming to an end, he extinguished the candle by pouring a little red wine over it, and turned to me.

'Havdalah means separation,' he said. 'These prayers separate our holy day from the mundane remainder of the week. Now that we have become mundane once again, let us proceed to have dinner. Shall you get it, Rivkele? I'll hold the baby.' Rivka disappeared into the kitchen, whither Amy followed her, not before a short whispered conversation with her brother whose words I could not catch. While the young women prepared the meal, we played with the two tiny boys who swarmed cheerfully over our knees and under our chairs, and tried to play successively with the fire tongs, the lamp and the bread knife. As sitting and dining room together, the place was filled with that type of appurtenance which is of essential use to adults and of great danger to children, so that I was continually on the *qui vive*, although their father seemed perfectly at ease letting them do exactly as they liked, contenting himself with removing from their little hands any object which appeared too pointed or sharp for comfort, and consoling the indignant cries which invariably followed this act with a sudden medley of songs and dances.

'Perhaps we could move into the nursery,' I finally said, after Samuel had brought a tin cup down energetically on little Eliel's head. 'Would not the babies be safer and more comfortable there?'

'There is no nursery here. Apart from this room, there is only the bedroom. Our home is very small, and we cannot yet afford anything better,' replied David in a relaxed tone of voice indicating neither surprise nor offence at my awkward miscalculation of the situation. Rising, he opened the door leading out of the modest sitting room and showed me a bedroom whose tiny proportions caused me a pang of mingled discomfort and guilt. The children's two little cribs were pushed into a corner, separated from the rest of the room only by a thick dark blue curtain looped onto a string nailed to the ceiling, which now hung open. A few, very few scattered toys lay on the floor around these little cribs. For the rest, the room contained only a larger bed, a row of clothes hung on nails and a rickety little dressing table with a crooked mirror. A door led into a tiny bathroom with a tin bath in the middle of it, and another led out into a small, dirty stone courtyard.

The boys scrambled into their familiar little space the moment the door was opened, but we could not follow them, as the bedroom was far too exiguous to contain us all. David pulled his chair near to the bedroom door to keep an eye on them, and we continued to talk cheerfully about children and sundry other subjects. Suddenly we heard a tremendous crash in the kitchen, followed by a cry of dismay.

We all jumped up, but before we reached the kitchen door, it opened from inside, and Amy, thrusting her head through the crack, said quickly and nervously, 'It's nothing, it's nothing. Rivka dropped the serving platter. She says can you get her the silver tureen instead.'

I saw Jonathan throw the briefest of glances in her direction, and their eyes met instantaneously. I thought she gave a minuscule nod, but it annoyed me to find myself unable to penetrate their singular mode of communication further.

Unaware of their little exchange, and seeing nothing more than a household accident where I suspected some sudden emotion, David reached up to the top shelf of a dresser which held a number of cheerfully mismatched dishes and glasses in its various recesses.

'Ah, I shall eat out of this with pleasure!' he said, lifting down an item certainly astonishing to behold in the modest, dark little apartment; a splendid, heavy soup tureen of silver, with handles richly decorated with entwined bunches of silver grapes and leaves.

'What a noble tureen you have there,' I remarked.

'It was our wedding gift from Jonathan and Amy's parents,' he smiled, handing it into the kitchen where it was received with eager hands. 'It is so impressive that we do not use it as often as we might. It certainly is Aunt Judith all over, isn't it,' he added, turning to Jonathan.

'You mean ostentatious and bourgeois?' said Jonathan, with a hint of coldness.

'Maybe a little taste of that, but above all something

solidly worthy, no cheating with appearances, and actually rather regal,' answered David, whose good humour was truly invincible.

Emerging from the kitchen, Amy and Rivka now cleared away the objects of the Havdalah ceremony from the table and, pulling it a little away from the wall, they redecked it with a gay embroidered cloth and set the tureen in the centre of it. David helped them lay the table with chipped and bent oddments from the dresser whose modesty made the table resemble a crowd of beggars besieging the Queen's carriage, and we settled around it, Rivka holding her older son upon her lap, while the baby crawled about at our feet with a crust of bread tightly clutched in his little fist.

Uncovered, the tureen revealed a meal of lentils, upon which swam a few lonely pieces of mutton. It was, however, comfortably warm and fragrant, and as hunger is the best sauce, we were soon regaling ourselves in communal pleasure. I knew that Amy was longing to introduce the subject which had brought us to her cousin's home, but she waited patiently until the meal had been consumed, the dishes carried away and a dense almond cake had appeared, accompanied by a pot of tea.

'Let us tell them now, shall we?' she said, when everyone was sitting around the table in a state of replete peacefulness. 'David, Rivka, now is the time to discuss the details of why we want to ask for your help. We hope that when you know exactly what is going on, you will feel as we do about what must be done.'

She described Professor Ralston and his murder in a few strong sentences, laying emphasis on the factual murder, and on the strange contradictory evidence about the timing, and stressing the anti-Semitic activities of the man, and the important role played by the mysterious rabbi. Rivka and David listened intently. Rivka made no comment, but pressed her lips together nervously and glanced at her husband. David, however, was extremely surprised by our tale.

'You don't think the man you saw was a rebbe from *here?*' he said, turning to Jonathan.

'I think it almost certain,' was the reply. 'From where else could he be? We absolutely need to find him.'

'Hmm,' said David slowly. 'Are you sure it wouldn't be best to leave the whole thing alone? What could a rebbe from here have to do with a murder? Why bring trouble on him?'

There was a moment's silence, then Amy, Jonathan and I all spoke simultaneously.

'I for one am duty bound to look for him as best I can, with or without help,' I said. 'It is my job.'

'The police are looking for him too,' said Jonathan. 'We need to find him first!'

'No, but David—don't you see?' burst out Amy. 'If he is being hunted for by detectives and by police, he will be found, sooner or later, and then he will certainly be arrested, and if he cannot tell the police who the real murderer is and convince them that he has nothing to do with it, he will be accused and brought to trial himself!'

'*That mustn't happen!*' cried Rivka, with a sudden look of pain.

'Vanessa has to do her best to find out what really happened,' said Jonathan, more calmly. 'And I think we must help her to go as far as possible while avoiding the police. Surely you do not want them invading the East End, searching houses, questioning people and making arrests, as is certain to happen soon enough if no progress is made—if it is not already beginning, without our knowing it?'

David threw himself back in his chair. Clouds passed in front of the sunshine.

'Even if you are right,' he said reluctantly, 'what do you think I could do? There are dozens, if not hundreds of rebbes in this part of town.'

'What we were thinking, though,' said Amy gently, 'is that most of the rebbes from here, the real Hassidim, I mean, are not likely to leave and go into town very often, are they? They scarcely ever do leave their homes or their *shul*—they could hardly do it without being noticed, could they?'

David writhed in his chair and grew a little hot, as the idea of actually participating in an investigation to locate an errant rabbi gathered reality.

'What is *shul*?' I asked, in order to distract him.

'It is our study house,' he answered me. 'It isn't exactly like a synagogue, which would be closer, I suppose, to your church. Synagogue is where the Shabbat and festival services take place. The *shul* is often in the synagogue, or next to it if there are two rooms, but it is the place where we students congregate to study *Talmud* and *Mishnah*, the texts and the commentaries on the Torah—the Law.'

'You are a student there? I thought you worked in the City,' I said in surprise.

'I do work in the City. But every Jew is a student,' he answered. 'I go to *shul* every free moment I have, though it is little compared to those who are fortunate enough to be able to study all day.'

'It must leave little time for your home and family,' I observed.

'David's home is always here, waiting for him. It is not going anywhere,' said Rivka. Her eyes met those of her husband lovingly, and her fingertips brushed his.

'I suppose it is not so very different from what my husband does,' I mused. 'After all, though he generally returns home after his day of work, often enough he goes racing out again if some idea for his mathematical research comes upon him. I suppose there are many ways of spending one's life in study.'

'Let us return to the rebbe,' said Amy with her usual single-mindedness. 'Listen, David. Suppose that your own rebbe suddenly upped and went off to transact some private business in the City? Wouldn't you hear something about it? I'll bet the students here gossip plenty, and discuss every little detail concerning their teachers, just like students everywhere else.'

'They do gossip,' said Rivka honestly. 'Gossip in this community is more than you can imagine. And the strange thing is, that there is so very little to gossip about. The people live the most regular lives, and almost everybody has far too much work to get into any kind of trouble. Yet the least little dispute in the marketplace gives rise to infinite discussion and analysis! Perhaps the most serious of the young men try to avoid engaging in gossip, in order to respect the Hassidic prescription against *Loshen hara*—"the evil tongue", meaning speaking ill of people. But everybody I know gossips anyway! I myself learn everything that goes on from your brothers, Dovidl,' she added, smiling.

'You have brothers?' I asked.

'I have two brothers, Yakov and Ephraim,' he said. 'They are fifteen and eleven; they are just schoolboys. My mother works very hard as a hand in a tailor's shop, and my father has a stand in the Sunday market and also spends much time in the *shul*, so the boys visit here very often. They love to come after school and play with their little nephews.'

The Library Paradox

'Your little brothers probably know just about everything that goes on around here,' said Amy firmly. 'If any rebbe disappeared for an afternoon, you could find out about it, or they could. You must imagine it,' she added, turning to me. 'A Hassidic rebbe is hardly a private person: he is entirely given over to his disciples and students, and his time belongs to them. Even his wife is lucky to spend any time alone with him. He is solicited all the time, by people asking learned questions, or needing help, or wanting his judgement on some problem. And when nobody is soliciting him, he is likely to be surrounded by eager students drinking the words of wisdom from his lips.' Turning to David, she added, 'Have you yourself heard nothing at all about an unusual absence?'

'No,' began David. Then he stopped. 'We-ell, not really. Funnily enough, there was something about a rebbe disappearing recently, but it's just a funny coincidence. It has nothing to do with what you're looking for. It's just a story.'

'What do you mean, just a story? Where did you hear it? Who was it about?'

'I heard Yossele, our local storyteller, giving one of his recitations last week. It was a new tale by Yitzhok Peretz published in *Kol Mevasser*—that's our newspaper—called "If not still higher", or something like that. It was really good and I enjoyed it. I wanted to tell it to my brothers, but when I started, they told me they had just heard the same story in school. And then someone else, I don't remember who, told me that they had just heard that wonderful story. Actually, I heard it mentioned several times last week.' He stopped suddenly, struck by a thought. 'I wonder why that particular story made the rounds?'

'What is it about?' said Amy.

'It's...well, that's just it. It's about a rebbe who disappears. He is absent mysteriously early every morning, and a foreigner—a Lithuanian—tries to find out where he goes.'

'It would be good to find out exactly who began telling the story, and why,' I said. 'I mean, most people probably heard it lately from someone who retold it because they themselves had heard it and liked it. The thing would be to work backwards up the chain to its source. It might be nothing more than the recent publication of the story—'

'But it might be that everyone is talking about it because somebody noticed something like it really happening!' cried Amy, picking up on the idea that David had half-expressed.

'I don't know, though,' he said. 'People tell stories around here all the time, and Peretz' latest can always be counted upon to get a lot of appreciation. Peretz is one of our great Yiddish authors,' he added, turning to me. Reaching up to a shelf, which held a pile of papers and well-thumbed tomes, he took down some old newspapers and glanced through them. I looked eagerly over his shoulder, but found myself confronted with Hebrew characters, as illegible to me as if I were staring at a blank wall.

'You won't be able to read this,' he said, smiling. 'Anyway, I don't think I have the story here, as it only just came out. Listen, I'll find it and translate it for you, and send one of my brothers to bring it over to you tomorrow. I don't know what conclusions you'll be able to draw from it; probably none.'

'I would very much like to read the story, nevertheless,' I said.

'But in the meantime, can't you also try to find out the source of the storytelling, as Vanessa was asking?' said Amy eagerly.

The Library Paradox

'I can try, I suppose, though I hardly see how. I only wish it were clear that it is the right thing to do,' he answered, looking rather unhappy. Sensing the reason, Amy tried to reassure him.

'David, not one of us here believes the rebbe Jonathan saw is the murderer. We proved to our satisfaction, from the evidence, that he can't be. But don't forget that the police are looking for him, too. And they may not accept our arguments. What we say depends on exactly what Jonathan remembers seeing, and when. We believe him, but the police may easily imagine that he is mistaken by a few seconds. Our finding the rebbe will help him, not hurt him, David, we are sure of it. You know it too, don't you?'

He did not answer, but his gaze met mine.

'Is what she says true for you, too, Vanessa?' he asked me.

For a brief moment, I hesitated. *Was* I completely sure? *Could* the rabbi not be the murderer? *Could* Jonathan not be mistaken by a few seconds? But no—he was clearly telling the truth when he described exactly what he saw and did that fatal evening.

'Yes, it is,' I said finally.

London, Sunday, March 15th, 1896

Sundays are sadly unproductive with respect to collecting information from official sources. I rose this morning somewhat later than usual, and set immediately to considering how I might best spend the intervening hours before the evening's dinner party at Professor Taylor's home, to which he had promised to summon as many of Professor Ralston's erstwhile colleagues as could be prevailed upon to attend.

It may have no apparent bearing on the investigation, yet I felt I must begin by going to church. The quietness of prayer, the respectful silence whose intensity is merely increased by the tiny rustles of quickly stilled movements, the echoing tones of the sermon, the abandonment of controlled thought to the familiar ways of hymn and prayer: all this is more conducive to concentration and insight than any other atmosphere I have ever encountered. Yet today, for the first time in my life, the collective yearning for God seemed too staid for me to be able to lose myself in it. The sermon was steady and noble, the listeners rapt, the singing inspired, and yet something was lacking: the joyful abandon, the radiant rapture, the sheer happiness of nearness to God that I had witnessed so recently...in another religion.

It occurred to me for the first time that I could not remember ever, for even one moment in my life, feeling myself to be personally and individually animated by the grace of God. I tried, as I stood and sat decorously upon my pew, to understand something of the deep hatred Christians manifest towards Jews (history having clearly proven that Catholics tend to sin more in this direction than Protestants). Brought up in ignorance, with nothing more than a kind of vague, undeveloped horror of the blasphemy of not worshipping our Lord, I had never actually asked myself what Jews worshipped instead. If I had, I could have easily discovered the answer, for they continue to worship as they always have, the very same Deity of the Old Testament as we do. The denial of Jesus Christ as his son and his Messiah, a gesture of love and pity for mankind that God sent to humanity, is sad for them, perhaps, for they are thus denied the hopes for eternal life offered to us by His sacrifice. One may consider them most unfortunate in this regard (although they in no way appear to share this conviction), but how can it be a cause of hate? Often they have been accused of being the murderers of Christ, yet this accusation seems more a consequence of hatred than its cause, for anyone who reads the Gospels, anyone with even a minimal knowledge of the reign of terror of the Romans in Jerusalem and the unlimited power and immense cruelty of Pontius Pilate, knows that only Romans, not Jews, had the power to execute. And from thence to accusations of ritually murdering children to drink their blood appears to denote a frenzy of hatred, which goes beyond any rational explanation. Perhaps one must seek within the psyche of each one of the individual Ralstons of this world, to understand what personal tragedy has provoked such bitterness.

I puzzled over this question for some time, and finally came to the conclusion that as I am not likely to be able to penetrate the complexities of the historical causes on my own, the most important thing to do is not to try, but rather to fight hatred as I find it, and to love my neighbour as best I can. This comforting thought brought me directly back to the task at hand, and emerging from the church, I felt my soul to be renewed and refreshed after all.

I greatly wished to continue the search for Britta Rubinstein, but could not see how to proceed, most particularly on a Sunday, during which I could not even have recourse to calling upon Mr Upp, or upon my old friend Detective Inspector Reynolds. Returning home, I addressed a note to the latter, reminding him of the interesting occasion of the lost emerald, and proposing to visit him on Monday afternoon in order to ask him for some help and advice about a search for missing persons. I then wrote a lengthy letter to Dora, filled with anxious questions about the twins. I went out to drop these in the corner post-box, and had only just returned to the house when the doorbell rang. Upon opening it, I perceived a small boy of eleven or twelve, whose angel face was smudged with London dust and grime.

'Are you Mrs Weatherburn?' he asked, looking at me curiously. 'I'm Ephraim, David Mendel's brother. He told me to bring you this,' and he handed me an envelope containing several pages.

'Ah, thank you!' I exclaimed, realising what the package

must contain, and taking it from him. 'It's very nice of you to come all the way here,' I added. He inspected me carefully, then burst out suddenly, in a half-whisper of awed respect, 'Is it true you're a *detective?*'

Was this a good thing, I wondered briefly? Yes, perhaps it was.

'Yes, it is true,' I replied seriously. 'How did you know?'

'I heard David talking with Rivka. He didn't mean me to hear! But when I asked him, he wouldn't tell me anything, except that I should bring you this.' His black eyes focused upon me appealingly. 'Won't you tell me? What is it all about? What's the mystery? Can't I know? I'd like to be a detective.'

'You would?' I looked him over carefully, pretending to size him up. He straightened himself and waited in eager silence. After a short moment, I nodded.

'Listen, maybe I can tell you, maybe not. A good detective has to be able to keep a secret,' I said importantly. It occurred to me briefly that David might object to my involving his little brother in a murder case, and I felt a quick pinch of anxiety. But the opportunity was golden, and there could be no possible danger in what I was going to ask him to do.

'I can keep a secret,' he said firmly. 'I promise!'

'All right then. It's a case of *murder,*' I whispered, leaning towards him with an expression of confidentiality which was rewarded by the size of his eyes very nearly doubling. 'But not of anyone in your part of town, of course. This man you wouldn't know.'

'Then how can my brother be helping you?' he asked, burning with curiosity. 'Is it someone from the City? What does he know about it?'

'He doesn't know anything,' I sighed. 'He isn't involved.'

'Then what's this?'

'This envelope? It's just a story he thought I would like, by an author called…Peretz, I think. Is that the name?' Pulling open the envelope, I extracted the sheets and showed him the title: 'If not still higher', by Y. L. Peretz.

'Oh, I know that story! I just heard it!' he observed. 'That's funny; I wonder why David is sending you that?'

'You heard it recently?' I said. 'That's very interesting. Who did you hear it from?'

'A boy in my class told it in the playground,' he said easily.

'All right. Now listen,' I told him seriously. 'You say you want to be a detective. So I'm going to give you a test. I'm going to give you something to detect. But you understand that you have to do this like a real detective. Everything has to be totally secret. Don't let a soul know that you're investigating. You can ask people questions, but you have to do it in such a way that they think you just happen to be curious, not that you're actually investigating with any purpose. Yet you must be quick. You have to try and do it within a couple of days, if you can.'

'What do I have to do?' he asked eagerly.

'Well, people all over your part of town have been hearing this story lately. Your job is to find out who started telling the story first. Start by asking where the boy who told you the story heard it, who told it to him. And then, find out where that person heard it, and see if you can work your way right back to the first person who told it. As quickly as you can manage it, mind. But make sure that you never, never let a soul suspect that you're detecting, all right? Can you do that?'

'Is that all?' he said, looking faintly disappointed. 'Well, I'm sure I can manage that. If I do, will you give me some real detecting to do?'

'We'll see!' I said. 'But you have to realise that there is

no difference between this job and "real detecting". Most of detective work is just this kind of work; finding out details, or looking up paperwork. If you want to be a detective, you have to be prepared to do little tasks in secrecy. And remember this: the secrecy is more important than the task itself. Don't make yourself look suspicious by insisting if it doesn't seem natural. Remember, spies and detectives must never court danger or reveal themselves!'

'What should I do if I find out the answer?'

'I want to know about anything interesting you find out, anything at all. But you go to school, so it might not be so easy for you to come and see me—and you mustn't write anything down, of course, ever! No, I think that if you want to let me know something, you should tell David. He'll know how to find me. Don't forget to be discreet. Promise?'

'Of course I promise,' he said, impressed in spite of himself. I was also impressed. His easy *I'm sure I can manage that* rang in my ears. Like a little mouse, he probably knows all the ins and outs of his maze-like little world. If anyone could find out where the story started—if David's sudden suspicion were right, and had some relation to reality—why then, Ephraim, not David, was the most likely person to discover it for us.

With these thoughts in mind, I settled upon Emily's comfortable little sofa to find out what the famous story was actually about. The handwritten sheets were accompanied by a short note from David.

Here is the tale I told you about, which I heard recently. It was written by Yitzhok Leib Peretz—if you knew what that name means to us! Our language is so humble that almost no one actually thinks of writing in it. I mean writing real literature, reflecting our beliefs and our lives. We call Peretz 'the father of Yiddish literature'. His tales are like drops of our essential truth. I have put it in English as well as I can, but so much is necessarily lost. Every phrase, every expression might have been taken directly from the mouths of us Hassidim.

I must tell you that around here, people tell stories all the time. And a recent story by Peretz will make the rounds faster than anything. So I just don't know if this can possibly have any significance. Yet it struck me as a coincidence, after our talk yesterday.

My very best to you,
David Mendel

Putting the note aside, I turned to the story itself with curiosity.

If Not Still Higher, by Yitzhok Leib Peretz

And every morning during the Days of Awe, at the time for the penitential prayers, the Nemirover rebbe would disappear; vanish! He was nowhere to be seen: not in the synagogue, not in either of the shuls, not at a prayer-gathering, and definitely not at home. The house stood open. Anyone who wanted to could go in or out; nobody stole from the rebbe. But not a living soul was to be found in the house.
    Where can the rebbe be?

Where could he be? In Heaven, of course. Do you think a rebbe doesn't have a lot of affairs to attend to during the Days of Awe? Jews, G-d save them, need to earn a living; need peace, health, good marriages for their children; want to be good and G-d-fearing. But their sins are great, and Satan with his thousand eyes watches, and accuses, and informs...and—who is to help if not the rebbe?

That is what the people thought.

Once, though, a Litvak (Lithuanian) arrived in town, and he mocked! You know the Litvaks: they don't have a high opinion of the books of ethics; instead they cram themselves full of Talmud *and* Mishnah. *A Litvak will quote a whole text and leave you with your mouth hanging open. Even Moses wasn't allowed to ascend to Heaven during his lifetime, but had to stop ten handbreadths below! Try to argue with a Litvak!*

'Where else does the rebbe go, then?'

'How should I know?' he answers with a shrug. And before the words are out of his mouth (what a Litvak is capable of!) he resolves to find out.

The very same evening, just after evening prayers, the Litvak steals into the rebbe's bedroom, creeps under his bed, and lies there. He intends to wait all night and see where the rebbe goes; what he does during the time of penitential prayers.

Another person might doze off and miss the opportunity, but a Litvak will always find a way. He repeated from memory an entire tractate of the Talmud! *I can't remember whether it was* Profane Things *or* Vows.

Before sunrise he hears the call to prayers.

The Library Paradox

The rebbe had already been awake for some time. He had heard him sighing for almost a whole hour.

Anyone who has ever heard the Nemirover rebbe sighing knows how much sorrow for the Jewish people, how much suffering there was in each sigh... Hearing the rebbe sigh would melt you with pity. But a Litvak has a heart of iron. He hears it and just keeps lying there. The rebbe lies there too: the rebbe, G-d bless him, on the bed, the Litvak under the bed.

The Litvak hears the beds in the house begin to creak; hears the occupants get out of their beds, hears the murmur of a blessing, hands being washed, doors opening and closing. The people leave the house, and once again it is quiet and dark. Through the shutter a small gleam of moonlight barely penetrates...

The Litvak confessed that when he was left all alone with the rebbe he was seized with terror! His skin prickled with fear and the roots of his earlocks pierced his temples like needles.

There's nothing to laugh about: alone in a room with the rebbe, before daylight in the Days of Awe!...

But a Litvak is stubborn; so he shivers like a fish in the water, but he continues to lie there.

Finally the rebbe, G-d bless him, gets out of bed.

First he does all the things a Jew is obliged to do, then he goes to the clothes chest and removes a bundle... Peasant clothes appear: linen trousers, great boots, a coat, a big fur cap, and a large leather belt studded with brass nails.

The rebbe puts them on. From the pocket of the coat a thick rope sticks out; the kind of rope peasants use!

The rebbe leaves; the Litvak follows.

On his way out the rebbe goes in to the kitchen, stoops, removes an axe from under a bed, thrusts it into his belt, and leaves the house.

The Litvak trembles, but he doesn't falter.

A quiet autumnal sense of awe hovers over the dark streets. Often a cry can be heard from one of the prayer groups reciting the penitential prayers, or a sickly groan through a window... The rebbe keeps to the edges of the street, in the shadow of the houses... He glides from one house to the next with the Litvak behind him...

And the Litvak hears his own heartbeats mingle with the heavy footsteps of the rebbe: but he continues nevertheless, and together with the rebbe he arrives outside of the town.

Beyond the town there is a wood.

The rebbe, G-d bless him, enters the wood. He walks thirty or forty paces and stops beside a young tree. And the Litvak is amazed to see the rebbe take the axe from his belt and begin to hack at the tree.

He watches the rebbe chop and hears the tree groan and snap. And the tree falls, and the rebbe splits it into logs and the logs into chunks of wood; and he makes a bundle of these chunks and ties it with the rope in his pocket. He throws the bundle over his shoulder, sticks the axe back in his belt, and walks out of the wood and back to town.

In a back street he stops before a half-collapsed house and knocks at a window.

'Who is it?' a startled voice calls from within. The Litvak recognises a woman's voice; the voice of a very sick woman.

'Me!' the rebbe answers in peasant dialect.

'Who "me"?' the voice from inside asks again.

And the rebbe answers again in Ukrainian: 'Vasil!'

'Vasil who? And what do you want, Vasil?'

'Wood,' says the supposed Vasil; 'I have firewood for sale. Very cheap. I'm practically giving it away!'

And without waiting for an answer, he walks into the house.

The Litvak steals in behind him and by the grey light of dawn he sees a bare room with rickety furniture... A sick woman lies in bed, covered with rags, and she says bitterly, 'Buy wood? With what should I buy it? I'm a poor widow, what money do I have?'

'You can have it on credit!' answers the supposed Vasil. 'It comes to sixpence altogether.'

'How will I ever pay that?' groans the poor woman.

'Foolish woman,' the rebbe lectures her, 'here you are, a poor sick woman, and I trust you for this bit of wood; I have faith that you'll pay me. And you have such a great and powerful G-d, and you don't trust Him, and you don't have faith in Him even for a silly sixpence-worth of wood!'

'But who will lay the fire for me?' the widow groans. 'Do I have the strength to get out of bed? My son had to stay away at his work.'

'I'll lay the fire for you, too,' says the rebbe.

And having placed the wood in the oven, the rebbe, with a groan, recited the first verse of the penitential prayers.

And when he had lit the fire and it was burning merrily, he recited the second verse, somewhat more cheerfully...

And he recited the third verse when the fire had subsided into a steady glow and he closed the oven door...

The Litvak who saw it all stayed and became a Nemirover Hassid.

And later, whenever a Hassid said that the Nemirover gets up every morning during the Days of Awe and flies up to Heaven, the Litvak would not laugh at all, but would add quietly,
'If not still higher!'

I emerged from the pages with a start, and looked around me quickly, getting my bearings. Amazingly, within the few minutes it had taken me to read the story, I had completely forgotten where I was, forgotten about the existence of such a place as London altogether, forgotten about the grey sky and the March drizzle, feeling myself, instead, wandering half-lost in distant streets, between dark tumble-down houses.

'This might well mean something, yes it might,' I said to myself, folding away the pages and slipping them into my notebook. 'We shall see, if only little Ephraim can discover something.'

I rose, and putting on my wraps, I went outside and made my way through the miserable, misty rain to Professor Ralston's library. I felt a wish to examine his papers again, and in particular, his professional writings. Indeed, I went through his personal papers with some care on my previous visit, in the company of Professor Taylor; I saw what there was to be seen there—only there was not much to get hold of! I did not realise then what is now becoming clear to me, namely that it was through his articles that the Professor had made the most enemies, and that I was wrong to neglect them.

It being Sunday, no one was about, and the Adelphi Street gate was locked. I let myself in, relocking it behind me, and entered the library and then the study discreetly. Once settled in, I began opening the drawers of the left-hand cabinet one by one. I took out each of the heavy files and looked through their contents methodically. One article made me smile, as I remembered the annoyance its thesis had caused Professor Taylor as he tsk-tsked about it on the floor under the window.

For more than two hours, I worked my way through the papers to the echo of drops beating against the large window, sometimes harder, sometimes almost ceasing. I scanned each one, wondering about its significance, yet none of them appeared to me to contain a possible cause of murder. That is, until I came to the folder devoted to the Dreyfus affair.

It contained nothing handwritten, nothing personal, only a large sheaf of press cuttings, many in French. Before examining them, I went back to the other cabinet, containing the personal correspondence, and extracted the file containing the two letters from the journalist Bernard Lazare, and sat down to remind myself of their contents.

In the first letter, dated March 1895, Mr Lazare reproached Professor Ralston, courteously and without undue bitterness, for an article he had recently published in *The Times*. The letter contained a concise but striking analysis of the negative effects of anti-Semitism, and a gentle but firm explanation that *monsieur le professeur* had not understood the true facts of the Dreyfus affair, which was a grave judicial error. Mr Lazare invited Professor Ralston to visit him and his friends in Paris at his convenience, in order to study the elements of the Dreyfus dossier. He was certain that *monsieur le professeur* would be influenced by what he read. The letter was written in elegant and rather difficult French, with no effort at simplification. The journalist seemed to take it for granted—or else he was aware—that Professor Ralston's French was very good. But it would be, I remembered. Hadn't someone told me that his mother was French? It was Mr Upp, or maybe Professor Taylor. I remember hearing something about Ralston's father: *the mother was a foreigner that he met and married on his travels to France and Poland...Catherine de Medici...*

The second letter by Bernard Lazare was dated September 1895, and took a very different tone. Clearly Professor Ralston had been to Paris in the meantime and the visit had not gone well, in addition to which he had continued to publish inflammatory articles in the British press, and established a friendship with the notorious anti-Semitic writer and newspaper director Edouard Drumont. All of these things were brought up in the letter, which accused the Professor explicitly of using his position as a *savant*, a renowned scholar, to wield undue influence on a subject upon which he had not taken the trouble to reach an objective conclusion, and furthermore—this must have piqued the Professor—of basing all of his research and scholarly work on a personal feud or animosity so bitter that it could not but have its roots in some subjective psychological experience. There was no record of Professor Ralston's answer, if any. I really wish I could meet this Bernard Lazare.

There were no letters from Lazare but these two and the one that had been on the desk at the time of the murder, and there seemed to be no reason to suppose that there had been others. I wondered yet again what the empty file marked 'B.L.' could have contained; a wealth of material, to judge by the thickness of the used binding. Putting away the letters, I took up the dossier on the Dreyfus affair.

It contained cuttings of a great many newspaper articles, some signed, some unsigned; some in French, others in English. They covered a period of more than a year; the earliest dated from December 1894. Many of them were signed by the same Drumont that Lazare had referred to so bitterly; he wrote exclusively for a newspaper called *La Libre Parole*, of which he was also the editor, and his articles invariably expressed a fever of generic anti-Semitism. I skipped quickly over descriptions of 'typical racial characteristics' of both physical and psychological types, searching for explicit references to the Dreyfus case. There were several of these but, somewhat to my surprise, I found them to be extremely unconvincing; it seemed strange to me that someone should attempt to persuade an entire populace of a person's guilt based on such vague, raving indications as I was now reading. Given that Dreyfus's guilt was now questioned or disputed by people as eminent as Bernard Lazare or Professor Taylor, I expected Drumont to give specific arguments supporting his conviction, but he did nothing of the kind, contenting himself with the type of railing that usually convinces only the already fully convinced. He was particularly enraged that the poor captain should ever have been allowed to make a career in the Army at all, the Army being, after all, the very seat of a country's honour.

This man is interested in making money like all the sons of Shem. You could shoot him by mistake, after having slapped his face with his own epaulettes—and it wouldn't be enough to put into his mind the ideas of honour, of duty, of patriotism that he cannot possibly have, because they are the legacy transmitted through innumerable generations, and cannot be improvised.

It could not have been more obvious that Dreyfus was here being tried and convicted for no crime other than his race and religion.

A number of articles signed Maurice Barrès, which I read with increasing disgust, were more underhanded in their insinuations, twisting as they did the unjustified assumption of guilt into a pretended presumption of blamelessness:

I don't need to be told why Dreyfus chose to become a traitor. Can one even speak of treason? Dreyfus doesn't belong to the Nation. He is but an uprooted plant, ill at ease in our old French garden. He is the representative of a different species. How could we expect this child of Shem to possess the beautiful traits of our Indo-European race? He is not permeable to all the excitement caused within us by our land, our ancestors, our flag, the word 'honour'.

Professor Ralston appeared to have been inspired by this style in his own writings, but being British, he did not allow himself to fill pages with swollen declamations of national superiority. His analyses were sharp and to the point and his adjectives were few; his theme was not so much the guilt of the traitor Dreyfus as the signification of this guilt in terms of the Jewish influence on the economy, and thereby on the culture and development, of an entire nation. Like Drumont and Barrès, he considered this influence to be pernicious, undermining the solidity of ancient roots based in the land and the cohesion of our people and our valiant Army. Had it not been for the streak of bitter irony, which permeated every line—*If not for the necessity of judging him according to French morality and the French system of justice, the Dreyfus affair would really be a case study for a Department of Comparative Ethnology*—I would have found his writings more convincing than those of the French. And yet, perhaps because I am a woman, I felt disturbed, not merely by the description of the Jewish threat to the national identity, but by the Professor's analysis of this national identity itself. I am English to the core, yes I am, indeed. I love my country deeply and passionately: I love its nature, its spirit, its language, its countryside, its traditions, its rich history, its defiant island soul, its little field creatures, and its wandering lanes and hedgerows—*This precious stone, set in the silver sea...this blessed plot, this earth, this realm, this England*, beloved of John of Gaunt—I love it with a feeling as elemental and beyond analysis as the love of a mother for her child. Yet I object to being expected to bend in worship to the British Army as a symbol. Am I truly expected to believe that every individual in the Army is a model of personal honour, and that to accuse any one of them of any crime whatsoever is a stain on the body as a whole? Is not the Army, after all, guilty of an infinite number of bloody horrors? Of course, in my humble ignorance, I am happy that our Army exists, and that it is there to defend me and mine from attack, but I am unspeakably wary of extending this feeling to a dangerous absolutism, and deeply resentful that this should be presented as a condition *sine qua non* for being truly English. All in all, Professor Ralston struck me as a fanatic with a dangerous obsession. Leaving the library and locking the door behind me, I found myself wondering what could possibly have made him become the way he was.

I returned home, damp and very muddy about the hem, just in time to find Emily charmingly dressed, with her prettiest hat in her hand, and hopping with impatience over my absence. I looked at her in surprise.

'I am coming to Professor Taylor's dinner party with you,' she said. 'Did I forget to tell you? He sent me an invitation because, ah, because I have friends who will also be there. Do hurry and dress! Shall I help you?'

'No, no,' I laughed, seeing her impatience. 'I shan't be long. I don't have anything so very complicated to prepare myself with, you know.' And removing the much-reduced day's wear, I arrayed myself rapidly in the dove-grey silk evening gown that Arthur particularly likes, and a single string of pearls.

The drizzle had turned into a downpour, and we were lucky to catch a four-wheeler trundling grumpily down Tavistock Street, as it passed in front of the house. We emerged in front of the Professor's house just off Russell Square, and dashed to the door as quickly as we could, avoiding the puddles, umbrellas raised.

I was surprised to perceive quite an astonishing number of people assembled in the elegant drawing room into which we entered. I had expected a small gathering of professors of history, but Professor Taylor, coming forward immediately to welcome us, told us that he had also invited professors from the mathematics department, as well as some distinguished foreign visitors. Many of these gentlemen were with their wives, and there were even some young people, so that the atmosphere was altogether sociable and friendly. Professor Hudson was present; he greeted us kindly and gestured his family forward to be introduced.

'My wife,' he said proudly, 'my son Roland, my daughters Phoebe and Hilda.'

Roland was an exceptionally handsome youth of about twenty. Seeing Emily blush pink as she shook hands with him, I felt suddenly enlightened as to her earlier excitement.

The Library Paradox

'Hello,' he said to her gaily. 'How are you getting on at King's? Does my dad's teaching still hold together?'

She laughed, a tiny bit more than necessary.

'Your father is the best teacher I've ever had,' she said contentedly. 'It's nothing for you; you've had him all your life. But I feel so lucky to be here! Roland is up at Cambridge now,' she added, turning to me. 'It's a funny thing. He grew up here, and I there, and now we've switched places.'

'Do you also study mathematics?' I asked him.

'Why, yes! Can one study anything else?' he said with amused surprise. 'No, I'm only joking. I can see you don't know our family, though. My mother read mathematics at Newnham twenty years ago, and all three of us children drank it with our milk, as you might say. Whenever she was too busy, Dad took over. My sister Phoebe will be going up to Cambridge next year for sure. As for little Hilda—why, Dad claims she's the cleverest of us all!' He smiled warmly in the direction of a snub-nosed and freckled young thing of fourteen or so, who although by far the youngest person present, was not in the least bit intimidated, but chatted cheerfully with the mathematics professors as though she had grown up among them, which indeed she apparently had.

Professor Taylor, who had moved away to greet some new arrivals, made his way back to me with some difficulty.

'Talk, talk to everyone,' he encouraged me. 'Everyone here has something or other to tell you about old Ralston. He'll come up naturally soon enough, I'll see to that. All the mathematicians here have had some contact with him over logic. We told you that he was bit of a maniac about that, didn't we? He took the advanced courses, and tried to argue with the people working on the new theories. Here is someone you must meet. This is Bertrand Russell, a fellow of Trinity. Your husband is at Trinity, isn't he?'

A presentable, almost foppish young man in his early twenties looked me up and down, and enquired who my husband was, politely enough, yet a little haughtily, as I thought.

'His name is Arthur Weatherburn,' I said. 'You are probably acquainted with him, although I do not believe that I have yet had the pleasure of meeting you.'

'Oh, Professor Weatherburn! I knew him, of course. I never took any of his courses, though. I'm not too interested in those matrix theories. I work in philosophy and logic. I don't actually live in Cambridge any longer.'

His tone subtly implied that there was no possible comparison in importance between philosophy and mere 'matrix theories'. I asked myself why Professor Taylor had insisted on my being introduced to this person, and concluded that he must have known Professor Ralston. I wondered briefly how I could lead the subject of conversation in that direction before the young man decided that I was not worth his notice.

'And here is Dr Burali-Forti,' Professor Taylor continued, drawing forward a rather tall and strong gentleman of a rustic, Mediterranean appearance, who had just approached our group. 'He is visiting our Department from Italy, and Russell has come down here to work with him.'

Professor Hudson and a few other mathematicians had by now collected about us, birds of a feather sticking together.

'Have you written up anything on your paradox, Burali?' asked one of them.

'No, no,' replied the person addressed, with a strong Italian accent. 'I have not understand it properly yet. It is a deep and strange thing. It-a does not make much sense, I do not yet see the real importance of it for mathematics. I must think. We are very much talking with Russell about this. He is trying to find ways of saying the same thing differently.' He smiled at his younger colleague, who frowned.

'A paradox?' I said, associating it instantly with my own paradoxical problem.

'Are you interested in paradoxes?' he asked me at once, clearly eager to talk about it.

'Ah, I have heard of some mathematical paradoxes already,' I stammered, 'you know what I mean, surely. Those stories that mathematicians use to torment us ordinary souls, like the one explaining that if the hare starts the race after the tortoise, he will never be able to catch up for some reason...'

He laughed. 'Zeno's paradox states that the hare—or the fast runner Achilles—will never catch up because whenever he reaches the place where the tortoise just was, the tortoise has already advanced from that place,' he said. 'Mine may not be so easy to explain as that one. But your husband is a mathematician? You are, perhaps, used to some mathematical terminology?'

'Well, yes, if it is not too difficult,' I admitted, wondering what I was letting myself in for.

'Then I shall be very happy to explain it to you!' he said with alacrity. A discreet, dark-clothed being floated by with a tray, and I found myself holding a fluted glass of champagne. Dr Burali-Forti took one as well, and tapped it gently against mine, producing the pleasing 'ting!' that only beautiful crystal can yield.

'Drink, drink,' he said happily. 'All definitions will then seem very simple! Now, do you know what a totally ordered set is?'

'Yes, I do know that,' I answered, feeling that I was passing an examination. 'It is just a set which is ordered by some order. I mean, if you take two different elements a and b in the set, then either a is less than b or b is less than a. That means you can line up all the elements in an ordered line, doesn't it, just like the ordinary numbers.'

'Yes, very good, very good,' he said. 'Now, such a set is also called *well-ordered* if it has a *smallest element*, and every one of its subsets also has a *smallest element*. That is not so easy to see, is it? The ordinary counting numbers 0, 1, 2, obviously form a well-ordered set.'

'Yes, I quite see that,' I concurred.

'Well, what you now need to know, and this is where it becomes conceptual, is that *every well-ordered set has a unique ordinal number*. If the set is finite, all is well, the ordinal number is just the number of elements of the set. But if the set is infinite? Wait—do not say that the ordinal number is then infinity! In this theory, there are no *infinite numbers*. If a set is finite and contains ten elements, its ordinal number is 10. If the set is empty, its ordinal number is 0. All the counting numbers 0, 1, 2 and so on are thus the ordinal numbers of finite sets. But there are bigger ordinal numbers! For instance, we write *omega* for the ordinal number of the set of all counting numbers. You can see that it is not the same as the ordinal number of the set of points on a line, for instance. God forbid you should say omega equals infinity! All these numbers measure different intensities, different quantities, different *types* of infinity. Every well-ordered set has its ordinal number, and these ordinal numbers themselves form a well-ordered set, with 0, the ordinal of the empty set, as smallest element.'

'You mean that you classify infinite sets into different *sizes* of infinity,' I said, catching something of his gist. 'I do see that one cannot say that there are as many counting numbers as there are points on a line, even though there are an infinite number of both. There seem to be far *fewer* numbers than points.'

The Library Paradox

'That is exactly it,' he concurred, 'different infinities can be compared. I said that the ordinal numbers form a well-ordered set, so they can be arranged in a row, starting with 0, the smallest one, and going up according to their order. And it is infinite. No matter how big an infinity you have found, there is always a greater one. Do you agree?'

'Insomuch as such a thing can be conceived,' I said, trying to visualise an infinitely increasing sequence of increasing infinities of infinity and succeeding only in imagining larger and larger versions of strange letters from foreign alphabets streaming before me.

'So, the set of these ordinal numbers, measuring the sizes of infinite sets, itself forms a well-ordered set,' continued the Italian professor with irrepressible aplomb, 'and thus, like any well-ordered set, it has an ordinal number.'

'Ye-es.'

'Then, let us have the paradox!' he said triumphantly. 'Start at the left of the row of ordinal numbers, with 0, and take everything along the line to the right as far as you like. Then stop. What you have taken is a subset of the complete, infinite row. This subset is of course also well ordered, just as the full set is.'

'It would seem so, yes.'

'But the ordinal number of any subset is greater than any of the ordinal numbers that are in the subset.'

'Ah, really?' I said.

'Yes! for instance, the set {0,1,2} has 3 elements, so its ordinal number is 3, which is greater than any element of the set {0,1,2}.'

'Oh, I see.'

'But now, what if the subset you take is the entire set? You start at the left, and move along to the right *all the way*. You include everything! Then you have a subset, which happens to be the full set, and so its ordinal number is greater than any ordinal number which is inside your subset, but your subset *is* the full set of ordinal numbers, so that none can lie outside it.'

Alas, my head was spinning by this time.

'I wish I could understand it better,' I said regretfully.

'You can,' said the young Bertrand Russell, who had been standing by, listening. 'Burali—I see what it is I've been trying to tell you. This makes it all much simpler! What you're really saying is that *you can't have the set of sets, which don't contain themselves*. Of course! That's what I've been trying to formulate clearly all these last weeks!'

He seemed surprised and amazed at his own remark. Dr Burali-Forti cast him a look of confused admiration.

'I don't quite understand what you mean,' he said honestly.

'Neither do I!' I chimed in, probably even much more honestly.

'But it's simple,' he told me. 'Yet no, you are not a mathematician. Let me think for a moment.' He pressed his hand to his forehead for a moment, then looked up, his eyes twinkling.

'Let me tell it this way, then,' he said. 'The story takes place in a country with many libraries. A Master Cataloguer tells each librarian in his land to make and send him a catalogue listing all the books in his library. But when the Master Cataloguer receives all the catalogues, he notices that in some cases, the librarian has included the catalogue itself in the list, and in other cases, he has not done so. The Master Cataloguer now wishes to list the catalogues he has received, and to begin with, he attempts to make a list *of those catalogues which do not list themselves*, by which I mean those which are not included in the list of books they contain. And here is the paradox: should the Master list the catalogue he is presently writing amongst those catalogues which do not list themselves, or should he not?'

'Well, if he does not include his own catalogue in his list, then his catalogue becomes one of those which do not list themselves—oh!' I said.

'Exactly,' he said, lifting his chin. 'And in that case, he should add his catalogue to the list of those which do not list themselves. But if he does it, then he should not do it, for he cannot include a catalogue, which lists itself, in the list he is presently making. That is really a new way of expressing the paradox!' He turned to the few people who were standing about us, listening to him, with the air of a successful conjuror.

'This is a very important discovery,' said Dr Burali-Forti.

'It is impressive,' said Professor Hudson, 'so easy to explain, and yet so peculiarly contradictory. But now that I see what you are saying, I can tell you something extremely surprising. I myself—a mathematician—did not spot anything extraordinary or important about it until this very moment! But as it happens, I have already heard this very same paradox, albeit in a different version, not such a pleasant one.'

'Who did you hear it from?' asked Russell sharply, looking displeased.

'From someone who is now dead, and who was not even a mathematician,' said Professor Hudson, with a slightly ironic expression. 'Your discovery is safe.'

I began to suspect something.

'Are you referring to Professor Ralston?' I asked suddenly.

'Exactly.'

'Ah,' said Professor Taylor. 'You must be thinking of that paradox about Israelites that he was so fond of telling. Are you saying that, logically, what he told is the same thing as this library story?'

'It's exactly the same,' he replied.

'Let us hear it,' said Dr Burali-Forti, with scientific interest.

'Well, I'll tell it to you,' said Professor Hudson with some distaste. 'Please bear in mind that it represents nothing of my own views and that its author has passed away. I am only repeating it because I have just realised that its scientific content is actually much more significant than I would have believed. His idea was to take a, ahem, well, a specific group of people, ahem. Israelites, for example. Now, take each person in the group, each Israelite as it were, and ask him the following question: does he feel himself as a member of some specific group, or not? Some will respond that yes, they belong to a group. Others will respond that they do not feel they belong to any group. Now, group together all those who reply that no, they do not belong to any group. Pick out any one of them, and ask him if he feels he belongs to that group; that group of non-belongers, as it were. If he says yes, as a non-belonger he is in the group of non-belongers, why, there is your contradiction. He should not be there, since he claims not to belong to any group. But if he insists that he does not belong to any group, then he cannot be in the group of non-belongers, so he must belong to the other group, namely the group of belongers. It is truly the same paradox. Ralston interpreted it as saying that the denial of the original belong-ing, the denial of the race, in fact, produces a contradiction. That was the aspect of it that he enjoyed; it seemed to say that a person's identity as an Israelite is not something which can be denied; it is not up to the members to choose. It was his way of saying that assimilation was meaningless. Well, that was the bee in his bonnet.'

The Library Paradox

'It's a little amateurish,' said Russell. 'What is really needed is to put the whole reasoning in the context of set theory. I must get to work on this.'

Professor Ralston was a revolting personage, I thought, but did not, of course, speak the words.

At this very moment, dinner was announced. Professor Taylor personally guided me into the dining room, and I found myself seated with him on one side of me and Dr Burali-Forti on the other. Professor Hudson sat across from me, flanked by his family. Emily sat next to Roland Hudson and continued to look pink. I glanced at them once or twice out of the corner of my eye. I thought of Jonathan's devoted gazes and felt a little sad.

'So you have heard all about the paradox?' Professor Taylor asked me as mock turtle soup was served.

'I believe I have heard more about it than I can possibly digest,' I replied. 'I feel I still have a lot to learn,' I added as significantly as I could, looking at him.

'Ah, I was forgetting!' he responded, nodding. 'I must tell you the most important piece of news. Bernard Lazare has answered my invitation positively. He welcomed the opportunity to lecture in London, as a matter of fact.'

'Oh, how exciting! When?' I asked eagerly.

'Tuesday. The day after tomorrow. He will lecture in our Department at three o'clock.'

The Professor spoke loudly enough to be heard by people all around the table.

'A lecture at three o'clock? What's it about?' asked several voices.

'A new light on the Dreyfus affair,' he replied. 'Lazare

is of course one of the principal proponents of the Captain's innocence. Some new document or other has appeared, supporting the claim, or so he says.'

I took this to be an adroit attempt to turn the conversation onto the subject of Professor Ralston. It was immediately successful.

'I heard about some such thing from Ralston before he died,' remarked a professor of history.

'Yes, he would have had plenty to say about it,' said another. 'He was very active in influencing public opinion in this country against Dreyfus, wasn't he? I saw an article he wrote somewhere. It was a little shocking, whether the fellow is guilty or not. Even if he did betray his country for money, a professional historian ought to avoid drawing general racial conclusions from it.'

'Oh well,' responded one of the women airily. 'He wasn't writing for a scholarly journal, after all, but for the newspapers. A man may be allowed to express his personal sentiments outside of his profession, I suppose.'

'Well, whatever a person does, one can ask of him to use good taste.'

'To require that, a man has got to *have* good taste, and I'll admit that Ralston was lacking in that particular attribute.'

'And he always would insist on using that fake method of logical argumentation that he invented,' said a thin man with a prominent Adam's apple, who had not been introduced to me, in an annoyed tone of voice. 'The fellow took my course in Intermediate Logic—did all the homework, and quite well, too. But then he took to coming to my tutorial room during the hours when I was supposed to be available for the *real* students, and try to get me to sanction his system for turning theorems in logic into rhetorical forms. He always wanted to talk about proof; he was obsessed with being able to *prove* all sorts of things that are simply not provable—as bad as Descartes with the existence of God!'

This conversation was continued at some length, while the soup was cleared away and a truly remarkable stuffed fowl appeared in its place, accompanied by a succulent medley of tiny new potatoes and glazed baby carrots. I studied the menu with care, and thought of cauliflower and spinach. I really should make progress in cooking and not leave it all up to Sarah.

I thought I was listening to the conversation quite intently, but the word 'murder', striking suddenly on my ear, awakened me from a cuisine-oriented reverie.

'Has anyone found out anything about what actually happened?' someone was asking.

'I am not aware that any real progress has been made,' said Professor Taylor impassively, avoiding any glance in my direction. I wondered guiltily if his remark hid a veiled reproach.

'Journalists, at any rate, do not know anything yet,' said young Russell. 'I know, because one came to interview me yesterday. He had caught onto Ralston's using logic and wanted to discuss the thing with a real logician.'

'Why would a journalist interview a student?' I whispered into Professor Taylor's ear.

'He's quite an important person, you know,' he replied in a murmur. 'One of our great families, very much in view.'

'I explained the basics of logic to him as best I could,' Russell was continuing. 'Not that he understood much. Still, he was less ignorant than most, and displayed a rudimentary capacity for reasoning. His article is to appear in tomorrow's paper, but as far as I know, there won't be any real information in it. He said that the public has got to be reminded, so that they won't have forgotten the problem when the solution really does turn up.'

'It was a load of rubbish, that logical bee in Ralston's bonnet,' said the same professor of logic who had spoken before. 'But the worst of it is, that kind of language actually convinces some readers. I don't know whether he did it consciously, but he played on the awed respect people feel whenever some scientific argument is brought out at them. Can't argue with science, can you? Most annoying. I highly disapprove. I told him so, but he begged to disagree. Said using highly structured logical arguments was a help to the reader and a sign of respect. Humph.'

Dinner had been cleared away at this point, but the dessert had not yet appeared, leaving an oddly empty little moment. The conversation lapsed, and Professor Taylor hastened to revive it.

'He was so different from his father,' he said. 'I wonder how the two of them managed not to clash, within the same profession. Such different methods. I don't know if Ralston's original interest in history came from his father—he certainly received an excellent education—but his methods certainly didn't. Not like you, Hudson,' he added, directing himself to that individual. 'You're bringing up your children properly, by all accounts. Not going to get any strange mutations with a chip on their shoulder, I hope?' He smiled benignly in the direction of the three youthful Hudsons, who burst out laughing at the allusion to Darwin's recent and controversial theories. It is an interesting fact that although all people who consider themselves modern believe firmly in the process of evolution insofar as it describes fish or alligators, it still seems like nothing but a great joke in reference to our supposedly superior species.

'I will not deny that I am most proud of them,' said their father with a layer of quiet poise over his secret delight, 'and furthermore, they all fortunately appear to be quite normal. But then, so did Ralston, perhaps, as a youth. Who knows when that rabid mania seized hold of him?'

The Library Paradox

'It was a long time ago, that is certain,' said Professor Taylor.

'That's true,' chimed in another Professor. 'Frankly, he was constantly causing uncomfortable situations. I don't know how many times I've sat at High Table cringing in front of guests, or had students complaining bitterly about him in my tutorial room. And one always has to keep up appearances and pretend it is all normal. Why, he sat on young Bryant's thesis defence not a year ago and tore him all to pieces, and the jury couldn't honestly give him his degree after that, even though the rest of us thought the thesis work was perfectly all right.'

'He prevented a student from obtaining his degree?' I asked. My ears had perked up at the name 'Bryant', and in any case I was always on the *qui vive* for news of anyone who had reason to hate or resent the deceased Professor.

'Temporarily, at least. Of course, he will redefend it this year, with a different jury. Still, it is most unpleasant. You know, a thesis defence is usually a formality. It is difficult, of course; the student must present his work excellently and be prepared for many questions and much criticism, however the actual refusal of the degree is almost unheard of! One does not allow one's student to defend his thesis if it is not absolutely complete. Bryant's work was good enough, but he is an opinionated fellow, and Ralston took exception to some of his statements. Bryant didn't sit down under it, and the result was an open quarrel. Most embarrassing. And we had offered Bryant a lectureship to begin directly after his defence, as well. He couldn't take it up, obviously, without having gained his degree, and as his scholarship had run out, he was left with no means of support. It's all the worse for him as he has to support his elderly mother. She is a widow, is she not?' and he turned to Professor Taylor for confirmation.

'I don't know—er, I believe so,' said the Professor, looking very uncomfortable.

I remembered the thin young man working in the library, and wondered about his choice of a job. Was there some reason behind it? Or did he merely find it a convenient way to tide himself over until, perhaps, a new lectureship should come up?

'It wasn't the first time we had such problems with Ralston,' said Professor Taylor. 'He's been difficult ever since he first came to King's, before 1880. It must have been in 1878. He was a young graduate then, so he'd have been about twenty-one or -two. He looked older than his age already. He had a most characteristic face, did he not? Lean-cheeked, a lone wolf. Indicative, perhaps, of the bitterness in his character. He finished his thesis in 1883, if I remember rightly. Yes, he can't have been more than forty or so when he died.'

'I never saw him,' piped up young Hilda, a bouncing girl who could never have been described as lean-cheeked. 'I never got to see the murder victim, it's not fair! I would so have liked to. I do wonder what he was like!'

'You little vampire,' began her father, humorously, looking faintly embarrassed. But Mrs Taylor smiled at Hilda from across the table.

'Why, if you want to know what he looked like, perhaps you can,' she said. 'He is in the group photograph taken on the day of the Honoris Causa ceremony, isn't he?' she asked her husband.

'Well, I don't know,' he said with a slight shrug. 'He might be there, I suppose. But who knows where that old photograph is now, anyway?'

'Why, it must be in the Chinese cabinet, with the other photographs,' she said, and rising, she crossed the room to a beautifully ornate cabinet, painted black with red figures, and opened a little door in it with a finely wrought key. She removed a handful of photographs from within and returned to the table, where she handed them to her husband one by one, smiling.

'Look, dear, here is our wedding day,' she said happily. 'I have not looked at these pictures for years!' The image made the round of the table, and I must confess that there was a certain amount of laughter, as the Professor's high domed forehead and bush of white hair was compared with the curly head of a youth from another time. Other photographs of the family followed, a portrait of the children, now grown up, and a picture of a house in the countryside.

'Here is the Department picture,' she said, handing him a rather larger photograph of a group.

He scrutinised it closely. Sitting next to him, I could see that though the picture itself was fairly large, there were a dozen people grouped within it, so that the faces were quite reduced in size.

'There he is,' he said, showing me the picture and pointing at one gentleman, dressed like the others in cap and gown, but somewhat shorter in stature than they.

I stared at the face intently, wondering what it could reveal to me. Yes, it was lean-cheeked, even hollow-cheeked, and the man in it could easily have been taken to be forty already, even though the picture was several years old. I wondered with a shudder if it did not date from the time when he had appeared in Court…to condemn another man to death on cruel and specious grounds. Fixing his features in my mind, I passed the photograph down to the young people, who were eagerly awaiting a sight of the murder victim, more exciting to their youthful minds than wedding pictures of a couple who had reached a peaceful old age with no mishaps.

'Did Ralston ever collaborate with his father?' asked someone.

'No, as far as I know,' replied Professor Taylor thoughtfully. I noticed that most people addressed their questions to him, as though he were undisputedly the person best acquainted with the dead man.

'Probably because his father couldn't stand him,' snickered the professor of logic.

'Well, they didn't have the same research speciality, of course. Ralston senior studies the history of Franco-Polish relations. He wrote a book on Henry III—theirs, of course, not ours. You remember—the one who was called upon to be King of Poland, and who had to sneak away and flee secretly in the middle of the night, and come galloping home to become King of France upon the death of his brother. He was the little favourite of his mother, Catherine de Medici. A well-known murderess in her own right, by the by; one wonders, rather, if she didn't have a hand in the brother's death. But do you know, I don't think Gerard Ralston was brought up much at home. His mother died when he was still quite small, and the boy was sent to school, of course.'

Maybe that explains it, I thought, thinking with a pang of plump little Cedric being removed bodily from my loving arms to a distant boarding school. Of course, he is only one and a half, the precious darling, but I cannot imagine that he will be so very different at six. He is tender and dreamy and needs his mother very much, and I hope he will stay that way for a very long time.

The subject of Professor Ralston and his untimely death eventually exhausted itself without my finding myself particularly enlightened. Somewhat to my relief, the remainder of the meal, accompanied by its three different kinds of wine, was devoted to conversation of a lighter sort. I felt a little like an overstuffed cushion, and was quite glad when the other guests began to depart, as I was looking forward to lying down and allowing the natural process of digestion to take its course. Yet something prevented me from politely taking my leave even after all the other guests had gone except for Professor Hudson's family, who could not tear themselves away from the tremendously amusing banter they were engaging in with Emily. I felt that I very much wished to talk more with Professor Taylor.

'I am delighted that Mr Lazare will be coming here,' I said to him. 'Do you think I will be able to talk with him privately? I would like to ask him a few things.'

'What things?' he said.

'Well, for one, I want to know what he can tell me about that empty folder marked with his initials that we saw,' I said. 'And also, whether he thinks there was anything in that last letter of his, the one to which Professor Ralston was replying when he died, which might have a connection to the murder. What a pity I know so little about the Dreyfus affair. I would like to know more about it before hearing tomorrow's lecture.'

'Well, I can tell you more about it,' he said suddenly. 'In fact, I can do even better—I can show you some documents you are not likely ever to see anywhere else. Come this way,' and he led me into a little study giving off the dining room. Sitting down at his desk, he began digging down in the drawers, and pulled out a file filled with papers.

'Yet I wonder if I should show you these,' he said. 'They are not for everyone. How much do you actually know about the case?'

'I do know the basic facts,' I told him. 'I read quite a number of contemporary newspaper articles on it that I found in Professor Ralston's study. I know he was arrested for treason after his handwriting was identified on a letter apparently found in the German Embassy, written in French and offering a list of important military documents to the Germans. I also know that his trial took place behind closed doors, and that apart from the letter itself, other secret documents were produced, although nobody seems to know what they were. And I know that he was condemned to public degradation, having his military insignia torn off, and to life imprisonment on Devil's Island off the coast of French Guyana, where he was taken about a year ago.'

'But do you know that he never ceased for a single moment to declare his innocence? and that his family and friends have sworn to fight to the death to have the trial reopened? Do you know that he was condemned on the mere evidence of handwriting experts whose conclusions were all wildly contradictory?'

'I did gather that,' I said. 'But I thought there were actually other documents besides the notorious *bordereau*.'

'Secret—probably fabricated,' he said. 'The man is innocent. He was selected as a culprit because of his race.'

'If journalists were the judges, I would say you are certainly right,' I said. 'In the newspapers race is the sole reason ever mentioned. Apparently he was too rich to have any need for financial gain. So they continually try to explain the treason by asserting that a Jewish person cannot be expected to have a sense of honour or love for his country.'

'Read these,' he said suddenly, pushing the file towards me. 'They are excerpts from the letters Dreyfus has written to his wife since his arrest. She has had copies made and shown them to—to a few of his—defenders.'

I glanced down at the letters, but hesitated, burdened by a peculiar feeling of indiscretion at not only reading private letters, but reading them in front of another person.

'Go on, read them,' he said. 'Dreyfus wrote these letters

knowing that they would be read. In fact, they are read by government censors before they ever reach his wife.'

I took up the first one and began to read, then continued to the others, turning over the pages rapidly.

My beloved, I think about you day and night. To be innocent, to have spent a life without any kind of stain, and to see myself condemned for the most monstrous crime a soldier can commit—nothing can be more dreadful! I feel like the plaything of a horrific nightmare.

I don't even want to tell you what I suffered today. Why make your misery even worse? I can only tell you this: when I promised you that I would continue to live and to resist until my name can be rehabilitated, I made the greatest sacrifice an honest man whose honour has just been torn away can make... Why can't we open people's hearts with a scalpel and read what is written within them? In mine, the people who watched me today would read 'This is a man of honour' written in letters of gold. But I understand them—I too would have been filled with contempt to see an officer called a traitor. The tragedy is that the traitor is another than I!

I keep thinking that I don't know how I found the courage to promise you to go on living after my condemnation. Last Saturday remains branded in my spirit in letters of fire. I have the courage of a soldier who can face danger, but I don't know if I really have the soul of a martyr... I live only for the conviction that it is impossible for the truth not to be revealed one day, for my innocence to be recognised and proclaimed by my beloved France, my beloved country…

…The other day, when the crowd covered me with insults, I would have liked to escape from the hands of my guards and offer my breast to those who were so indignant at the sight of me, and tell them: 'Don't insult me, you can't see my soul, but it is absolutely pure of any stain; if you still believe I am guilty, take me and kill me.' And if they heard me shout 'Vive la France' even under physical torture, perhaps then they would believe I am innocent!

I wanted to die, I wanted to kill myself, until you, my darling, so devoted, so courageous, brought me to understand that I didn't have the right to give up, to desert my post. I was terrified of the unendurable moral suffering…yet I gave way, and I lived. I underwent the worst torture a soldier can be made to endure, torture worse than any death, and I followed the terrible road from court to degradation to prison to here without ever yielding to the shouts and the insults, without ever ceasing to proclaim my innocence, loud and clear to all who could hear me. But I left behind a shred of my heart at every station on the way.

I am desperately ill and feverish; in between the torrential rains the humidity is hot and heavy; at ten o'clock in the morning the temperature is already unbearable. I am shaking with fever, but I have asked them to send me a doctor. I don't want to die here!

The Library Paradox

We are in the season of dry heat; I am covered with insect bites—yet that is nothing, compared to the moral torture! My brain, my heart scream with pain. When will they find the real traitor? Will I manage to live until then? Sometimes I am afraid that I won't. My whole being dissolves into despair. Yet I refuse to die. I want my honour back; my honour and my children's honour.

They don't let me sleep. All night the guards move around, clanking chains, banging doors and changing shifts. When will it end? When will it end? They have locked me into my cabin now, because there are workers on the island. I think my brain will burst.

My darling, the boat has just brought me your letters. Still nothing—the traitor has not been discovered! My heart keeps boiling with rage and indignation.

Today is the 14th of July—they have put up our tricoloured flag. I served it so long, with honour and loyalty. I feel so much pain that the pen just falls out of my hands. There are no words for this.

The nights are horrible. I am shaken by the insane desire to sob, my suffering is so intense, but I swallow it down, because I am ashamed of my weakness in front of the guards who watch me day and night. I am not alone with my pain even for a single minute!

This torture is beyond human endurance. Every day the same anguish, the same agony; I am buried

alive in the tomb. What is happening within the con-
sciences of those who condemned me on a miserable
piece of handwriting, with no proofs, no witnesses,
no possible motive for such a heinous crime?

I put down the last letter. The sounds of laughter from
the other room floated eerily through the closed door.

'It seems impossible to continue to believe in his guilt after
reading these,' I said. Very quietly, the Professor piled them
all together and put them back into their folder. He did not
speak, but a glistening in his eyes made me suddenly aware of
an intensity of emotion which surprised me.

'Did you not show them to Professor Ralston?' I asked,
perhaps (with hindsight) a little tactlessly.

'I did. It was one of the biggest mistakes I ever made,'
he replied with cold hatred, pushing the folder back into the
drawer and snapping it shut with a gesture that precluded further questions.

I took my departure with a meek exterior but a seething
mind. There is more to Professor Taylor than meets the eye.

London, Monday, March 16th, 1896

I spent a night of strange and dangerous dreams, many of whose images remained with me even after I had arisen. The flat was empty and quiet. I made a cup of tea and, sitting in front of it, I let its warm, fragrant vapour float comfortingly into my face for a moment, before drawing pencil and paper towards me and writing the following list.

> *Suspects:*
> *(1) Britta or Rebecca Gad or any other relation of*
>   *Baruch Gad*
> *(2) the rabbi*
> *(3) Edmund Bryant*
> *(4) Professor Taylor*

I then rubbed out the fourth name, blushing at being the author of such a ridiculous idea. Yet it was all so strange. How did the Professor come to possess copies of the intimate Dreyfus family letters he had shown me? Moving as they were, yet why did they provoke him to such strong emotion? What was the cause—and what was the true intensity—of the flash of anger against Professor Ralston that I had clearly detected in his voice? I wrote his name back onto the list.

Yet if he were guilty, would he have come to call upon my services? It was really absurd. I rubbed out the name again.

Still, if Jonathan, all fired up by Emily's account of my exploits, had joined with Professor Hudson to persuade Professor Taylor to consult me, it might have seemed suspicious to refuse. He may, indeed, have thought it was for the best; in spite of his politeness, I suspect him of lacking a sincere belief in my capacities, and I remembered how he had summarily rejected the idea of consulting Mr Sherlock Holmes. I wrote his name again.

Yes, but would he then be helping me in my researches, inviting guests, introducing me to Bernard Lazare, lending me the keys to the library and study? I took up the rubber.

But perhaps someone was aware that he had the keys—his wife, for example. In that case, he might logically consider that it would be safer not to hide the fact from me. And for that matter, had he shown me all that he had? Could he not, for example, also possess a copy of the key to Professor Ralston's private rooms—and might he not have used it? And as to the guests and the rest, could he not be killing two birds with one stone by appearing to help me while in fact leading me actively up the garden path? I put down the rubber.

Well—Professor Taylor may be on my secret list, but he is not its foremost member. I set out of the house, determined to locate Britta and Rebecca Gad without delay.

I had plenty of time before my planned visit to Inspector Reynolds, who had answered my note with a confirmation brought in late yesterday evening. I employed this intervening time in trying to advance my search. I first visited Somerset House to look up other Rubinsteins and try to discover anything about Britta's family. But I failed, for the opposite reason from last time; there were too many Rubinsteins for it to be feasible to trace them all. I then went to Mr Upp's office and had the freckled urchin carry him a note containing a request for information on the subject of the present location of Britta Gad and her daughter. He contented himself with sending me back a brief answer to the effect that unfortunately he had no information on the question, but that had he himself been in the position of the widow of a man executed for murder, he would undoubtedly have changed names, a notion which discouraged me. After having wasted my entire morning in this manner, I wended my way on foot through a chill mist to the Victoria Embankment, and entered the premises of New Scotland Yard with damp shoes, soiled hems, and black thoughts.

My only consolation was in the thought that it might be possible to obtain help from the Inspector not only in locating the two missing ladies, but perhaps even in obtaining permission to visit Baruch Gad in prison. Indeed, this kind of thing, which is practically inconceivable for ordinary mortals, is a mere matter of routine for the police.

I walked into the building and enquired for the Inspector with a lady seated behind a counter, wearing a forbidding expression on her face. 'I believe he is out on a case,' she said with asperity, but disappeared nevertheless into the inner reaches of the building.

The Inspector himself returned with her to greet me, and he was neither out nor forbidding; he seemed quite pleased to see me.

'Mrs Weatherburn, what a pleasure,' he said. 'You visit London very rarely, don't you? Why, I can't remember ever seeing you here before. Do let me show you around. We're quite proud of our location; we've only been here five or six years, you know. "New Scotland Yard", we insist on calling the place, although there's no more Scotland Yard here than Buckingham Palace. I rather miss the old Scottish Kings' courtyard and its legends, but we're much better off here, of course. We'd become very cramped in Whitehall. Now we can work properly. Do come along to my office. I ought to be able to scare up a cup of tea. Now, tell me what you are doing here. Is this holiday or business?'

'Business,' I said firmly. The relationship between the police and private detectives is always, at best, ambiguous, so I thought I would do as well to take the bull by the horns straight away.

'Is that right?' he said cheerfully. 'Getting under our feet again in some way, are you? Do I know the case?'

'You probably know of it, at least,' I said. 'I am investigating the murder of Professor Gerard Ralston of King's College.'

'The Ralston murder! Why, I've heard about nothing else since I got here this morning. There's to be a breakthrough today, it seems. Are you behind that, then? I might have known.'

'But I'm not,' I said, amazed and alarmed. 'This is news to me. Dear me, what can have happened all of a sudden? Do you know?'

'Well, to start with, there was a fairly nasty newspaper article on the front page of the *Illustrated London News*, more or less accusing our services of incompetence. I've got it upstairs; I'll show it to you. I'm not on the case myself and I'm not quite sure what's going on with it, but according to what I've been hearing in the corridors, our people are ready to react.'

'React? How?'

'By making an arrest.'

'An arrest! Who will be arrested? Do they know who to arrest?'

'I'm afraid I don't know the details. All I can tell you is that the newspaper article talked about logic, and logic is apparently the order of the day. How is your own investigation going?'

'Not too well,' I admitted, as we continued down hallways and up stairs, arriving finally in the Inspector's comfortable quarters. 'Actually, I wanted to ask you how you think I might go about finding a person who might be anywhere.'

'Locating lost persons; a difficult task. What exactly do you know about this person?'

'It is two people really: a woman and her daughter. I know their names, or at least, I know the names they went by ten years ago: Britta and Rebecca Gad. I haven't been able to find any official record, or anything at all, in fact, after the marriage of Britta Rubinstein to her husband Menachem Gad in 1874 and the birth of their daughter in 1875.'

'Menachem Gad? Now, that name rings a bell. What is it? An old criminal case, wasn't it? The murder of a child. He hanged, didn't he?'

'He did. But—but I have honestly begun to wonder whether he was really guilty. There was apparently no real motive, except for some sickening rubbish about ritual murder.'

'Motive, motive,' he said. 'There goes the amateur. It's means that count, means and opportunity.'

'There goes the policeman,' I said, only half-smiling.

'And why exactly are you looking for this man's widow?'

'I have a feeling there might be some connection with the Ralston case,' I said a little reluctantly. 'But I could be wrong.'

He whistled slowly. 'I won't ask how you dug that out; I

expect you wouldn't say it if you didn't have good reasons. I haven't heard a whisper of anything about that old case here.'

'I might be mistaken,' I said quickly. 'It's just a faint lead.'

'So the wife and child have disappeared from view?'

'Well, they do not seem to be in London; not under the same names, at any rate.'

'That doesn't mean much; they could easily have changed their names. They could have done anything, couldn't they? Even gone to live in a foreign country. What did you say the woman's maiden name was?'

'Rubinstein. But I haven't been able to locate her even under that name.'

'Rubinstein; she may have been foreign herself. Perhaps she went back to Poland or Russia or wherever they all come from. There isn't going to be too much I can do to help you. I can send someone to check that there is no criminal record under those names,' and he scribbled a short note which he delivered to a young man who answered a bell.

'What would the police do in a case like this?' I asked.

'Well, we'd be methodical. We'd start with all the bureaus of public information in the country; we'd tackle the nearest family members we could find, and failing specific information, we'd cover everyone in the area bearing the same family name, both maiden and married. Rubinstein is common among the Jews. There was someone else in the family involved in the Gad case, wasn't there? Wasn't it a trial of brothers?'

'Yes. The other brother is in Dartmoor.'

'Well, then, that's the person to start with.'

'I would like to! But how could I obtain the authorization to visit him? Only family members can visit a prisoner, in general.'

'Well, the police can certainly visit a prisoner if we judge it necessary,' he began. 'Ah, you're back,' he added, as the young man he had sent out with the note returned and thrust his head around the edge of the door.

'Yes sir, but nothing to report. No criminal record associated with either of the names you wrote down.'

'Thank you, Johnson. Well, that was to be expected. Still, as we were saying, there is still the brother in Dartmoor. Let me handle this for you, Mrs Weatherburn. I should be able to arrange visiting rights. Coming from Scotland Yard, that should not be a problem, even though you do not have official status. But we'll brush that under the rug—you've been helpful in the past, so I'm happy to be able to do you a good turn now. I'll communicate with the governor of the prison and fix a time for your visit. I suppose it's rather urgent?'

'Oh, yes.'

'Come back and see me tomorrow after midday,' he said. 'I'll send a telegram or two and see what I can do before then.'

I contained my enthusiasm with difficulty. Finally, a ray of light in the darkness?

'Don't be too optimistic,' he cautioned me. 'The prisoner might refuse to talk to you, or he might know nothing about their whereabouts.'

'I'll cross that bridge when I come to it,' I replied.

'Well, if you believe in this thing, you had better work as fast as you can, because as I told you, an arrest is imminent.'

'Oh, yes! Who can it be? I almost forgot—you were going to show me the article that caused such a stir.'

He reached over to a chair near his desk, upon which he had laid his coat, hat and stick in a precarious pile. They all fell off as he unceremoniously dug the newspaper out from underneath them.

'Bother,' he said, handing it to me.

The article leapt to the eye. A blaring headline entitled it:
LIBRARY PARADOX STILL UNSOLVED

Interviewing a logician? Why, this must be the article
written by the very journalist that Bertrand Russell mentioned
yesterday. What had he suddenly understood? Was it Russell
who had indicated the solution to him? What could it be? I
read the description of the crime and its discovery once again,
and tried to apply a fresh eye and logical reasoning. But my
mind remained perfectly blank.

'Do you understand what the famous loophole is?' I asked
the Inspector, feeling a little envious of the anonymous journalist whose boasts—or whose prowess—I was not able to
match.

'No, but I haven't thought about it. The fellows on the
case saw what he meant right away, I believe,' he replied. 'At
least, I assume they did, since they've been talking about an
arrest. But they're not telling details at this point.'

'I do wish I knew,' I said.

'You'll find out very soon,' he assured me, handing me
the paper and guiding me kindly to the exit. 'But one never
knows—this doesn't mean you should stop your own work,
not yet. Go on and follow up your lead.'

I reached home, worried and harassed, to find Amy waiting
for me in a state of great excitement.

'Look—we must go back to Settles Street tonight!' she
exclaimed the moment I came in. 'Can you? We received this
note from David. Do you think he's found something out?'

The note read: *Come down tonight if you can—urgent.*

'Of course we shall go. When do we leave?' I said reassuringly, taken aback by her excitement almost verging on panic, as she unconsciously crushed the little note into a ball.

'Right now, if you will. I've sent to Jonathan to tell him to go directly there.'

'And what about Emily?'

'Oh, Emily!' A look of intense annoyance crossed her face briefly, then she shrugged and smiled. 'She won't be in this evening—she won't come with us. She's busy. She's at the Hudsons' again. It's for the best.'

'For the best? What do you mean?'

'Oh—nothing. I wasn't talking about tonight—I was talking about Emily and Roland Hudson. But it doesn't matter. It doesn't matter whether she comes with us or not, or what she does. You see, she isn't really one of us. Emily is a dear friend and I love sharing the flat with her, but when it comes to questions of life or death or one's whole future, then...'

She did not finish her sentence, and I did not take her up on it. I thought I understood that when she spoke of 'life or death or one's whole future', she was not referring to our investigation, but to something else, something I had also noticed. However, as it seemed to be no business of mine, I did not comment, but merely took up my shawl, which I had only just put off, and prepared to depart.

The aspect of the sordid, tumbledown tenement in Settles Street seemed more depressing than ever, and the contrast with the radiant warmth and liveliness within was all the more striking. Already before Rivka opened the door for us, a great racket of shouting and playing and tumbling about was to be heard. I do believe I have never seen a woman happier in her interior than Rivka Mendel, as she rose like an angel from amidst a medley of scattered toys, spoons, rolling balls, half-eaten children's meals and mending, to say nothing of what appeared to be an unbroken sea of boys, complete with crashing waves. Her own two were directly in the process of riding on the back of a youth whom I immediately recognised as cheerful little Ephraim. He was galloping about on all fours, knocking into the furniture, while a second, somewhat older youth galumphed after them, holding the littlest one in place to prevent him from tumbling off, and generally aiding the whole pyramid in its endeavour to remain upright.

'You know Ephraim already, and this is Yakov, David's other brother,' said Rivka, tranquilly indicating the thumping, bumping four-headed beast. 'David is not home yet; he is still in *shul*. But it is Ephraim who says he really has something to tell you.'

'Did you succeed in the project I gave you?' I said eagerly, addressing the red-headed youngster. He looked up from his activities and smiled.

'Yes! We did it! And we worked hard, I can tell you,' he answered. 'I told Yakov about it—I hope that's all right—and we sleuthed together. We kept on asking everybody where they had heard the rebbe story, and we talked to everybody—I mean everybody! We talked to boys from five different *shuls*! And we found out something.'

It was at this precise moment that Jonathan and David arrived together, having met each other in the street outside. Unlike his younger brothers, David looked serious. He glared at me.

'The boys say they have found out something important that they want to tell you,' he said severely.

'Yes,' I said meekly.

'You put them up to this, didn't you, Vanessa? You know that I didn't want them mixed up in it,' he began.

'Oh, David, don't start!' shouted both his brothers in chorus. 'We had fun! We loved it! And it's silly to think it was dangerous. It was just a test!'

He said some scolding words to them in Yiddish, but they were undaunted and answered back loudly, without losing their cheerfulness. Finally, David shrugged and turned to me.

'Well, they haven't told me what it's all about, so I don't know,' he said. 'Do I have the right to find out, or is this for your ears only?'

'No, I think we should all hear it. Ephraim, tell us what you have discovered,' I said.

'Everybody was telling the rebbe story last week, because—there really *was* a rebbe who disappeared!' he cried triumphantly. 'For a whole afternoon! Nobody knows where he went! And then he came back and everything went on just the same as before. There's a song about it, too, that they're singing now.'

'When did this happen?' I said quickly.

'It was *iom shishi*—the eve of the Shabbat,' he said. 'That means it was the Friday before last.'

'It is the one!' exclaimed Jonathan.

'Have you simply heard about him,' I said, 'or have you actually found out his name?'

'We've found out his name, of course,' said Ephraim indignantly. 'What do you take us for? It's Reb Moyshe Avrom.'

'Moyshe Avrom!' said David. 'I can't believe it—Moyshe Avrom is one of our best-known and most revered rebbes. He is known far and wide for the extent of his knowledge and the depth of his interpretations.'

'All I need to do is lay eyes on him,' said Jonathan, unimpressed by the praise. 'I would know him again at once. I *must* see him.'

There was a short silence at this remark, during which the two boys fixed us with large, astonished eyes.

'Why do *you* need to see him?' asked Yakov.

Nobody answered. Ephraim turned to Yakov with an air of utter delight, and said, 'Why, it wasn't a test after all! It was real detection, for the *murder mystery*! Wasn't it?' he added, turning to me for confirmation.

'Well, it was,' I admitted, feeling a little guilty. 'But *keep the secret*, whatever you do.'

'Be quiet, boys,' said David severely. 'I'm sorry you ever got into this at all, but since you did, just keep quiet about it. No more meddling.'

'But we want to help!' wailed Ephraim.

'When can we see the man?' asked Jonathan impatiently.

'Well, I've told you this would not be so easy,' said David thoughtfully. 'I've explained to you already what the life of a rebbe is like here, I mean a real Hassidic rebbe like Moyshe Avrom. His time is not his own. There isn't one moment when he isn't surrounded by his pupils or his disciples or his family. His disciples live in his house, and follow his every movement, word and gesture, trying to learn something from them. He never has a casual conversation, because everything he says is taken to have tremendous meaning. In fact, for this rebbe to have left for an afternoon must have been quite difficult.'

'We heard that he just told his students to stay in the *shul* and simply walked out the door, and none of them even thought of following him, because they always do as they are told,' said Yakov. 'They probably thought he went out to breathe the air, but in fact he did not return for several hours.'

'Why can't we just go and knock on his door?' said Jonathan.

'I'm afraid you wouldn't get near him. His disciples would receive you, and never let you get near their holy man.'

'Can we not get a message to him?' I suggested.

'But how would you deliver it? Even if you delivered it

by hand, you'd still have to give it to one of the students. They probably take care of his mail for him as well,' said Rivka.

'I have an idea!' said David suddenly. 'What about the Purim festival, Rivka? It starts Thursday. You probably don't know what the Purim festival is, Vanessa; I'll explain it to you later. But it's the one day in the year in which all houses are open. People wear disguises, and mummers and musicians go in and out of the houses playing and dancing. Why, probably anyone will be able to enter the rebbe's home that day!'

'But entering his home is not enough,' I said. 'I am going to need to speak with this man in private.'

'That seems practically impossible, Vanessa. I don't mean this offensively, but he would not speak alone to a person like you; in fact, you would be expected to stay in the women's section of the room. I don't know how you can manage it, but at least I think I can get you inside.'

'All I want right now is to *see* him—to see if it is the right man,' said Jonathan. 'I don't need to talk to him—I wouldn't even know what to say. Vanessa can do that afterwards, if he is the one.'

'I hope so,' said David, then glanced at me. 'You think this is strange, don't you? I understand that in a way it is absurd that it should be difficult just to get near enough to someone to speak to him about something important. The thing is, it isn't a question of individuals. Life here is so different from life outside. The meaning of people's lives is different. I mean, people's lives have *meaning*. Rivka, for instance—she isn't just a married woman raising a family like thousands of others, doing her best to get the children fed and to bed on time. Not here. Here, everything you do is for the glory of the Lord. Everything you do counts and your time, your efforts and your words are not your own. You just have to trust me that it isn't a simple matter. I can't think of anything better than the Purim festival.'

'To talk to him, maybe. But I just want to lay eyes on him from a distance,' said Jonathan. 'I can't wait till Thursday. I need to see him *now*.'

'We heard he walks home from *shul* at the same time every evening,' said Ephraim helpfully. 'Of course, he leaves together with the whole group of students, but perhaps if we go and stand near the *shul*, Jonathan can get a glimpse of him.'

'What time does he go?' I asked.

'Seven o'clock exactly.'

'Let's go now,' said Jonathan immediately, glancing at his watch, and David nodded and led the way outside. Amy remained to help Rivka with the small children, and David tried to forbid his brothers from joining us. Yakov complied with a shrug, but Ephraim attached himself to us irrepressibly, with the excuse of being the only one who knew exactly where the rebbe's *shul* was situated.

'If it is really the right man, we must make some kind of a plan for me to be able to do more than merely enter his house,' I said to David as we walked.

'Even if you did manage to approach him, and to talk to him directly about the murder, which seems almost as unlikely as flying to the moon, you almost certainly would not obtain a straight answer,' he answered quietly. 'Rebbes speak in parables and ask questions instead of answering them.'

'Ugh,' I said. 'We'll just have to cross each bridge as we come to it. First things first, then: let Jonathan identify him! Is the place far?'

'No, it's just off Brick Lane,' said Ephraim. 'It's a good thing it's not too dark yet.'

Although not dark, the light was dimming. Poor people

hustled along the dirty streets in the chill, and comforting lights showed at a multitude of windows along the way. I tried to imagine many little homes all as snug as Rivka's, but the task was impossible, so powerful was the impression of poverty and misery given by the cold, huddled people in their ragged coats and the half-naked, bare-legged children who ran about the streets. We crossed Whitechapel and turned down Old Montague Street and then up Brick Lane, Ephraim gambolling happily ahead of us, and reached the tumbledown little house that served as synagogue and *shul* for the rebbe's community at a few minutes before seven.

'That's the place,' said Ephraim in a whisper, pointing. We stopped, and peering at its dimly lighted windows with interest, we tried to find a place to post ourselves near enough to see, but not so near as to attract attention. It seemed strange to be standing there doing nothing. Several people passing stared at us with some hostility, and indeed, Jonathan and I in our city clothes fitted badly into the general atmosphere, even though Rivka had bound my hair up under one of her own kerchiefs before allowing me out of the house.

'Where has Ephraim got to?' I wondered, looking around for him.

'Shhh!' David admonished me. The door of the prayer house was opening.

In front of my fascinated eyes, there emerged a gaggle of young men wearing clothes and aspects so outlandish as to give David, by contrast, almost the air of a typical British man-about-town.

Dressed in black from head to toe, with long coats and big hats, they wore their hair in long curls falling on either side of their cheeks. Without exception, their faces were pale and wan. All of those faces were turned towards one exact point in the middle of their group; they surrounded their rabbi and had eyes only for him. Alas, he was rather short in stature, and it was impossible to see anything more of him than the large, wheel-shaped fur hat he wore on his head.

I glanced at Jonathan, who made a gesture of frustration. I was just wondering if we should not try to create some diversion to shake apart the tightly bound group, when we saw that Ephraim, who had moved right up to the door, had understood the situation and was in the process of taking this task upon himself. Throwing the merest twinkling glance in my direction, he burst suddenly forward, and running up to the tightly knit, slowly advancing knot, he called out a few names in a loud voice—'Hey, Shimon, Reuven!' and began to babble something in his own language, in loud and excited tones. David shook his head in amazement.

'Shh, shh,' said several of the earnest young men, pushing Ephraim away and murmuring, in low voices, little phrases which sounded for all the world like 'Who are you?' and 'What do you think you are doing?' He struggled and continued to shout. Several of the young men undertook to hustle him aside, and in doing so, they actually increased the distance between themselves and their revered leader—and he became, momentarily, visible! He was quite an old man, nearer eighty than seventy, with a spreading grizzled beard on his chest and a wholesome face whose sternness was relieved by a faraway, almost ecstatic expression. Although short, he walked with a steady step, and seemed firmly built, although this was somewhat hard to judge as he was well-wrapped up against the weather with greatcoat, scarf wound many times about his neck, boots, and gloves. *Gloves.* I thought about the gun, about its strangely smudged-over fingerprints.

I felt someone grab my arm. 'It's the same man! It is!' Jonathan was whispering urgently into my ear. 'There's no question about it. I recognise him absolutely. Oh, my God.'

'Then let's go,' responded David immediately. 'Our task is accomplished for the present. We don't want them to notice us. Let Ephraim find his own way back. He can deal with it,' he added ruthlessly, as his brother received a resounding smack for some insolence and rubbed his cheek ruefully. 'Don't worry about him! There never was such a survivor. He'll know his job is done when he sees us gone.'

His attitude surprised me for a moment, when I remembered how annoyed he had been at my inveigling the child into helping, however harmlessly, with the investigation. But I suppose that then he was imagining his brother being led into all kinds of unknown dangers, whereas the mere falling into the hands of a group of ultra-religious Hassidim obviously constituted no danger at all in David's eyes.

I disliked leaving the child behind, but followed David nonetheless as he walked quietly away and turned the corner into Brick Lane. There, to my surprise, I saw a man standing still and waiting, just as we had being doing a few moments earlier. I looked straight at him, and his gaze momentarily met mine. There was something disagreeable about it. I did not know the man, but I knew the look.

'That man is from the police,' I murmured to David, as low as I could, hurrying to catch up with his rapid steps.

'The police?' he said, glancing back without slowing down. 'What makes you say that? He looks perfectly ordinary to me—more so than you do, at any rate.'

'I don't know how I know. I just feel it. I've met so many policemen! And he's there, waiting, watching. Do you think the police can possibly have succeeded in identifying the rabbi? Oh, I forgot to tell you—but just this morning I heard from the police that there was going to be an arrest today. Can they have found him themselves? How can they have done it? And how could they possibly justify an arrest? We *know* he cannot be the murderer!'

Jonathan turned to me, looking worried.

'Can we warn him?' he suggested.

'I wish we could, but it would not change anything. He would not heed a warning,' said David. 'A rebbe does not flee. If he is arrested, he will defend himself with the truth.'

'You don't understand!' I said. 'If the rabbi is on the point of being wrongfully arrested, he is in serious danger! Jewish people are convicted of crimes just because they are Jews! Don't you know that?' I was surprised by the urgency in my own voice. All that I have learnt about the Dreyfus affair, on top of my increasing doubts about the Gad case, has shaken me to the core.

'Vanessa is right! He mustn't be arrested!' said Jonathan suddenly, in a voice so choked with passion that I stared at him in amazement.

'What happened? Was it the right man?' said Amy, hastening towards us as soon as we stepped into the little flat, which was warm and steamy with cooking.

'It was, Amy!' said Jonathan. 'If only we could talk to him soon! But Vanessa thinks she saw a policeman watching him as we came away. She's afraid the police might have identified him too, and be getting ready to arrest him.'

'No-o-o,' cried Rivka. 'I can't believe that—it just isn't possible. Why, how could they have ever identified the rebbe? They can have no spies or informers here.'

'The police have a lot of methods,' I was beginning, but Jonathan interrupted me.

'*If* the rebbe is arrested, we will save him,' he said firmly.

'After all, we can prove that he is innocent, can't we? Our reconstruction shows that he can't possibly have done it.'

It was true, and I wondered again, as I had many times already, what 'logical loophole' the *Illustrated London News* journalist had been thinking of, that I had not yet been able to see.

'And if the rebbe is not arrested,' Jonathan was continuing, 'Vanessa will have to approach him during the Purim festival, the day after tomorrow. Now that I've seen him, I understand why David says that it's our best chance of getting near him. It seems practically impossible to approach the man for a private conversation.'

Ephraim entered the flat at that moment, laughing.

'I ran all the way home,' he said. 'Oooh, they were mad at me! Did you get a proper look at him?'

'Yes. It is the man we were looking for,' said David soberly. Ephraim joined us at the table and served himself some food.

'When are you going to tell me what it's all about?' he said.

'As soon as we can; as soon as we know enough ourselves,' I began.

'That's enough,' said David firmly.

'Well, if you won't tell me about this case, do tell me about another one, at least!' he insisted pleadingly. 'Tell us about a mystery that you solved. I want to learn,' he added slyly, 'you know I want to become a detective myself!'

'Ah,' I began, wondering if this was the right place and time to recount the stories of other crimes. But everyone else seemed to think the idea was an excellent one.

'Well, let me think,' I said, quickly reviewing some past cases in my mind for something that I could reasonably recount in front of children. 'I once had an interesting case about a woman who disappeared. I am afraid that the police suspected she had been murdered. As all the people who could possibly have been concerned seemed to have an alibi, the police came up with the theory that the murder was a collusion between at least five people, each of whom, I admit it, was in possession of a very valid motive. The woman was extremely rich, and her two grown children would have inherited her money. She had had a...ahem, there had been a story with a...well, her husband was actually quite angry with her. Furthermore, her own two brothers had a serious grudge against her because she had inherited a large fortune from an old aunt who had disinherited her nephews on account of their dissolute ways.'

'And what had really happened to her?' asked Ephraim.

'Well, in fact, she had had enough of being harassed, disliked and resented by her family, which was also in the bad habit of constantly pestering her with demands for money. So she had purchased a house for herself in the south of France under another name, and quietly departed thither. You know, Ephraim, the majority of the cases we private detectives are called in to investigate end up being more mysteries than crimes. The number of true crimes is much smaller than the number of mysterious occurrences, which may take on the appearance of crime.'

'That poor lady,' observed Ephraim, 'she lost her family. Even if it wasn't a very nice family.'

'Perhaps life is nothing but a long series of losses,' said Rivka, 'and we only notice it in this story because we do not have the habit of seeing it in our daily lives. It is unavoidable, even for us, who seem happy now. I know it.'

Amy and Jonathan both reacted to this gloomy statement by voicing vaguely consoling murmurs while hastily gathering up their things. It was indeed a good time to depart, as it was becoming quite late.

'And the rebbe? Should we not go and see whether he has been arrested?' said Jonathan, without much hope.

'It is no use now,' I said, 'we will just find ourselves in front of a darkened house with no way of telling what has happened. Listen, I will try to find out what has happened first thing tomorrow, and if necessary, we will go to the police together.'

After walking a short distance, we hailed a cab, and trotted quietly through the dull-coloured evening, speaking little. The cab slowed down as we moved up Tavistock Street, and drew up in front of our door. I alighted and saw, to my surprise, another cab in the process of drawing up behind us, just as Jonathan emerged from ours. At the very moment that he set his foot upon the pavement, two things happened.

First, a man jumped out of the cab which had stopped behind ours, and dismissing it with a word, smartly greeted two other men who had been standing in the shadows near our doorway. I recognised him at once—it was the very man I had seen on the corner near the rabbi's little synagogue.

Second, one of the two waiting men stepped forward towards us.

'Mr Jonathan Sachs?' he said.

'Yes,' said that young man with a justifiable air of alarm.

'Police,' said the man. 'You are under arrest for the murder of Professor Gerard Ralston. I will ask you to come along with us quietly'—and in the blink of an eye, Jonathan found himself in handcuffs and being pushed rudely in the direction of a waiting police vehicle further up the road, while I stood by feeling stunned, shocked and impotent.

'Don't just stand there! *Do* something!' cried Amy, jumping to the ground beside me and shaking me violently by the arm. 'You know the police—speak to them!'

'So we got him,' murmured the gentleman I had seen earlier

to one of those who had been waiting for us, while the other gave Jonathan the usual speech contingent upon an arrest. 'I followed him back,' he went on, 'I've been tailing him about London all day. I've got every one of his movements written down.' And he smiled with the satisfaction of a professional after a job well done, exactly as though Jonathan had been a hardened criminal who had gone into hiding and been tremendously difficult to find.

Amy and I hastened up to them as Jonathan was being hustled into the carriage.

'Where—where are you taking him?' I stammered awkwardly to the policeman making the arrest.

'Bow Street,' snapped the officer, climbing in.

'Jonathan!' cried Amy desperately.

'Amy—I didn't kill him!' he answered hoarsely, leaning across the policeman towards her for a moment, before the carriage door thumped shut upon them. She did not answer.

How blind I have been! I remained on the pavement, thunderstruck, unable to move, rooted to the ground, staring blankly, physical existence forgotten, while a great light was suddenly lit in my mind, throwing aside the shadows. *This*, nothing other than this, was the famous 'loophole' in the logic of the case. Jonathan was lying—the whole of his story was a tissue of fabrications—there was no rabbi! At the moment when the other young men came running around the house, he was halfway down the path *leaving* the building, and simply turned around upon hearing them coming, pretending to be walking *towards* it. Here, indeed, was a simple, complete, indisputable solution to the incomprehensible paradox.

I turned to Amy as the carriage rumbled away, and was frozen by what I saw in her face.

I expected to see shock; I expected surprise, distress, horror, anger even. But her expression showed something completely different. How can I describe the look in her black eyes as deep as wells? Unfathomable sadness, immense weariness, wordless fear and dull despair, the crushing weight of the world—she had the kind of eyes with which one contemplates living death. And it dawned upon me slowly, my hair rising on my scalp, that she knew all about it—she knew it, she knew it all along.

As though knowing what her face must reveal to me, Amy turned away into the darkness, her hand in front of her mouth.

'I must go to my parents,' she said in a muffled voice, and the sound of her quick steps was lost to me within a minute.

London, Tuesday, March 17th, 1896

It took me a long time to come back to myself, to bring myself to walk to the door, open it, climb the stairs, and unlock the door of Emily's little flat. I entered stiffly, awkwardly, feeling unlike myself, not knowing what to feel, so shaken was I by what I had witnessed.

Emily was sitting at her desk, her burnished hair shining in the light of a little lamp, having a late cup of tea all by herself, and labouring over a heap of papers filled with scribbled calculations. The fire had died down to a mass of embers, glowing mysteriously from within as though communing with themselves, and the rest of the room was in shadows. She looked up with pleasure at my entrance, and rose to throw a little more coal on the shivering flames.

'Why, are you alone?' she asked, noticing it suddenly. 'Where is Amy?' Then, catching sight of my face, she came towards me quickly. 'Vanessa, what has happened?'

'Jonathan has been arrested for the murder,' I said heavily.

'No!' she cried. 'Oh, Vanessa, it can't be! Jonathan—but why Jonathan? *Why?*'

'Think,' I told her. 'His having done it explains everything.'

'You mean…' I saw her expression change slowly as she tried to imagine what might have happened.

'He could have been leaving, not coming, when the others saw him. And invented all the rest,' I told her. 'At least, that explanation would fit the facts. And that is what the police think, and this journalist as well,' and I pulled the morning's newspaper out of my bag and showed it to her. She read over the article quickly.

'You read this this morning?' she asked.

'Yes—and my inspector friend actually told me there would be an arrest today. But I did not understand what it meant until this happened, just now. I have been very stupid.'

'No, you haven't! Vanessa—the police are wrong, of course! They are making a horrible mistake! You don't *believe* that Jonathan did it, do you? Do you? Vanessa—how can you? Is it because there is no other explanation?'

'Well, that and something else,' I said slowly. 'I saw Amy's face when they took him away. She *knows.*'

'I don't believe it, no, I don't,' said Emily stoutly. 'Not just because I know Jonathan and like him and cannot believe for a second that he would ever murder anyone. It isn't just that, Vanessa. It's everything together; it makes no sense. Just think! Why would he have been so eager to have you come and solve the crime? When I told him about you, he was so keen on your coming! He pressed me into writing to you, and persuaded the professors to go and see you. Why would he have done that—out of some kind of insane hubris? No, that just isn't possible. And then, what about the rebbe that he saw? That wasn't a lie, you know it wasn't—that man was seen in the street by other people.'

'It could have been a coincidence,' I murmured reluctantly. 'Or it could have been witnesses reacting to suggestion. Or maybe Jonathan even saw the man he described, but a few minutes earlier, when he was *really* going into the library.'

'But Vanessa, Jonathan was looking for that rebbe, and making you, and Amy, and David and Rivka look for him! Why would he have wanted so much to find him? If you had managed to locate him, and then he had stated that he left the grounds at a few minutes before five and saw Jonathan going in, it would be horribly dangerous for Jonathan—it would as much as accuse him of the murder! Surely he wouldn't have been trying to find the rebbe, if he really was the murderer.' She looked at me suspiciously. 'But perhaps you think that he has been leading you up the garden path all this time, by pretending there was a rebbe when really there was none, or by pretending to search for the rebbe while making sure that in fact nobody would ever find him.'

'No-o,' I said thoughtfully, realising that she knew nothing of our activities of the evening. 'It isn't that. We did find him.'

'You did? What do you mean? When? How did you do it? How can you be sure it's the right man?'

'Jonathan recognised him,' I said confusedly. For Emily was right; this behaviour would be quite inexplicable if Jonathan were really guilty.

'How did you ever manage it?' she asked. 'One rebbe among thousands?'

'David's little brothers did it. At least, they found out about a rabbi who had seemingly disappeared for a whole afternoon, the Friday before last. So we went to see if we could have a look at him. And he came out of his house, and Jonathan recognised him.'

'There!' she said triumphantly. 'You see? That would make no sense if he had invented the whole story. He wouldn't have identified him. It would have been a crazy thing to do! He would simply have said it wasn't the right one. This *proves* that he's innocent. I hope you believe me now.'

'You sound like a mathematician,' I smiled. 'Real life is not always that simple.'

'But why not? Proofs are proofs, whether in mathematics or in life!' She touched the pages scattered on the table in front of her. 'And do you know,' she continued, 'it's not just the proofs that can be similar, but the whole situation of having a problem and wanting to solve it. I imagine that what you feel when you are on a case is not much different from what I feel when I work on a problem in maths—it becomes an obsession, and I turn it over and over in my head, looking at it from every angle, searching out every tool I can possibly use. I never thought of being a detective myself, and I've always admired you for all the ways you have of reasoning that I would probably never think of. But now it's different—Jonathan has been arrested, and he is my friend! I want to work with you, think with you, think *like* you, use the fact that I can think like a mathematician to help you solve this case! And that's what I'm trying to do. I'm pointing out something that would make no sense if Jonathan were really guilty. He just wouldn't have identified that rebbe.'

'What you say does make sense, Emily,' I said. 'It's not that I disagree. I want to agree. But people do very strange, illogical things sometimes, according to their character, and particularly when they are in danger. It might just be that Jonathan didn't realise the danger, and tried to convince us of the truth of his story by trying to prove the elements of it which really were true.'

'At the risk of having his story disproved and immediately causing his own arrest? No, Vanessa. Jonathan is not that stupid. He can think.'

'But this explanation solves the paradox,' I said anxiously, as the force of her argument sank in. 'There isn't any other possible solution.'

'There must be,' she said. 'We just don't see it yet. We didn't think of this possibility either, until now.'

'I don't know about "we",' I said. 'You and I did not, certainly. But what about Amy, and Jonathan himself?'

'You really think they might have been expecting this?'

'I am certain of it, and so would you be if you had seen how they reacted to the arrest.'

'Did Jonathan say anything?'

'He said "I didn't kill him",' I admitted, remembering his face, his voice as he spoke those words, trying to analyse what they signified. He had not spoken them to the world at large; he had addressed them specifically to Amy, as though they contained some kind of personal message. Why? Because he saw that she believed he had done it? But why would she believe that, she, his own sister, when Emily remained staunchly defensive?

'I think Amy knows something she isn't telling me,' I said.

'And what about the rebbe? *He* must know something important! Are you going to talk to him, Vanessa?'

'Yes,' I said. 'I mean to see him on Thursday.'

'Thursday! But that's ages away! Why not tomorrow morning?'

Why not, indeed? David's explanation seemed so complicated, and yet, when I remembered the gaggle of students and the manner in which they had unceremoniously chased away little Ephraim, I believed him.

'I will do everything I can,' I said. 'I have three days before Jonathan will be had up before the magistrate. If I find out the truth by then, he will not be committed to trial. Emily, I won't stop looking, I promise you.'

I went to bed, but could not sleep for seeing Emily's large, accusing eyes. I tried to recapture the immediate sense of conviction and enlightenment that I had felt when Jonathan was taken away, but it was too late; Emily had succeeded in diluting it with a heavy dose of doubt. Jonathan, firing a gun at Professor Ralston? Impossible to visualise. I remembered my list of suspects: Edmund Bryant, Professor Taylor, Britta Gad. Yes, but those hypotheses had not allowed me to solve the paradox. It had never occurred to me to think that the witnesses might be lying. Least of all Jonathan; I had not doubted his word for a moment. And what if he were not lying? Could it be the other two witnesses, Mason and Chapman?

I lay back in the dark, and tried to work out the possibility. To begin with, they were together, so they must at the very least have been accomplices. Fine, they were accomplices. Yes, but the caretaker had declared that he had accompanied the two students to the back gate and locked it behind them at five o'clock precisely. They would have had to run inside, kill the Professor, and return outside, going towards the back for some reason, then come running back to the front even more incomprehensibly to 'discover' the corpse. If Jonathan had not been there, this behaviour would have been foolish and dangerous. Had they been meaning to flee out of the back gate? But it was locked. Had they bribed the caretaker to leave it open? Much too risky, once he heard about the murder. Was the caretaker also an accomplice, nourishing a secret hatred of Professor Ralston?

The Library Paradox

Nothing was beyond belief on that score, perhaps, yet this was much too complicated, and anyway it totally failed to explain why they should have changed their minds and come running back. Could they have heard Jonathan coming? Not from that distance, and even if they had, it would have been wiser to continue out the back gate and away. Could they have heard the rabbi leaving? But what nonsense—if my construction were true, and under the hypothesis that Jonathan was speaking the truth, the rabbi was in the library during the murder.

Absurd!

Mason, Chapman and the caretaker were obviously telling the truth.

So then? Jonathan was lying? Friendly, smiling, dark-eyed Jonathan. I began to think over Emily's arguments in his favour. Why would he have pressed her into calling me in to solve the case? He would have done better to quietly ignore the situation. Why would he have identified the rabbi? It would have been so much safer to say it was the wrong man, and leave us searching. His behaviour made no sense if he were guilty—yet how could he be innocent? Round and round circled my tired brain, like a ferret in a cage.

I slept a little towards morning, but woke early, feeling troubled and anxious. Emily was still in bed, and the flat was strangely silent. Rising, I dressed in the chill and went to make tea and consider my plan for the day. I had meant to visit Inspector Reynolds to see if he had been able to obtain the authorisation for me to visit Baruch Gad, as he had promised. I had also meant to listen to Bernard Lazare's lecture at three o'clock, and to try to talk to him privately afterwards, in order to probe the link between the Dreyfus affair, which was the ostensible subject of his dealings with Professor Ralston, and the list of ritual murders contained in the file marked 'B.L.' Under the assumption that Jonathan was innocent, these tasks were indispensable, and I meant to accomplish them. But was he innocent? I decided to begin my day by going to visit him. Guilty or not, he was not going to avoid some pointed questions.

I left the house as soon as I had finished my cup of tea and a slightly stale raisin bun, and proceeded immediately down Tavistock Street and up Wellington Street, then on to the Bow Street Police Station, stumbling along through a heavy fog which caused me to step accidentally into the road more than once, so that my boots were soon squelching with muddy water. I tried in vain to recover the feeling of delight at having the chance to visit London that had filled me as I took the train from Cambridge, failed utterly, arrived at the station frowning, and demanded to see Jonathan with a sharpness that the policeman took for authority. As a result, less than ten minutes later, I found myself face-to-face with the newly detained suspect.

I have been in prisons many times in recent years, to see prisoners accused of various crimes, or people who might hold some key to the investigation in which I was engaged, and the surroundings no longer hold much awe for me. Yet I was strangely moved as I saw Jonathan led into the room. He looked sorrowful and gloomy, his face drooped, his eyes drooped, his tail would have drooped if he had had a tail. I felt a sudden pang as I remembered my very first visit to a prison, so long ago, and another young man behind a wire mesh… Jonathan's dark eyes seemed to merge with another pair, from my memory, as I gazed into them, and I was fired with the same urgent desire to defend him that had seized me eight years ago when I first saw Arthur behind bars. Oh, I am easily moved by young people in distress!

'Why have they arrested me? What do they have against

me?' he asked me, before I had a chance to speak. The words were not at all what I expected. I looked at him thoughtfully.

'As far as I know,' I told him, 'you have been arrested purely on the grounds that your having lied appears to provide the only possible explanation of the library paradox.'

'Oh!' he said, looking startled, and yet strangely relieved, as understanding swept over him. 'I see. I didn't think of that. I thought—I thought it must be something else altogether. Yes, I see it now. How awful—it's true! My lying would explain everything, wouldn't it? Good heavens! Only I'm not lying, Vanessa.'

'No?' I said. 'Are you sure?'

'I swear it! Vanessa—don't you believe me? Everything I told you is the truth. They can't arrest me just because if I were lying, it would solve the puzzle, can they? They have to prove I'm lying, and they can't prove it, because I'm not!'

'They most certainly can arrest you on those grounds, and for that matter, they can try you and even convict you,' I said severely. 'Being the only person with opportunity is the single major factor in a murder conviction. A second important factor is motive. That is what they will look for next.'

He remained silent, looking at me apprehensively. *Motive.* What was in Amy's mind?

'Listen to me, Jonathan,' I said. 'If there is anything else against you—any evidence, any past event whatsoever that could be construed as motive, or any reason for suspicion of wrongdoing on your part, you *must* tell me.'

I saw him flinch.

'Don't lie,' I said quickly. 'I know there is something.'

The silence grew deafening. I mistrusted him, and yet oddly, his reaction reassured me more than a wordy, fulsome and immediate denial would have.

'Do you know,' I said after a moment, 'I have never asked

you exactly what you were doing in the grounds of Professor Ralston's library that day. Why did you go there at all, you, a mathematics student? Were you going to see him?'

'No, I—I never saw him,' he stammered. 'I—I was going to look something up in the library.'

'What was it?' I said sharply, feeling a finger of worry creeping up my spine.

'It was, it was something to do with Judaism.'

'Jonathan, you don't know how to lie. Don't try to do it! Don't you realise that the police will tear you apart when they interrogate you? Don't you realise that if you hide something now, when it comes out it will make your case much more serious?'

'I can't tell you, Vanessa,' he said desperately. 'I can't, I just can't. It doesn't matter, does it? I swear to you that every single thing I told you about what happened as I was going up to the library is true, exactly the way I said it. I swear that I didn't murder the Professor and have no idea who did. All of that is the straightforward truth. Somebody else murdered him, and the important thing is to find out who it was and how he did it! You can find out, Vanessa, you're a detective. What I was going to the library for is personal, and I didn't get it done anyway. So how can it matter? Vanessa, *somebody else murdered him*! That rebbe that I saw, Reb Avrom, he *must* know something—he came from the room where it happened! He can't be the murderer himself, we proved that. He could confirm my story. I'm sure he saw me just as I saw him. He must remember it. I could tell the police about him, maybe it would help me. But I don't want to. I—I hate the idea of a man like him being…being where I am now, or worse. Vanessa, you must go to see him. Find out what he knows! It's the only thing that can help me.'

The Library Paradox

I frowned at him, disappointed and disapproving. Yet there was something in what he said. If I chose to believe that his statements as to the events on the day of the murder were true—and I did find myself believing him, a little in spite of myself—then I needed to investigate all the possibilities, to follow up all the threads. And there were still several. Britta Gad. Bernard Lazare. The rabbi.

And then—whatever Jonathan was hiding, Amy knew it as well. I remembered the look in her eyes as the policemen took him away, and mentally added her as a fourth line of enquiry to my list.

Jonathan bid me goodbye with a chastened air. I responded a little coldly. I do hope he will not make a fool of himself in his interrogation by not being able to answer simple questions such as what he was doing at the library at all, or by trying ineffectually to withhold some information that is probably bound to come out anyway. If I ever fail as an amateur detective, perhaps I could turn to the task of preparing prisoners for their interrogations.

Emerging into Bow Street, I was struck, as I had been many times before, by the contrast between the hidden shadows of prison life, and the sunny freedom of the busy citizens without. There have been times when I have seen a man captured and led off by policemen with his hands in handcuffs, and it has seemed to me that I saw that man cross the invisible boundary between two parallel worlds. I looked around me, savouring, as I always did, the ability to walk whither I would, before going to see Inspector Reynolds at Scotland Yard. I felt a great need to stretch my legs to the full extent of their possibilities, a reaction, no doubt, to the claustrophobia of the police station. The distance from Covent Garden to the Victoria Embankment did not seem far enough, and the time was too near the midday meal to visit the Inspector immediately, so after a moment's reflection, I decided to go round by way of Piccadilly Circus, where Emily had told me that a quite suitable and agreeable tea shop called Lyons had very recently opened its doors. The idea of finally discovering a decent solution to the daily problem of luncheon was tempting enough for me to take the long route with pleasure.

I walked along rapidly, feeling a hint of springtime piercing delicately through London's persistent dinginess, located Lyons, found it to be a pleasant enough place indeed, just what London's ladies are sorely in need of. I emerged refreshed and renewed, ready to set off courageously on the long walk down Haymarket and Cockspur to New Scotland Yard. The Inspector was in his office.

'So,' he greeted me as soon as I made my appearance within his doors, 'how is your investigation progressing? Has the arrest of the Sachs youth clarified things for you?'

'Yes and no,' I said disapprovingly. 'I will admit that I was perfectly blind not to predict his arrest from the newspaper article at once. But I still suspect that it may be a mistake.'

'Well, well,' said the Inspector not unkindly, although with a rather annoying smile, 'we have our methods and you have yours, to be sure. With all due respect, I myself am more likely to believe in logical reasoning than in feminine intuition, though my wife would probably beat me about the ears if she heard me say so. Well, it isn't my fault; I've nothing to do with the case myself. So you have other ideas in mind, do you?'

'They are not ripe yet,' I said. 'It is useless to discuss them on a theoretical level without any proof. I need to investigate further.'

'It isn't useless to discuss a theory,' he said hopefully. 'We do it all the time, how else do you think we work?'

'Well, the police make their own theories, but past experience has already shown me that they are not too keen on listening to mine,' I replied. 'Remember your colleague Inspector Peters in the emerald case.'

'Yes, I remember it well,' he smiled. 'That was the first time we met, you and I, wasn't it? I remember Peters expressing doubts…' His voice trailed off, perhaps because he sensed that his remarks were on the point of becoming tactless.

'I know, I know,' I said, unable to resist the expression of a latent resentment which I usually manage to forget. 'Policemen always seem to have doubts about me. If I were a tall, unsmiling, square-jawed man with a cigar and a trench coat, the police would be happier listening to me, I suppose. The problem comes from the skirt, perhaps, or the general lack of authority. I don't know. But that isn't the issue right now—you for one have never treated me that way, and I am grateful. It is I who don't want to talk about my theories quite yet. I need more information. Please, do tell me if you have managed to arrange for me to be able to visit Baruch Gad in Dartmoor.'

'Yes, yes, of course I have,' he said. 'We police are not so useless as all that, you see?'

'I never said you were useless!' I protested vehemently.

'Well, let us not spar,' he laughed. 'I have your visiting pass right here, with tomorrow's date on it. You will have to make your own way down to Dartmoor.'

'I can't thank you enough!' I exclaimed, my good humour all renewed. 'Please forgive my asperity. This may be immensely useful! Oh, I do hope I find out something from the poor man.'

'So do I, indeed, and if you do, I hope you will be kind enough to let me know,' he said, handing me the paper, and I bid him goodbye and took my leave feeling that I had obtained everything I needed in spite of the awkward moment caused by my too-pointed tongue. I set out immediately to walk to King's College, hastening my steps.

The College building is enormous, but thanks to the careful instructions provided by Professor Taylor, I found the history department without difficulty. It was still reasonably early, but the large lecture hall was already buzzing with curious listeners. I took a seat in the most thickly populated part of the room, and began listening to the medley of different conversations, snatches of which struck my ears from all sides. I soon distinguished three major themes: first, the question of why exactly Mr Bernard Lazare had been invited to give this lecture today, and whether there was some relation with the mysterious murder of Professor Ralston; secondly, was Mr Bernard Lazare correct or mistaken in his well-known position with regard to the innocence of the Jewish captain; and thirdly, were the Captain guilty, what was his motivation? Some thought that he was guilty because he was Jewish, and as such, naturally devoid of patriotic feeling. For others, he was not guilty, but accused in good faith because he was Jewish, and as such, assumed to be devoid of patriotic feeling. And there were those for whom he was not guilty, and his accusation had been made in bad faith, by those who wished to make a scapegoat of a member of the Jewish religion. It seemed quite inconceivable to anybody present that whether guilty or innocent, his acts or the accusations against him might somehow be entirely independent of his religion. This struck me as a strange and rather sad state of affairs. Upon the stroke of three o'clock, Professor Taylor entered the lecture hall, accompanied by a short-legged, stoutish man wearing a pointed beard associated with a well-furnished moustache, a small pair of spectacles, a balding forehead, and a general air of intense thought and willpower. Professor Taylor introduced him sagely, with little commentary, as a French journalist of repute who had come to tell us about the current state of the Dreyfus affair, which is at present an issue of such urgent divisiveness in French politics. We applauded politely, he sat down, and the stout gentleman took his place behind the lectern, and began to speak in rather heavily accented but perfectly fluent English.

'Ladies and gentlemen,' he began, 'I am not here merely to inform you of a grave injustice being perpetrated *at this very moment* upon French soil. I will inform you, certainly; I will give you every known detail about the situation. But I will do more than merely inform you: I will ask you for your active and vocal support of the sacred cause I am defending here; your support as Englishmen and Englishwomen, citizens of a country whose great history proves that it is less deeply troubled than my own by the fatal and destructive disease of anti-Semitism.'

He proceeded to give a shocking description of the general movement in France against the Israelite population, illustrated by French newspapers which he held up to our view and whose front pages were decorated with lurid titles and drawings dripping with hatred.

'As the English befriended the beleaguered French aristocracy during the Revolution, I expect them to befriend the beleaguered Jewish population of France today,' he said incisively. 'France is stripping its Jews of their rights, and all but forcing them to leave, just as England is opening her hospitable arms to tens of thousands of those who are fleeing the despair and destruction of the East.'

He spoke as if the phenomenon of anti-Semitism were unheard of in England, something that is obviously false given all that I have learnt lately about Professor Ralston. However, I thought that his attitude of assuming beyond even a moment's doubt that the English were on a higher moral plane than their traditional enemies across the Channel—a doubtful fact in itself, I suppose—was probably a wise enough manoeuvre to arouse a feeling of support. Besides, it is undoubtedly true that England has accepted many thousands of Jewish refugees in the last ten or twenty years; enough, as I had seen with my own eyes, to form almost a complete city within a city in the East End of London.

Now Mr Lazare left the subject of anti-Semitism in general, to turn to the Dreyfus affair in particular. He introduced the case as a figurehead for the expression of all the pent-up hatred for the Jews seething within all the different layers of French society, and openly declared Dreyfus himself to be nothing more than an innocent scapegoat.

'All Paris, all France is divided over the guilt of this man,' he exclaimed, 'guilt whose proof was deduced falsely, based on racism, inference and dishonesty. Let me now describe the facts.'

I pricked up my ears, wondering if it was conceivable that some titbit relevant to my investigation might be forthcoming, and scooping out my notebook, prepared to take notes of the salient aspects of the case. Let me set them down here in detail.

September, 1894: In the wastebaskets of the German embassy, a French spy discovers an unsigned letter, the *bordereau*, containing a list of military classified documents. Mr Lazare read it out:

Sans nouvelles m'indiquant que vous désirez me voir, je vous adresse cependant, Monsieur, quelques renseignements intéressants:

1. *Une note sur le frein hydraulique du 120, et la manière dont s'est conduite cette pièce;*
2. *Une note sur les troupes de couverture (quelques*

modifications seront apportées par le nouveau plan);
3. *Une note sur une modification aux formations de l'artillerie;*
4. *Une note relative à Madagascar;*
5. *Le projet de Manuel de tir de l'artillerie de campagne (14 mars 1894)...*
   Je vais partir en manoeuvres.

This letter apparently accompanied several documents delivered to the German Embassy, which were not discovered. Captain Alfred Dreyfus is selected by the French Army as the most likely culprit, because he has been in contact with the Army divisions dealing with artillery, the hydraulic brake and the negotiations on Madagascar—but above all because he is Jewish.

October 1894: Commandant du Paty de Clam tricks Dreyfus into writing down some of the same words as those which appear in the *bordereau*, decides on the basis of a certain superficial similarity that Dreyfus is guilty—goodness, do not spies even take the trouble to disguise their handwriting?—and has him arrested and sent to prison.

October 31, 1894: The French anti-Semitic newspaper *La Libre Parole* somehow obtains this secret information and publishes it on the front page, which Mr Lazare held up to our astonished eyes:

HAUTE TRAHISON!
ARRESTATION D'UN OFFICIER JUIF!
LE CAPITAINE DREYFUS!

thus simultaneously revealing open anti-Semitism and state secrets.

November–December 1894: A brief and secret investigation into the case ends with the recommendation for a court-martial.

December 19–22 1894: Dreyfus is tried in a secret court-martial behind closed doors. Handwriting experts all contradict each other. Those who do not agree with the desired analysis are sent away, some are removed from their official positions. It leaks to the public that an unidentified letter on an unidentified topic, shown only to the judge (and certainly not to Dreyfus' defending lawyer), is a key incriminating document; the public learns only that it contains the words 'that scoundrel D'. Dreyfus is pronounced guilty of high treason and condemned to military degradation and perpetual deportation.

January 5, 1895: His appeal rejected, Dreyfus is degraded in a public ceremony where his buttons are removed—goodness, the imagination pales—and his other military insignia, and his sword is broken. He remains calm and firm throughout the entire ceremony, regularly proclaiming his innocence in a ringing voice. Yet the crowd of onlookers outside the fence surrounding the courtyard ceaselessly screams racist insults. I recalled the Captain's own terrible description of the experience...*last Saturday remains branded in my spirit in letters of fire...*

The Library Paradox

April 1895: Dreyfus is placed in solitary confinement on Devil's Island, a sweltering rock off the coast of French Guyana, where he remains under close and hostile surveillance every minute of the day, in constant danger of death from exhaustion and tropical diseases. Unspeakably horrible.

March 1, 1896: A new document is apparently discovered by the same French spy, in the same place as the *bordereau*. But unlike the *bordereau*, this document is addressed to an explicitly named person. And that person is not Captain Dreyfus.

'I cannot give you the name at this point,' said Mr Lazare, 'for under the rules of democracy, the addressee must be presumed innocent until proven guilty, and to have him prematurely condemned by public opinion would be equivalent to the crime against Dreyfus himself. I will, however, give you the nature and text of the message discovered. It is a telegram, a so-called *petit bleu*, which was written and addressed but for some reason thrown away and apparently never sent. The contents are as follows: *Monsieur, I await before anything a more detailed explanation than the one you gave me the other day on the question in suspense. Consequently I pray you give it to me in writing so as to be able to judge if I can continue my relations with the house of R. or not.*

The contents of the telegram seemed meaningless. Mr Lazare was sensitive to this impression.

'To experienced eyes, this is very obviously an espionage document,' he announced firmly, and in spite of the fact that this theory supported his personal views almost too perfectly, I felt inclined to agree with him. The peculiar message did seem to be purposely couched in a language of disguise and double play which did not obviously correspond to any normal way of writing.

'What it means is simple: the *bordereau* formed part of a correspondence between an officer of the French Army and a German member of the Embassy, which has continued to this day, uninterrupted by the arrest and condemnation of Dreyfus! What conclusion could be clearer?'

Indeed.

'I learnt of the existence of this document almost immediately,' he continued, 'for fortunately, France and its Army contain many honest people, who are aware of the injustice committed against Alfred Dreyfus, and are working together to overturn it. But do you think it will be easy for me to use this new discovery to advantage? No—it will be not only difficult, but dangerous. First of all, I have never seen the document, but only a hasty copy made by my informant. If it becomes a serious threat to the upper echelons of the Army, nothing could be easier than to destroy the original. Secondly, if it becomes too well known to be destroyed, the person who takes it upon himself to make it officially public runs a serious risk of being accused of having forged it. All dealings with this new document contain a tremendous risk of backlash. For indeed, to any objective observer, it *proves and confirms* the innocence of Dreyfus, and indicates the guilt of another. But for those whose main goal is to confirm his condemnation and foment enmity against the Jews, it is nothing but a danger.

'Before taking any other action, I must try to prevent the negative reaction I predict, by calmly apprising as many individuals as possible of the existence and reality of the *petit bleu*, in order to avoid them learning about it by some kind of public announcement such as a newspaper headline, which would only increase the intensity of the polemic. That is my purpose here today: to give you an objective version of events before you will learn of them through articles written by journalists, each of whom has a racist theory to prove.'

He bowed, to signify that he had finished, and the audience proceeded to applaud politely. I remembered Mr Lazare's letter to Professor Ralston. The beginning of the Professor's answer gave a fair idea of what the rest would have been like; I remembered his qualifying the news as 'vague nonsense' and saying the telegram was sure to be 'a forgery'. Out of pure indignation, I surprised my neighbours by suddenly redoubling my applause. Professor Taylor stood up, calmed the noise with a gesture, and invited the audience to ask questions.

The exchanges continued over the next half an hour or so, and Mr Lazare filled in a good many details, telling us where and in what conditions Alfred Dreyfus is being held at this instant, the unceasing activities of his brother and his wife in his defence (what his wife must be living through at this very moment—it does not bear thinking about!) and a good deal of generality about the shameful wave of anti-Semitism in France and the shocking role of the newspapers in its development. Finally, the questions were over and the audience filed out. As the room emptied, Professor Taylor beckoned me forward and introduced me to the illustrious journalist, with no frills, as the private detective investigating the death of Professor Ralston.

'That is very interesting,' he said to me, raising his eyebrows. 'But is there some way in which I can be of help to you in the matter?'

'I do have a few questions I would very much like to ask you,' I began hopefully. 'He was one of the people to whom you wrote about the *petit bleu*, was he not? We found your letter in his study after his death. It seems as though he was in the process of answering it when he was killed.'

'How terrible,' he said. 'There was a letter to me? What did it say?'

'He hadn't written much,' I said. 'But he said something to the effect that if the *petit bleu* existed at all, it was probably a forgery.'

'I know this is a difficult thing to say of the dead,' said the journalist slowly, 'but I must tell you that my correspondence with Professor Ralston had led me to believe that he was becoming slightly mad. Not only did he suffer from a degree of anti-Semitism whose rabidity denoted some form of paranoia, but his correspondence had lately taken on a tone of insult and provocation which went beyond the limits of decency.' Glancing at his watch, he added, 'I must hurry away now, for I have a meeting with several journalists in half an hour. But we can meet again tomorrow morning, if you wish, before I return to France. I will show you some documents to explain what I mean. I propose that the three of us meet together at ten o'clock in the foyer of the Savoy, where I am staying.'

We nodded our heads, and the overworked gentleman bid us goodbye and dashed off into the street with an energy unexpected from one of his rather portly girth. Professor Taylor accompanied me to the exit at a calmer tempo, but his eyes were full of urgency.

'Finally, we can talk,' he said. 'I heard this morning that young Sachs has been arrested for Ralston's murder. Do you know anything about this? Are you connected with it in some way?'

'No. The police arrested him on the grounds that the only logical solution to the mystery is that his testimony must be false. However, he insists that he is speaking the truth,' I told him calmly. But my heart was beating wildly. Professor Taylor could be the murderer—for powerful reasons of his own—yet he did not seem the kind of person who would allow someone else to be condemned in his stead. Was he going to confess?

'Is it possible? Could he really have done it? I don't know him well at all, yet it is hard to believe. Could they not be making a mistake? Have you discovered anything yourself?' he continued anxiously.

'I have other leads,' I said feebly, wondering inwardly at the rigid unwritten social rules that made it impossible for me to ask him directly whether his was not, after all, the hand that had held the gun. Yet the eyes that were looking at me were blue and kind, and expressed only a distressed worry.

'Is Mr Lazare one of your leads?' he asked.

'Not exactly—not as the murderer, I mean—yet I do have some questions to ask him,' I said.

'I will be pleased to join you tomorrow morning, then,' he replied, and shaking my hand courteously, he departed before I could ask him anything more, even if I had been able to formulate a question.

I looked at the time, and seeing that it was nearing five o'clock, I decided to go to David and Rivka's house immediately. Stepping smartly into the first dingy four-wheeler that passed, I directed him to Settles Street and sat back thoughtfully as we rolled off, trying to plan how best to tell them what had to be told. I wondered hopefully if they might not have learnt it already, by a telegram or a visit earlier in the day, but when Rivka opened the door in answer to my quick knock, I saw at once that she knew nothing. Amy must have had her hands full dealing with her distraught parents.

'I am very sorry to be the one to bring you bad news,' I said quickly, drawing a chair towards her. 'It is about Jonathan: last night, after we left you, he was arrested.'

'Arrested!' she gasped. 'Jonathan! But why? What have they arrested him for?'

'For the murder, Rivka. Do you remember that I thought I saw a policeman spying on the rabbi last night? Well, he really was a policeman, but in fact he was spying on Jonathan. And others were waiting for us at our flat. They arrested him as soon as we arrived.'

Rivka sat down; her face turned pale with horror, then chalk white. The baby sank in her weakened arms, and I hastened to bring her a glass of water and gather him up myself as she struggled to regain her composure. I worried that the little fellow might burst into shrieks, but he remained perfectly still, fixing enormous eyes on his mother and reducing the expression of his own little existence to the silent watchfulness that tends to overtake small children in unfamiliar circumstances. I watched her also, and the blank, childish terror in her eyes suddenly made me wonder, as I had the first time I saw her, how old she actually was.

'Jonathan arrested—for murder! No, it's impossible, impossible. No, this can't be happening!' she said in increasingly desperate tones, pressing her hands to her heart.

'It doesn't mean that he is guilty,' I said quickly, unable to seriously entertain the possibility aloud in the face of such a reaction. 'We need to help him by finding the true murderer. I need your help, Rivka, yours and David's. We need to work together; we need to see the rabbi, Rabbi Avrom. Will David be home soon?'

'I don't know. I don't know when he will come. He is in *shul*,' she said, her emotion giving way to a kind of exhausted dullness.

'Is it nearby? Could I fetch him? It is an emergency,' I said, beginning to feel slightly worried. Her face was whiter than ever. I stared at her, and it dawned on me with increasing dismay that what I was seeing was similar to what I had seen in Amy yesterday evening. Like Amy's, Rivka's reaction did not appear normal to me. I would have expected indignation, even anger, and a solid declaration of belief in his innocence. Instead what I saw was excessive shock and fear. Was she fending off the unbearable notion that Jonathan might actually be guilty?

'Don't be so frightened,' I told her. 'The rabbi will surely give us the proof that Jonathan is innocent. Rivka, what is the matter?'

For answer she burst into tears.

I felt a little at a loss; I could see there was something I should know, but I could not see how to get it out of her; the more she was frightened, the more she sank into incoherence, and the more I reassured her, the more she would be likely to take hold of herself and say nothing of whatever family secret I now began to suspect her of sharing. I hesitated, and at that moment, to my relief, the door was flung open and David himself burst into the room.

'I couldn't stay in *shul*, Rivka,' he cried, rushing towards her. 'I felt so uneasy—I felt something was wrong! I left suddenly and came running home. Oh, what is it, what is it?' and he knelt next to her and took her in his arms.

'Jonathan has been arrested,' she said in a voice muffled by the shoulder against which her face was buried.

'Jonathan! For our murder? That's—why, that's crazy!'

He turned to look up at me. 'How can it be? I didn't know anybody suspected him.'

'Nobody did, I think, until yesterday,' I said, and recounted yet again the story of the newspaper article and the paradox.

'That's terrible,' he said. 'But he didn't do it, of course. He shouldn't be in much danger. We will have to confront Reb Avrom, come what may. We will find some way to tell him what's going on. If he knows it's a question of life or death, the rebbe will listen!' He turned back to his wife with a look of tender concern. She was sobbing harder than ever.

'Rivkele, what's the matter? It will be all right, you'll see. We'll get Jonathan out of there. The police have made a mistake, that's all. What's wrong?' he added, in a strange tone, suddenly perceiving, as I had, that something deeper was upsetting her. I moved a little farther back, holding the baby—the older boy was nowhere to be seen—and made myself as inconspicuous as possible, for I thought that David had a better chance than myself of persuading her to express what was in her heart.

'Arrested for murder,' she wailed incoherently. 'Oh, I should never have married you.'

'What are you talking about?' he said, amazed. 'Just because your cousin has been arrested by mistake? Rivkele, that's nonsense. Of course you should have married me. I need you—aren't you the one who draws water for me from the well? from the source of life?' He put his arms around her shoulders more closely. I paused in my thoughts, struck by what he had just said. Was he referring to something from the Bible?

'We must see what we can do to help your aunt and uncle,' David continued. 'I suppose they know of it already?'

'Yes,' I said, 'Amy went to them immediately after it happened, last night. I have not heard from her since.'

'Poor Aunt Judith,' said Rivka, making an effort to speak

more normally. 'She will be desperate. But Uncle Simon will take control. Perhaps they can visit Jonathan.'

Everything came together in my mind at once. It was Rebecca with her pitcher who drew water from the well—*Rebecca!*

And Uncle Simon, and Aunt Judith—Simon and Judith! I remembered the marriage certificate I had seen in Somerset House: *Judith Gad and Simon Sachs, married in the Synagogue, in 1871.* And I had not made the connection, because I had never heard the name of Uncle Simon, and Sachs was said to be a typical Jewish name.

'Rivka'—nothing but the Hebrew form of Rebecca. Rebecca, Judith Gad's niece—Rebecca, Menachem Gad's daughter! I have been scouring London for this girl, while seeing her every day.

My God, I have been so blind! I turned to her, and the baby transferred his startled gaze from her face to mine.

'You are Rebecca Gad, aren't you?' I said. 'I have just realised it—I should have known it before. You are Menachem Gad's daughter. Now I understand why you and Amy are so frightened about Jonathan. You think he killed the Professor *because he had a good reason to do it.* Is that what it is?'

'No!' she cried loudly, and sank half-fainting into her husband's arms. 'No, it isn't that! Innocent, guilty, it doesn't make any difference. It's too late, too late. Arrested—put on trial—condemned!' And she uttered a choked cry and closed her eyes, pressing her hands to them as though to shut out the vision. And I understood what it was that she feared. It was that which she had already lived through once.

'What does this mean? Who is Menachem Gad? What are you talking about? What about your father?' said David urgently, staring back and forth between the two of us. 'Rivka, what is this all about?'

There was a silence while Rivka struggled with herself.

'It would be better for you to tell your husband,' I advised her softly. 'If your father was innocent, then there is no dishonour in his death.'

'Do you think so?' she said. 'Then you are the only person I have ever heard say so. Dishonour—I don't know, but there is pain. Too much pain,' she continued, her face still buried in her hands. 'Pain and terrible memories. I can't bear to talk about it, after so many years of silence.'

Pulling her hands away, he captured them in his, bending towards her with an expression on his face that reminded me of a half-forgotten moment in my own experience.

I lay on my bed, the midwife near me; the birth pangs had been upon me for many hours already, and I was exhausted. Each one was followed by a little oasis of calm, but these oases were becoming shorter, and I did not know how I should find the courage and the strength to continue enduring the ever increasing pain. I saw the door of my bedroom open suddenly, and Arthur, entering and crossing the room with a firm step in spite of the midwife's annoyed exclamations of 'Mr Weatherburn, sir! You must not come in here now!' came up to me. Taking my hand in his, he bent close to me and said...some of those words which the normal course of daily life gives so few occasions to hear. They filled me with joy, they heartened and encouraged me, and I turned to him with a smile to tell him so, when I was suddenly submerged in a wave of pain stronger than ever. His face changed as he saw, and he looked at me with exactly the expression I saw on David's features now, as he held his wife's hands in his and looked into her eyes.

'Tell me,' he said softly.

'My father was hanged, he was hanged for murder, for the horrible murder of a child,' she cried, suddenly breaking down, 'but he was innocent, David, he was innocent, I swear it. My father would never have killed a soul! He was a victim, no less than the little boy he was accused of murdering. They said—at the trial, David, they said—they said that he had done it for me, so that I should eat the matza with…with the blood in it!'

She stopped, overcome. David stared at her.

'It was because of things such as these that we left the old country,' he said.

'They can happen everywhere, David,' I said. 'I wouldn't have believed it before, but I know it now.'

We jumped, all three of us, at the sound of a sharp knock on the door. Nobody moved, and after a moment it was pushed open from outside. Amy entered, and stopped short at the sight of us.

'Oh, I came to tell you myself,' she began.

'Vanessa told us,' said Rivka. 'Amy, she knows all about my father.'

Amy stared at me, dismay filling her features.

'How did you find out?' she stammered.

'Why didn't you tell me?' I countered.

'Why should we tell you?' she said, almost angrily. 'So that you could become the first to believe that Jonathan murdered that monster? That's what you think now, isn't it? Anyone would.'

'Do you?' I said quickly.

Her eyelids lowered suddenly. 'Of course not!' she said.

'Yet you are frightened, very frightened.'

'Vanessa—do you have no imagination? Can't you under-stand that my family has already been through this? It will destroy my mother, it will destroy us all. It's obvious that the case against Jonathan is serious, horribly serious. They say he had the opportunity, and now they will say that he had a motive, too. We realised right away, he and I, that anyone could say he must have been lying. But as long as no one knew that he had any connection with that horrible Professor, we thought he would be safe from suspicion. We've just been waiting and worrying…and hoping that you would find the true murderer before anyone found out about this.'

'You've known all this the whole time and never said a word,' I marvelled, not knowing whether to be angry with her or with myself. 'And when I asked you if you knew anything about James Wilson—you said nothing!'

'You gave us the shock of our lives!' she exclaimed. 'We thought no one would ever find out, and you discovered the connection in less than one day! You really frightened us. We had been so keen on your coming, because we hoped you would find the true murderer before anyone noticed that Jonathan could be accused if his statement were considered untrue. Instead of that, you started to find out just what we didn't want you to know. It was horrible! You mustn't be angry with us, Vanessa. We were silly to think we could fool you, but you must understand why we tried.'

'You did fool me,' I said, but her words comforted me a little. They had tried, and succeeded for a certain time, but in the end, I had discovered the truth by myself. Yet something troubled me in her words. What did she mean, when she spoke of Jonathan's 'connection with that horrible Professor'? What could that connection be—unless they were aware of Professor Ralston's role in the trial of her uncles? If Jonathan knew that, then he had a motive indeed.

'Amy,' I said, 'even if the police learn that Jonathan is related to the Gad brothers, what motive would they attribute to him for the murder of Professor Ralston?'

She hesitated, looking at me, then glancing down again. 'The anti-Semitism…' she began.

'No, Amy,' Rivka intervened suddenly. 'No, tell her. It's no use hiding it any more. If anyone can help us, she will. I'll tell you myself,' she added, turning to me. 'Our Uncle Baruch went to prison ten years ago, and Jonathan is the only person in the family to have visited him during all that time. Since Jonathan turned sixteen, he has been to Dartmoor Prison every three months. He was always especially close to Uncle Baruch as a child, and Aunt Judith and Uncle Simon decided to allow him to go when he would be old enough. They never wanted Amy to go, though, because of her being a girl. As for me, my mother and I had moved away from London. After my father—died—' she winced at these words, 'my mother and I went to live in Brighton, far from everything we knew. She took her own name of Rubinstein back and found employment in a hotel, but her health became worse and worse until she could barely do her work. She used to take me to the synagogue often; she became more and more devout with the years. She died when I was seventeen, and I didn't know what to do, so I wrote to Aunt Judith. After all, she was my father's sister and my only near relation. And I went to live with her and Uncle Simon. They were wonderfully kind to me. Because I had become more religious than they were, they allowed me to attend a different synagogue than theirs, and that's how I met David, almost right away.'

'You were married under the name of Rebecca Rubinstein?' I asked.

'Rivka Rubinstein,' she replied. 'My mother changed my name with hers when we moved to Brighton. But that is not what I meant to tell you. I wanted to say that I was just a child when it all happened, and even though I thought of Uncle Baruch sometimes, I never dared mention him to my mother, and she never spoke of him. So I knew nothing until I arrived at Aunt Judith's, and then I learnt from Amy and Jonathan that Jonathan had been visiting him for years, and—this is the important thing—that Uncle Baruch had made him swear to try to find out who the anonymous witness at the trial was; the one whose false testimony caused the jury to bring in a verdict of guilty. And Jonathan had promised.'

'He made him swear it at Jonathan's very first visit to the prison,' said Amy. 'Jonathan was just sixteen, and I was twenty-one. He told me about it as soon as he came home. We got all fired up and felt noble. He wanted to search for the mysterious witness right away, and I wanted to help him. But we had no idea how to go about it. We didn't find out anything for ages. We did try; we tried to see the judge, but he had died, and we tried to find out who had been on the jury, but no one could tell us. I didn't see what else we could do; I was ready to give up. Jonathan didn't want to give up, but he didn't know what to do either. He ended up deciding to start frequenting anti-Semitic circles, in the hopes of hearing something. He took to reading their newspapers, and going to their lectures and meetings. He would come home furious, lock himself in his room for hours; I've seen him cry, Vanessa. You have no idea what it's like to be one of us! Each and every one of us has a battle to fight, no matter what circle of society we live in. It's easy to see what can happen to people like my uncles—foreigners, penniless immigrants, only good enough for the rope. My mother thought she was escaping all that when she managed to marry into a wealthy, established bourgeois family. But our class has its own problems. We're educated, and although Jews finally obtained the right to take degrees at Oxford and Cambridge—not thirty years ago, mind—we're still shunned there in a hundred ways you couldn't possibly understand. We learn to love refinement and nobility, yet we see ourselves reflected in the eyes of gentry like vermin. We want to welcome our persecuted co-religionists from Eastern countries, but it is no easy task, when their miserable masses cause the people among whom we live to turn against all Jews with a hatred that overflows even onto those who belong to the same set as themselves. When you've been given as many cold shoulders, and seen as many turned-away faces, when you've heard as many sniggers and snide remarks as we have, you start wondering and doubting—about yourself and yours. No one knows those feelings as we do. If you want to understand our story, you have to understand this. Have you ever heard of Amy Levy?'

'I have,' I said, surprised at the sudden change of topic. 'I remember reading an exquisite story by her in *Woman's World*. Why do you mention her?'

'Because she is the writer who has best expressed what I'm trying to tell you. Have you read her novel *Reuben Sachs*? No relation—except for the race.'

'No,' I admitted. 'I didn't realise she was a Jewish writer.'

She laughed bitterly. 'She isn't any more,' she said. 'She committed suicide, and no wonder. And that's why I want to become a writer. I only wish I could express, in my writing, something of what she did. Read what she wrote, Vanessa. I have her book at home; I'll give it to you. You have to know what it's like. I'm telling you this because you have to understand why, when Jonathan came to King's three years ago and heard about Professor Ralston, the famous anti-Semite history professor, he started going to his lectures. And he came to believe that Professor Ralston was the anonymous witness.'

'How did he find out?' I asked, reluctant to know, reluctant to hear the answer.

'I don't know exactly,' she replied. 'He went to several lectures; he became familiar with the Professor's library, and figured it out somehow. He told me over a year ago. He said that he didn't have any proof, but felt certain.'

'Amy—he hadn't promised your uncle to take revenge, had he?'

'I don't think so,' she said desperately. 'I can't believe it. I can't believe my uncle would ask him to do that! And if he had—if he had, I'm sure Jonathan would have told me.' But her voice shook with doubt.

'Do you know why I was looking for Rebecca Gad and her mother?' I asked. 'Because I thought that one of them might have killed the Professor. And do you know why? Not because of their grievance against him. That would hardly explain why the murder should happen now, ten years later. Of course, the identity of the witness might have only just been discovered, but it seems too much of a coincidence that this would happen just when Baruch Gad was about to be freed. It occurred to me that someone who loved him, knowing he would be out of prison in another month, may have wished to prevent him from taking justice into his own hands, avenging his brother and, as a consequence, returning for the rest of his life to the prison cell from which he had only just emerged. That is why I was looking for Britta and Rebecca.'

'I didn't do that!' cried Rivka, starting out of her chair. David, who was listening silently, took her hand reassuringly.

'No—she's asking if that is what Jonathan did,' said Amy.

'I am asking you if you know the answer,' I said. 'Who killed Professor Ralston?'

'How can I know? It couldn't have been Jonathan, and it wasn't me—I don't know. I don't know!' Rivka said desperately.

'I don't know either,' whispered Amy. 'Vanessa—I have asked myself about Jonathan, honestly, I have. Yet—he's my brother! I'm five years older than he is, I've known him since he was a baby. He can't have done it. It's impossible.'

'Have you really asked yourself about him?' I said. 'Have you asked yourself exactly what he was doing, why he was going to the Professor's library on that day? I saw him this morning, and I asked him, but he refused to say.'

'I have thought about it. I have wondered. But I think it must have been a coincidence,' she said after a moment's hesitation. 'I told you that he went there sometimes, because he tried to frequent anti-Semitic circles, in order to seek... for...'

'To seek for the identity of the witness,' I completed. 'But you told me he knew it already over a year ago. Why go to the library now?'

The two girls faced me silently.

'Did Jonathan tell his uncle that he had discovered the witness?' I asked.

'Yes, he did, right away. My uncle thought of nothing else. He lived for that; he pressed him at each visit,' said Amy. 'Jonathan told him as soon as he was sure.'

'What do you think your uncle would have done when he came out of jail, if the Professor had not been killed?' I asked.

'I don't know, how can I know? I have not seen my uncle since I was a child. I can't say I know him any more. I don't know what he would have done,' said Amy with anguish.

'Our family is not made of murderers!' exclaimed Rivka with a fury that sat oddly, and rather tragically, on her sweet features. 'And anyway, whatever he *would* have done, he didn't do it!' Standing up, she took the baby back from me and hugged it defensively.

'If Jonathan intended to—or thought he would—do something—for Uncle Baruch, then surely Uncle Baruch would know it,' said Amy. 'If only we could ask him.'

'Perhaps I can ask him. I am going to see him tomorrow,' I

said, remembering it suddenly. 'I meant to ask him where Britta and Rebecca were, but I don't need to ask him that now.'

'Tell him what has happened to Jonathan!' exclaimed Rivka. 'Ask him, ask him if he knows anything at all about all this. I don't know what he asked Jonathan to do, or why Jonathan was going to see Professor Ralston, but Uncle Baruch may know. And if he knows that Jonathan has been arrested, he will tell us!'

'I will ask him,' I said. 'But it is awkward. Prison visits are overseen by a guard who listens to every word. In fact, how could Jonathan ever tell him about the witness? That was very risky, wasn't it? Even if your uncle did not care about his own life any more, should he have attempted anything at all against the Professor later on, Jonathan's words would have been recalled and Jonathan would undoubtedly have been arrested as a party to the murder.'

'Of course. They both realised that. They had a code word,' Amy told me. 'And they never used names. That was the rule.'

'What was the word?' I said quickly. 'I will need to use it. I cannot ask him anything directly, in front of the guard.'

'They always referred to the witness as "the black dog",' she said. 'They talked about him as though it referred to a dog that my uncle cared about, and he wanted to know what had become of it. And sometimes they referred to Professor Ralston as though he was the owner of the dog.'

'So for instance, I can tell him that the black dog is dead?'

'Oh, yes,' said Amy. 'He is certain to understand that. But how can you tell him that Jonathan has been arrested? How can you tell him that Jonathan was visiting the black dog and we need to know why? How will you ever make him understand? The black dog isn't enough! How will you refer to Jonathan?'

'Call him "Yoni",' said Rivka quickly. 'Our uncles always called him that when we were small. It's short for "Yonatan", the Hebrew form of Jonathan.'

'Yoni,' I said. 'That will be useful. You'll see, I will manage to ask him, by hook or by crook.'

'But he won't know the answer,' said David, intervening in the conversation warmly and unexpectedly. 'Because there isn't anything to know! Jonathan didn't kill that monster of a professor. I can't guess what happened that day, or what he was doing there, but it wasn't for the reason you think. You girls are blinded because you're so afraid for him. But I know that Jonathan is not a murderer. He does not have the temperament, the spirit of a killer. Trust me, the truth is something different. We'll see Reb Avrom on Purim—and we'll find it out from him!'

London, Wednesday, March 18th, 1896

I awoke with my mind full of anxiety about the coming visit
with Baruch Gad, a visit whose goal had been entirely modified by yesterday's discovery. Looking at the clock, however,
I remembered suddenly that before that, I was scheduled to
meet Bernard Lazare at the Savoy.

I dressed with extra care, partly in order not to feel shame-
fully out of place in such a grand place as the Savoy, and partly
in the hopes of impressing the prison officials with a sense of my
distinction, so as to avoid any possibility of a last-minute refusal.
After some hesitation, I even took the gold locket containing min-
iatures of Cedric and Cecily—a jewel I never leave behind and yet
very rarely wear, so precious is it to me—and tied the black velvet
ribbon around my neck. Thus protected, I descended, relieved
to perceive that it was not exactly raining, although the air was
damp with a tiring grey fog. Making my way to the Strand, I
entered the imposing doors somewhat nervously. The grand

entrance, the sumptuous decor, the elegant guests and the discreet but observant footmen impressed me greatly, but the consciousness of the locket and the rich but sober dark-grey stuff of my dress aided me to remain as dignified as though I were used to such places. I worried that my boots were muddy, although I had scraped them conscientiously on the mat before entering, but as they were entirely invisible in any case, I tried to forget about them, and stood scanning the area for those I had come to meet.

I saw Mr Lazare almost at once, hurrying towards me with his quick, lively step, holding his cane but not using it. He transferred a folder containing a sheaf of papers from one hand to the other as he approached, and shook mine vigorously.

'How are you, how are you?' he said eagerly. 'I have received a message from Professor Taylor. Unfortunately, he will not be able to join us here after all. His wife is unwell. It is a shame. Still, let us talk without him. Come here, to one of these little tables.'

Some half-conscious scruple caused me to hesitate for the briefest moment. To meet a distinguished London professor and a well-known journalist in the public foyer of the Savoy for an important discussion was one thing, whereas to have a rendezvous alone with a mysterious foreigner in a place where I was acquainted with no one was another. Already I feel often enough that I am treading on the very edges of what is considered proper—tea alone at Zoedone's, taking four-wheelers across London by myself (although not hansoms—those two-wheelers are really suggestive beyond even the most permissive bounds of propriety), dropping into Scotland Yard...but as long as no one is explicitly observing or reproaching me, I tend not to bother about it. Now, however, I wondered what Mr Lazare would think of the situation. I did not want our conversation to be rendered awkward by disrespect for the social conventions.

However, he was smiling and beckoning me forward with no sign of being ill at ease, and I really had no intention of cancelling our meeting, so I pushed my scruples aside and followed him into the inner part of the foyer. He is a Frenchman anyway. It is all probably entirely different over there.

'Let us settle here,' he said, drawing me towards one of the many low tables surrounded by armchairs which filled the immense, luxuriously chandeliered and carpeted area. We sat down, and taking his large folder upon his knee, he began to undo its clasps with eager fingers.

'I have brought some things to show you,' he said, opening it, but then he covered the contents quickly with his hand, as a feather-light step sounded near us and a smooth voice enquired if we wished for tea.

I felt that Mr Lazare wanted no interruptions, but I really wanted a cup of tea, so I intimated as much to the waiter discreetly, then composed myself again to seriousness.

'I first want you to have a look at these,' he said when silence had returned. 'They are copies of the letters that Dreyfus has written to his wife since he has been incarcerated.'

'I have seen them already,' I said, glancing at the first one.

'Ah, is it Professor Taylor who showed you the copies I gave him?' he asked.

'Yes, he showed them to me. He is deeply moved by them,' I said.

'Professor Taylor is a very interesting person and a valuable ally,' he said. 'Although he believes in Dreyfus' innocence and even wrote an article or two in the early days of the conflict, he has not joined our group, nor does he openly take any action now. Yet I feel that he follows the story with a deep personal concern. I do not know exactly why, but I am glad to keep in contact with him. I feel that the day may come when he may be of great help to us.'

'Yes,' I murmured, wondering suddenly.

'And you?' he continued. 'Are you also on our side in the Dreyfus affair?'

'Yes, I am,' I said resolutely, even though I had not explicitly asked myself the question until that very moment. 'If you mean, do I believe that he is an innocent victim of error, yes, I have come to believe that now. I don't know if there is anything I could do to help your cause, though.'

'The intention is enough. I shall be happy if I am able to help you, in your own cause. Would you like to ask me any particular questions?'

'I have two questions to ask you,' I said. 'The first concerns a certain folder I found in Professor Ralston's study, bearing the initials B.L.'

'Ah, my initials,' he said with a small smile.

'It was well used,' I continued, 'and had clearly once held a rather thick sheaf of papers, but it had been emptied out. Only one paper had remained inside, having become caught on the inner part of the clasp. I copied it here.' Opening my notebook, I showed him the list of ritual murder cases. He scanned it with an air of open disgust which overlay something less visible but equally present: sadness.

'What can I tell you about this?' he said finally. 'Even though I did not know that Ralston had done research on these things, I am not at all surprised by it.'

'I have discovered that he was interested in these cases for a more practical reason than just research,' I said, wondering how much I ought to tell him about the Professor's participation in the Gad trial, if he were not in fact aware of it.

'Is that so?' he replied.

'You don't know anything about it?' I asked him. 'I thought you might, because of the initials B.L., which made me think that the folder contained material that had something to do with you. The same initials appeared on the folder containing your correspondence with him. He was a very organised man. In fact, he seemed to preserve and classify all his papers very carefully, so I am not sure why he emptied out this one particular folder. I really hoped you might know something about it.'

'I have no idea, and cannot explain why my initials should be there. It is most strange—and even rather offensive, if I may say so,' he exclaimed indignantly. 'Could it not simply have been an old folder affected to a new usage?'

'I really don't think so,' I said, 'all the folders were labelled with care, and there were some whose labels had been modified, but this one bore its original inscription.'

'I cannot explain it,' he said again. 'Perhaps he saw the Dreyfus affair as being a case of this type, although it is not really comparable. Yet if that were so, he would probably have added it to the list.'

'He was actually particularly interested in this last case, the James Wilson one,' I told him. 'I don't suppose there could be some connection between the two cases?'

'They are both cases of victimisation of Jews,' he said, 'but all of the ones on this list are blood libel cases. Even the biggest stretch of the imagination cannot make the Dreyfus affair into a blood libel case. The man is accused of treason, not murder.'

'Oh!' I exclaimed suddenly, as his words sank in. 'What did you call these cases?'

'What? What did I say?'

'These cases here—these ritual murder cases. What did you call them? Blood libel?'

'Blood libel; that is a common term to describe such cases,' he said, looking at me in surprise. 'Have you never heard the words before?'

'Maybe I have,' I said, wondering if I had not heard those words from Rivka yesterday. 'But I didn't pay attention. Usually I have seen them referred to as ritual murder,' I said. 'Blood libel—I just noticed those words.'

'Ah—I see what you mean.' He looked at me with sudden understanding. 'It is an unpleasant association with my initials,' he added with a disgruntled air. 'I never thought of it before. It is not at all pleasing. However, the observation appears to have answered your question. The B.L. on the folder containing this paper is unlikely to have referred to anything else.'

'I am afraid so,' I said with a sigh. 'That means that the folder bears no relation to you whatsoever.' Another clue gone, I thought sadly. 'Well, I must put that idea aside, then, and ask you my second question. I told you yesterday that Professor Ralston appeared to have been in the process of writing to you when he was killed. I want to examine the possibility of whether the letter you sent to him, or the information it contained, had any bearing on his death. I do know that he published a number of virulently anti-Dreyfus articles in the British press. He hadn't done so in many months, but I presume that the document you wrote to him about, that you mentioned in your lecture of yesterday, might cause the case to be reopened, and therefore might also have made him begin his public activities again?'

'Undoubtedly,' he replied. 'From everything I have been able to learn—my knowledge is not yet as detailed as it should be, for information only reaches me through several layers of leaks from within the department of secret services of the Army—still, it appears to be certain that the document that has been discovered is of great importance, not only for Dreyfus himself, but for our national security, since the traitor appears to be continuing his activities. I intend to leave no stone unturned until I find out everything there is to know about it.'

'So you believe that it is really serious, and you communicated this feeling to Professor Ralston in your letter, and it seems as probable to you as it does to me that he was going to fight it.'

'More than probable. It is certain. On the day he received my letter, instead of replying to me at once, he dashed off a letter to a person in Paris who is especially concerned with attempting to obtain a revision of the Dreyfus trial.'

'Who was it?' I asked quickly.

'The chief rabbi of France, Zadoc Kahn. He is an extraordinary man, as he should be, for it is not easy to be a chief rabbi nowadays. We have the same problem in France that you have here in England; massive immigration from the East. Large waves of Jews have arrived in the last ten or twenty years. Rabbi Kahn has formed a massive organisation to relocate them in friendlier countries: Argentina, Brazil, Canada.'

'Perhaps that is better than keeping them and accusing them of crimes,' I said crisply. 'But tell me this: why do you think Professor Ralston chose to write directly to the Rabbi and put off his answer to you until later?'

'Well, I cannot say for sure, but I can think of several possible reasons. First of all, he had a relation of particular enmity with Rabbi Kahn. He had provoked him into serious open disputes while he was in Paris. Ralston believed him, as chief rabbi, to be the architect of the efforts in favour of Dreyfus. This is not actually the case; I have worked much harder on the case than Rabbi Kahn, and even my role is not comparable to that of Captain Dreyfus' own brother. However, it is not so strange that Ralston attributed this major role to the leader of our community. Also, I myself never openly quarrelled with Ralston, because it is not my way. He was certainly provocative and aggressive, but

I would not rise to the bait, preferring to stay calm and see all sides of the question. And as you may know, before the Dreyfus affair began, I published an analysis of anti-Semitism in which I tried to give a fair presentation of all the different views. This made me less of an ideal enemy for Ralston. That is why it does not seem to me unnatural that Ralston should react instantly to my letter by addressing the Rabbi, and accusing him. The Rabbi allowed me to take a copy of the letter when I told him that Ralston had been murdered, and that I was going to see the detective in charge of the case. Let me show it to you; you will understand why I told you yesterday that I wondered if Professor Ralston were not becoming slightly mad.'

He extracted the letter from his folder and handed it over to me.

So, Rabbi—

I hear that the BEAST is about to rear up its ugly head again: I refer to your famous little Captain (the Jew, not the Corsican). A pity—I had hoped the affair would be settled for good once he had been sent off to his lonely island. But what a piece of luck for you: a new document, so they say, but you probably know exactly what it is and where it comes from, don't you? Better than anyone else, I should guess. And how useful for you it will be, as under the guise of the noble endeavour of rescuing your fancy boy from his island, you can get back to the kind of work you and your people do best: creeping and penetrating into old, established societies, undermining them, rotting them, and causing them to decay, by dividing their people, sowing enmity and fomenting discord, all in order to grab a little material advantage for yourselves. Just the usual phenomena to be observed wherever the Jews have managed to gain a foothold. Bravo! Don't be too sure of success this time, though. I will fight you every step of the way, and there are plenty in France who think as I do.

—G. Ralston

'Goodness gracious!' I exclaimed, after perusal of this shocking epistle.

'You see what I mean?' he said.

'Yes, I do indeed. Why, he was worse than a fanatic. This does sound nearly insane! But Mr Lazare, listen. Underneath the raving, Professor Ralston really says as clearly as possible that he intends to take up the cudgel against Dreyfus once again, if the case is reopened. Do you think it conceivable that he was murdered in order to prevent him from doing that?'

He reflected for a moment. 'It seems difficult to believe that someone would have killed Professor Ralston in order to prevent him publishing new articles against Dreyfus,' he said finally, 'given that a large number of such articles were certain to appear very shortly, at least in French newspapers, written by the people in France to whom he refers in the last line of his letter.'

'Well, I agree it is unlikely that a French person would come all the way over here to silence him, when there are already such excellent targets as Barrès or Drumont to hand. But Professor Ralston was in England, and from all I have read, it seems to me that he was one of the chief proponents here of anti-Semitism, and anti-Dreyfusism in particular.'

'Well, perhaps some English person killed him for that reason. I really don't know,' he said, politely restraining further expression of his obvious doubt.

'How did the Rabbi react to Ralston's letter?' I asked.

'Not by coming over to kill him, I think,' he said.

'No, no. I am not suggesting such a thing. But did he tell anyone about it? Did he have any contacts in Britain to whom he might have mentioned it?'

'I have no idea.'

'Can we find out?' I said, as a sense of urgency began to make itself felt within me. 'Could you ask him? It suddenly occurs to me that this, or something like it, might be the explanation of the fact that an elderly Hassid was visiting Professor Ralston just before his death.'

'So that story is true? I thought it was just calumny,' he said.

'No, I *think* it is true,' I said quietly. 'He was observed by the young man who has just been arrested. He insists he is telling the truth.'

'Well, but this is very dangerous. If this man were visiting the Professor because Rabbi Kahn asked him to exert some influence, and it becomes known, then it is he who will be arrested, and it will all end up with yet another Jew on trial for murder.'

'But that is already the case. Jonathan Sachs is Jewish, too.'

He threw up his hands in a gesture of weary despair.

'They may both be innocent. If so, my task is to prove it,' I said. 'And if one of them is guilty, well then a trial is not only inevitable, but just. However, I do not believe the rabbi seen by Jonathan Sachs can be the murderer, and I will tell you exactly why. If Jonathan is speaking the truth, then it is absolutely impossible for the rabbi to have been the murderer, on a question of timing. And if Jonathan is lying, that would be more likely to imply his own guilt than someone else's. And even if he were lying about the timing in order to protect the rabbi, why, it would be much easier to deny ever having seen such a person.'

'You are very logical,' he said with a smile.

'I am learning,' I responded. 'Logic is the keystone of this case. But I need more than logic; I need information. I need to know if there is any connection between your Rabbi Kahn and Jonathan's rabbi.'

'Well, I will ask him the question,' he said. 'I will send him a telegram today before leaving for France, and you may have an answer by tomorrow.'

I thanked him warmly. I was impressed by his intelligence and kindness, and by the many things I had just learnt from him, and excited over what struck me as an important new idea. Yet as we said goodbye, I could not prevent myself from glancing anxiously at my watch. The coming visit to Baruch Gad was causing me increasing tension and nervousness, and I could not wait another moment before hurrying off to Paddington. On the way there, I tried to prepare myself mentally for the transition from luxurious hotel to prison ward.

The trip to Exeter, and from thence through Devon to Princetown was rather long, but my time was well occupied, first in inventing ways to express what I wanted to ask in front of the prison guard, and when I had settled that in my mind, in reading the novel by Amy Levy which I had found in the flat and taken along with me. I read it quickly; it was a short book, expressing mingled bitterness and sadness with virtually no lightening moments.

Following the fortunes of various members of a well-to-do family of bourgeois British Jews, the novel placed each one of them, separately, face-to-face with the fundamental dichotomy of their lives as Englishmen, and their lives as Jews. Reading along, I saw the title character, Reuben Sachs, condemn to oblivion all of his deepest spiritual needs for his milieu, his family, his religion, and the deep, quiet understanding of the beautiful Jewish girl he secretly loves, in order to achieve outward success by being elected to Parliament. More complex and appealing was the personality of his cousin, Leopold Leuniger; a brilliant student and sensitive violinist, to whom every aspect of life showed its face of suffering more easily than its face of joy. At home, the gross materialism, the vulgarity, the worldly values rendered him ashamed, miserable, and sarcastic, whereas at Cambridge, in spite of his brilliance as a student and an artist, and his success in entering an aristocratic social circle, his religion and his background left him feeling like an eternal outsider. I remembered what Amy had tried to tell me, and the young man's anguished self-contempt seemed a perfect illustration for it.

> Leo had taken in the slight, brief, yet significant episode in all its bearings, hating himself meanwhile for his own shrewdness, which he considered a mark of latent meanness... 'Ah, look at us,' he cried with sudden passion, 'where else do you see such eagerness to take advantage; such sickening, hideous greed; such cruel, remorseless striving for power and importance; such ever-active, ever-hungry vanity, that must be fed at any cost? Steeped to the lips in sordidness, as we have all been from the cradle, how is it possible that any one among us, by any effort of his own, can wipe off from his soul the hereditary stain?'

For a Jew to remain cloistered within his own racial group, or at least in a sufficiently middle-class and well-protected part of it, is to remain a prisoner, but has the advantage of dulling the consciousness of the opprobrium of the outside world. For him to strike out and emerge into the wider society, on the other hand, while bringing all the joys of discovery and giving the momentary illusion of belonging, cannot but lead in the end to an exacerbated sensitivity to that opprobrium, encountered in every social contact, with varying degrees of subtlety. Leopold, who had left the comfortable nest of the family circle and the family business to study at Cambridge, could not meet a new person without immediately feeling the secret stab of knowing that the other thought of him as a Jew, even if he gave no visible sign of it. Dreyfus, who had also left the reassuring circle of the family business to join the Army in which he believed he could express his soul as a Frenchman, had encountered the very worst manifestation of prejudice against his race that could be imagined. I thought fleetingly that the real story was far more like a novel than the fictional one. The whole complex question of this contrast between belonging and exclusion reminded me sharply of Professor Ralston's paradox; I began to understand how he might have come to invent it. I thought of Jonathan, and his carefree, smiling ways; he had struck me as more easygoing, less anguished than his sister, for instance. But did he not harbour the same fundamental contradiction within himself? He had been hiding so much from me, and all of it was sheer pain; his uncle's fate, his visits to the prison, his obsessive researches into anti-Semitism.

What else might he not be hiding?

Could I hope that my visit to his uncle would shed any light on the question?

I arrived in Princetown somewhat later than I had intended, but thanks to the foresight which had made me telegraph for some conveyance from the local inn before leaving London, a small and nondescript vehicle was awaiting me outside the station. The driver looked at me pityingly, no doubt taking me for a distraught wife or sister exercising her rare visiting rights. I would very much have liked to chat with him during the ride, and ask him if he frequently brought visitors to the prison, but felt it would appear impertinent and unseemly. It seemed clear enough that he went regularly to the prison, for he clucked and the horse trotted along calmly as though he knew the way only too well.

The prison is farther than the edge of the town, near no other building, but already out upon the vast expanses of the moor. The cab left me at the main gate, an imposing angular stone archway. 'Here is where the visitors enter,' he informed me casually. 'Prisoners go in through another door.'

I was accosted immediately by an official of some kind, and upon introducing myself and showing him the telegram which the prison governor had sent Inspector Reynolds confirming my visit, I was led inside and escorted into the said governor's office, not without first being subjected to a rapid search in a little cubicle by a dour lady whose unique task in life was to ensure that female visitors bore no weapons with which to launch a sudden attack upon Authority.

My interview with the Governor was short and to the point. He looked at me with surprise and disfavour as my presence was announced.

'You are V. Weatherburn, Private Investigator?' he said, looking me up and down.

'Yes,' I responded shortly, rather disliking his tone of frank contempt.

'I was expecting a man,' he said with annoyance.

Well, that shows a certain prejudice upon your part, I thought, but restrained myself from speaking the words aloud. I was not surprised that Inspector Reynolds had chosen to frame his telegram ambiguously. This man would probably have refused me access to his prison if he had known I was a woman. He looked both annoyed and disgusted, but said nothing, contenting himself with ringing a bell and barking to the prison guard who promptly appeared, 'Bring this person to room 10. Have the prisoner Gad brought there and remain present for the fifteen minutes' duration of the visit.'

It struck me as I followed the guard that, although in the course of the last few years I have visited quite a number of prisoners, I have never yet seen a single one who was actually condemned. All of my visits have been to people who were accused and awaiting judgement, and most of them have not taken place in real prisons, but in police cells, which is quite different. I remember feeling long ago that it was like visiting a nether world; I had lost that impression with habit, but it came back to me strongly now. A prison, a true prison, a high-security prison for murderers and dangerous criminals condemned to many years of confinement, is another matter altogether from the chaos of the cells where accused people may be held for a night or two, pending appearance before a magistrate, and where, at least according to the humour of the police officer on duty, the prisoner is not always treated like a criminal.

Here, the very corridors held an atmosphere of frightful repression; the tones, the gestures of the guards bespoke a state of permanent tension and enmity. I thought about Baruch Gad spending ten years within the silence of these walls. My conviction of his innocence, which had begun as the faintest echo of a doubt on the first day I read of the trial, and which had increased with each of my successive discoveries, was now as solid as a rock. Baruch Gad was no grisly murderer, but a victim of anti-Semitism and the machinations of maniacs like Professor Ralston. He was the only prisoner I was to see, yet as

I walked along the corridors, I felt, like an alchemical mixture, the tension of mingled evil, fear, and power which dominated the entire closed-off prison society.

I do not know about the other visiting rooms, but number 10 turned out to be not a room, but a cage. With walls and ceiling of wire mesh, it sat within a larger room; the interior of the cage was divided into three sections by two parallel walls of mesh forming a corridor running down the middle. Each section contained one chair. The guard introduced me into one section through a little door which he locked behind me. He himself then entered the little corridor which divided the two sections, pushed the chair there to one end of it, and sat down with a carefully cultivated lack of expression on his face. I waited, and he waited. Nothing happened for several minutes, and I felt uncomfortable, exposed, and somehow deeply ashamed for myself, for the prison, and for humanity in general that such cages should exist. I cringed secretly, while remaining outwardly composed, and sat motionlessly without a sign of impatience. Time passed, but I refused stubbornly to look at my watch. It struck me that the guard had a dreadfully boring job. We both waited.

After what seemed like an endless time, I heard sounds and saw the slight figure of a man being led towards the opposite side of the cage between two guards. He was handcuffed and they pushed him along with an inhuman rudeness and lack of ceremony which disgusted me. I tried to tell myself that like the screaming crowds who mocked Dreyfus, the guards believed him guilty, guilty of the murder of a little child, and that were I personally to encounter the murderer of a child, I would not be tempted to treat him with any particular delicacy.

The door of the cage was opened, and the prisoner was introduced inside and locked in. His two guards moved off a very short way. The situation was awful. There was at least a yard's distance between us, the width of the corridor where the guard was sitting stolidly, and every word we spoke would be overheard by at least three people. I felt awkward and tongue-tied for a moment. Then the prisoner crossed his part of the cage to the barrier which divided us and, leaning against it, he looked directly across at me, fixed me, in fact, with a look so direct and so intense that my inhibitions dropped suddenly away. Two paths crossed in my mind, and I seemed to be standing in front of the prisoner Dreyfus on his desert island, pleading, shouting his innocence to the four winds, standing alone on the rocks as a symbol of injustice and persecution. The man in front of me was a broken man, his shoulders bent, his face drawn, the spark of life dimmed yet not extinct. Kept alive, perhaps, I thought suddenly, by nothing other than his terrible grievance. I felt a little shudder run through me. Rising, I went to stand directly across from him and looked back at him, meeting his eyes. Erasing the very consciousness of the guard from my mind, I spoke the words I had carefully prepared.

'Mr Gad,' I said, looking at him, 'I must inform you of something which will mean a great deal to you. The black dog is dead.'

He looked up suddenly, stared at me in amazement, but said nothing.

'Yoni went to see the dog on the day he died,' I continued. 'He says he never did see the dog, but others say he did.'

'Yoni—Yoni is accused of killing the dog?' articulated the prisoner suddenly, in the hoarse voice of someone unused to speech. It was obvious that he had caught on to my meaning instantly; the code was working. I responded with a brief nod, wishing that I could tell him to avoid the word *killing*. I did not want anything of the kind to remain in the memory of the guards.

'He claims he didn't see the dog,' I went on. 'I want to

help him; I wish I knew if it were true, or if in fact he did see the dog—maybe because…someone asked him to.'

'Asked him to?' he repeated, and his eyes filled slowly with a look of horrified consciousness; I could see the idea forming in his mind as clearly as it was in my own, that Jonathan might have gone to kill the Professor in order to offer his uncle a future, however heavy the price.

Jonathan, so cheerful and so full of life—spending the rest of it here, in this hell!

He blanched. The expression on his face alone was enough to convince me that the man in front of me knew no more about Jonathan's purpose in visiting Professor Ralston than I myself did. Yet I tried to ask him again.

'Yes—was he asked to go *see the dog*?' I insisted.

'No, never, never,' he said with such horror that his hair seemed literally to be rising upon his scalp, and his voice rose to a dangerous pitch of excitement. 'I would have given my right hand, I would have given my life to avoid this.'

It was borne in upon me that his words were not a mere expression; he meant them literally. I felt no doubt that he would, as he said, have given his life, have chosen death, rather than see his nephew condemned for murder, whether innocent or guilty. I sighed.

'You never thought this might happen?' I said. He shook his head, and suddenly, as I stared at him, his eyes rolled upwards under their lids, revealing only the whites in a horrific image of blindness, and he fell to the floor like an inert mass.

'Fainted,' said the guard in the corridor with scant interest. 'They often do, during visits. It's too hot. End of visit, that means, I guess.' And releasing me, he guided me firmly back to the Governor's office, with much clanking of keys and metallic doors.

'Well?' said the Governor, ignoring me and looking at him.

'They only talked about a dog, like the other fellow, except now the dog is dead,' said the guard laconically.

'What is this about a dog?' said the Governor to me, eyeing me coldly.

'This dog was very important to Mr Gad before he went to prison. It was the one attachment he preserved to the outside world, except for his nephew,' I said firmly. 'However, the dog has died. I felt it my duty to tell him before his release, so that the news would not come as too great a shock to him once he is free.'

'This telegram says you are here to investigate a murder,' he said angrily.

'The murder of a dog,' I replied unmovedly.

'What kind of investigation is this? What could he know about the death of a dog?'

'Not much, indeed,' I replied.

'I consider this a hoax,' he said icily. 'Thanks to this, Gad's visiting rights are cancelled from now until the end of his term of imprisonment.'

I reminded myself that he had visiting rights only every three months anyway, and would be released in much less than that. There was clearly nothing to be gained by sweetness, so I allowed my natural impulses to take over.

'Inhumanity is probably not the best way to govern a prison,' I said frigidly. 'Fortunately it is not my concern if it is the principle upon which you wish to establish your authority.'

We glared at each other in silence.

'Show this woman out,' he said finally, turning away from me and indicating the door to the guard. And I was pleased enough to rise and leave, to emerge into the outside world, to capture the waiting cab, to listen to the smart clip-clop of the hooves trotting away from the dreadful prison, and then to the soothing rumble and whistle of the train as it carried me through the Devon countryside towards Tavistock Junction. Once safely settled on the express for Paddington, I began to reflect upon what I might conclude from my visit, but fell asleep instead out of pure emotional exhaustion, and did not wake until the train pulled into the station.

As it stopped with a shudder, I started awake from a dream so vivid that I had to shake myself to return to the present. I had been standing in the shadows of a darkened room, holding Cecily and Cedric by the hands. It was eerie, but their presence warmed and protected me (although in reality, in that situation, I should have been terrified threefold). The room was lit only by a shaded lamp which threw a dim glow onto the motionless, standing figure of a man. He looked at us wordlessly, we looked at him, and I tried to make out his features in the gloom. That sharp nose, those sunken cheeks—why, it was Professor Ralston, returned to haunt his own study! Yes, that is where I was standing. I recognised it now, saw the desk and chairs, returned to their upright positions. I saw, also, the bleeding wound in his chest.

Who killed you? I asked him, but he did not answer. Of course not, I thought reasonably. How silly of me to ask questions to a dead man. I squeezed the children's warm little hands, tiny anchors linking me to the world of the living. He could not tell me how he had died. Yet his eyes were fixed upon me.

It was actually more of a powerful image than a dream.

As I gathered my wraps and descended the steep step onto the quay, part of my brain was still under the spell of the strange vision. It was evening, but not very late. There was no reason not to…

I found myself on my way to the Professor's library.

The Library Paradox

With no fixed purpose, I let myself into the building and, unlocking the door of the study, I stood where I had been in my dream and looked towards the place where I had seen the Professor standing. There was no lamp, but the dim evening light was grey, not black, and I tried to conjure up his presence within it. I remained concentrating, calling him forth with all of my powers. I stood silently, evoking his presence, receptive, asking for communication. The minutes passed slowly. And I heard a faint noise.

And then another one. The sound of steps overhead, in the flat above me. Slowly, these steps began to descend the stairs leading to the door behind the desk, the door to the Professor's rooms.

Can I describe my feelings? I believed, yes, I truly believed that I had conjured the dead. I stood frozen, too petrified to take note of the many physical manifestations of fear which flooded me; a kind of horrified fascination glued me to my spot. I would not have fled for the world. I expected no grinning death's head or rotting flesh, but let me admit it openly and frankly—difficult as I myself find to believe it now, as I write it—I did, truly and completely, expect the Professor, in the dim, shadowy incarnation I had seen in my dream. The steps reached the bottom, the door opened quietly. My eyes were fixed upon it.

It was Edmund who stepped into the study.

He leapt back, violently startled at seeing someone standing there, knocked himself sharply against the door jamb, and stood breathing heavily, one hand rubbing his head. His other hand, which clutched a piece of folded paper, was pressed to his pounding heart. He looked completely undone by the shock, and the sight of his state brought me to myself.

'So you do have a key to Professor Ralston's private rooms,'

I said. 'I thought there must be a double somewhere. No one takes the risk of having a single key to an important lock.'

'Professor Taylor had it together with the others,' he said faintly.

'And he gave it to you? To look for something? What?'

Edmund did not look capable of any vigorous reaction after the shock my presence had given him, which seemed to far outweigh the shock he had caused me, in spite of the fact that he had unexpectedly encountered a mere solid human, whereas I was expecting to come face-to-face with a ghost. Taking advantage of his weakened state, I crossed over to him and removed the paper firmly from his hand. He did not resist. It was a short letter, written in the cramped handwriting of someone ill and weary.

Dear Professor Ralston,

I am aware that your father's wishes in a certain matter concerning me are of great annoyance to you and that you have strong objections to his plans. I fear, indeed, that these feelings have led you to regard my son with an enmity that he does not deserve. I wish to inform you herewith that although your father is a kind, admirable and noble man, I have no intention of acceding to his wishes, now or in the future. I sincerely hope that this will not cause him pain or disappointment, for I should not wish to be the cause of unhappiness in any person. But what he asks is impossible for me. I feel that a woman can marry but once in her lifetime, be that marriage before God or before society. I beg of you, therefore, to put aside all worry on that score and, if possible, to influence your father to forget me, and to find it within yourself to treat my son as you would any other student, with no regard to these private events that have disturbed our lives, but in which he plays no part.

Sincerely yours,
Emilia Bryant

'What does this mean? Professor Ralston's father wanted to marry your mother?' I said, lifting my head in surprise and looking at the pale, still motionless young man who stood facing me, leaning against the doorjamb.

'Yes,' he said, with the ghost of a shrug.

Time seemed to have stopped in the darkening room, and the atmosphere breathed no violence. I knew I should be afraid of Edmund, yet I found it impossible.

'Did you kill Professor Ralston because of this?' I asked.

He looked surprised, and roused up a little.

'Of course not!' he said. 'What an idea!'

'Did you kill him because of your thesis?' I continued.

'I didn't kill Professor Ralston at all, and nor did my father,' he said. 'You're barking up the wrong tree.'

'Your father?' I said, taken aback, even astounded by these unexpected words. 'What do you mean, your father? I thought—Professor Taylor had said that your mother was a widow. If you have a father, why—then how could Professor Ralston's father have wanted to marry your mother?'

'Don't be stupid,' he snapped. 'Haven't you ever heard of illegitimate children?'

'Oh,' I said, embarrassed. 'And Professor Taylor knew about it?'

He had obviously thought that I knew more than I did. Now he seemed to regret having spoken. He did not answer, and I stared at him, thinking.

Why was he here, searching for this letter? Why did he have the key? Who had given it to him? Who had I seen searching, searching among papers and documents, in this very room?

'Professor Taylor!' I said suddenly. 'Professor Taylor has had a second family all this time, growing up alongside the real one!'

'No, it isn't like that,' he replied quickly. 'My father is an honourable man.'

'Hmm,' I said doubtfully, trying to adjust myself to this new vision of the white-haired history professor as a rake. My expression seemed to stimulate Edmund to defend him.

'This all happened when my father was very young,' he explained. 'He did not intend to be a Professor; as a young man, he entered the Army. When he was only in his early twenties, he fell in love with my mother, who was the daughter of the captain of his regiment out in India. Something happened—I can't explain it,' he went on, blushing. 'But the captain was furious with him. Right around that time, the regiment sent a small group of soldiers out to reconnoitre, and they had fallen into an Indian ambush. The captain accused my father of having colluded with the enemy, and having given them information. There was a court-martial. Had he been found guilty, he would have been executed. But the charges were patently false, there was obviously no proof of any kind. In the end he was accused of negligence and disobedience, and given a dishonourable discharge. He returned to England an embittered man, and started a new life, attending university. My mother and I returned to England only several years later. She looked everywhere for him, but when she finally found him, he was married to someone else. He had had no idea that I existed. It was too late. Yet he did what he could for my mother and me, discreetly.

The Library Paradox

It was thanks to him that I became interested in studying history. He has been a father to me in spite of everything. I—I cannot criticise him for what happened when he was barely twenty. He has been in a difficult situation for the last twenty-five years, and he has handled it with as much dignity as he could.'

'So that explains why the Dreyfus affair rouses him to such fury!' I exclaimed, suddenly enlightened.

'Oh yes. The injustice and the shame of his dishonourable discharge left him with a bitterness that has never been effaced,' Edmund replied.

I was touched by his spontaneous defence of Professor Taylor's behaviour, and disinclined to make any moral judgement. Indeed, it was difficult to see how the Professor could have acted differently, once the mistake had already been made. He almost certainly thought that he would never be allowed to see the young girl again, knew nothing of the coming child, and could be justified in leaving the error behind him and beginning a new life on a solid basis of scholarship and marriage. But how dreadful for him when the young lady suddenly appeared, having borne all the terrible consequences of the mistake alone, still in love with him, the mother of his eldest son—and he could do nothing for her, or almost nothing, for what is a little help and friendship to a woman who loves?

'Did Professor Ralston know about this?' I wondered suddenly.

'He did, because my mother told his father why she could not and would not marry him, and he told his son. I don't think Professor Ralston cared much. But he liked knowing, and let my father know that he knew.'

'Blackmail?' I said quickly.

'Oh no. He neither used nor even mentioned the situation except for a hint here and there. As I said, I don't think it meant much to him. Ralston's mind was on other things. However, it made my father uncomfortable. He was afraid that Professor Ralston might have written something down somewhere—in a diary, or something—and wanted to search his papers to find anything of the kind. He was really afraid that if some document were found by the police, or by whomever should sort Professor Ralston's papers later on, the story could not but come out, and his wife and all his colleagues would learn of it. The first few days after the murder, he couldn't search, he could only wait, because even though he had the keys, the police were there every day, and they left a constable at night to keep the place safe. But it seemed that they found nothing; at least they questioned no one about it. Then he became hopeful that there was nothing, only I knew that my mother had written a letter to the Professor—that letter there. But the police clearly never found it, for I am mentioned in it explicitly, and they would certainly have questioned my mother and me about it. When the police finished their work, my father began to search for it. He could not risk it during the day, there were too many people in the library, but he managed it once or twice at night. He looked through the flat and the study before you arrived, especially through the letters. The day you came, he searched through all of the articles and publications. But he found nothing, not even my mother's letter. Professor Ralston might have destroyed it, of course, but we were sure that he had not. He was proud of never destroying any document. My father was convinced that the letter was hidden somewhere, and became more and more nervous about its being found. He gave me the key to the flat and asked me to search for it. I did, many times, after hours, but I never found it until today. I used to wonder if it wasn't hidden in the pages of some book, even though it seemed impossible that he would leave such a letter in a place where anyone might find it—but I used to take every opportunity to open the books in the library and look inside them, except that there are far too many of them, and usually I just ended up reading them for pleasure. That's what happened the evening you were here, studying medieval saints. I couldn't help getting interested in what you were looking up.'

'And where was the letter in the end?'

'It was hidden behind a framed photograph of his father. It's an odd thing to do, to have put it there, isn't it? It's almost like he thought perhaps his father was lonely.'

Edmund had become strangely loquacious; I felt that it was a relief to him to tell me all this. He came towards me, and reached to take the letter back.

'This belongs to my mother,' he said. I read it through again quickly, fixing its contents in my mind, before handing it over to him.

'Edmund,' I said, 'could that key have ever left your father's possession? Do you realise that anyone who held it could have shot the Professor and then quickly run upstairs?'

He looked surprised.

'Nonsense,' he said, after a moment. 'My father had this key all the time, and found it where he had put it. But in any case, everybody knows that the police opened the door with the key that was in Ralston's pocket and searched upstairs. There was nobody.'

'Windows?' I said tentatively.

'These enormous windows don't open,' he said. 'They're the same upstairs. I'm sorry, but I'm afraid you must look for your murderer elsewhere. Come—there is nothing more for us to do here. Let me get you a cab.'

I followed him outside, seething inwardly. Whether or

not the strange story of his mother constituted a motive (and it was not clear that it did, barring the hypothesis of blackmail) Edmund was right. It was impossible for the key to have been used for the murderer to hide upstairs. I had known that already. The case abounded with motives—if anything, there were too many of them by now. Yet the paradox remained complete.

London, Thursday, March 19th, 1896

I sat over my breakfast tea, smoothing out and marvelling over the telegram which had only just been delivered for me, and which excited me so much that Edmund and his story were pushed to the back of my mind. The message was from Bernard Lazare, according to his promise, and fitted like a puzzle piece into the scheme that had sprung up in my mind while I was talking to him.

On receipt of Ralston letter Zadoc Kahn communicated with rebbe Moses Avraham now in London asking Avraham to make some attempt pressure Ralston stop working up British public opinion against Dreyfus.

David pronounced his rabbi's name as Moyshe Avrom; but I hoped that the difference was but a matter of pronunciation, and hastened to David and Rivka's house to show it to them, and to prepare for my visit to the rabbi. David, who had remained home from work to celebrate the festival, confirmed this. 'Avrom,

Avrohom,' he said, 'it's our Ashkenazi pronunciation that changes some a's to o's. The correct transliteration is Avraham; the English would say Abraham. As for Moyshe, it's the Ashkenazi pronunciation of Moshé, the Hebrew form of Moses.'

Rivka pressed her hand to her heart nervously, reading the telegram over his shoulder. 'But David,' she said, 'doesn't it seem strange that a rebbe from some little *shtetl* in Poland would be in contact with the chief rabbi of France?'

'I think it must be the same man,' he said. 'He may come from a little *shtetl*, but according to what Ephraim has heard about him, he is considered to be one of the most learned rebbes of his generation; "his fame has travelled far and wide", as they express it here. He studied both in *yeshiva*, the school for the study of the *Talmud*, and in a regular Polish gymnasium, obtaining the highest honours in both. They say he speaks seven languages. I can very well imagine him never leaving his own tiny community, whether in Poland or here, but corresponding with well-known personalities all over the world. That is important for you, Vanessa,' he added, turning to me, 'because it means that he will have studied English. He may not speak it too well, because he would not have much daily opportunity to speak it, even here in London, as strange as that may seem. But it solves one of our problems for this afternoon. If you get to speak to him at all, you won't need a translator.'

'If only this turns out to be the proof that Jonathan is telling the truth,' said Rivka, taking the telegram from David and clutching it. 'And what about Uncle Baruch? What happened yesterday, Vanessa? Were you able to see him? Were you able to ask him anything?' She sounded nervous and I hastened to reassure her.

'Yes, I was. And Rivka, he said that he never asked Jonathan to see the Professor, and never would have. I made him understand what had happened and he said he would have rather died. And then he lost consciousness.'

'What can it all mean?' she said wonderingly, as though not daring to be hopeful.

'I sincerely hope and believe that it means Jonathan—is in the clear,' I said, hesitating a little crossly as I remembered his annoying refusal to tell me the *whole truth*, but completing my sentence anyway, out of kindness. 'At any rate, the rabbi holds the crucial piece of evidence, and we must find out exactly what he knows today, for Jonathan is to appear before the magistrate tomorrow morning, and he *must not* be committed to trial. It is too dangerous; juries are too unpredictable, and even at the very best, a trial means many days of painful accusations and public revelations.'

'No—anything but that!' said Rivka.

'Well, then let us decide how I am to approach and talk to this rabbi, and what I am to say.'

'Yes, we must think,' said David. 'I've already told you why it will be difficult. It would be simply unthinkable for you, a strange woman—and you are obviously a stranger and an Englishwoman here, even if we do cover up your hair—to simply go up and speak to him. First of all, he will certainly not be alone, but surrounded by devoted members of his family and the students and disciples you saw. The trouble is that even if you do get into the room and approach him, chances are they will treat you more or less in the same way they treated Ephraim the other day, before you ever get a chance to say a word.'

'But Ephraim provoked them,' I said. 'If I were to speak calmly and tell them that I have something important to say to the rabbi, would they not behave more reasonably?'

'Vanessa—no! You, an unknown *woman* pushing your

way into their group would be perceived as far more offensive and provoking than Ephraim's silly words.'

'But you said that for today's festival there will be all kinds of people going in and out of the house. That means women as well as men, doesn't it?'

'Yes. Doors will stand open today for the mummers and players going from house to house, and the people watching them. That will certainly help, as it means that you will probably be able to enter the rabbi's house, and slip into the part of the room reserved for the women. But what then?'

'Could I give him a written message, perhaps? Asking to speak with him alone?'

'Vanessa, you really are naive! I keep telling you that the rebbe would not go anywhere, alone, with you or any other woman, except for his own wife, of course. Not even into the next room. In fact, he would not so much as look at you directly.'

'Bother being a mere woman! I simply *must* speak to him, come what may!' I cried impatiently.

Unexpectedly, David burst out laughing at my words. 'I never heard the Bible so aptly paraphrased,' he said. 'That's just what Esther said, in a nutshell!' Suddenly, he stopped laughing and stared at me. 'Why, of course,' he said. 'It's so simple. What you should do is go to the rabbi's house disguised as Esther.'

'Disguised? Is it all right for her to wear a costume?' said Rivka quickly. 'The men here usually do, but the women?'

'Well, now that you ask me, it is true that one does not see many women in disguise, though little girls certainly do it,' answered David thoughtfully. 'Yet there are some, I am sure of it. It must be all right. Let me just check something,' and he went to the shelf containing books in Hebrew and lifted down one or two heavy volumes, through which he shuffled rapidly.

The Library Paradox

'*Mateh Mosheh* 1014, Yehudah Mintz says that women may disguise if they do not take the guise of men,' he announced after a few minutes. 'And look—here in *Hagim uMo'adim*, Maimon writes that women may even disguise as men, and men as women, if it is purely for the purpose of entertainment.'

'Then it must be all right,' said Rivka.

'But who is this Esther I am to disguise as?' I said curiously.

'Esther? Don't you know who Esther is? Oh, how stupid I am! You don't know what the Purim festival is, do you? It's the festival commemorating the death of Haman; it's in the Bible.'

'Oh—you mean the Book of Esther!' I exclaimed. 'Of course, I should have realised it when you mentioned the Bible.'

'Disguised as Esther, you can pretend to be a player, and stand up and tell a tale! People will be running all over the streets in disguise today, dressed up as Vashti or Esther in old silks and veils, or wearing crowns as Ahasuerus, or three-cornered hats like Haman, or even just dressing up as clowns with jangling bells and playing instruments and singing wild songs—sometimes they even dress as Hassidim—those who are not actually Hassidim, I mean—and rush about making fun of them, imitating their wild ways, the way they rock back and forth when they pray, and go into trances. Players in groups go into the houses and sing songs, or make music, or act out the Purim play itself. Dressed as Esther and wearing a veil, you could simply stand up and speak out like a performer. It would have to be English, of course, but that may be just as well. It may prevent some of the students from realising what's going on. Rivka—can we disguise Vanessa as Esther?'

'I would have to borrow some things,' she said, looking me over. 'Let me run over to Sheyne's, her husband is the rag-and-bone man, she has a lot of old robes and dresses and things.'

She hurried out, the baby bouncing on her arm. Little Samuel followed her quickly, clinging to her skirt.

'I will need to think about what to say and how to say it, if I am to make myself clearly understood by the rabbi, but not by the people around him,' I said thoughtfully, visualising myself standing in front of the rabbi and a roomful of people, disguised as a veiled queen. 'This is even stranger than yesterday, when I had to communicate with Baruch Gad in code. I seem to be doing this every day now. Well, what would Esther say?'

'*If I perish, I perish!*' he quoted. 'Those are her most famous words. How well do you know the Esther scroll?'

'Scroll?' I said.

'I mean the book in the Bible,' he said. 'We have it printed out on separate scrolls for this festival. Rivka has one in English, somewhere, I know she does. She does not read much in Hebrew yet, except for the basic women's prayers. She is putting her best efforts into learning Yiddish.'

'Oh,' I said, as he scrabbled about in the heap of books again, and dug out what he wanted from underneath the tomes he had just put back. 'Well, Esther is not one of the books in the Bible I know well. We Christians seem to greatly prefer Job, for some reason.'

'I can imagine. Well, here it is, read it, so you can see what it was like to be Esther,' he said. 'It is not long.'

The quaint scroll was written out in many columns along a long, thin rectangle of paper which was all rolled up on a wooden rod attached to one of the short sides of the rectangle. The other short side was attached to a second wooden rod, around which one continuously rolled the part of the scroll one had just read.

The Library Paradox

'What an intelligent system,' I observed, after getting used to the motion.

'All books were this way in antiquity,' said David. 'The sewn parchment codex—that's a book with pages—was invented by the Romans. *Caudex* is the trunk of a tree, you know, and the pages were called "leaves", as they still are. They found it took up less space, and you could write on both sides of the parchment.'

'Well, I like this method,' I said, beginning to read the sacred text and rolling it up progressively as I went.

Now it came to pass in the days of Ahasuerus... in the third year of his reign, he made a feast unto all his princes and his servants... he shewed the riches of his glorious kingdom and the honour of his excellent majesty many days... white, green and blue hangings... pillars of marble... drink in vessels of gold... On the seventh day the king commanded the seven chamberlains to bring Vashti the queen before the king with the crown royal, to shew the people and the princes her beauty: for she was fair to look on. But the queen Vashti refused to come at the king's commandment by his chamberlains: therefore was the king very wroth, and his anger burned in him... The wise man Memucan said... Vashti the queen hath not done wrong to the king only, but also to all the princes and to all the people that are in all the provinces of the king Ahasuerus. For this deed of the queen shall come abroad unto all women, so that they shall despise their husbands in their eyes, when it shall be reported: the king Ahasuerus commanded Vashti the queen to be brought in before him, but she came not. Likewise shall the ladies of Per-

sia and Media say this day unto all the king's princes,
which have heard of the deed of the queen. Thus shall
there arise too much contempt and wrath.

'Well, well,' I thought. 'This sounds like quite a familiar
story.' Some words of Shakespeare's came into my mind:

Biondello: *Sir, my mistress sends you word*
That she is busy and she cannot come.
Petruchio: *How! She's busy, and she cannot come!*
Is that an answer?

The Taming of the Shrew is a play for which I have always
entertained a sincere and spontaneous dislike, in spite of a sneak-
ing conviction that Shakespeare wrote the entire thing with his
tongue in his cheek. The same cannot be said of the Bible, I
suppose, yet it contains its own form of humour. Vashti humili-
ates the king, and instead of hushing it up quietly, he makes a
tremendous song and dance about it, with the result that every
woman in the world for all of the countless following generations knows exactly what Vashti did and feels an irrepressible
sympathy for her. Well, I expect that Vashti had to pay the price
of her independence, as women always have had to from the
dawn of time. Memucan continues his lecture:

If it please the king, let there go a royal commandment
from him...that Vashti come no more before king Aha-
suerus; and let the king give her royal estate unto another
that is better than she.

Ha, my mind thought, running irresistibly upon its own
track as I read. Good riddance. She probably found him repul-

sive. 'Better than she', indeed. More docile, or more slavish, you mean. Ahasuerus, meanwhile, continued to behave in unsurprising ways for a biblical king.

> *Let there be fair young virgins sought for the king... gather together all the fair young virgins...and let the maiden which pleaseth the king be queen instead of Vashti... Now in Shushan the palace there was a certain Jew, whose name was Mordecai...and he brought up Esther, his uncle's daughter, for she had neither father nor mother, and the maid was fair and beautiful... So it came to pass, when the king's commandment and his decree was heard, and when many maidens were gathered together unto Shushan the palace...that Esther was brought also unto the king's house...and the maiden pleased him, and she obtained kindness of him... Esther had not shewed her people nor her kindred: for Mordecai had charged her that she should not show it...the king loved Esther above all the women, and she obtained grace and favour in his sight more than all the virgins; so that he set the royal crown upon her head, and made her queen instead of Vashti.*

This is followed by more typical behaviour by Ahasuerus: Mordecai discovers a plot against the king to which he responds by immediately hanging the conspirators from a tree, after which he proceeds to honour and promote Haman the son of Hammedatha the Agagite to the highest position in the land and promise him anything he wants. And what does Haman want?

> *And all the king's servants, that were in the king's gate, bowed, and reverenced Haman: for the king had so*

commanded concerning him. But Mordecai bowed not, nor did him reverence... And when Haman saw that Mordecai bowed not, nor did him reverence, then was Haman full of wrath. And he thought scorn to lay hands on Mordecai alone, for they had shewed him the people of Mordecai: wherefore Haman sought to destroy all the Jews that were throughout the whole kingdom of Ahasuerus...

Wonderful, I thought to myself sourly. Has anything changed since?

Mordecai gave the copy of the writing of the decree that was given to destroy the Jews, to show it unto Esther, to charge her that she should go in unto the king, to make supplication unto him, and to make request before him for her people... Esther spake, saying...All the king's servants, and the people of the king's provinces, do know, that whosoever, whether man or woman, shall come unto the king into the inner court, who is not called, there is one law of his to put him to death, except such to whom the king shall hold out the golden sceptre, that he may live... Then Mordecai commanded to answer Esther, Think not with thyself that thou shalt escape in the king's house, more than all the Jews... Who knoweth whether thou art come to the kingdom for such a time as this? Then Esther bade them return Mordecai this answer... So will I go in unto the king, which is not according to the law: and if I perish, I perish.

Fortunately, Esther succeeded in approaching the king without perishing.

The Library Paradox

*Then said the king unto her, What wilt thou, queen
Esther? and what is thy request? it shall be even given
thee to the half of the kingdom. And Esther answered,
If it seem good unto the king, let the king and Haman
come this day unto the banquet that I have prepared for
him.*

A banquet? My detective instincts stirred. Was Haman
to fall suddenly and strangely dead after drinking from a
bejewelled goblet? No, I reminded myself sternly. This was
not *Arabian Nights*.

Haman was delighted at the invitation, to be sure, but he
could not get over Mordecai's lack of respect. His wife consoled him with the following suggestion:

*Let a gallows be made of fifty cubits high, and tomorrow
speak thou unto the king that Mordecai may be hanged
thereon: then go thou in merrily with the king unto the
banquet. And the thing pleased Haman, and he caused
the gallows to be made.*

In the meantime, however, the king learnt of Mordecai's
good deeds on his behalf and asked Haman's advice on how to
honour such a one, but without naming him:

*Haman came in. And the king said unto him, What shall
be done unto the man whom the king delighteth to honour? Now Haman thought in his heart, To whom would
the king delight to do honour more than to myself? And
Haman answered the king, For the man whom the king
delighteth to honour, Let the royal apparel be brought,
and the horse that the king rideth upon, and the crown*

royal which is set upon his head: and let this apparel
and horse be delivered to the hand of one of the king's
most noble princes, that they may array the man withal
whom the king delighteth to honour, and bring him on
horseback through the street of the city, and proclaim
before him, Thus shall it be done to the man whom the
king delighteth to honour. Then the king said to Haman,
Make haste, and take the apparel and the horse, as thou
hast said, and do even to Mordecai the Jew, that sitteth
at the king's gate.

Once again the notion of murder flitted through my mind.
But no. Haman obeyed the king and promenaded Mordecai
safely through the streets of the city, returning home, needless
to say, in a foul mood, 'mourning and having his head covered', to be precise.

So the king and Haman came to banquet with Esther
the queen. And the king said again unto Esther on the
second day at the banquet of wine, What is thy petition,
queen Esther? and it shall be granted thee: and what is
thy request? and it shall be performed, even to the half
of the kingdom. Then Esther the queen answered and
said, If I have found favour in they sight, O king, and if
it please the king, let my life be given me at my petition,
and my people at my request: For we are sold, I and my
people, to be destroyed, to be slain, and to perish... Then
the king Ahasuerus answered and said unto Esther the
queen, Who is he, and where is he, that durst presume in
his heart to do so? And Esther said, The adversary and
enemy is this wicked Haman. Then Haman was afraid
before the king and the queen.

So should I be in his place, indeed.

And the king arising from the banquet of wine in his wrath went into the palace garden: and Haman stood up to make request for his life to Esther the queen; for he saw that there was evil determined against him by the king. Then the king returned out of the palace garden into the place of the banquet of wine; and Haman was fallen upon the bed whereon Esther was. Then said the king, Will he force the queen also before me in the house? As the word went out of the king's mouth, they covered Haman's face. And Harbonah, one of the chamberlains, said before the king, Behold also, the gallows fifty cubits high, which Haman had made for Mordecai, who had spoken good for the king, standeth in the house of Haman. Then the king said, Hang him thereon. So they hanged Haman on the gallows that he had prepared for Mordecai. Then was the king's wrath pacified.

This part of the story reminded me of Grimm's fairy tales. I remember various scenes in which evil stepmothers are asked how erring persons should be punished, only to find their precise recipes applied to their unwilling selves.

'You can stop reading there,' said David, who was peering over my shoulder, 'that's all the part that we celebrate today. There isn't anything else about Esther after that.' I glanced up at him as he spoke. He looked just a tiny fraction too hopeful.

'I'm nearly at the end, I'll finish it,' I said firmly.

... The king granted the Jews which were in every city to gather themselves together, and to stand for their life, to destroy, to slay, and to cause to perish, all the power of

the people and province that would assault them, both little ones and women, and to take the spoil of them for a prey, upon one day in all the provinces of king Ahasuerus, namely, upon the thirteenth day of the twelfth month, which is the month Adar... Then the Jews had light, and gladness, and joy, and honour. And in every province, and in every city, whithersoever the king's commandment and his decree came, the Jews had joy and gladness, a feast and a good day. And many of the people of the land became Jews; for the fear of the Jews fell upon them.

As well it might, before the fatal day had arrived. But can the Jews be blamed for a commandment which after all reveals more about the procedures of Ahasuerus than their own? And would they, after all, execute it?

Now in the twelfth month, on the thirteenth day of the same...the Jews gathered themselves together in their cities throughout all the provinces of the king Ahasuerus, to lay hand on such as sought their hurt: and no man could withstand them; for the fear of them fell upon all people. And all the rulers of the provinces, and the lieutenants, and the deputies, and officers of the king helped the Jews; because the fear of Mordecai fell upon them... Thus the Jews smote all their enemies with the stroke of the sword, and slaughter, and destruction, and did what they would unto those that hated them... And they kept the fourteenth day of the month Adar, and the fifteenth day of the same, yearly, as the days wherein the Jews rested from their enemies, and the month which was turned unto them from sorrow to joy, and from mourning into a good day... Wherefore they

*called these days Purim, after the name of Pur, that is,
the lot that had been cast to consume them and destroy
them…*

'These things always seem to end with a triumphal slaughter on one side or the other,' admitted David sadly.

'It does alter one's perception of the Jews as a victimised people,' I said, remembering that Professor Taylor had once made
the same remark. 'After all, he who laughs last laughs best.'

'Yet they—we—we are, we always have been a victimised people,' he exclaimed passionately. 'I don't say this out
of pride, I wish to God that it weren't true. But the Bible
tales that end this way do not disprove it; they are merely
signs of a desperate optimism, the hope for triumph and survival, in the language of the time. The status of victim has no
value for us—it has no value at all in our Bible. It was *your*
Christ who created that notion: that the victim is to be hon-
oured, that the last shall be first. We don't have that notion
to comfort ourselves in our misery. We have only constantly
shattered dreams of victory and triumph over our oppres-
sors. But there have been no such triumphs in living memory,
and in much, much longer than that. Only the persecutions,
the Inquisitions, the pogroms—and these ancient, legendary
memories.'

There was no possible answer to this: he spoke the simple
truth. I rolled up the scroll to the beginning and tied it with its
ribbon, thinking about Esther, imagining the struggle between
her fear before the king and her fear for her people. I forgot
altogether where I was, and jumped at the sound of the rickety
door being pushed vigorously open.

'Look at all that I've brought!' rang out Rivka's youthful
voice, as she made her reappearance, her arms loaded with a

big bundle of old garments in the middle of which nestled the baby, who was twisting a mass of gold-tinted tulle happily in his fat little hands.

'I got some things for myself as well,' she added. 'And Sheyne said we can leave the babies with her when we go out. She won't leave the house today.'

She laid her finds out upon the table. David immediately pounced upon a long, somewhat tattered black velvet dress of a loose and flowing cut.

'She can't go there with this rip,' observed Rivka. 'I'll sew it up.'

'Sew it up as best you can, and she can wear a shawl or something over it.'

'I'll lend you my silk one, and we'll cover your hair with something pretty. Then you put this veil over everything; I took it on purpose. Eliel is quite attached to it, dear me, I do hope he'll allow us to have it back.'

She tugged gently, but the baby tugged harder and looked stubborn.

'Leave it,' I laughed. 'It's too early, anyway. He'll forget all about it later on.'

'Yes, if only he doesn't tear it. Sheyne wouldn't like that; I'll need to give the things back this evening,' she replied, eyeing the little tot suspiciously. But he showed no sign of tearing the veil, contenting himself with turning it and plucking at it delicately, and examining it with deep concentration for all the world like a tiny scientist.

Young Ephraim joined us for a convivial midday meal, during which I continued to ruminate over the best way to present my story, wondering if the whole thing were not completely absurd and unrealistic, and how on earth I seemed to continually find myself in such theatrical situa-

The Library Paradox

tions, something which had never happened to me in any of my previous cases.

'David,' I asked suddenly. 'If I manage to explain the whole situation to the rabbi so that he understands it, how do you think he will actually answer me?'

'It depends on what you ask him,' he said. 'I hope that he will give you an answer of some kind, but it may not be easy to understand. Rebbes speak in hints and parables. I wish I could tell you that he would just describe exactly what he saw in the library that day, but it is very unlikely to be so simple, especially before other people. In fact, I don't advise you to ask him openly about the library or what he was doing there on that day. Remember how his absence was turned into a myth. Whatever he may say to you, no matter how mysterious and irrelevant it may sound to you, don't dismiss it, study it. One thing is certain: he will not fob you off with an empty response.'

After lunch, Rivka and I donned our gowns and drapes, and the four of us sauntered out into the street together, the babies in tow. I felt peculiar and slightly foolish, but put a good face on it, and quite soon forgot all about looking strange, as the streets were altogether full of people in all manner of disguises.

Children rushed about making tremendous rackets with wooden noisemakers, which they shook violently as they ran. Musicians passed with tambourines and flutes, and stopped in little groups to play melodies under windows or in open doorways. The weather was balmy and everyone was in a festive mood. Smells of delicious baking wafted from the kitchens. These smells, and their sources, a multitude of warm little baked pastries, were of particular efficaciousness in convincing Rivka's two little boys to remain with the lady called Sheyne.

'We needn't be in any hurry,' remarked David, 'let's take

a roundabout way to the rebbe's house, and see what's happening in the streets.'

I was anxious to arrive at the rabbi's house, but on the other hand, I wanted to blend in as well as possible with the typical behaviour on this special day, so I moved along with them, without saying anything, keeping my eyes open and watching everything about me.

I was by no means the only Esther upon the streets; I saw several others, garbed in varying degrees of finery, some of whom were obviously men. Each time two Esthers encountered each other, salutations were exchanged. We were surrounded on all sides by kings and queens, prime ministers, executioners, and evil Hamans with weird masks and three-cornered hats. Groups acted out the famous scenes on some of the street corners, or entered people's houses in order to give their tiny play; individuals strolled about, carrying harmonicas or accordions, and stopped to tell their stories in a sing-song voice, accompanying themselves with tunes. All were surrounded by groups of children, who at regular intervals burst unanimously into shrieks and vigorous agitation of their rattles and noisemakers.

'They do it to cover the name of Haman every time it is pronounced,' David explained to me as we passed a story-teller whose voice was drowned by a particularly loud commotion. 'The children know exactly when his name is about to occur, and they make the racket just in time to pretend not to hear it.'

'And were they really not to hear it, all the pleasure would be gone,' I laughed.

Upon this one day, it seemed as though all the weariness and misery, the grey mud, the dirty tenements and their penniless and ragged denizens had completely disappeared, to be replaced by gaiety and music and even, astonishingly, pale rays of sunshine.

'Purim is our happiest festival,' observed Rivka. 'Even as children, we loved it best of any. I expect I shouldn't say this, but it contains less prayer than most of the other festivals.'

'*Nem a Hummentaschen*,' said a woman near us, wearing a flour-bedaubed apron and holding out a large tray loaded with the same little triangular pastries that had so charmed Samuel and Eliel. I took one and bit into it, smiling my thanks from under my gold-tinted veil. It was stuffed with poppy seeds. The lady smiled back, and for the first time, a little feeling of rightness and belonging crept over me, and I stopped cringing inwardly like a usurper about to be discovered and deposed.

'They're called *Hummentaschen*, Haman's pockets,' said Rivka. 'But they're supposed to be shaped like his hat.'

'What is that man doing?' I asked curiously, as we moved on. He was giving a remarkable performance of tumbling, with rapid series of somersaults and cartwheels, and stopping between them to entertain the usual motley group of eager children with bursts of speech.

'He's telling some story or other,' said David, stopping to listen for a moment. 'Obviously this one is not about Esther. Anything goes on a day like this.' He glanced at me significantly. 'That's why I think our plan may work.'

We came, eventually, to the rabbi's home on Brick Lane, just around the corner from the little *shul* outside which we had waited for him three days ago. Like most of the others up and down the street, the door was flung wide and people were running in and out. Besides the tight, severe group of black-clad, earlock-wearing disciples, who were massed inside the room, I perceived several other guests, many of which were children in gales of laughter over some skit played by a couple of actors. Through the door, I was able to perceive the rabbi himself, enthroned in a large armchair, listening to the actors with benevolence, although without laughing.

David stepped inside, and then beckoned to us. 'The women are in there,' he said softly, gesturing towards the far end of the room, where a curtain divided off a portion of the large room from the rest. Ephraim joined the other children immediately. David stationed himself near the wall, among a group of other listeners, and Rivka and I slipped across the room and entered the women's section. It was here that the women of the household and their many visitors congregated to enjoy the festival. The segregation was not complete; groups of young people in disguise moved in and out; whole groups disguised as the characters in the story circulated together, singing or chanting and playing instruments. The younger boys and girls dashed about freely in all parts of the room.

After some time during which we watched the mummers in the main part of the room through gaps in the curtain, Rivka led me away from the curtain towards the farther wall, where there was a large table upon which lay several tattered Esther scrolls and prayer books written in Hebrew for the use of the women visitors, who were taking them up and putting them down constantly, as they entered the room or left it to go into the inner portions of the house or capture a stray child.

'There are players all the time,' she said, fingering the books absently. 'How will you get a chance to intervene?'

'I'll wait. There will be a gap at some point, surely,' I said. 'I think we are too early. People must begin going home at a certain point.' Seeing that some of the women were watching us, I picked up a prayer book as well.

'That is a beautiful one,' said Rivka, taking the well-worn little volume of blue leather embossed with gold letters from

me. 'I wish I had one like it. You can see that it has lived.'
She riffled through it gently, but her gesture caught the eye
of a lady who had been in the room the entire time, checking
on an impressive brood of noisy little ones, dragging them
back from the front part of the room when they became too
rowdy, giving them cakes when they whined, and otherwise
taking on the responsibility of keeping the festival cheerful
and lively. She seemed to be of the household, and this idea
was confirmed as I saw her turn towards Rivka and reach
out to take the prayer book from her, not rudely, but with a
few quiet words. Stammering an apology, Rivka reacted too
quickly, letting go of the book before the other woman had
grasped it, so that it fell to the floor. Unexpectedly, an old
photograph slipped from between the pages and lay face up
on the ground, where the three of us stood staring down at
it in surprise.

The picture showed a vigorous couple in the prime of
life, of which the man was clearly recognisable to me as the
rabbi himself, although he was much younger, probably in his
middle thirties. Between them stood a group of four children.
The tallest one was a girl of about sixteen; a medium-sized boy
was on her left and a smaller one on her right, and she held a
little girl of about three in her arms. With her pale colouring
and fair hair, her strangely slender, dreamy face, she stood out
in the photograph almost like a being of another world. It was
difficult to concentrate on any face but hers. I stared at her,
fascinated. It seemed to me that she reminded me strongly of
someone; another face I had seen somewhere, that had that
slender line, that strange fixed gaze.

The woman who had spoken to Rivka, a heavy, dark and
somewhat worn-out looking creature between forty and fifty
years of age, looked more surprised than any of us; bending

down, she retrieved the picture and held it to her face, inspecting it closely.

'That is the rabbi,' I said in English, identifying him with a forefinger, and hoping she would not take the gesture as offensive prying. She nodded in answer.

'*Die kleyne bin ich*,' she added, planting her own finger on the littlest child, who wore her hair in a dark cask framing her heart-shaped face.

'She says that the little one is herself,' Rivka translated. 'The prayer book is her mother's. We shouldn't have touched it. No one uses it but her mother. We ought to put it back,' she added, picking it up from where it lay at her feet.

'These are your brothers and sisters?' I asked the lady, reluctant to interrupt what appeared to be a moment of discovery.

'Yes,' she answered in hesitant, broken English. 'Two brothers; here.' She pointed vaguely towards the outer room, then, turning towards Rivka, she suddenly burst into a short speech in Yiddish, as though she wished to disburden herself of an anxiety which was exerting some irresistible inner pressure upon her. Several times I caught the word *schwester*, like the German word for sister, and I waited impatiently for Rivka to provide me with a translation.

Suddenly she started and stopped speaking. Rivka also looked up guiltily.

'The *rebbetzin*!' she said.

The shadow of the elderly rabbi's wife fell upon us as she approached. At the sight of the book and the picture, a look of fear came over her features. Snatching both with a word of anxious reproach, she thrust the picture out of sight and hurried out of the room, looking badly upset. Her daughter followed her hastily.

'What was she telling you?' I asked Rivka quickly.

'She said she had never seen a picture of her eldest sister before, that she hardly remembers her; she has only a few memories of her up till the time she was about five years old. Then her sister seems to have disappeared. She told me that if it were not for the fact that her two older brothers have much more precise memories than hers, she would hardly be convinced that the beautiful princess she remembers admiring really existed elsewhere than in her dreams. The parents never, ever mentioned the girl after her disappearance; not even one single time, and this lady never dared ask them. She did talk about it with her brothers, but more and more rarely; it seems to have ended up turning into some kind of dread family secret. She seemed deeply moved that her mother had kept a picture of the lost daughter for all these years, even though she never spoke of her.'

'Perhaps the girl died suddenly, and the parents could not bear to think about it,' I said.

'That is impossible. There are burial and mourning ceremonies and prayers for a dead child. And it is a *mitzvah*, a good deed, to recall her memory lovingly.'

'But then what could possibly have happened, to make parents behave that way?' I mused.

She hesitated. 'It's not easy to imagine what a girl can have done to deserve such treatment. But…there is something like that in a book I read, a novel in Yiddish which is much loved by the people here,' she said. 'It is a story by Sholem Aleykhem, and it tells about a poor milkman with many daughters, and each of them gets married, one by one.'

'A Yiddish version of *Pride and Prejudice*,' I observed.

'In a way,' she responded, smiling. 'But so different! Every marriage contains a heartbreak. And the father ends up treating one of his daughters exactly like the rebbe and his wife. He says: once and for all, she doesn't exist any longer.'

'But why? Why?'

'Because she marries a Gentile.'

Shylock's cry of despair—*O my daughter! Fled with a Christian!*

'And in the story,' Rivka went on, 'he never mentions her again, and forbids his wife and children to mention her, and never goes to see her even though she lives very nearby.'

'That seems heartless,' I said.

'No—it is terrible for him—like a wound every time he thinks of her, like a death for which one cannot mourn because it is always fresh and never finished. But he cannot bear the marriage. His religion, his faith, his God, his whole life would lose their meaning, and all the suffering, all the persecutions and misery and poverty and injustice that he and all the Jews have had to bear just for *being* Jews. If you no longer care about preserving it, then where is the meaning of it all? Even modern Jews like Amy's parents would suffer if she were to marry a Gentile. As for a rebbe like this one—I think it would be death to him.'

'You really think the girl in the picture married a Gentile?'

'No, I don't think anything, I am just imagining and guessing. But you know, it could be. It is not so terribly unlikely; it does happen. And it is difficult to imagine any other reason for such a reaction.'

'Suppose she had a…an illicit love of some kind?'

'With a Jewish man? If he were not already married, the whole community would force them to marry. But then the father would not cut her off. All marriages are arranged within this community; such a marriage would be not be worse than any other. If the man was already married, the daughter would probably be shut up at home until a new marriage could be arranged, probably with some horrible old widower who wouldn't care. Those are grave sins, but they are not unforgivable; they are part of the human condition.'

'Suppose she converted to Christianity?' I asked.

'Then the father would probably react the way he did! But what Jewish girl would convert to Christianity for any reason other than love?'

'Does the girl in the picture remind you of anyone?' I asked her suddenly, feeling a little spurt of suspicion that there might be some connection between the rabbi's family and the Rubinstein or Gad families. Britta Rubinstein? No, the mother of a young girl like Rivka would not be old enough to be the girl in the picture, who, if she were still alive, would have to be nearly sixty.

'Not particularly. Does she remind *you* of someone?' she countered. I looked at her sharply, but her natural expression of surprised interest was convincing.

'Yes, she does,' I answered honestly, 'but I can't remember who it is. I have become sensitive to such resemblances. I feel that I saw a face like hers recently somewhere; very recently. If only I could think who it might be! You are sure that her face recalls nothing to you?'

'Nothing at all,' she said. 'It is a shame. It would have been exciting to be able to help you.'

'But you have been helping me a great deal,' I replied. She didn't answer, and in the brief moment of silence, I noticed that no more sound was coming from the other side of the curtain, and hastened back to it.

'The play is over,' I said, peering through a gap. There were still several men milling about, but most of them seemed to be the rabbi's disciples, easily recognisable by their black garb, and their hats and fringes and long side-curls. David and a few other guests stood out in their more ordinary clothing, the more so as the disciples did not mingle with them at all.

One of them began a song, and the others soon picked it up. It grew and swelled into a loud, tuneful and rhythmic chant, containing only one word, repeated over and over.

'What are they saying?' I asked Rivka.

'*Rebbenu*,' she answered smiling. 'It means "our rebbe".'

'*Rebbenu, rebbenu, oy rebbenu-u-u-u-u,*' sang and chanted the group of disciples, more and more loudly, and they surrounded the rebbe, still sitting tranquilly in his armchair, and danced around him in increasingly wild circles as they sang, swaying and flinging their arms about.

> '*Oy, oy, rebbenu, oy, oy, rebbenu— Rebbenu-u-u-u-u-u-u—u-u.*'

I watched in fascination as they became more and more uncontrolled; many were dancing with their eyes closed, their faces upturned towards Heaven. Several of the women and girls on our side of the curtain took up the chant, albeit more softly, but they too lost themselves in the joy of it and swayed back and forth freely as they sang. The melody was an easy one and before long, to my own surprise, I found myself singing along, abandoning myself to its invincible attraction. The wildness of it swirled through the room, snatching up the guests one after the other; it seemed that no one could escape it.

> '*Rebbenu, rebbenu, oy, oy, rebbenu,*
> *Oy, oy, rebbenu, rebbenu, rebbenu,*
> *Rebbenu-u-u-u-u-u-u—u-u.*'

On and on it went. As though in a trance, I melted completely into the collective spirit of it, totally forgetting about my mission and my reason for being there; I believe I might have remained singing and swaying with the others until evening. But my melodic reverie was broken quite suddenly by a hand seizing my sleeve and giving it a vigorous tug.

I opened my eyes, startled. It was little Ephraim, mandated by his brother, who was eagerly pulling me by the arm.

'David says—now or never!' he whispered dramatically.

A powerful wave of nerves washed over me as the memory of my task returned. I felt as though I were about to step on a stage. Worse, in fact, for at least the actress about to perform her role has rehearsed it thoroughly and benefited from the counsel and advice of the theatre director, and even more importantly, she will play for a house full of people who are expecting to see that very performance, and at least a portion hope to like it. Whereas I, with only the most summary preparation, was about to infringe every rule of the household in which I found myself. Deep in my mind, I repeated to myself a little phrase which has reassured me many times in similar situations.

After all—what is the worst thing which can possibly happen?

To be summarily ejected by the disciples with the sidelocks and flung rudely out upon the pavement, I concluded quickly. Horrid, but I would survive it. I yielded to Ephraim's hot little hand and, lifting my chin under the golden veil, I emerged from behind the curtain, thinking of Esther, and trying to look both humble and courageous. Upon my appearance, the song stuttered to a halt.

In spite of the gauze veil which entirely covered my head, the flowing black robe, and the silk shawl which wrapped my shoulders, all of which together allowed no hint of impropriety, I perceived immediate shock and, let me own it, horror and even disgust painted upon all the masculine faces in the room, as I stepped out amongst them. I resisted the urge to flee or hide and, approaching the rabbi, I stood facing him. He alone accepted the fact of my arrival without changing expression, but he did avert his eyes from my face.

So did all the others, but they did not stop there. There was a general rustle of movement towards me, and various angry, half-whispered orders and probably insults were flung in my direction. I ignored it (or pretended to), and spoke clearly and steadily the words David had taught me.

'If I perish, I perish.'

And to complete the illusion of Esther, I knelt in a queenly fashion and tried to look supplicatingly at the rabbi without staring.

The disciples stopped rustling and looked at their master for a clue to his response. They all had turned away their eyes and even their heads to avoid the sight of me, yet I felt their attention fixed inimically upon me. The few children still trailing in the room grouped silently in a corner or disappeared behind the curtain to watch the strange events from a safer nook. Suddenly, for the first time since I had arrived, I heard the rabbi's voice.

'Let the Gentile woman rise and speak,' he said, in the careful, heavily accented yet perfectly comprehensible English of people who have studied the language in books in a foreign land, but never spoken it in its native country.

I felt a little twinge of something irritating, almost humiliating, in his immediate identification of my modest self as an outsider. How could he tell? After all, Amy, for instance, would have spoken exactly as I had, and surely he would not have referred to her as a 'Gentile'. Did I radiate in some particular manner—or on the contrary, did I *not* radiate in some way undetectable to my inexperienced sensitivity? It was, I must admit it, annoying.

However, the main thing was that he had invited me to

speak. Seeing that the disciples were now all fixed in various attitudes of studied absence, albeit they were still listening closely, I stood up, and swaying very slightly like the storytellers I had seen at work earlier, I began my tale.

'I am here to tell you the tale of a powerful rabbi and a young man in danger,' I said, pronouncing the words slowly and distinctly, and then I waited until complete silence reigned.

'Long ago, there was an evil man who lived locked inside a heavy stone castle working black magic. This man hated Jews above all other peoples and ceaselessly worked for their disgrace and death.'

Stopping for the merest second after this introduction, I gave a tiny glance about me. A few of the children had edged forward, others had lost interest; clearly not everyone in the room understood much English. I continued to speak, even more slowly and clearly than before.

'At the same time, in a different part of the same large town, lived a respected and powerful rabbi. This rabbi was beloved and surrounded by family and disciples who listened to his every word and never left his side. He had important, influential friends in many countries who sent him letters. He heard of every event in the world concerning Jews, of all that they had to endure in each country, of every scandal perpetrated against individuals or entire villages or cities, every accusation, every murder, every pogrom. He suffered from these things and surrounded himself with holiness in order that at least one spot in the world should remain pure.

'One day, the rabbi received a letter from another rabbi, a very important rabbi, who lived in a large country across the sea. The rabbi spoke of the horrendous trial of a Jew who had been condemned to spend the rest of his life on an island in the sea no bigger than a large rock. The man was innocent and many people tried to save him; not only Jews, but righteous men of all nations and religions. Yet many other people worked against him, desiring to keep him imprisoned forever on his island. The man had become the symbol of all Jews, polarising and dividing the populations. Father quarrelled with son, brother with sister, friend with friend.'

I glanced around me surreptitiously. By now, everyone in the room was listening raptly.

'Among those who worked particularly hard to poison the mind of the populace against the innocent man was the evil magician who lived in the stone castle. This is what the rabbi from across the sea wrote to the rabbi who lived in the large city, and he asked him if there was anything he could do to stop the evil magician from preventing the rescue of the innocent victim from his terrible fate.

'The rabbi normally never left his home, which was one of the few spots of stainless purity on the face of the earth. Yet, pondering over the letter, he saw that he could, perhaps, wield some influence, because of his extraordinary knowledge and power. He saw that it would be possible for him to confront the evil magician, face-to-face, and perhaps cause him to see the error of his ways. He saw that this would be a *mitzvah*.

'Saying nothing to anyone, the rabbi, one day, quietly disappeared from the house and the *shul* where he spent all of his time. His disciples missed him, his family missed him, but all day they did nothing. They did not search for him, because they knew that he was a saintly man and whatever his business was, it was high above their comprehension. So completely did they believe in their rabbi that they had no fear at all and were quite ready to believe that he had gone to visit Heaven, which indeed, was in some sense not so far from the truth.

'The rabbi made his way to the evil magician's stone castle. I cannot tell you what happened inside that castle, because nobody knows, nobody except for the rabbi himself. It is a great mystery. The rabbi departed, his work complete, and returned quietly home, where he took up his usual life.

'As it is, on his way out of the castle, he had passed a young Jewish man who was going in. This young man entered the castle and—he found the evil magician lying on the floor, dead! Secretly, deep in his heart, in spite of the horror and distress of the discovery, the young man felt a stab of joy, because he was well aware, in his own flesh, of the hatred that the evil magician had for all Jews, and the infinite harm he had done them.

'However, the young man was not alone to discover the dead magician. His servants arrived, and they called in the— the soldiers.' (This was a sudden improvisation; I preferred to refer to servants and soldiers rather than witnesses and policemen.) 'The soldiers arrested the young man and took him away. They threw him in a dungeon and accused him of murdering the magician. He shouted his innocence, but no one believed him, because the servants had found him alone in the room with the dead magician. A date was fixed for his trial, though in fact, the outcome was already clear to everyone. It was obvious that the young man would be condemned and executed.'

I paused to let a little tension gather.

'Only the young man knew that the rabbi had been with the magician before he came, because he had seen him leaving. He knew the rabbi, from a distance, and was filled with love and respect for him, and it never occurred to him even for a single moment to imagine that the rabbi might have killed the magician himself. Nor did he think even for one second about mentioning the rabbi. His greatest care was to protect the rabbi from the horrors of a trial like the one he himself was about to undergo, like the one which had condemned that other innocent Jew to spend the rest of his life on a deserted rock. So he said nothing.'

A longer pause.

'The trial was fixed to begin at *ten o'clock in the morning* of a certain day. *Ten o'clock in the morning*. The day approached, yet the mystery remained complete, at least to the friends of the young man, who were convinced of his innocence, if not to the soldiers who arrested him, or to the judges who were already prepared to convict and hang him. Finally, as no clue appeared nor anything which could reveal the truth, *on the very day before the trial was to begin*, a lady who wished to aid the young man went to see the rabbi and ask for his help. The rabbi should help as he saw fit; he knew better than anyone else what the truth was, and what it would be best to do. It was enough for her to relate the whole story to the rabbi. The rabbi was a holy man and would not leave an innocent Jew to be condemned.'

I stopped speaking. It was not quite the end of my story, but I desired some kind of response. For a long moment, none came, only total silence. I was just about to speak again, when the rabbi lifted his head and looked up at me. His piercing eyes met mine for the briefest moment.

'Where did the trial take place?' he asked quietly.

'In a grand courtroom, the grandest in the city,' I replied quickly. 'It was a great heavy building of grey stone, with thick and frightening walls, closer to a prison than a castle. Austere, forbidding, dangerous. It was in a street in the middle of the city, a curved street in the form of a *bow. Bow Street*.'

Again I stopped. This time I was helped by Ephraim, who took the entire story literally, and was eager to hear the end.

'Did the rabbi go there?' he asked when he couldn't bear the silence any longer, which was after but a very short time.

It was now up to me to predict the future. I did so firmly.

'The rabbi went, and there he told the secret which he alone knew, which cleared up the entire mystery, and the young man was saved. I wish I could tell you what the rabbi said, but I cannot. It is hidden behind a veil which the rabbi alone has the power to rend. The rabbi went there, and then he returned home, and his disciples said that he had surely visited Heaven during the morning. Which was indeed not so very far from the truth.'

My tale was over. I had delivered my message, and it must have been unmistakable. It was up to the rabbi to act now. Almost to my own surprise, I no longer felt the urgent desire to obtain some admission or some explanation from him at once. Under the influence of his personality, I felt no desire to press or insist, but only to wait; I was filled with a quiet certainty that he would not fail us. Making a deep and graceful reverence, I trailed as regally as I could to the back of the room behind the curtain. Rivka seized my hand joyfully.

'That was wonderful,' she whispered. 'He surely understood. I wonder what he will do. Will he speak to us? We had better not leave yet.'

We did not leave; the four of us remained in the rabbi's house until the very end of the festival. Finally, the other guests from outside were all gone, there were no more songs or plays, and the smell of dinner began to waft through the front room. A couple of the young disciples took down the curtain and began to move the furniture which had been pushed to the walls back to its place, and to prepare the table and chairs for the evening meal. The rabbi heaved himself out of his armchair. 'We must go,' said David, pulling us towards the street door. I followed him, yet could not resist casting one look backwards. The rabbi bid us goodbye with a small movement of his hand and a little nod. Did I imagine it, or did that nod mean something special, something addressed to me alone?

Outside, the dusk had fallen, and although a few disguises and musicians were still to be seen, almost everyone had gone indoors by now and few traces of the morning's chaotic and joyful carnival remained. The dim light, the dirty pavement were depressing. I felt as if I were standing at a crossroads between two worlds. The whole of the afternoon I had just lived through seemed unreal, and my tranquil confidence ebbed away rapidly, leaving a residue of dissatisfaction and worry at the thought that I had, after all, learnt and accomplished nothing.

Rivka did not feel any of this. 'He understood you, I know he did,' she insisted enthusiastically. 'If he didn't speak today, it just means that we have to wait until tomorrow morning. I am not so afraid any more, now that I have seen what you are able to do. I can hardly believe that you managed to speak to the rebbe for so long! What outsider could ever have managed that!'

'It was perfect,' agreed David as we took the direction of their home. 'You couldn't have done it better. Our plan was brilliant. Come along with us now—you shall put your own dress back on and have some more *Hummentaschen* and some dinner. I suppose you will go to Court tomorrow?'

'Certainly,' I said. 'I hope that the rabbi will come, I hope so with all my heart. But to be honest, I am maddened by the idea that I have now seen and spoken with the rabbi, yet do not know anything more than what I knew before. There is still a missing piece to this puzzle! Perhaps we shall learn it tomorrow morning, and perhaps not. Yet we hold so many of the threads in our hands already. We ought to be able to understand what happened by ourselves at this point! What is the matter with us? Why can't we solve this problem?'

'It is true that we still don't know the most important thing of all: what did the rebbe see and do in the library?' said David thoughtfully. 'Yet we cannot say that we know nothing more than we did yesterday. At least now we know why Reb Avrom went there.'

'But do we?' I said.

'Of course!' he replied in surprise. 'It was in that telegram you received this morning.'

'Well then, tell me why he went?'

'Because he received a letter from the chief rabbi of France asking him to. Isn't that what you told us?'

'Yes, I did, but I don't consider that it explains much. What did he think he could accomplish? What did he mean to do there? What could he *say* to Professor Ralston? The rabbi is a man who reflects deeply about what he does. He wouldn't just dash off and try to convince him to stop being anti-Semitic. It's perfectly obvious that that would have no chance of working. If anything, it would just enrage the Professor even more. What did the rabbi go there to say?'

'I see what you mean,' admitted David after a moment's reflection. 'I'm trying to imagine what he might have thought he could do, and I realise that I have no idea. In fact, now that you mention it, what could anyone possibly say, to try to stop a man like Ralston? There's no way to silence that kind of person short of killing him—oh! No, I didn't mean that.' He stopped, embarrassed. There was a rather long silence.

'We learnt another little fact,' said Rivka meekly. 'Maybe this has nothing to do with anything, but we learnt that the rabbi had a daughter who disappeared.'

'Really?' put in Ephraim, interested by this revelation of something more dramatic than the rest of the day's fare had been. 'Disappeared? How? When?'

Rivka told him about the finding of the photograph and the comments of the rabbi's other daughter.

'Oh,' he said with some disappointment. 'You mean she disappeared a hundred years ago. No point looking for a corpse, then.'

'Not a hundred. More like forty or forty-five,' I said. 'I wonder where she is now?'

'Didn't you say her picture reminded you of someone?' said Rivka. 'Perhaps you have actually met her, and you don't realise it. Who could she be?'

I ran all the elderly ladies I could think of that had any connection with the case through my mind, unsuccessfully. Mrs Bryant? I had never met her, and besides, she was certainly too young. Mrs Taylor? No, she really did not look at all like the girl in the picture, nor did Mrs Hudson. Had I met anyone else? I could not think of anyone. Yet that face...

'Oh, this is awful,' I moaned. 'I ought to know! That makes two different mysteries surrounding the rabbi. What we have to do is find the link between them.'

London, Friday, March 20th, 1896

The gavel banged on the magistrate's desk and the proceedings were opened.

I, as a member of the public with no official status of any kind, sat upright in my gallery seat, stiff with anxiety, staring at the door, wondering whether the rabbi would come, and trying, unceasingly and desperately, to find the key which would simultaneously solve all the questions which still eluded me.

I had returned home last night so weary that it was difficult even to concentrate on answering all of Emily's eager questions, the more so as I clearly perceived that my replies and my continuing ignorance disappointed her. I left her as soon as I could and flung myself into bed, too tense, too overexcited, too deeply troubled to sleep. I had cast my line, but I couldn't know if it would bring up any fish. There was nothing more I could do now, except hope and wait and think. I was overwhelmed with nerves and unable to settle my mind to any one train of thought. I tossed and turned on the narrow sofa, and the events of the day ran over and over, obsessionally, through my brain. Over dinner, Rivka had told me the story of Chava, Tevye's daughter, and how she chose to leave her father's house, abandoning her past in order to marry the Russian boy Fedka who had captured her heart. According to Rivka, the story dealt essentially with Tevye's heartbreak, and the unbearable pain of being torn between the religion that was his whole life and the daughter who was still, to him, the precious treasure he held, consoled and rocked in his arms as a baby.

I drifted to sleep, and baby Chava became baby Cecily in my dreams. I felt her presence so close to me that I was warmed by her firm little body. I reached to plant a kiss on her round cheek, and encountered only emptiness. I jumped awake in a shock of dismay and found myself alone in the unfamiliar bed. No tender little girl, just the empty darkness.

I fell asleep again, and Chava returned to my dreams, no longer as little Cecily, but now inextricably identified with the young girl in the picture at the rabbi's house. I seemed to see her living in her village, going out of her house, perhaps, to draw water or tend geese or run errands, meeting a young man from a place so near and yet so far, falling in love, and turning away forever; yet looking back at her father, perhaps, like Chava, with tragedy in her eyes.

Then it seemed to me that she died, but it was not really death; her living body turned into a photograph, she became the photograph. I stared at her features, stared at them; the rest of the picture, the people grouped around her, became blurred, and only her face stood out. The features shifted slightly, and her face became another face: Professor Ralston, also dead, looking out of another photograph, also surrounded by a group of indistinct people.

The Library Paradox

Again and again, through the course of the night, I dreamt the same thing. The young girl's face in the photograph melted away and became that of Professor Ralston. I was exhausted by the time I awoke, and relieved to see that it was already light outside. My bed had become a place of torment and I desired only to leave it. A glimpse of my dream came back to me briefly, but I chased it away like a cobweb. It made me shiver; it felt strangely abnormal, like the delusions of fever.

I washed and dressed quickly. Emily was already up and preparing tea.

'Of course I'm coming with you,' she said quickly, as soon as she saw me. Why was she coming, I wondered. What did she feel? Was it curiosity? Friendship? Was it something more? But I was too preoccupied to probe, and merely nodded.

We were silent as we made our way through the streets toward Covent Garden in the morning freshness. My mind was on the events of yesterday and those to come this morning, and I tried to force myself to concentrate, feeling that this was my final chance to fit the scattered pieces together into a coherent whole. Yet my eyes could not help straying to my surroundings, and noticing the tiny leaves beginning to bud on the bare branches of the trees. I felt something like that inside my own head: exactly such a little, budding thought seemed to be trying to push its way up through the confusion in my brain, with the stunning tenacity of a little green shoot trying to break the surface of the hardened ground. I speeded up my steps nervously, dragging Emily along pitilessly, and wishing that I could stop asking myself a thousand times whether the rabbi would or would not come.

I would not have thought that the case was sufficiently interesting to attract much of an audience—after all, one comes before the magistrate merely to determine whether or not there is enough evidence to send one to trial—but a medium-sized cluster of people had already gathered at the door and was beginning to edge its way inside. I suppose there are always spectators available for this kind of thing.

Emily and I took places in the public gallery. We soon saw Jonathan, entering with his solicitor, a distinguished gentleman quite unknown to me, probably an expensive expert hired by his parents, whom I took to be the handsome and well-dressed couple I saw flanking Amy, sitting some distance away. I observed their faces with great interest. None of them noticed me in the least; all three were staring intently at the scene below.

The magistrate looked distant and pained. The prosecutor was a personage so pointed, so severe, so glaring and so inimical as to cause my spine to prickle: no leniency, no tolerant broad-mindedness was to be expected here. Repressing my distaste, I leaned over to a lady sitting near me and asked her if she knew who he was.

'That's Mr Andrews, a Scotsman,' she replied with the knowledgeable air of a familiar of the place. 'And it's Sir Morris Hirsch for the defence! Well, he would defend this case, wouldn't he?' She sat back, laughing unpleasantly.

I turned away from her, and set to observing the witnesses for the prosecution, grouped together below. To my surprise, I recognised Mr Upp. Sitting next to him was a bony gentleman with a domed forehead, greying hair and unhappy eyes. I guessed that this must be Professor Ralston's father, finally arrived from overseas, and felt acutely sorry for what he must be going through. The rabbi was nowhere to be seen, although I searched for him anxiously and ceaselessly until the gavel banged, and proceedings commenced.

The Prosecution began by calling as a witness the doctor

who had attended the corpse. He described the exact nature of the victim's death, following instantaneously from a gunshot wound to the heart. Mr Andrews then called the police inspector who had been summoned to the scene, who gave a complete description of the state of the room at the time, which corresponded in every way to what I had myself observed. The magistrate was interested above all in the position of the murder weapon.

'The weapon was undoubtedly Professor Ralston's property?' he asked, even though this piece of information had only just been stated as fact.

'It was, my Lord, and I will presently have a witness who will attest to the fact,' replied Mr Andrews.

'And it was found lying, you say, near the doorway of the Professor's study?'

'Yes, my Lord,' replied Mr Andrews. 'Just about a yard inside of the door. The desk, tipped over, stood about two yards from the door and the Professor's body had fallen behind it.'

'So you assume that the criminal, standing on the other side of the desk from the Professor, snatched the Professor's gun from him and shot him—'

'—at close range, my Lord—'

'—at close range, then turned to flee, dropping the gun.'

'Yes, my Lord.'

'Very well,' said the magistrate. 'Let us have the next witness.'

The next witness was Mrs Forbes, housekeeper of the murdered man. She spoke very little, asserting that she knew nothing, nothing at all. Yes, the gun was the Professor's, he kept it with him, usually in the same room, at all times, and occasionally, although not always, took it out with him. Yes, the Professor thought he had a lot of enemies, and by the look of it, he was not wrong. No, she did not see how it could be something to do with his personal life. As far as she knew, his personal life was of the simplest. No, he kept neither letters nor papers in his house; everything was kept in his study below, which needed no more cleaning than an occasional sweeping and dusting. The door leading from his study upstairs to his rooms locked automatically when it closed. The Professor opened it with his key when he wanted to go upstairs. He did not mind the automatic locking, quite the contrary. He disliked the idea that if he were out of his study for a minute and someone entered, they could slip upstairs to his rooms. The Professor thought it possible that this might happen; he had enemies, remember. No, she did not see how the murderer could have slipped upstairs to the Professor's rooms, since so far as she knew, there was only the one key that the Professor had, which was found in his pocket. And anyway, the police had searched upstairs directly upon their arrival. No, she herself did not have a key to the rooms. The Professor let her in when she arrived. If he was already down in his study, he let her in, and if he was upstairs, she knocked and he came down to open the door for her. No, she always came after the library was already opened. It was opened every day punctually at nine o'clock by the Professor himself.

Sir Morris Hirsch raised a new point during his cross-examination. Could someone have been in the Professor's lodgings upstairs before the shooting, slipped down and killed him, blocking the door open with some object, and then gone quickly back upstairs when the witnesses ran in? Yes, it would have been possible, except that how would the murderer have ever got away? Could he have been sitting on the roof the whole time? But he could hardly escape up the chimney, and the windows didn't open. How did one air the rooms? Well, the windows had tiny sections at the top which one lowered with a stick. But no, they were no higher than a hand's breadth. No, certainly no one could pass through them. He could not have got onto the roof.

Mr Andrews then called the detective inspector from Scotland Yard who was in charge of the case. I recognised him as the man who had arrested Jonathan. Quietly avoiding any mention of Bertrand Russell, journalists or newspaper articles, he explained how he had himself discovered the logical flaw in the perfect paradox with which the case had at first seemed to confront him.

'To begin with, you had not thought that the witness Mr Sachs was lying?'

'I had no particular reason to think so. In principle, when we begin work on cases, we assume that the witnesses are speaking the truth and try to confirm their statements. However, when confronted with an obvious contradiction, we are in the habit of making the hypothesis that any one of them may be lying. In this case, we delayed working on that assumption because the witness claimed to have a witness to his own statements, namely the Orthodox Jew he met on his way out. If we could have located and identified that individual, and if their stories agreed, it would have diminished or possibly even excluded the probability of the witness' statement being a lie. So we allowed ourselves a waiting period while searching for that person.'

'But you were unable to find him.'

'He had, seemingly, vanished into thin air. Or rather, not into the air, but back into that part of town where Jews come cheaper by the doz—where there are a great many foreign Jews and many people do not speak English, and even when they do they are most reluctant to aid the police in any way. The search began to appear hopeless, and I came to the decision that the possibility of the witness being a liar must be confronted. That was when we proceeded to an arrest. At that point, the Ralston family lawyer came to see me with a threatening letter directed against the murdered man, and I was able to discover almost immediately that the author of the threats was closely related to the man I had arrested.'

This information caused a stir in the public gallery, and a terrific stir in myself. So the police knew about Jonathan's relationship to the Gad family! Yes, of course they must. It was easy enough to establish a relationship once one had the idea that it might exist. I remembered my own search in the birth records for Rebecca Gad. I had started searching in her parents' marriage year of 1874. But if I had been more thorough—if I had taken the time to search for every child born to the married couples in my entire list of Gad spouses, I would soon have found Amy and Jonathan, born just a few years earlier, and realised the connection myself much sooner than I did. Of course, I had acted logically enough, but I had lacked the thoroughness that the police automatically bring to their research. It was a bad thing for Jonathan. They could easily construe a motive out of it. More distraught than ever, I looked around for the rabbi.

Ignoring the rustle of interest in his statement, Mr Andrews proceeded to call the next witnesses, who were successively Mr Mason, Mr Chapman, and the college caretaker who had accompanied them to the gate on the evening of the murder. All three told the same story; it was simple and straightforward and matched what we already knew in every particular. Before turning over Mr Mason for cross-examination, Mr Andrews said that there was one point which he greatly wished to elucidate.

'As you came running around the house and reached and turned the front corner, you saw the accused and called out to him?'

'Yes,' replied Mr Mason soberly.

'What did you say?'

'I said, "Someone's been shot!" and ran on inside.'

'Did you pay attention to whether the person you saw on the path came running after you?'

'Not at all. I didn't look back. However, I certainly assumed that he was following us, and he came rushing in barely a few moments later.'

'Now, Mr Mason, I wish you to answer the following question very carefully. When you saw the accused, what exactly was he doing?'

'Walking up the path,' said Mr Mason in surprise.

'You are sure of that.'

'Quite.'

'He could not, for example, have been walking *down* the path, away from the house, and have just turned around.'

Now he hesitated a little.

'I don't know. My impression was very certainly that he was walking up the path when I saw him. It never occurred to me that he might have been doing anything else.'

'How long would you say you actually had him in your vision?'

'That's hard to say. A very short time. A second, perhaps.'

'So it is impossible for you to say what he was doing, one or two seconds before you appeared around the corner of the house. In assuming that he was walking towards the house, you are projecting the image of what you saw, namely a man facing you, into the previous few seconds.'

'I suppose so,' said Mr Mason, confused.

Sir Morris Hirsch began his cross-examination by asking about this same detail. He made Mr Mason visualise the scene in his memory and describe exactly what he remembered. He made a great deal of the fact that Mr Mason believed he had seen Jonathan actually taking a step, and that his shoulders were not twisted, as they would have been if he had been turning, but full-face forwards. Sir Morris experimented by taking a few steps, turning on his heel rapidly and walking in the other direction, while the magistrate counted seconds.

'That is conclusive,' said Sir Morris Hirsch smugly. The result did not appear to me to be so convincing, nor so great a victory. He tried a similar tack with Mr Chapman, but Mr Chapman said only that his view was obstructed by Mr Mason as they ran, and he was only barely conscious in his haste and worry that someone else was present and Mr Mason had called out to him. He described in detail the manner in which he and Jonathan had both rushed out of the house and turned around it in different directions, meeting at the back a few moments after, and how he had then left Jonathan and gone for the police, locating and bringing back a constable on the beat just around the corner, who had then had other officers summoned. He asserted firmly that there was not a soul in view, front, back or side of the house, and that in a perfectly flat square garden containing not even a shrub, it would have been impossible for anyone to hide.

'Unless he was pressed against the wall on Mr Sachs' side of the house, and they were accomplices,' he said. It seemed unkind, but I think he said it more out of thoroughness than out of malice, particularly as he immediately added, 'But if that were the case, the person would have had to leave the premises by the front gate, and he did not, because Mason said he was standing looking out of the front door while I ran for the police. When I returned with the officer, we told him the murderer might still be on the premises, and made a complete search once again. There was no one.'

The caretaker's testimony proved beyond any shadow of a doubt that Mr Mason and Mr Chapman themselves could not have been personally involved with the shooting.

'Before calling my next witness,' said Mr Andrews, 'I would like to remark that according to the testimonies we have already heard, the accused stands in the dock as a consequence of the purest logic. According to the circumstances we have heard described, no other solution is possible. And pure logical reasoning is sufficient to prove our case. However, I am as firm a believer in the importance of establishing a motive and comprehending the origin of the crime as any member of the legal profession. And that is the purpose of my next witness. I would like to call Mr Abel Burton to the stand.'

I recognised the man at once. It was no other than the prison guard who had sat in the centre section of the visiting cage at Dartmoor, listening to my interview with Baruch Gad.

After asking for his name, age and profession, Mr Andrews proceeded to the point.

'You have heard conversations between the accused and a prisoner at your institution?' he asked.

'Yes.'

'How many such conversations have you heard?'

'The prisoner came every visiting day, that is, once every three months, for the last several years.'

'How many years?'

'I do not remember precisely, but certainly at least five if not somewhat more.'

'The prisoner has, in fact, been visiting the inmate at

Dartmoor regularly for six years,' Mr Andrews informed the magistrate, 'from the time he reached the age of sixteen.' Then, turning back to the guard, he asked, 'What is the relation between the accused and the inmate of Dartmoor?'

'I was informed by the Governor that the inmate, Baruch Gad, is uncle to the accused,' replied this gentleman, 'his mother's brother, to be precise, and that this relationship was the basis of his visiting rights.'

'I object,' said Jonathan's solicitor, rising suddenly. 'This is not direct evidence.'

'It can be directly confirmed,' said Mr Andrews quickly.

'Let it stand, subject to confirmation,' said the magistrate.

'What were the main subjects of conversation between the prisoner Gad and the accused?' asked Mr Andrews.

'They talked about the family; the accused told his uncle about his parents, his sister, his studies and his friends. And they talked frequently about a black dog.'

'A black dog?' the magistrate observed in surprise. 'What dog was that?'

'What did they say about the black dog?' asked Mr Andrews.

'The prisoner Gad used to ask his nephew where the black dog was; this dog was apparently lost or had disappeared and he wanted him to find him. That went on during the first few years. Then one day, one or two years ago, the nephew came and told his uncle he had found the black dog.'

'And what was the reaction of the prisoner Gad to this information?' said Mr Andrews.

'He was very excited. I never saw him react so strongly during the entire ten years I have known him. The prisoner is habitually a very quiet man, but that day he was beside himself.'

'And during the following visits, the accused gave his uncle regular news of the black dog?'

'Yes. He also spoke sometimes of the black dog's owner.'

'What did he say of the dog's owner?'

'As far as I can remember, in answer to his uncle's pressing questions, he told him the owner was a university professor teaching history in London.'

Mr Andrews suddenly changed his demeanour. Leaning forward, he lowered his voice and adopted a tone of meaningful significance.

'Did it ever occur to you that the black dog was not a dog, but a person?'

'I object!' said Sir Morris Hirsch, bounding to his feet. 'This is a leading question.'

'It is,' admitted the magistrate. 'Strike out the question and pose another.'

'Did you ever wonder why the prisoner cared so much about a black dog?' said Mr Andrews.

'No,' said the prison guard bluntly, with a slight shrug. 'The answer to the other question would have been no as well. I thought that the prisoner may have been deeply attached to this dog before going to prison, and still cling to his memory. Prisoners often do. I did wonder why the dog had no name.'

'And you never asked the prisoner about the black dog?'

'No. We listeners are discreet. We are obliged to overhear conversations to counteract any plot to escape or other criminal actions. But we try to keep our presence unnoticed. Those are the rules. The purpose is not merely politeness. In theory, if we are sufficiently discreet, the prisoner and his visitor may come to forget our presence, and we may pick up something important.'

'So,' said Mr Andrews, highly disappointed by this answer, and turning to the tactic of sarcasm, 'we are to understand that you never, for one moment, realised the obvious fact that the prisoner and the accused were fooling you, and using a simple, basic code to communicate fundamental information about an impending murder.'

'I object!' interjected Sir Morris Hirsch loudly, at the same time as the witness said, 'No, I never thought that.'

'But I claim it is the case,' said Mr Andrews firmly. 'I claim that the black dog referred to no other than Professor Gerard Ralston, the victim of murder. I claim that the prisoner Baruch Gad, whose nephew stands in the dock in front of us, planned the murder of Professor Gerard Ralston and had it executed by his nephew, the whole of the planning having taken place by the use of a simple code: referring to the Professor as a black dog and a few other key words. In order to justify my statements, I will ask this witness to stand down and call Mr Charles Upp to the stand.'

Mr Upp appeared. His brow was shiny; the role he was about to be compelled to play obviously went against the grain.

Mr Andrews began by asking questions to establish the fact that Mr Upp had received, from the judge at the trial of Baruch Gad, a letter addressed to him by the condemned man. The letter, the same one I had seen and written down from memory in my notebook, was brought out and read. A gasp ran around the assembled personages. Mr Andrews then proceeded to elicit from Mr Upp the story of his decision to take the letter to the police. I was at first surprised to learn that he had done it after all, but soon understood that he had been impelled to this action by the news of Jonathan's arrest, which had made it impossible for him to continue to doubt that the letter was relevant. He was then asked to explain the reference to the anonymous witness, and to identify him. His description of the Gad trial caused rustling and whispering in the Court.

The Library Paradox

'So Mr Jonathan Sachs became aware, a year or two ago, that the anonymous witness his uncle wished him to locate and identify, the very man who had testified against both of his uncles during their trial and had been instrumental in causing a conviction, was none other than the deceased Professor Ralston. Does it not seem clear that his uncle, in his bitterness and frustration at his own inability to act due to his incarceration, proceeded to push the young man to accomplish the second part of his vengeful project: murder, as he had already accomplished the first: identification?' concluded the prosecutor triumphantly.

It certainly did not constitute a proof, but then, no proof was needed; in order to send Jonathan to trial, it was only necessary to establish sufficient evidence. Even motive is but a cherry on the cake. The magistrate's face was serious. He enquired courteously but doubtfully if Sir Morris Hirsch wished to call any witnesses for the defence.

It seemed to me to be out of the question for Sir Morris Hirsch to call any witness; not Jonathan himself, nor any member of his family, nor any colleague of Professor Ralston. For under Mr Andrews' cross-examination, it would be impossible to avoid bringing forth the facts of Professor Ralston's raging anti-Semitism, and confirming Jonathan's close attachment to his uncle, its victim, and his discovery of Ralston's identity as the famous witness. All of this, it seemed to me, could only worsen the case against him. The situation appeared desperate. For the fiftieth time, I strained my attention towards the entrance to the courtroom, imagining that I heard some sound, some sign of the rabbi's sudden arrival. Yet I jumped in surprise when the door behind the magistrate's seat opened from without, and a note was delivered to him. Emily seized my hand.

'Did you see that? What do you think it means? Has he come?'

'It could be anything,' I said. 'It might not even have anything to do with the case. But it could be the rabbi—it could be that he has arrived and wishes to present evidence. Emily, if only it were so!'

Rising, the magistrate announced a ten-minute recess. Everyone relaxed momentarily as he rose and exited, calling Sir Morris Hirsch to join him. My heart leapt. Could it be? Were we, finally, about to understand?

Amy had seen me, and was making her way towards me, her face filled with anxious and bitter dismay.

'Vanessa, it is going as badly as it possibly could. Is there nothing you can do?' she said accusingly. I felt that I had failed her indeed. Yet all was not lost—if only…

'We succeeded in seeing the rabbi yesterday,' I told her quickly, 'and I believe I managed to make him understand the situation. He did not tell me anything, but we hope that he will come here to testify. Perhaps it is his arrival which has caused this interruption.'

'Do you think so?' Her eyes lit up momentarily, then darkened again. 'But will it be enough? What if he simply says that he talked with the Professor for a while, then left, noticing nothing. It would probably be the truth—people like him are in the clouds. Oh, Vanessa, what we need is to understand who murdered that monster!' She looked at me pleadingly, and I felt a little stab of guilt. Why, why was this problem proving so intractable? Why was I unable to solve it? Her gaze, fixed upon me, startled me. Suddenly and for no discernible reason, a little snatch of my dream came back to me; I remembered those two other pairs of eyes, from the two photographs, who persisted in confounding and identifying themselves. I tried to put the image aside.

'Rubbish,' I murmured to myself. 'And yet…'

'What did you say?' said Emily politely.

The Library Paradox

The sensation of revelation, like a wave, was so incredibly strong in me that I felt as though I should faint. I leaned backward in my seat and closed my eyes for a moment, remembering, visualising. Surely, surely dreams are the word of God.

'The girl in the picture looks exactly like Gerard Ralston,' I said. 'I realise it now; they have the same face, the same eyes, the same fanatic look. They are too similar—she was or is related to him. Who can she be?'

'What girl are you talking about?' said Amy.

'A girl in an old photograph we saw yesterday at the Purim festival in the rabbi's house,' I explained. 'It was a picture of the rabbi himself, but much younger, and his children. One of them was a girl of about sixteen. It is she whose face reminds me of the photograph of Professor Ralston that I saw at Professor Taylor's house.'

'Vanessa, are you sure? Can it be possible?' Emily was saying, pressing her hands to her forehead in order to concentrate. 'So there *is* a connection between the rabbi and the Professor.' She paused for a moment, thinking as always in terms of numbers. 'Listen, how old do you think that girl would be today?'

'Let me try to be as precise as I can,' I said, calculating quickly. 'The trouble is that I have to guess all the ages. The woman who showed us the photograph yesterday is probably between forty and fifty. Let us say forty-five—and she was about three in the picture. So it would have been taken forty-two or -three years ago. That corresponds more or less with the father's age, I think. He must be practically eighty now, and he looked in his mid-thirties in the picture. The girl in the picture looked about sixteen, so that would mean she would be nearing sixty now.'

'Nearing sixty… and how old was Professor Ralston?'

'He was forty. Emily—she could be his mother. She could.

It is possible, indeed, it must be so! I remember now that Professor Taylor told me that his father married a girl from "over there", where he travelled for his research, and all this time, I have been assuming that he married a Frenchwoman, because of Professor Ralston's knowledge of French. But he studied both French and Polish history! He must have married a *Polish* girl! Emily, *the rabbi was the Professor's father-in-law*. I feel as certain of it as though I had always known it! His daughter was Ralston's mother. Rivka told me that she must have married a Gentile to have been rejected from her father's family. And she died when her little boy was only five or six.'

'Vanessa,' said Amy slowly, 'what you're saying is perfectly impossible.'

'Why?'

'Because obviously, if the Professor's mother had been Jewish, he could not have hated the Jews so. In fact, he would have been a Jew himself. Judaism passes through the mother only.'

'But perhaps she converted, and the child never knew that she was Jewish,' said Emily. 'She must have converted in order to marry the father, and they came to live in this country, and she died when the child was small. Perhaps she never told him a word about her origins.'

'That seems likely,' I agreed. 'Perhaps she resolved to forget them just as her father resolved to forget her. And the rabbi only came to England himself a few years ago. If he knew that his daughter was long dead, or even if he didn't know, I can well imagine that he would make no effort to contact her Christian family.'

'It is still hard to believe,' said Amy slowly. 'Even if he didn't know it, still, of all people, why should the son of a Jewish woman become so rabidly anti-Semitic?'

'I don't know. I have wondered what made him become

so,' I said. 'But listen: this may explain why the rabbi went to see the Professor!'

'He went because the chief rabbi of France asked him to intervene, didn't he?' said Emily.

'Yes, I know that. But up to now I couldn't understand what he could have hoped to actually *tell* the Professor, which could have any hope of persuading him to stop his activities. But now I can imagine that when the other rabbi asked him to try and stop the Professor from his anti-Semitic activities, our rabbi decided to talk to him about the fact that his mother was Jewish. If, as we imagine, Professor Ralston had no idea about that, it would be a powerful argument to change his attitude. Surely he would be obliged to feel differently after learning *that*—otherwise all that enmity would come down to hating himself!'

'Jews know how to do that well enough,' said Amy softly. I remembered thinking the same thing, while reading the novel she had given me. But Emily was speeding forward with her reasoning.

'So let us accept the hypothesis that the rabbi went to tell Professor Ralston that his mother was Jewish. And perhaps the Professor became so angry at the news that he took out his gun to attack the rabbi in a fit of rage, and there was a fight and the rabbi snatched the gun—' She stopped suddenly as she noticed Amy glaring at her.

'That explanation is unlikely,' I said. 'First of all, even if the rabbi lost his temper or resorted to self-defence, it is hard to believe he would have quietly walked away afterwards. And Professor Ralston was only forty, while the rabbi is twice that. How could he have had the strength to wrest the gun away? But above all, how could he have reached the street gate so soon after the shot? We cannot get away from that difficulty. It's the thing that has convinced us of his innocence from the start.'

'They're coming in again,' said Amy, turning towards the magistrate's door. 'Look, Vanessa, you were right! It is the rebbe! He's coming in. I must return to my parents. Oh, what is he going to say?' She hurried off, edging between the gallery seats, and I leant forward in my seat and fixed my attention on the rabbi. He stepped forward, heavily dressed in his black clothes, the wheel-shaped fur hat upon his head, his thick grey beard pouring over his chest. Although he was old and walked slowly, his step was firm and his look was clear and direct. The magistrate called the Court to order once again, and Sir Morris Hirsch ushered the rabbi to the stand respectfully.

'I call this witness for the defence,' he said formally to the magistrate. I had the impression, however, that he looked rather taken aback. Obviously he had no idea what role the rabbi played in the tale unfolding before us. He glanced quickly at Jonathan. I followed his look, and saw that Jonathan's face had lit up with eager hope.

There was a slightly embarrassing pother while the rebbe was sworn in. A Bible was produced and hastily put aside. The magistrate had a Torah brought out, and the swearing took place.

'Do you speak English?' was Sir Morris' first question.

'I speak some English,' was the quiet reply.

'What is your name?'

'Moyshe Avrom.'

'Your age?'

'Seventy-nine.'

'How long have you been living in this country?'

'For six years now.'

'Where did you live before?'

'In Poland.'

'Why did you emigrate?'

'Life was too difficult, and the danger of pogroms was too great.'

'Did you bring your family with you?'

'Yes, I came with my wife, two sons, one daughter, and their nine children.'

'Where do you presently reside?'

'Brick Lane, in the East End of London.'

'What is your occupation?'

'I am a Hassidic rebbe,' he said quietly.

There was a pause, as Sir Morris seemed to decide that the time had come to broach the question of the man's involvement in the case presently before the Court.

'Do you know some fact or some piece of information concerning the death of Professor Gerard Ralston of King's College?' he finally asked, point-blank.

'Concerning his death, I know nothing. But I was with him briefly on the evening of March 6th,' replied the rabbi calmly. 'I have heard that he died immediately after my departure.'

A murmur ran around the crowd.

'Are you able to tell us exactly at what time you saw the Professor, how much time you spent with him, and at what time you left the library?'

'I arrived at about a quarter to five. I left at five o'clock exactly.'

'How can you be so certain of the precise time of your departure?'

'I looked at my watch as I walked away.'

'Did you see anyone on your way out of the library?'

'I remember passing a young man, who was coming in at the street gate just as I was going out of it.'

'Were you acquainted with that young man?' asked Sir Morris.

'No. I do not know who he is.'

'Do you see that young man in this room now?'

The rabbi looked slowly around the assembled lawyers and witnesses before raising his eyes to the dock. 'He is there,' he said finally, pointing to Jonathan with quiet poise.

Sir Morris then took a deep breath.

'When you left Professor Gerard Ralston at five o'clock,' he enunciated clearly and purposefully, 'was he alive and well?' An infinitesimal flicker of time passed before the rabbi responded,

'Certainly.'

'Are you aware that when Jonathan Sachs, the young man sitting in the dock over there, whom you saw entering the gate, reached the library and went inside, he found the Professor dead, shot through the heart?'

'I had heard only a rumour of this fact. I do not know precisely what occurred. But that rumour is what made me come here today.'

This answer caused a stir of approval among the assembled listeners. Sir Morris took advantage of it immediately.

'You were not summoned by the police?'

'Certainly not. I have had no contact with the police.'

'That answer corresponds with what we heard before,' said Sir Morris with satisfaction. 'Indeed, the police have shown themselves to be singularly incapable of discovering this witness, and even shed doubt upon his existence.' He smiled and looked around to see the effect of his words, but nobody else was interested, because they were merely impatient to hear the continuation of the rabbi's story.

'Can you tell us exactly why you went to see Professor Ralston, and what occurred during your visit?' was the next question.

The tension in the room increased considerably. There was a little buzz.

'I had heard that Professor Ralston was a well-known anti-Semite,' said the rabbi. 'I had been told that in reaction to the discovery of a new document, he was preparing to renew his attacks against Captain Dreyfus, a French Jew wrongly convicted of treason. A French colleague of mine close to Captain Dreyfus asked me if I could attempt to persuade the Professor to cease his attacks against our community. So I went.'

'You wished to persuade him to stop his anti-Semitic activities?'

'Yes. In particular those he was preparing against Dreyfus.'

'Did you expect him to listen to you?' said Sir Morris, visibly surprised.

'Certainly.'

'And he did listen?'

'Certainly.'

Emily squeezed my hand, containing her excitement with difficulty. 'Of course, he *had* to listen,' she whispered into my ear.

'And how did he react to your suggestions?' asked Sir Morris.

'He was very angry,' said the rabbi, causing a small commotion.

'I can imagine that,' said Sir Morris, ignoring it. 'And how did your interview end?'

'When I had finished telling the Professor what I wanted to tell him, I said goodbye and left,' said the rabbi simply.

'You left? You walked away?'

'Yes. I walked out of his study and down the path and out of the gate and down the street and took the omnibus home.'

'You saw no one, apart from Mr Sachs there?'

'No one at all until I reached the street.'

'And you had no idea the Professor lay dead behind you?'

'No. Otherwise I should not have left, but remained to aid the dying man.'

'Too brazen!' murmured the woman sitting near me. 'And Sir Morris is helping him. Well, he would, wouldn't he?' She aimed a vinegary sneer in my direction but I ignored her wrathfully.

'There was no one in the library? Are you sure? No one else in the Professor's study?'

'No one. Both rooms were absolutely empty. If they had not been, I would not have spoken to the Professor.'

'Did you hear anything in the room behind you after you left it?' insisted Sir Morris. 'Voices or cries?'

'I believe I heard the Professor shouting something after me as I walked out,' he replied. 'But I am somewhat hard of hearing. I did not catch the precise words.'

There was a silence.

'We appear to be at a standstill,' observed the magistrate dryly.

'Let me cross-examine, my Lord!' cried Mr Andrews.

'Are we ready to proceed to cross-examination?' enquired the magistrate of Sir Morris.

Sir Morris wiped his forehead and sighed.

'Yes,' he said wearily.

'Are you acquainted with the accused?' said Mr Andrews aggressively, pointing a crooked finger at the dock.

'No. I have never met him.'

'I put it to you that you are acquainted with him, or at least with relatives or friends of his, and that they organised your appearance here today in order for your testimony to exonerate him. I put it to you that you were never at Professor Ralston's library.'

'That is false,' said the rabbi.

'I put it to you that you are an accomplice of the accused and your purpose here today is to give him an alibi.'

'That is false,' he said again.

'Then tell us how you come to be here today?'

'I heard about the arrest of a young man for the murder of Professor Ralston, and learnt that the murder had occurred just after I was with him. I did not know exactly how my testimony could be useful, but I felt it a duty to present it here. I meant to arrive at the beginning of the proceedings, but I had some difficulty in finding my way here. I do not go about much in London.'

'Yes, but *who told you*? Who told you about it? Who told you it was here? Who told you to come?' persisted Mr Andrews.

'A young woman unknown to me,' replied the rabbi.

'A young woman unknown to you,' repeated Mr Andrews sarcastically. 'Can you tell us what she looked like?'

'She was veiled,' he replied.

'A mysterious veiled young woman! Well, well. And under oath, you swear that you do not know who she was.'

'Yes. I did not know her at all. I do not know who she was, nor how she was able to guess that I was the rabbi seen coming out of the library. This is as mysterious to me as it is to you.'

'Fishy, rather than mysterious, I would call it,' said Mr Andrews. 'I put it to you that you were nowhere near the library on March 6th, and had never heard anything about it, and that the young woman, some friend of the accused in the dock here, came to persuade or bribe you to say that you were, in order to get him out of trouble.'

'That is false.'

'Can you prove it?'

'The young woman spoke to me in front of a large number of witnesses, in front of a room full of people, in fact, who can describe to you exactly what she said.'

'And what did she say?'

'She told the story of the murder, the rabbi seen coming out of the library by the young man going in, the young man discovering the body and then being himself arrested. She told me that the case was to come before the Court on this day, at this time, in this place. All of this was said in public.'

Mr Andrews turned suddenly and sharply towards Jonathan.

'Who was she?' he barked.

Almost involuntarily, Jonathan glanced up towards me. Mr Andrews looked up, following his gaze. I stood up.

'It was I,' I said.

'And who are you?'

'Wait, wait,' said the magistrate. 'If this young woman is a relevant witness, we must have her called and sworn in.'

An usher came to fetch me and led me downstairs and along corridors to enter the courtroom by the door used for witnesses. The rabbi was sent to sit on the witness bench, and I was sworn in. The Torah, which was lying on the clerk's desk next to his hand, was mistakenly offered to me for use instead of the Bible. I said nothing and swore by it quietly.

Under Mr Andrews' sharp questioning, I explained that I was a private detective who had been called in to investigate the murder. I said I had been employed by Professor Taylor and Professor Hudson, omitting any mention of my personal acquaintance and friendship with Jonathan. I then proceeded to explain how, with the aid of 'friends in the East End', we had traced back the telling of the Peretz tale in order to discover the rabbi. I took care to avoid any allusion to the relationship between Rivka and Baruch Gad and Jonathan, for I knew that if this fact came out, my own testimony would become highly suspect. But my apparently objective involvement spoke for me. The magistrate appeared to accept my testimony as truth, which more or less obliged Mr Andrews to reluctantly do the same. Disgruntled, he sent me to sit down upon the witness bench, and called up the rabbi once again.

'There is another question I would like to ask you,' he said. 'I want to know exactly what arguments you presented to the Professor to induce him to cease those anti-Semitic activities of his that you disapproved of so highly. You say that he was angry at what you told him. What did you say to make him angry? Why did he not simply dismiss your arguments with a laugh?'

The rabbi did not say anything.

'Answer the question,' said the magistrate.

'He cannot answer it,' said Mr Andrews. 'There is no answer. It's all a put-up job. This man ought to be arrested as an accomplice.'

'Will you answer the question?' said the magistrate again, a little more sharply.

'I cannot,' he said.

He would not speak of his daughter!

Yet there was someone else here who knew the truth. I stared anxiously at the man I took to be Professor Ralston's father. He, of all people, *must* know what the rebbe had come to tell his son—must he not? Why did he not speak? To my surprise, his face was blank and weary and showed no sign of recognition nor of understanding. What was happening? Was this some other man, not the Professor's father? Or was my idea that the rabbi's daughter was the Professor's mother entirely wrong? Or could it be that he simply did not recognise his wife's father? Why, of course! They had probably never met! The rabbi would not have frequented the home of the Christian man who had stolen his daughter, either before or after their marriage. He would never have wanted to see him. The rabbi was almost certainly unaware that he stood facing that very man at this moment, only a few yards away. And Professor Ralston's father was equally unaware that he was vaguely staring at his own father-in-law. Of course he knew that he had married a Jewish girl, but he probably did not imagine that anyone else could know of it.

'This man should be arrested!' said Mr Andrews again.

I felt that I *must* intervene. Only the full truth could elucidate what had really happened! Because of his refusal ever to mention his errant daughter, the rebbe would not explain what he had said to the Professor, and what had passed between them.

The magistrate was becoming impatient. Turning rather coldly to the rabbi, he said, 'Your silence is most suspicious, and your story is subject to doubt.'

'They are accomplices. Do not allow them to go free by swearing to a story in which each of them provides an alibi to the other!' said Mr Andrews shrilly.

The rabbi's stubbornness was too much for me. He may not have fully realised his own danger, but I did. At this rate, he was certain to be arrested the moment he left the courtroom. I rose to my feet.

'I can tell you what he told Professor Ralston!' I cried loudly.

Everyone in the courtroom gasped. The magistrate banged his gavel out of pure reflex, then looked at me.

'Put this woman back on the stand,' he said.

I joined the rabbi on the stand.

'The rabbi told Professor Ralston that he was his grandfather. His daughter was the Professor's mother,' I said concisely, trying to remain poised and hoping that I was not making a gigantic mistake based on a dream and a vague photographic similarity. My words caused the greatest commotion in the public gallery that had been heard yet.

'How can that be?' said the magistrate, looking at me as though I must be insane. But the elderly gentleman next to Mr Upp was slowly rising from the bench.

'I am Gerard Ralston's father,' he said. 'I have something to say.'

'Call this witness to the stand,' said the magistrate with annoyance. 'I wish to have all these witnesses confronted.'

I sat down, and the Professor was sworn in.

'I call Professor Ralston senior, father of the deceased,' said Mr Andrews, 'in order to confront his statement with that of the witnesses previously heard. Is this rabbi your father-in-law?'

'I never met my wife's father,' said the grey-haired Professor, scrutinising the rabbi. 'But his name was Moses Abraham, and he lived in the Polish village of Dembitsa. Are you he?'

'I am he,' replied the rebbe. The two men stared at each other, each with the memory of ineradicable suffering.

'Surely Moses Abraham is not the name you gave when I asked for your identity,' said Mr Andrews angrily, and turning to the stenographer, he added, 'Please read out the witness' declaration of identity.'

'What is your name? Moyshe Avrom,' read out the stenographer.

'It is the same name, spoken with the Ashkenazi accent in Yiddish,' said the Professor. 'I did not recognise it.'

'So this man is the father of your wife, the grandfather of your son, the deceased Professor Gerard Ralston?' said the magistrate, not troubling to conceal his intense surprise. And indeed, the contrast between father-in-law and son-in-law was such as could easily astonish.

'It seems so,' was the simple reply. 'But my son was never aware of his mother's origins. She died when he was only six.' Whispers and murmurs were to be heard, as the public became aware that the notorious anti-Semite Gerard Ralston was, without knowing it, the grandson of a Hassidic rabbi.

'I wish to ask Rabbi Abraham once again what he went to tell Professor Ralston on March 6th,' said Mr Andrews. 'I ask him, specifically, if he informed him of the fact that his mother was Jewish.'

'I did,' replied the rebbe simply.

'And he was previously unaware of the fact?'

'He knew nothing of it,' confirmed the elderly professor.

'And he had no idea that his grandfather had arrived in London? You had no contact with him, your own grandson?'

'When my daughter left our home in Poland to marry a Christian, she died for me,' said the rebbe with a look of rigid bitterness that seemed to have remained undimmed over the forty-odd years that had elapsed since. 'I knew nothing of her life, of her husband, of her child, not even their names. I did not know when they left Poland to live in England. My wife, however, remained in contact with my daughter until her death. I did not know it; we never spoke of her. I forbade the family to speak of her. I have not mentioned her for more than forty years. I was not aware that she had had a son. Nearly three weeks ago I received a letter from Rabbi Kahn of France, in which he spoke to me of this Gerard Ralston and of his anti-Semitic writings. He asked me if there was anything I could do to influence him to stop leading the fight against Dreyfus in England. I talked to my wife about the letter from Rabbi Kahn. And that is when my wife told me that Gerard Ralston was the name of our daughter's child. She confessed to me that she had never obeyed my command to forget our daughter, that she had continued to see her daughter after her marriage, and to write to her after she came to live in England, until she died. I knew nothing until that day of the existence of my daughter's son. And now that I know, what can I say? Such a son was a punishment for her sin.'

The Jews are perhaps the most uncompromising of people. If they were not, their race and their religion would have slipped into oblivion long ago. *Then must the Jew be merciful,* Portia said. Then, perhaps, would the Jew no longer exist.

'So you think he deserved to die?' interjected Mr Andrews quickly.

'It is the Lord and not men who must decide such questions,' replied the rabbi.

'And you still claim that you do not know how the Professor met his death?'

'I do not *know*. No.'

But is it not obvious by now? I wanted to scream. I longed to speak. My anxious gestures finally succeeded in catching the eye of Sir Morris Hirsch. He raised his eyebrows. I nodded quickly and urgently, and he called me once again to the stand. The rabbi and the Professor sat down.

'The manner in which the Professor met his death is now clear,' I said.

The magistrate looked up at me in surprise. 'Well then, will you condescend to explain it to the Court?' he said.

'Yes. It is very simple if one separates the two strands which appeared inextricably intertwined around the Professor. On the one hand, the Professor was a particularly fanatical anti-Semite who used all of the power and influence he held as a Professor of repute in a distinguished university to attack the Jewish community. It is important to realise that his actions were not limited merely to generic activities such as publishing articles. He was personally responsible for sending at least one innocent Jew to the gallows and another to Dartmoor, and he had contributed with all the means in his power to the movement which sent Captain Dreyfus to Devil's Island and is keeping him there. He was probably the author of any number of other acts of this kind.

'On the other hand, unbeknown to himself, the Professor's mother was Jewish, which in fact by the tenets of the Jewish religion meant that he himself was also a Jew. Confronting these two facts makes it easy to imagine that the rabbi's information must have been a severe shock to the Professor, the destruction of the very meaning he had chosen to give to his life. It now seems clear that he took his gun and shot himself.'

'Shot himself? But the witnesses heard the sounds of a fight going on in the room. They heard shouting and the crashing of furniture before the shot.'

'As the rabbi left, he heard Professor Ralston shouting violently after him. The desk in front of him, with its articles and letters lying on it, would mock him as a symbol of his life's work, and it is easy to understand that in a gesture of violent rage, he heaved it over, and it fell onto the chair standing on the other side of it. He then picked up his own chair and flung it against the wall, where it crashed into an engraving. The idea of the gun in his desk drawer probably came to him at this point, and he snatched it out with sweating, slipping hands, smudging the traces of his own fingerprints. It is quite possible that he actually caught up the gun with some idea of running after the rabbi, but of course it was too late. So he turned it against himself.'

'But the gun was found near the door,' the magistrate continued to argue.

'The Professor was standing behind his desk, which had

fallen and was lying obliquely supported on a chair. The gun fell onto it and glanced off, projected a yard or two in the direction of the door. Have you ever dropped something onto a slanted surface? It will glance off at the reflection of the angle from which it fell. There was a fresh dent in his desk, actually. I didn't realise until now how it must have been made.' I regretted my words instantly, fearing that I would be asked how I had managed to be inside the Professor's sealed study, but fortunately nobody raised this delicate point. The magistrate was considering my words.

'You have no proof of all this,' he said finally.

'What I am giving you is a proof by logic. It is the only possibility. We saw that neither Jonathan Sachs nor Rabbi Abraham can be guilty, because each of their testimonies exonerates the other.'

'Unless they are accomplices and both lying!' insisted Mr Andrews tenaciously.

'Well,' I said, 'if that were the case, then it seems to me that the whole point of their plan would have been for each of them to make a statement exonerating the other from the start. But the rabbi did nothing of the kind. He remained at home and let Jonathan be arrested. In fact, he was serenely ignorant of everything that took place after he left the Professor's study.'

'But he came here today.'

'Because I asked him to.'

'You don't know that he did not mean to come anyway, or perhaps to present himself to the police with his statement in his own good time.'

'But that doesn't make sense! Obviously, the longer the rabbi waited to give his evidence, the more suspicious it would look. Even today you find it suspicious, and cannot resist wondering if he has not been somehow bribed or persuaded to invent his role. The natural thing for him to do, if this were a conspiracy, would be to "find out" about the Professor's death from the next day's newspaper and present himself spontaneously to the police with his story, in a context having no relation to Jonathan Sachs at all.'

The old gentleman, Professor Ralston's father, suddenly stood up from the bench, and turned towards the magistrate. His face was grey and drawn.

'I should like to say something, if I may,' he said. There was a kind of deathly despair in his voice.

'Certainly,' said the magistrate courteously.

Stepping up to the stand, the Professor leaned his hands on the bar wearily. He looked down painfully for some time, collecting himself, before speaking.

'I feel as intimately persuaded as a man can, that what this young lady is saying is the truth. It gives me great pain to say this, but I know that I am deeply to blame for what my son became, and for everything that has happened. I allowed my son to remain totally unaware of his mother's Jewish origins. It never occurred to me when he was a child; she converted to Christianity, and we were a Christian family. But she never ceased to suffer terribly over her father's severity and rejection. Her pain and resentment at this treatment grew as she saw even her mother's kindness tempered by feelings of guilt and fear of discovery. She spoke bitterly of the Jews, and complained often and passionately of their harshness, yet without ever explaining the full and true circumstances to our child. I believe that without fully realising it, my son came to blame the Jewish people for her suffering and her early death. They became the focal point of the resentment caused by the loss of his mother. I feel largely to blame for letting this happen. I never told him the full truth, nor helped him to overcome his sadness at his mother's death. I felt incapable of it. I thought that in order to become a man, he should bear her loss in silence, just as I myself was doing. At least, that is what I told myself. But I realise now that bearing the loss in silence was the easier way, for me, than talking about it would have been.

'Later, when my son became an adult and began specialising in the study of the Spanish Inquisition and other historical iniquities, I wondered if I should speak to him. But I put it off for too long; also, I did not generally read his scholarly publications, and did not realise to what point he had become engaged in the direction of ferocious anti-Semitism. We were…we were not close. Yet one day after a colleague drew my attention to a particularly virulent article by him in a well-known intellectual journal, I decided that I must broach the subject. I went to see him, and in attempting to introduce the topic gently, I found that his prejudice was so severe that he could not even hear the word Judaism without flying into a kind of rage. I had barely begun, by delicately allowing that the contribution of Jews to our society may not be all negative, and this alone brought a storm of what I can only call hysteria upon my head. I tried to induce a state of imagination in my son by such phrases as "Imagine that you yourself were Jewish". He answered—I will never forget this phrase—"If I were a Jew I would commit suicide." It was then that I decided there was no point in ever telling him the truth. I had left it too late.'

The Professor's voice was broken and weary. He paused and sighed, then added sadly, 'There is no case against the accused, nor against my father-in-law. I have no reason to doubt that their stories are true.' He sat down and looked at his knees.

Needless to say, the magistrate discharged Jonathan without a stain on his character. He seized my hand and shook it gratefully as he was leaving, surrounded by his loving family. I thought he was going to stay and talk for a while about the meaning of it all, but no.

'Where is Emily?' were his only words.

EPILOGUE

Cambridge, Sunday, April 12th, 1896

Nearly a month has passed since I last wrote in my journal. March, with its crop of daffodils and crocuses, has gone, leaving only the long green blades behind. April has come, filling my little garden with its own personal selection of flowers; purple pansies, blue muscarii, violets and pink bells bloom in lost corners, while the carefully planned beds produce groups of fat-petalled and civilised hyacinths and tulips. The old garden walls are dripping with wisteria, whose dry stalks are already heavily loaded with enormous, promising buds. Arthur is sitting near me—he has quite forgiven me for making him desperately anxious by my sudden disappearance. Upon receiving no letters from me during his absence, he became worried and sent three increasingly urgent telegrams before it suddenly occurred to him to try at Dora's, whence he received full reassurances, at least concerning the children.

'But I'll never feel secure when you are investigating a

case of murder,' he said, brushing a little moss off the stone bench, and drawing near to me.

'It wasn't really one, after all,' I said consolingly, picking a flower and tucking it into his buttonhole.

The two most precious flowers of all the garden frolic about like happy lambs. Here in the midst of all this, my own Eden, I am absorbing the last rays of late afternoon sunshine, and preparing to dot the i's of the story recounted in these pages by writing down an account of the visit I received earlier this afternoon.

It was an unexpected one, yet expected and unexpected are all the same to me; whoever comes, planned or unplanned, finds the same odd mixture of peaceful tranquillity and permanent chaos, and a cup of tea is always available. There is no time here; time, and urgency, exist for me only when I am investigating. At home, each day is just a poem; some speak of rainfall, others of sunshine, and all of them contain the same echo of tenderness.

When guests join us, the children gambol around them, deeply interested yet keeping a suspicious distance unless mollified by particularly tactful personal communication. If a guest is particularly loud or overexcited, they cling very tightly to their parents.

Jonathan did not cause them to cling; he sat, long-legged and relaxed, upon a garden chair, smiling valiantly. He was up in Cambridge for mathematical reasons, he explained, and could not resist the impulse to drop by.

'To think I haven't seen you at all since that last moment in the courtroom!' he said.

'No,' I said. 'The moment I walked out of there, I had nothing else in my mind but taking the first train down to Kent to recover my babies. I can't think how I managed to

spend so many days away from them. They're very addictive,'
I added, clutching little Cedric, who presented himself at that
precise moment holding a large and impressive pink blossom
which he had torn from its stem.

'No no no, mustn't pick flowers,' I told him. There was
not much authority in my tone. The pink tulips are not at
all my favourites, anyway. He paid but little attention to my
words and, inserting the end of a petal delicately into his
mouth, he sampled it with concentration. I kissed the top of
his soft head.

'You seem to have survived the separation well enough,'
said Jonathan agreeably. 'And how did you find the children?
Were they upset at your long disappearance?'

'Not much,' I admitted. 'To tell you the truth, when I
arrived at the house where my sister and her husband live—it
is the house I grew up in—I found the babies in a state of perfect delight, as their father was there, devoting himself to them
adoringly, while my sister and the nurse had gone off on a
well-deserved outing. I did feel guilty when I saw him! He
was supposed to be doing mathematics in France.'

'And what was he doing instead—taking a secret holiday?'

'Well, he had discovered that I was gone, and that the children were at my sister's, so he went there to be with them. He
meant to come up to London to look me out, but the babies
having once got hold of him would not brook the idea of letting him go, so he stayed and waited to see how much time I
would take before putting in an appearance.'

'And how long was it?'

'Oh, I came the next day. I did feel like a terrible mother
when I saw them!'

'Nonsense. It was probably good for them—teach them

to appreciate their luck,' said Jonathan, tickling Cecily with a long blade of grass, as she stood staring unwinkingly at him, planted on a pair of solidly parallel little legs.

'Well, in any case, I have made up for it since,' I said. 'I spend all my time with them, and Cecily has learnt to say "mamma is back" as I have repeated it so frequently.'

'Mamma back,' said that small person obligingly. Jonathan smiled.

'It is interesting, this learning to speak,' he observed. 'I must have done it myself at that age, yet I occasionally have the unfortunate impression that I did not do it quite right. I wish I could express myself better.'

'What would you express, if you could?' I said, sensing some deeper meaning behind his words.

'I would convince Emily to marry me,' he said. 'She would, if she saw inside me.'

'She doesn't want to?' I said. It was very sad, but I was not completely surprised. Emily was as fond of Jonathan as could be, perhaps fonder even than she realised. But there was some-one else who made her cheeks flush and her eyes sparkle.

'I think she is in love with young Hudson,' said Jonathan gloomily, as though reading my thoughts. 'And what can I say?' he added after a short pause. 'He's brilliant, attractive, a nice fellow altogether...and not Jewish.'

'I'm sure that has nothing to do with it!' I exclaimed indignantly. 'We Gentiles are not all like Professor Ralston, you know!'

'Oh, him—he wasn't a Gentile,' he responded bitterly. 'He was one of us. Now that I know it, I almost wonder how I never saw it before. That single-minded fanatical rigidity of his was really a twisted version of something uncompromising and even obsessional in us, that I recognise...only too well.'

'That is what Darwin would call the survival instinct,' I said. 'In a situation where survival is not threatened, it becomes a danger. Jonathan, the world is full of beautiful things—why, here you are in this garden, free as air! Just think that you might have been in prison at this very moment. You have been inside Dartmoor. You know what it is like.'

'I know, I do know. I often think that very thought,' he said. 'I'll be forever grateful for what you did. It's incredible, though, that none of us understood sooner what actually happened. There was obviously only one possible answer.'

'Ye-es,' I said. 'And yet, I find myself wondering just a tiny bit about it. Would the Professor really have shot himself just because he found out his mother was a convert from Judaism? I know he told his father that he would commit suicide if he were a Jew, but I can hardly believe that he really meant it. His father took it seriously because it was his own son, and because he felt guilty. But it's probably just as well that it never came to trial. I wonder if a jury would have accepted that as a motive for suicide.'

'Oh!' he said. 'Actually, we talked with Reb Abraham afterwards much more. He told us all about his interview with the Professor. He feels responsible for what happened. He has sent all of his disciples away to study with other rebbes. You see, he—he actually said more to Professor Ralston than we thought. He told him that he had to entirely cease all of his anti-Semitic activities instantly, or else he would make the information public—tell everybody that Ralston himself was Jewish. A lot of people deeply disliked Ralston. They would have made mincemeat of him, professionally.'

'I see,' I said. 'And I am not completely surprised. It was almost a kind of blackmail. That raises an extremely difficult moral question. Did the rabbi do right, or wrong?'

'I think he did right, and I told him so,' he said. 'Ralston was himself a murderer, don't forget that!'

'I know why you say that, and you are right,' I said softly. 'That reminds me that your uncle must have come out of prison by now. Tell me about him.'

'He was released less than a week ago,' he replied. 'He has gone to live with my parents now, while looking for a little place of his own. It's strange; freedom is…not as easy as you might think. Prisoners think of nothing else, and yet, when they emerge, they are like lost souls. But that is what a family is for. His story has cost us all so much in indignation and fury and worry and fear that we are spent, and now only wish to welcome him and make sure that he finds a little quiet con-tentedness, a little tranquillity.'

'How—how did he react to Professor Ralston's death?' I asked, a little timidly. 'It seems strange to think that he said he meant to kill him.'

'I wonder what he would have done, in fact,' mused Jonathan. 'It is easy to think of killing someone in the heat of despair, or from the depths of a prison. It is surely not so easy to do it when push comes to shove. He did not say what he would have done had none of this happened, but he did tell me that when he learnt that I had been arrested and realised that I was in danger because of that letter he wrote, he suddenly knew that he would have chosen to do none of it rather than have me risk what he has undergone. It seems silly now; hard to believe there was any real danger. Yet there was, I think. At least, I was terrified enough! Believe me, I saw those prison walls closing around me. The old rebbe was the only arrow in my quiver, and I was afraid that he would not come, or would deny everything, or worse, that he would be arrested as well. It never occurred to me that he could have had the power to say something to Ralston that would have such an effect on him. I admit that I saw no way out of it; I almost wondered if I hadn't committed the murder myself unconsciously, somehow.'

'Done it unconsciously, or meant to do it?' I said. 'Do you know, Jonathan, you never told me why you were going to the library that day. You never told anyone. But I have wondered about it a great deal. What were you doing there?'

He squirmed about a little.

'Well, I will tell you the truth,' he said at length. 'I do think you have deserved to know, and I can trust you. But please, never tell anyone what I am about to tell you. I don't want my family to know, above all not my uncle. I don't know what he would think of me. You see, I was becoming obsessed with the fact that he was about to be released, and that he would be free, and that he talked and thought about nothing but the Professor—the black dog, as we called him. I was terrified that he would immediately go and slaughter him and then perhaps commit suicide, or go back to prison forever. Not only my uncle, but my mother would have been destroyed by it. I have to admit that I felt that I couldn't let it happen. I went through a very difficult period trying to come to a decision.'

'Yes?' I said encouragingly, as he came to a standstill. 'I suppose that after all that has been said, you are not going to tell me that you decided to kill him in your uncle's stead, after all!'

'No, of course not. I'm no murderer,' he said. 'I was going to warn him, actually. I was going to tell him that my uncle was about to come out of prison, and that he was in mortal danger. I imagine he knew that my uncle was due to be released, and he knew about my uncle's letter to the judge, but he did not know that my uncle and I knew his identity, so I assumed that he must feel quite secure.'

'So you meant to warn him for his own safety?' I said.

'Well, yes, I meant to warn him, but to be completely honest, I also intended to reveal my knowledge of his role in my uncle's trial in a dramatic kind of way—to frighten him, to put him in the position of being accused. I wasn't just going to say, "My uncle wants to kill you, so go somewhere where you'll be safe". If I had said that, he would probably just have had my uncle put under police surveillance or even rearrested. I meant to make him feel frightened and threatened. I wanted him to fear for his life. I wanted him to wake up at night, hearing noises, terrified and not knowing what he was afraid of or where the threat was coming from. I really hated him. God knows how it would have turned out if I had done what I meant to. I can tell you that when I saw him lying dead, I was terrified. I literally wondered for a moment if my thoughts couldn't have had such an effect. But then I remembered that he must have had any number of enemies who mortally hated him.'

'He did,' I said. 'Isn't it strange that he himself was his own worst enemy in the end?'

MATHEMATICAL HISTORY IN
THE LIBRARY PARADOX

THE FAMOUS LIBRARY PARADOX of Bertrand Russell (1872–1970) is generally thought to have been discovered in 1901. Russell was a young man of excellent family; his paternal grandfather, Lord John Russell, had been a Prime Minister. He completed his studies and left Cambridge in 1894, turning to philosophy.

At about this time, probably in 1896, Cesare Burali-Forti (1861–1931), an assistant to Giuseppe Peano—and a mathematician whose interests, being ahead of his time, prevented him from ever obtaining a university position—discovered the first version of what became later known as Russell's paradox. As described in the book, his observation was that since the set of ordinals is a well-ordered set, it must have an ordinal; however, this ordinal must be both an element of the set of all ordinals and yet greater than every ordinal: a contradiction. Russell, a recent graduate from Cambridge, must have learnt of Burali-

Forti's work, which would naturally have influenced him in the discovery of his own version, which he made public in 1901.

The content of Russell's paradox is essentially identical to Burali-Forti's, however it has the advantage of being expressed only in terms of common notions rather than specifically mathematical ones. The version of librarians and catalogues is one of the commonest methods used by mathematicians for explaining the paradox to laymen. In terms of simple set theory, one considers the problem of sets which are, or are not, members of themselves (for instance, a catalogue of books in a library which lists, or does not list, itself as one of the books in the library). The paradox arises when trying to define the set of all sets that are not members of themselves. A moment's reflection will make it clear that if such a set is a member of itself, then it cannot be a member of itself, and vice versa: hence the paradox.

Russell's paradox is considered to have been of fundamental importance in the development of modern axiomatic set theory and logic. Gottlob Frege (1848–1925) was finishing up an enormous treatise on logic, the *Grundgesetze der Arithmetik*, when he received a letter from Russell containing the paradox. The paradox showed that Frege's work was based on axioms that were inconsistent and caused a sort of revolution in the way mathematicians considered logic and set theory. Any collection of objects was no longer considered worthy of the name 'set'. A set now had to be formulated as a collection satisfying certain basic axioms, and the principles of set theory apply in a consistent way only to these sets and not to collections in general. As is well known, Bertrand Russell went on to do more foundational work in logic, and then became deeply involved in affairs of global peace, winning the Nobel Prize in Literature in 1950.

Afterword

On the subject of taking degrees at Cambridge, the Jewish mathematician J.J. Sylvester was Second Wrangler in 1837, and was refused a degree. Another Jew, Numa Hartog, was Senior Wrangler in 1869; he participated actively in an effort to change the rules, testifying before the House of Lords. These efforts culminated with the passing of the Universities Tests Act in 1871, allowing students of all religions to graduate from Oxford and Cambridge by abolishing the requirement that they sign the Thirty-Nine Articles of the Church of England. Note that the act was passed just two years after a Jewish student became Senior Wrangler. However, although the brilliant young mathematics student Philippa Fawcett was classed *above the Senior Wrangler* in 1890, it took several more decades before women obtained the right to take degrees at Cambridge.

Incidentally, the fascinating history of the Dreyfus affair is exactly as recounted in the book, except that this was only the beginning. The full story, filled with spies and secrets, stunning reversals, sublime nobility and treacherous villainy, lasted until 1906, and ended with Dreyfus being awarded the Légion d'Honneur. It makes a more extraordinary tale than many a novel, and constitutes one of the most important and profound political events of *fin-de-siècle* Europe.

I would like to extend my warmest thanks to Peter Kenyon, a retired history lecturer whose main interest is in late nineteenth and early twentieth century social history, for his invaluable advice, suggestions and corrections on dozens of historical details throughout the manuscript. They ranged from questions of language to matters of law to details of carriages, trains, post offices, newspapers, and even chimneys and coals.